D1121043

The King's Warrior

By

Donna Fletcher

Donna Fletcher

The King's Warrior

Cover art
Kim Killion Group

Ebook Design
A Thirsty Mind

Visit Donna's Web site
www.donnafletcher.com
http://www.facebook.com/donna.fletcher.author

Chapter One

Wrath cursed the swirling snow. He had hoped the flurries that had begun falling early this morning when he and his troop had broken camp would be all the snow that followed them the rest of the way to Pictland. His hope had died shortly after when the snow turned heavy. Now they would not arrive home until it was near dark or later if the snow worsened.

He had been away from home too long, though he had accomplished what King Talon had sent him to do, quell the unrest and misunderstanding with the Drust Tribe to the north. While his mission had gone well, he had learned that there was still a group of Picts plotting against the King. At least, there was no longer any threat from the Drust. They were one of the fiercest warriors of the Pict Tribes and their location so far north was important to the King. Northmen came to trade from across the sea and seeing the Drust, their bodies covered from their head to their feet in intricate body drawings with barely a garment on them, kept the mighty Northmen from engaging them in battle.

Now that the problem had been settled, Wrath was eager to be home and find himself a willing woman to keep him warm for the night. He was not interested in finding himself a mate to join with for life. He was leader of King Talon's imposing personal guard and his position came before anything else. It had annoyed him to be sent on this mission, away from the King, but the King had felt Wrath was the only one he could trust with it.

A sudden strong wind whipped at Wrath's face and had him lowering and turning is head to avoid another icy slap. He did not keep his head turned away long. In a snowstorm as bad as this one, it was wise to keep focused on the horse in front of you or you could easily be separated from the others in the troop and chance getting lost in the snow and freezing to death. And since he was in the lead, he had to keep his troop on a steady course.

It was not long before Wrath brought the warriors to a halt. It was difficult to recognize his surroundings through the rapidly swirling snow. The familiar markers that let one know how far they were from the Pictland stronghold were impossible to see, forcing Wrath to rely more on instinct than a sharp eye to remain on course. That instinct is what had him halting the warriors, following in a single line behind him.

He dismounted and grabbed the coiled rope he had hung on the hilt of his sword strapped to his back. He knotted it around the leather belt at his waist and proceeded to have his men do the same down the line. When the rope fell short, he had more rope added to it until the whole troop was fastened to each other. If the whipping snowstorm forced one warrior off course, another would know about it. He refused to lose even one warrior. They all would return home together.

The bitter cold and falling snow made it difficult to judge how long they had traveled. Or was it eagerness to be home that made the journey seem endless? Wrath mounted his horse when all was done and kept his troop on a steady pace, his eyes on his surroundings to make certain they did not wander off course, and hoped the forest spirits were watching over them. He would take whatever help he could get to see them home safely.

They rode on with no complaints, at least no complaints that could be heard. The fierce wind whipped the words up and away as soon as they left the mouth.

The sky darkened after a while and Wrath was not sure if it was because it was growing late or the snowstorm was about to worsen. He hoped it was not the latter, since it would be impossible for them to continue.

He turned his head away when he was once again slapped with an icy blast of wind and in that moment he thought he caught movement in the snow. Had the wind whipped at the snow by the boulder? It would not be an animal. They would have sensed the storm and taken shelter. He looked again as his horse drew closer and again he saw movement. Or was it the ruthless wind?

Wrath watched as they were near on top of the spot and when he saw movement again, he brought his horse to a stop. He dismounted and went to the warrior riding behind him. After telling him what he thought he had seen, a line was formed so that Wrath could reach the boulder without getting lost in the blinding snow.

He saw no movement as he fought against the wind and he wondered if he had been foolish to stop, but then he saw it again. He had not been mistaken. Something was buried in the snow that had drifted up against the rock.

Wrath pushed against the wind and almost stumbled when his fur encased shoe caught on something beneath the snow. He kicked at it, thinking it was a fallen branch, but it did not feel like a branch. He squatted done and brushed the snow away to reveal a leg partially wrapped in worn cloth. It was a slim leg, too slim to belong to a man.

He quickly dug at the snow and when he uncovered the edge of a cloak, he yanked at it, sending the snow flying to reveal a thin body, though shapely enough to know it was a woman. He let the cloak fall to cover her body once again and hurried to brush the snow off the cloak's hood that completely covered her face, then he carefully eased it away.

The face lacked color and the full lips were tinged blue. What hair peeked out from beneath the hood was the color as bold as the sun. She had features that would have a man looking more than once at her and he squinted several times, then he finally leaned closer to look at what was around her neck. A red, raw mark circled her neck and that could be caused by only one thing—a noose.

Had she escaped a hanging only to fall prey to the snowstorm?

There was nothing he could do for her now but see that she was buried properly. A task in itself, since by the time he sent warriors to retrieve the body the forest animals would have feasted on her. It was not what he would want for her, but he would not endanger his warriors' lives when she was already dead.

Wrath stared at her for a moment. He could not help but wonder about her. Who was she? Why did she have the mark of a hangman's noose around her neck? Why was she here, so close to the Pictland stronghold? He would never know and for some reason that troubled him.

He went to tug the hood down over her face, when her eyes suddenly sprang open.

Wrath almost fell backward from the shock that she was not only alive, but from her eyes. They were the deepest blue he had ever seen. He was jolted by another shock when she spoke.

"Wrath!"

He stared at her, thinking he should know her since she had spoken his name, but nothing about her was familiar.

Her eyes closed again and while there were many questions he wished to ask her, now was not the time. He had to get her out of the snow and get her and his troop home before they all froze to death.

Wrath signaled to the warrior behind him and together they dug her out of the snowdrift. She was no burden to lift and carry to his horse. He handed her to the warrior tied to him and after he mounted, he took her from him, fighting against the punishing wind as he did. He placed her across the front of him, tucking her tight against his shoulder so that her head rested on his chest. He drew his fur-lined cloak around them both, keeping her covered from the shards of icy wind and bitter, swirling snow.

Her body was so cold that he worried the heat from his body would not be enough to warm her and she would die before they reached home. But then she was a stranger, so why should it matter to him? Was she a stranger to him? She had spoken his name as if relieved to see him. But she was not familiar to him, so how did she know him? And the marking around her neck nagged at him. It was the mark of the hangman's noose for sure. Or was it?

She stirred in his arms, drawing his attention and he thought he heard her say his name once again. The sooner they reached home, the sooner he would have his answers. He forced his thoughts away from the woman in his arms and on the difficult task in front of him...the blinding snow.

Their pace was slow and seemed to grow slower as the snow continued to rage around them. The darkening sky worried Wrath. If they did not reach Pictland soon they would have to make camp and try to survive another night in the worsening snowstorm. While his men had been trained to face such harsh conditions, the woman was not and he doubted she would make it through the night if exposed to the cold.

They continued to plod along and when Wrath spotted a faint light in the distance, he hoped it was not his eyes or thoughts playing tricks on him. He kept his horse steady toward the flickering light and was relieved when another light came into view.

It was the torches, burning brightly, atop of the tall enclosure that surrounded the Pictland stronghold. They had made it home.

The sound of the men's joyous roars as they spotted the lights pierced the mighty wind and was carried off on it. The warriors continued to roar and for a good reason. They wanted to make certain an open stronghold gate greeted them upon reaching it. And it did.

Wrath spotted Broc standing just inside the gate upon entering. He was one of King Talon's six personal guards that Wrath had trained to protect the King and give their lives for him if necessary. Seeing him there meant only one thing, King Talon wanted to see him immediately. That left no time to deposit the woman with the healer. He would have to take her with him.

Two torches burned brightly in front of the feasting house, a two story structure that King Talon had designed. It stood proudly amongst smaller dwellings. Wrath drew his horse to a stop and Broc, having followed alongside him, was quick to assist him with the woman.

"A mate?" Broc asked with a grin, holding the woman as Wrath dismounted.

Wrath winced. "Do not wish such a terrible fate on me."

"On any of the King's personal guard," Broc said with a laugh.

Wrath had agreed with a nod. It was not a spoken law that a member of the King's personal guard could not wed, it was a silent one. The King's protection came first, above all else, and a wife would distract from that.

The woman did not stir when Wrath took her in his arms and entered the feasting hall. Seeing the King had yet to arrive there, Wrath laid the woman on a table closest to the large fire pit in the corner of the room.

He was about to slip off his cloak and cover her when a shiver ran through her. Her garments were wet from the snow and doing her no good. The only thing he could do about that now was to cover her with his cloak, hoping the fur lining would warm her some.

"What have you there?"

Wrath turned to see King Talon descend the steps from the second floor. One look at the King and one understood why he ruled over the Picts. He was a man of immense power; tall, lean, and hard with muscles, he possessed the strength of ten or more men. He was a man to fear and respect. His fine features attracted endless women, but it was the strange markings on the right side of his face that captured the eye.

Most Picts had several body drawings significant to their tribe The King had only one and most believed he was born with it and meant to be King.

Wrath had known King Talon before he became King. They had fought together to defeat foreigners and force them off their shores. He was lucky to not only call him his King, but also his friend.

Wrath stepped aside as King Talon approached so he could see for himself.

King Talon gave the woman a quick glance when he stopped near Wrath. "You can tell me about her after you tell me how your mission went."

"Irongrey, the Drust leader, was pleased to learn that you had not deserted his tribe and was grateful for your generosity in the supplies you sent to help them survive as the land grows dormant and the cold descends. He was not pleased to learn that some in his tribe had plotted against you. He reaffirmed his tribe's allegiance to you and assures you that the Drust will stand with you against any and all enemies."

"The Northmen?"

"Trading continues and all seems fine with them. I have your share of the traded items, which Irongrey supplied without question or protest. Spices, wine, and fine cloth are a few of them."

"What does he intend to do about those tribesmen who betrayed him and are still at large?"

"He assures me they will meet their fate as soon as they are captured," Wrath said. "Irongrey made certain to announce to his tribe that their own tribesmen stole the supplies and the animals you sent to replace their aging ones. The tribe's people, all fierce warriors, were eager to begin hunting those who had betrayed them."

"Did you learn of anymore unrest among the tribes on your journey?"

"I learned that someone is enlisting those who are not pleased that you unified the tribes, took the throne, and became first King of the Picts."

"Someone believes himself more suitable to be King. We will discuss the problem when next the High Counsel meets. Now tell me, who is this woman," King Talon ordered with a nod at the table.

"I do not know. I found her buried in a snowdrift, barely alive. I am surprised she still lives. I was also

10

surprised to see that her neck bears the mark of a hangman's noose."

The king stepped closer to have a better look. "I will know what happened to her. No one is hung without my permission."

Wrath thought of Paine's wife, Anin. She had the power to touch someone and know what they felt. "Anin could touch her and tell us something about her."

"Anin asked permission for her and Paine to visit with her grandmother and her people, the Wyse Tribe. I granted her request. Anin has grown in her abilities since you took your leave. I am sure if she senses she is needed, she and Paine will return." The King looked at the woman again. "Did she speak at all to you?"

Wrath reluctantly said, "She spoke my name."

"Then the problem is solved. You know her. You find out what happened to her and I place her in your care."

"I do not know her," Wrath argued.

"Or you do not remember her, since you have known your share of women."

"I knew none of them well," Wrath protested and almost cringed at his own words.

"You must have left a good impression on this one, since she remembers you. See to her, she is your responsibility now."

"I could take her to the healer. She can tend her properly."

"Did I not say she is your responsibility?"

Wrath wanted to argue, but the threatening look on the King's face warned him against it. Instead, he nodded and said, "As you say, my King."

King Talon turned and stopped before climbing the stairs. "Do not join with her, Wrath. We do not know who she is or what problem she brings with her." He continued up the stairs, expecting no reply only obedience.

Wrath shook his head. He had no desire to join with her. She was nothing more than a problem that he wanted to be rid of and he was annoyed that he would have to tend her. He should have left her where he had found her. He shook his head again. He could be heartless when necessary, but it had not been necessary to leave her to die. Besides, he was curious about her, but then look where his curiosity had gotten him? He shook his head again and grabbed his cloak, roughly yanking it off her.

Her eyes flew open large with fright and she reached out to him. "Wrath, help me."

Chapter Two

Snow fell on Wrath as he carried the woman, wrapped snugly in his fur-lined cloak, to his dwelling. Her eyes had not remained open long enough for him to question her and heavy sleep had claimed her once again. It troubled him that she should seek his help since it meant she trusted him. Try as he might, he could not place her. But there had been many women he had shared not more than a brief, mutual coupling with and never knew their names.

It had been before Talon had become King. Talon, Paine, and he had been busy fighting endless battles and enjoying the free favors of the women of various tribes.

Tribes.

Various tribes were identified by their body drawings. The Drust were easy to spot since body drawings covered their enter bodies. He, being part of the King's personal guard, had distinct body markings across his back, chest, arm, and neck. All he had to do was find out what body drawings she wore and he would know her tribe. At least, it was a start in discovering who she was.

He was glad no one was about to see him carrying the woman to his dwelling. Tongues would wag, though if she remained with him too long talk would soon spread that he had taken a wife. And that was something he would not allow to happen.

She is your responsibility.

13

He shook his head, being reminded of King Talon's command. He needed to see this done and be rid of her soon.

Wrath laid her on his sleeping pallet once inside his dwelling. He left her there and turned to get a fire going in the fire pit in the middle of the small room. He needed no more than what he had—a place to sleep and to couple. He took his sustenance in the feasting hall and shared drinks and tales in there as well. He had no wont or need for more.

He returned to her and quickly relieved her of his cloak and her wet one. Her shift was another matter. It was soaked from the snow and difficult to get off her. He lost his patience after struggling with it and getting nowhere, he ripped it off her.

She was thin. He had seen such thinness before from those who had been deprived of food. Studying the length of her, her head would reach just past his shoulder. Her skin was pale, her breasts plump, which meant she had sizeable breasts at one time. The golden thatch of hair between her legs matched her hair on her head that was plaited in a long braid. Her body would be quite appealing once filled out. He was surprised to see that she bore no body markings. He turned her gently on her side and found no markings on her back as well.

The only mark on her was the burn mark from the rope that had been around her neck at some point.

She shivered and he hurried to cover her with a blanket, then placed fur hides on top, wanting to warm her as much as possible. There was no telling how long ago she had collapsed and been buried in that snowdrift. She had to be chilled to the bone.

He had built his sleeping pallet wide enough for two, intending to not always sleep alone, though not intending to sleep at those times either. He eased her closer to the wall and sat beside her on the bed to look more closely at the mark around her neck.

The skin was rubbed raw, more so in some spots than others. With gentle fingers, he touched along her neck just below the red mark and found that his touch turned to a caress, her skin so soft it enticed.

He pulled his hand away at the tempting thought, though more so since he felt himself growing slightly aroused. He did not need to add to his problem. Besides, she was far from a willing woman and he preferred women who were not only willing, but who enjoyed coupling as much as he did.

She had asked for his help and if possible that, and only that, was what he would give her.

He looked at the mark on her neck again. Something about it disturbed him. It took a moment for him to realize it was similar to ones he had seen before on captives, after battle. Prisoners of the conquering tribe would be tethered to one another with a rope around their necks and forced to march in a long single line. But there was no need for that now in this area, so did she bear a hangman's mark or the mark of a captive?

A sudden yawn reminded him that he needed rest. It had been a long, tiring, and burdensome journey, and he was glad to be home and sleeping in his pallet. And while he had not planned on sleeping alone, he certainly had not planned on sleeping with a woman unknown to him.

With his plans gone astray and sleep creeping up on him, Wrath shed his garments and climbed in naked beside the woman he knew nothing about. He no soon as lay on his back, then the woman turned and curled herself around him. She nestled her head on his chest as if it was something she did often and pressed her body next to his as if it belonged there. Her arm drifted over his middle, as if laying claim to him, and her leg slipped over his one until her knee rested just below his manhood as if it had found its way home.

Wrath thought to move her, but her body still held a chill and with his own body heated, more than he would have liked, it would help warm her. He eased his arm around her shoulder and laid his hand on her arm.

He shut his eyes, trying to force himself to sleep, but every time her body stirred the slightest against him, his manhood stirred as well. He had to fight to keep himself from growing more aroused and grew more annoyed with himself for having to do so.

After a few moments of complete torture and fearing he just might disobey the King's order, he decided to ease her off him. He looked down as he made ready to move her and saw her staring at him wide-eyed.

She smiled softly and it stole his breath. She was far lovelier to look upon than he had first thought.

"Wrath," she whispered gently. "I am safe with you."

Once again her eyes closed and she fell into a deep slumber, cuddling even closer to him.

He wanted to shake her awake and demand to know who she was and how she knew him, but her words, said with such conviction, had him keeping a firm hold on her and doing as she said—keeping her safe. But from who?

He finally slept. How long, he was not sure. Her stirrings woke him again. This time he found himself wrapped around her, with her back to his front, his leg over her two, and his arm snug around her middle, keeping her locked against him as if he had claimed her. Surprisingly, the thought did not disturb him and he fell back to sleep.

"Wrath!"

He woke with a jolt and seeing that she was curled tight against the wall away from him, he hastily reached out, slipped his arm under her and pulled her against him. She went without protest, turning and pressing herself against him until she was once again wrapped solidly around him.

She looked up at him and whispered, "Finally, I am where I belong—with you."

Wrath watched her eyes close again and he was stunned at the thought that hit him suddenly.

Aye, you belong with me.

He shook his head and blamed the foolish thought on his lack of sleep and let himself drift off once again.

His sleep was restless, mostly because of the stranger in his arms. She would cry out as if demons haunted her sleep. He would soothe her with a gentle touch and she would calm. It was the tears she cried in her sleep that upset him the most. Women who shed tears easily annoyed him. He preferred a woman who argued with him and showed strength than one who teared every time something upset her. Yet her tears disturbed him, twisting at his insides, causing him to silently swear and promise himself that he would find the culprit who had brought her such suffering, and kill him.

What woke him next startled him. The woman straddled him as if she intended to mount him. She dropped down over him, her hands on either side of his head so that she hovered slightly over him. Her hard nipples faintly poked at his chest, teasing, tempting, and demonstrating what they could offer, but not letting him have a taste. With her backside nestled nearly on top of his manhood and her nipples grazing his chest, he could not stop himself from growing hard.

She lowered her head toward his, her golden braid slipping past her shoulder to fall upon his chest, its silky softness only adding to his already aching manhood.

He thought she intended to kiss him, but she halted a short distance from his lips. He stared at her lips, her bottom one plumper than her top one and so shiny and moist that he wanted to reach out, grab her around the neck, and yank her to him, claiming her tempting lips in a wicked kiss.

"Promise me," she whispered. "Promise me."

"Promise you what?"

"Promise me. Promise me," she said again, though more urgently. She lowered her brow slowly to rest on his and whispered, "Promise me, Wrath. Please promise me."

"I promise," he said, wondering not only why he promised, but what he promised.

She raised her head and brushed her lips across his. "I am grateful." She slipped off him to rest herself comfortably against his side.

Wrath did not move, except to raise his arms above his head and lock his hands together. It was the only way to stop himself from climbing on top of her and poking her. Her faint kiss, so soft and enticing, had grown him harder and had him aching like never before. But then it had been days since he last joined with a woman and while it had been enjoyable, he had felt nothing close to what he was feeling now.

He wanted to bury himself in her and ride her until they both collapsed in pleasure. But he would not dare, not yet. He needed to know who she was and how she knew him and what it was that he had promised her. When that was all settled, then and only then would he join with her and settle this ache he feared would remain with him until he did.

How long he laid there with his eyes open, his arms stretched above his head, and his hands locked together, he did not know. Perhaps it was fear of falling asleep and waking to find her on top of him again and this time surrendering to his need that kept him awake. He waited to hear the sounds of first light, when the stronghold woke and the voices of the villagers were heard as they got busy with their daily chores.

He lost his fight to remain awake to the fatigue that finally took hold and perhaps by instinct or possibly familiarity, he lowered his arms to wrap around the naked woman pressed against him.

Wrath's eyes shot open, as if shaken from his sleep, to see the woman who had pressed herself against him all night, sitting with her back against the wall, the blanket clutched against her naked chest, her cheeks stained soft red, and her eyes spread wide.

"Who are you? Where am I?" she said with a quiver to her words.

Wrath wondered if his own surprise showed on his face when he asked, "You do not know me?"

She shook her head and clutched the blanket tighter.

"You called me by name when I found you buried in the snowdrift."

She lowered her head, her brow drawn tight, trying to remember.

He thought to remind her and learn her name as well. "I am Wrath and you are?"

She tilted her head as she raised it and looked upon him, uncertainty in her eyes. "I am Verity."

"Verity, the bearer of truth and not a name often heard, for it is a heavy one to own." He nodded at her. "Tell me, *Verity*, how did you get that red mark around your neck?"

19

Her hand went to her neck and she winced when she touched the raw skin. She turned her head away and chewed at her bottom lip, uncertain how to answer.

"You told me you were safe with me and that you were where you belonged...with me."

She remained silent, not turning around, not looking at him as she continued to nibble at her lip.

Wrath sat up. "Look at me, Verity."

She did not want to look at him. She had been looking at him ever since she woke, which seemed an endless time ago. She had been shocked when she laid eyes on him, a face more handsome than she had ever seen, long dark hair that gleamed in the fire's light, and a body more sculpted with muscle than most men. And he was a good size for mating, though she had covered that part of him fast enough. It was his body drawings that fascinated her the most. They covered his neck, both arms, and across his chest with a single swirl running down his middle. He was impressive to look upon while frightening as well. It was easy to see he demanded respect and admired strength.

Verity had neither.

She jumped when his hand took hold of her chin, not tightly, but with enough strength that warned her against fighting him as he turned her head to look at him. She almost shut her eyes, not wanting to meet his dark ones that had intimidated as soon as he had opened them.

"You begged a promise from me last night, and I gave it to you. What was it that I promised you?"

Her eyes held his, though it was more that his eyes had captured hers and refused to release her. She felt her breath catch in her throat and her chest tightened.

"Breathe," he ordered, though softly, and she did. "Another breath."

Again she obeyed until her breathing calmed and all the while, he never released the hold he had on her chin.

"Now tell me of this promise."

She took another breath before responding. "I know of no such promise."

Wrath brought his face closer to hers. "You are the bearer of truth, Verity, do not speak falsely to me."

"It must have been a dream. I dream often."

"A dream in which you know what I am called?" He stared at her eyes, the dark blue color he had seen when she had first opened them and throughout the night was gone. They were now a softer, lighter blue. But how could that be?

"I cannot explain it," she said.

He released her chin. "I think you can, but for some reason you choose not to." He tossed the blanket aside and swung his long legs off the sleeping pallet to stand and face her. "You can either tell me or tell King Talon and he will not take kindly to false words."

Verity kept her eyes focused on his face and tried with all her might to keep her wits about her. "I am a slave to a Northmen family. Many Northmen treat their slaves well, I was not so fortunate."

"A rope was kept around your neck?"

"At times, when I did something that displeased them."

Wrath clinched his hands, wishing the ones who had treated her so badly stood in front of him. He would beat them until there was nothing left of them and with the fury that was mounting in him simply pondering the thought, he would need no help to do it. His rage would give him strength as it usually did.

"Were you forced to mate with any of them?"

She shook her head. "I was not to their liking."

21

He found that difficult to believe. She had a pleasing face, a soft voice, and a body that aroused, though once fed well would be even more difficult to ignore.

"I thought often of trying to escape and I finally did, but the sea turned angry, as did the wind and the rain. The small vessel I had taken could not withstand the brutal beating of the sea. I thought for sure it would be a watery grave I would suffer, but I woke on a sandy shore."

Wrath could not imagine the horrifying ordeal she had gone through, but she had proven strong and courageous enough to survive.

"You are free now. King Talon will offer you shelter and protection here in Pictland."

"That is kind of him, but I cannot stay here."

"Why not?" Wrath demanded angry that she would think to refuse the King's kindness or was it that he did not want her to leave? The foolish thought stirred his ire even more.

"I did not escape alone. My sister was with me and I must find her."

Chapter Three

"You saw no sign of your sister when you woke on the shore?" Wrath asked.

Verity shook her head. "I searched the surrounding area, but found nothing. I came upon a tribe, though remained hidden, not knowing if I would be welcomed. I watched from the woods to see if my sister was there and when I saw no sign of her, I left to continue my search. The snow made it difficult, covering any tracks she may have left."

"Is she a child or grown like you?"

"She is grown, though has not seen as many moon cycles as I have."

"King Talon has begun trade with the Northmen and has forbidden them to enslave the Picts. You must have been taken when you were wee bairns."

"I barely recall my parents, but I do remember the day the Northmen came and swept me and my sister away." She did not tell him how ill she had gotten on the Northmen's mighty vessel as they journeyed across the rough sea or how she had cried in fright. Or how she ached when she realized she would never see her home again.

"The Northmen kept their attacks to the far northern isles. You and your sister must have been from those isles to have been captured by them."

Verity shook her head. "No. We were not from the northern isles that much I know."

"How could you be sure of that?"

"The tribe to the north of us would come to trade. I could never forget them. They wore little clothing and drawings covered their entire bodies."

Wrath's brow wrinkled. Had the Northmen journeyed further into Pict territory than was first known? No tribes south of the Drust had ever made mention of Northmen attacking them or taking anyone as slaves. Perhaps she had been too young to remember things as they truly had been.

"What brought you here to Pictland, home of the High King, when your tribe lies just south of the Drust?" Wrath asked, seeing her hand cling more tightly to the blanket that covered her naked breasts. His question had upset her. Why?

"I suppose it was the snow. It blinded me and set me off course."

Wrath placed his hands on the wall behind her and brought his face close to hers again. "You lie to me, Verity, but I will get the truth from you one way or another." He watched her face turn pale and smiled. "You wear your thoughts open for me to see."

She shut her eyes, as if it would close her thoughts to him.

Wrath pushed away from her. "Shutting your eyes against me will do you no good, especially if you want help in finding your sister."

Verity eyes shot open. "You will help me?"

"When you are completely truthful with me, I will help you." He moved off the pallet.

Verity watched as Wrath slipped on a long sleeve, black shirt that fell to the middle of his upper leg. She continued to stare as he proceeded to clothe himself. There was strength in his every movement. With one yank, his strong hands cinched the leather strip he wrapped around his waist, then he hastily applied his foot and leg coverings. He stretched his broad shoulders back before running his fingers from the top of his head down the length of his hair. Then he took the two long braids that hung on either side of his head and drew them back into knot.

He stared at her as intently as she did him. "Will you now tell me the truth?"

No one could know the truth.

"What is your sister called?"

"Hemera," she said. "And I fear for her safety being in unfamiliar land."

"Then the sooner you are truthful with me, the sooner we will find her."

"My garments," she said, feeling much too vulnerable with only a blanket covering her nakedness.

"I had to rip them off you." Wrath ignored her eyes that rounded so wide they appeared ready to burst from her face. "Wait here while I see about getting garments for you to wear. Then I will see that you have food. Afterwards you will speak to King Talon and tell him your tale."

She wanted to shout at him that it was no tale, but part of it was a tale and so she remained silent as he grabbed his fur-lined cloak. When he finally closed the door behind him, she let her shoulders slump from the burden she carried.

Wrath was her only hope in finding Hemera and once found what they would do she did not know.

Verity let the blanket fall off her. She refused to glance down at her body. She would be reminded of the past moon cycle, and it had not been an easy one. The Northmen wanted her dead for what she knew or what they thought she knew. She would have continued to starve to death if the escape had not gone so well, but she feared what the Northmen would do once they discovered that she and Hemera were gone.

Not wanting to think on her problem, she got busy unbraiding her hair. The golden strands were still a bit damp and some spots were knotted, but Verity kept at it until every strand ran easily through her fingers. She dropped her head forward to run her fingers through her hair again. She tossed the long strands back as she snapped her head up and her hair fell in soft waves past her shoulders, over her chest, to cover her breasts like a gentle blanket.

Verity yanked the blanket up against her chest when she heard the door about to open.

Wrath stopped abruptly when he entered to stare at her. Her golden hair, falling loose around her face and onto her shoulders, stunned the eye like the bright sun when it warmed the soil. When she shivered, he realized the cold wind was whipping past the door he had yet to close, and he shut it firmly.

He placed a bundle, beside her, on the sleeping pallet.

She reached with one hand to examine the bundle while her other hand kept the blanket firmly in place.

"There is no reason to hide yourself from me. I have seen all of you," Wrath said.

"Without my consent."

He caught the touch of sorrow in her eyes. Slaves obeyed, consent was not theirs to give. He wondered how often she had been stripped naked without her consent and the thought angered him.

"Don your garments and we will go eat," he said and turned his back on her, giving her what little privacy he could.

Surprised that he turned away from her, she hurried into a dark long sleeved, ankle length shift much softer than any she was accustomed to wearing and a pale-colored wool tunic to slip over it. They were a bit big for her slim frame, but warm and for that she was grateful. The foot coverings fit a bit snug once slipped on and tied, but again she was grateful for the warmth.

"I am appreciative for your generosity," she said as she draped the dark hooded, wool cloak, the items had been bundled in, over her shoulders.

Wrath turned, ignoring the tug at his insides when he looked upon her. The faster he saw this matter settled the better off he would be.

"We will go to the feasting house to eat," Wrath said and walked out of the dwelling, waiting outside for her to join him.

Verity hurried after him, eager to eat, since she could not recall the last time that she did. She pulled her hood up over her head, snow still falling, though not as heavily and glanced around as she followed his hasty steps.

They passed many well-structured dwellings as they followed a trampled path through the snow. Children, bundled well against the cold, ran about playing in the snowdrifts. A few men and women saw to essential chores and warriors roamed the area, their eyes on all that went on.

Verity stared amazed when they reached the feasting house. It looked as if one dwelling sat on top of another. Never had she seen anything like it before and, once inside the feasting hall, she could not stop glancing about. A huge fire pit sat off to a corner and kept the room comfortably warm. Stairs, combined of wood and stone curved up to the dwelling above. She marveled at the skill it must have taken to fashion such a mighty structure.

A delicious scent soon had her turning her attention to food the servants carried into the room in baskets, without handles, that they placed on a table close to the fire pit. She hurried to take a seat on the bench, but stopped, waiting for Wrath to sit and eat. She only hoped he would leave her enough to fill what felt like a large hole in her insides.

"Why do you wait? Sit and eat," Wrath said.

"You have yet to eat?"

"You are no slave here and need not wait for your master to leave you scraps. Sit and eat your fill."

Verity did not hesitate. As soon as she sat, she reached for a small egg and hurried it into her mouth. She wanted to sigh with delight at the taste, but was too busy reaching for a piece of the warm bread nestled in a basket.

Wrath joined her, realizing it had been too long since last he had eaten. He watched her reach for piece after a piece as if she feared it would disappear in front of her or that she might suddenly be deprived of it. It made him wonder and finally he asked, "Were you starved on purpose?"

Verity stopped from taking a bite of the meat she held in her hand, the delicious scent teasing her nose.

"Eat, then you will answer me," Wrath said, seeing the hunger in her eyes and not wanting to deprive her as he suspected others had done.

When she finished the piece of meat, Wrath handed her another one and she smiled as she took it and spoke before taking a bite. "Aye, I was starved."

"Why?" Wrath asked, hating the Northmen even more for treating her so badly.

"The King wishes to see you, Wrath."

Verity jumped and hurried off the bench to rush around behind Wrath. A man with white hair and a look of not only superiority but authority stood a short distance from the table.

"He will see you now in the High Counsel Chambers."

There were times Wrath wished he could squash the irritating man, not that it would take much, since he was not very tall or thick in shape. But the King would not take kindly to him harming Gelhard, his High Counselor.

Wrath stood, slipped his arm around Verity and she quickly pressed against him as if seeking his protection. He eased her down to sit on the bench where he had been sitting, though she seemed reluctant to leave his side. "You will remain here and eat until I return. No one will harm or bother you." He raised his head to look directly at Gelhard. "Is that not right, Gelhard?"

"The King informed me that the woman you found is under your protection. I will make it known," Gelhard said with a slow nod. "King Talon is impatient to speak with you." Without further acknowledgement, Gelhard walked off.

Wrath leaned down. "Worry not, you are safe here."

"You will not be long?" Verity asked, suddenly fearful of being separated from him.

"That depends on the King. Let no troubles disturb your repast. I will not be far." He pointed to a door to the left of where they had entered. Two warriors, wearing dark garments similar to his stood guard to either side of the closed door.

Her nod may have shown she understood, but the uncertainty in her eyes spoke differently. He walked away reluctantly, for some reason thinking he needed to stay and keep her safe. But from what?

One of the warriors who stood guard opened the door for Wrath as he approached. Wrath acknowledged both guards with a nod. He was their leader. He had trained them to protect the King and give their lives, if necessary, to save him.

"Tell me what you have learned about this woman you brought home with you," King Talon said, pointing to a seat to the right of where he sat at the long and narrow High Counsel table.

Wrath sat, knowing the King expected answers. He was not always a patient man, but he was a wise one. Wrath had recognized that in Talon when they had first met, long before he had become King. It had been obvious the man had been born to lead. "Her name is Verity and she has been a slave to the Northmen until she and her sister escaped."

"Sister? Where is this sister?"

"Verity searches for her and seeks a safe home for them. I told her that she is safe here."

"And was it a good poke that had you promising her sanctuary here?"

"I did not join with her, nor did she offer herself to me. She and her sister are Pict taken from this land before you were King and forced to serve the Northmen."

"If that is true, then she and her sister will be protected and offered a home here. Her body drawings will tell us the tribe she belongs to."

"She has no body drawings. She and her sister were taken well before they could earn their markings."

"The Northmen left her parents behind? How many others besides her and her sister were taken in the raid?"

"She did not say?"

"What of the mark around her neck? Was it a noose or had her owner kept her tethered and if so, why?"

"From what she has said, she did not always do what pleased the Northmen and so was tethered as punishment."

30

"The mark is raw, so the punishment had to be recent. Does her neck show remnants of previous punishments?"

Wrath frowned as he thought about Verity's smooth, soft neck and grew annoyed with himself for not having considered it. He grew even more annoyed when he had to admit it. "None that I saw."

"Why after so long did she and her sister finally attempt an escape?'

"I believe it has something to do with the Northmen trying to starve her to death."

King Talon titled his head, his brow narrowing. "A slave would have to have done something offensive to suffer such a punishment. If that is so, then the Northmen may pay me a visit and demand her return."

Wrath found it difficult to believe that Verity was capable of anything offensive, but what did he truly know of her? Everything she had told him could be a lie. If that was so, then who was she?

"You are aware of how long it has taken me to stop the Northmen from pillaging our northern tribes. We have finally established an agreement—tenuous that it may be—that allows trade between our northern tribes and the Northmen, with limited journey further into Pict territory. Some of the Northmen have even joined with our people in marriage to live among the Picts.

"If this woman has done something terribly offensive to the Northmen, they may demand her return, and I may have no choice but to return her to them in order to keep peace. The truth of her situation would be of great help to me if the Northmen do demand her return. You must find out the truth and not trust her until you do."

"The truth will not be easy to find when I have only her telling of the tale."

31

"That is why you will go find her sister and see what story she has to tell."

~~~

Verity kept steady eyes on the door as she ate, though she had felt full after the last two chunks of meat and bread she had eaten. She had thought she would eat more, having eaten so sparingly of late. Hemera had managed to scavenge and store some food before their escape and they had eaten before the angry sea had struck. Verity had also managed to steal some food from tribes she had passed while in search of Hemera that had helped sustain her, but then the snowstorm had hit and food became difficult to find.

She jumped when a servant leaned over from behind her to fill her vessel with wine. She had heard how the King of the Picts traded often with foreign merchants besides the Northmen, so she was not surprised that there was wine to be had here. Though, she had never expected it to be served to her or to be eating in the King's feasting house.

Verity had always been the one to serve and having never been acknowledged kindly by those she had served, she did not want to do the same to another. She went to turn around to face the servant just as the woman stepped around the table.

Verity almost gasped when she looked upon the woman. A single scar ran across her face from high on her cheek to down across her mouth, ending at her jaw. You could see that she was once beautiful, though no longer, her face distorted by the scar.

"You are a fine looking one. It will not be long before the King takes you to his private chambers. I served him once and see what it got me," she said with stinging bitterness.

"I have no wont to mate with the King," Verity assured her, certain the King would find no interest in her. Despite the ugly scar, the woman had a full and lush body whereas Verity was far too thin to please any man.

"Tell me that again after you lay eyes on him and he speaks to you."

"My words will ring true then as they do now. I am sorry for your misfortune. No one deserves what has been done to you. Perhaps someday you will find a man who will take kindly to you and—"

The woman snorted. "Kindly? Men only come to me for a poke when they are too drunk to see who it is they poke. Then there are those who are eager to poke me, but insist on covering my hideous face. I deny them all."

"And so you should. You deserve better."

"I have had the best. I have had the King. There is no man whose skills can compare to the King when it comes to pleasing a woman. I joined with him day and night, his thirst for coupling unquenchable, though I kept him appeased more often than not." Her shoulders sagged and her head drooped. "Now I am nothing more than a servant that everyone avoids looking upon."

"Stop blaming others, Atas," Gelhard snapped. "You got what you deserved for betraying the King and lying with another man, a man who proved to be an enemy of the King. You are lucky the King did not condemn you to live out your life with a tribe far removed from Pictland, which can still be arranged if you continue to complain to anyone who will listen to your foolish whining."

Atas retreated quickly after leaving the container of wine on the table.

If Verity had not been sitting, she would have retreated as quickly as Atas had done. He obviously was a man of some power, since Atas had paid heed to his threat and said no more.

"Do not think of giving yourself to the King. He will soon take a wife and she will see to pleasing him."

A snort came from the shadows and Atas emerged. "No one woman will ever be able to keep the King satisfied. It is good his seed is not strong enough to take root or his bastard bairns would be running wild around Pictland."

"What is that you say, Atas?"

Verity saw Atas pale so badly that it made her scar look as red as the day she had received it and knew it could only be King Talon who had spoken and put such fear in her. And while Verity was in no hurry to face the King, Atas was quick to apologize.

"My King, I am truly sorry, I meant—"

"Every word you spoke," King Talon finished, "Gelhard, see that Atas is escorted to a tribe as far north as possible."

Atas stepped forward. "Please, my King, please do not send me away. This is my home."

"You do not treat your home or those who have been good to you with respect. Perhaps a new home will teach what you have failed to learn." King Talon turned to Gelhard. "See her made ready to leave as soon as the snow stops. Have some warriors take her to the nearest tribe with instructions that she is to be sent north from tribe to tribe, when the weather permits, until she reaches the first outer isle where she will make her new home."

"Is this hideous scar I must bear not enough for you?" Atas cried. "Must you torture me more?"

"That scar is of your own foolish doing and how you carry it, with pride or regret, is up to you," King Talon said.

Verity did not hear a hint of concern in his powerful voice. He cared nothing for Atas or what would happen to her. She stayed as she was, her eyes lowered to the table, too fearful to look upon such an unmerciful man.

"Please, my King, I have served you well. I beg you to take pity on me," Atas pleaded, tears beginning to run down her cheeks.

"I did, and how do you repay my kindness? You say disparaging things my enemies hope to hear and use against me. Be glad I do not send you to the executioner. Now be gone out of my sight." He flicked his hand, summoning two of his personal guard that remained close by him and they stepped forward and took hold of her.

"Your enemy is right," Atas screamed as she fought the guards as soon as their hands took hold of her. "You are no man. No matter what woman you plant your seed in, it will never take root. Your seed is barren."

"For that, you may just lose your head," King Talon said, his icy tone sending a shiver through almost everyone in the room.

Atas fought the guards and Verity had no choice but to move or be caught up in her struggle. She hurried off the bench, away from the three and reluctantly turned when she reached the far end of the table.

Her breath caught when her eyes settled on the King. He was taller than many Northmen and solid in body. His features were exceptional, far finer than Verity had ever seen and it was easy to understand why women would find him appealing. But just as there had been coldness in his voice, there was also coldness in his eyes.

The guards got Atas under control, though she swore as they led her from the room.

The King looked her way and spoke, but Verity did not hear him. Sound had stilled and she felt darkness begin to creep over her. She silently begged for it to stop, a useless plea for it never stopped once it started. The darkness spread around her, encasing her like a shroud. Her eyes fluttered and her limbs turned weak. Soon she would no longer be able to stand. Wishing she could do something to stop it, yet knowing that was not possible, she waited for the inevitable.

Wrath did not hesitate when he saw Verity's eyes flutter closed and her body sway. He ran past the King and caught her before she could hit the floor.

Chapter Four

Atas gasped. "The stranger has brought illness to Pictland. Soon it will strike us all."

Wrath heard several servants begin to whisper and with good reason. It was known that one ill person could devastate a whole tribe within a moon cycle. He was quick to take charge before fear and foolishness could take hold. "Hush your mouth, Atas, this woman suffers no illness. Her long journey has weakened her."

"Take her out of here!" the King ordered sharply with a nod at Atas. "The rest of you get to your chores."

Once everyone hurried to obey, the King turned to Wrath. "Have the healer look over her and pray she has spoken the truth to you and that the Northmen have not sent a sickness to spread amongst us."

Wrath carried Verity out of the feasting hall and when he was only a few steps from his dwelling, her eyes suddenly sprang open. He was surprised to see the color of her eyes was now dark blue as it had been when he first found her.

"It cannot be," she no soon as whispered then her eyes closed again.

He laid her on his sleeping pallet, covering her with the blanket. He pressed his palm to her forehead and felt no warmth. There was always worry when heat settled in the body and feeling none brought some relief. What had she meant by *it cannot be*? And would she remember saying it? The King was right. He did not know this woman well enough to trust her. Why then did he feel that he could?

37

Wrath hurried to get the healer, Bethia. Before anything, he wanted Bethia to confirm what he already believed. Verity was not ill, weakened by her arduous journey perhaps, but not ill.

Verity woke with a start when the door closed. She stared anxiously at her surroundings before she realized where she was and recalled what had happened. She sat up and brought her knees up to her chin, hugging them.

She could not believe what she had seen. It was not possible, but her visions had never been wrong. She remembered the first vision she ever had. It had frightened her and she had shared it with Hemera. Hemera had warned her to tell no one about it or else she would be sent away to live with the seers, older women who lived only to predict and advise. Verity had been much too young to be forced into such a constrained life.

She and Hemera had kept her secret, and it was Hemera who had advised her to fake a vision now and again so it could be explained away as an odd attack that took hold of her on occasion. She had been wise in suggesting it and even wiser for Verity to have listened to her, for when a vision did strike her, no one had paid heed to it. It was also the reason not one Northmen would mate with her. They did not want their offspring suffering such an oddity.

It was what had brought her to Wrath. It was in a vision she had first seen him and had begun to feel safe with him. It had shown him protecting her and Hemera. She could not believe what her vision had revealed to her in the feasting hall. She shivered, recalling it.

The Northmen were coming for her and Hemera.

The door opened and a woman entered, and Wrath followed in behind her.

The woman approached the sleeping pallet. Her gray hair was shorter than Verity had ever seen on a woman. It barely brushed her shoulders. She was tall and thin and there was kindness in her eyes and a smile on her face. Verity was about to return the smile, when Wrath's words sent a chill through her.

"This is Bethia our healer."

Verity hugged her knees tighter to her. "I need no healer."

"You look well enough," Bethia said, pulling a bench close to the sleeping pallet and sitting.

"I have strange attacks on occasion. I am used them. They are nothing and they harm no one."

"They just come and go?"

Verity nodded and looked to see that Wrath leaned casually against the closed door, his arms crossed over his chest and his eyes steady on her, listening to her every response.

"How long have you suffered them?"

"Since I was young."

"Before the Northmen took you?" Wrath asked.

"No," Verity said, shaking her head. "They came long afterwards."

"Do you suffer any pain when they take hold of you?"

Verity was surprised it was Wrath that asked and even more surprised that he sounded concerned. "No, I feel nothing." That was not quite true. Some of her visions left her in fear, just as this one had. Most left her feeling tired.

"Then why do you hug yourself so tightly?" Wrath asked, pushing away from the door with his shoulder and approaching the sleeping pallet.

Verity was grateful to the healer for answering.

"What would you expect from her after her wits are stolen from her? It must leave her a bit confused."

Wrath stopped at the end of the sleeping pallet. "Does it leave you confused?"

"It depends on how long it takes me to wake from one. Longer attacks leave me more muddled." That was the truth, though she had never confessed that to anyone but Hemera.

"It must leave you tired as well, especially so after your difficult journey," Bethia said, reaching out to pat Verity's arm. "I believe a nice warm brew and some sleep will see you fit again."

Verity was quick to respond. "I need no brew."

Bethia patted her arm again. "I think perhaps that a healer did not treat you well."

Verity shivered and gave her knees another hug as she nodded, having no wont to speak about it.

"My brew soothes, nothing more, but if you prefer not to drink it that is your choice."

"If it will help her, she will drink it," Wrath said and was puzzled by the strange look Verity turned on him.

"The brew will do her little good if she is forced to take it," Bethia said and reached for the pouch hanging from the belt at her waist. She opened it and drew out some dried crushed leaves. She held them out to Wrath. "Take these to Simca, you will find her—"

Wrath took them from her. "I know where to find Simca."

"Yes, you would know where to find her." Bethia grinned. "She will know how to prepare the brew. Wait and bring it back here, if you will?"

"You will stay with Verity until I return and you will see if there is more you can do for her."

Bethia agreed with a nod, though she knew it was not a request.

"You are safe with Bethia," Wrath assured Verity before he left.

Verity hoped so, but she worried. Some healers had a way of knowing things and if it had not been for Hemera, the Northmen healer would have seen her dead.

"I have seen your kind of attacks before, where a woman suddenly slips into a deep slumber and cannot be woken." Bethia said once they were alone. "They come upon women who have visions. Some tribes fear the women who can see what is to come, other tribes revere them, though isolate them, since they also fear them. After all, who wants to be around someone who knows your fate?"

Verity remained silent, fearful this woman would divulge her secret.

Bethia patted her arm for a third time and smiled. "But you need not worry about that, since your attacks stem from illness." Her smile faded some. "Wrath sees things others do not. It is how he keeps the King protected, safe from those who wish him harm. He does not trust easily and does not tolerate fools and liars. He also has a temper that once let loose is not easily contained. But mostly, he is a man of honor and you can ask for no better man to call friend."

"I am grateful for your wise words and I will remember them well."

It was not long before Wrath returned and when he entered, he went directly to Verity and handed her the vessel he carried, not giving her a chance to refuse it.

Bethia stood. "It has a fine taste and will soothe you."

"She will drink it," Wrath said, sending Verity a stern look.

41

Accustomed to obeying, Verity sipped at it and was pleased by the pleasant taste and scent that drifted up her nose.

"She is well?" Wrath asked of Bethia.

"She is fine and, as she told us, she is accustomed to the attacks. She deals well with it when it overpowers her and now that you are aware of it, you will know what to do when it happens again."

Wrath had his doubts about that, since his insides had knotted when he had seen her about to collapse. "There is nothing that can be done to help her?"

Bethia patted his arm and smiled. "Be there to catch her."

Wrath did not find Bethia's response humorous, since he worried what would happen to Verity if he was not there to catch her.

Bethia stopped at the door. "An attack such as hers can rob her strength. See that she rests." She sent a smile and nod to Verity and left.

Wrath sat beside Verity. "Drink, it will help you."

He did not sound like those who had ordered her about with almost every word they spoke. There was concern in Wrath's voice and, of late, she had known little of that.

"You challenge me, Verity." Her eyes showed surprise at his words. "I want to believe what you have told me about yourself, but I wonder if I would be a fool to trust you until I have learned more about you."

Verity wished she could be truthful with him, but it was how he would respond to the truth that she feared the most. He would know all sooner or later, but until then she had to hold her tongue.

"The King wants to hear what your sister has to say. He has instructed me to go in search of her."

"When do we leave?" Verity asked anxiously. The sooner they found Hemera the better. Her visions did not always allow her to see when things would happen, so she did not know if the Northmen were making plans or had already left to come after them.

"You are not well enough to travel."

"You must take me with you. How else will you know my sister?" she begged.

"You will tell me about her and there must be traits you both share that I would recognize."

Verity reached out to rest her hand on his arm. "Hemera is different from others. She is often lost in her own thoughts and is slower to respond when spoken to. I worry how she will survive in a strange land on her own, and I fear that I will be too late in finding her. Please you cannot leave me behind. I must be there when you find her, however it is we find her."

Wrath had felt her hand tighten on his arm with every word she spoke. Her concern and fear were real, yet he felt there was something more she was not telling him.

"What were your plans once you reached our shores?" he asked and watched a brief flicker of doubt flash in her eyes. It was clear that she was hesitant to speak.

"We were not sure, safety from the Northmen was our first concern," Verity said, seeing no harm in telling him that.

"You believe the Northmen will bother to chase after two slaves that escaped? That does not seem likely unless of course you have done something so offensive that the Northmen seek reprisal."

Verity wanted to bite her tongue for not having thought on her words. "We are property and the Northmen do not like to lose what belongs to them."

43

"You are Pict. This land is your home. The King will see you are safe as long as you are truthful." It made no sense to Wrath that she should worry that the Northmen would come for her and her sister. They would not dare arrive on Pict shore and demand the King return two of his own people and even if she had done something to offend the Northmen, King Talon would be the one to see her punished.

"It is hard for me to believe that my sister and I are finally free after all these years. I worry that I will wake and discover it is all a dream."

"It is no dream. You are home now and have nothing to fear."

If only that were true, Verity thought as she drank more of the tasty brew.

"Tell me the last thing you remember before the sea claimed your vessel," Wrath said and moved his arm so that her hand fell off it. Surprisingly, her hand quickly latched onto his hand, as if she feared him leaving her side.

"The clouds were so heavy above, that darkness covered whatever there was of the moon. The swells grew larger and we hung on tightly. Then out of the pit of darkness came a huge wave and suddenly we were being swallowed by the icy sea. The next thing I remembered was waking up on the shore, wet and cold, Hemera nowhere to be seen. I needed to get warm before I could do anything else. I was lucky to come upon an empty dwelling. It took some time, but I got a fire going in the fire pit. It took several settings and risings of the sun for my garments to dry and for the cold to leave my insides. Only then did I begin my search for Hemera, and it was not long after that that the snow began to fall."

Wrath had known strong, courageous women and had fought beside many, but they had been trained since they were young, not so Verity. Her life had been one of servitude and obedience. How she had gained the courage and strength to plan an escape, brave the unpredictable sea, and survive a watery grave was remarkable. Or there was more to her story.

"I thought I found a torn piece of Hemera's cloak, but the wind snatched it from my hand."

"Where was that?"

"I wish I knew," Verity said with a sigh that spoke of frustration. "The snow was falling heavily and I was barely able to see where I walked. The dark piece of wool was like a beacon in the storm. It was caught in a bush and as soon as I grabbed it, the swirling wind robbed me of it."

"It sounds as if your sister was searching for you as well. Do you know how long after that I found you?"

"I am not sure, perhaps one or two sunrises." Verity shook her head. "It could have been more. The snowstorm made it difficult to tell."

"As soon as the snow stops, we will take our leave and search for your sister. Until then, you are to rest so that you are not more burden than help to me."

"I will be no burden," Verity said sharply and hearing her curt tone quickly apologized. "Forgive me, I meant no disrespect."

"You are not my slave, Verity, and while I will not tolerate a snappish tone from anyone but the King, I understand the reason for your curtness. I warn you, though, use it sparingly with me."

He stood abruptly and their hands parted with the same suddenness, causing them both to exchange surprised glances. Or had the sudden parting left them feeling as though they had been torn unwillingly apart?

"You need to rest and regain your strength for our journey."

She would have argued that she was strong enough whether she was or not, but a yawn settled it for her.

Wrath took the vessel from her hand. "Sleep, I have matters to see to."

"I cannot continue to intrude on your generosity. There must be some other place I may dwell until we take our leave."

"As the King has decreed, you are my responsibility, and since I am still not sure if I can trust you, I will keep you close."

"You cannot mean that I am to continue to share your sleeping pallet?"

Wrath leaned over her, bringing his face so close to hers that she thought for a moment he meant to kiss her, and she shivered.

"You keep something from me and until I find out what it is, you will stay by my side whether it is in my dwelling or sharing my sleeping pallet. He took hold of her shoulders and pushed her down to lie flat on her back. He then leaned over her, placing his hands on either side of her head. "You will not move from here until I return."

Verity nodded slowly and after staring at her for a few moments with dark eyes that reminded her of the sky during the raging storm at sea, he moved away and hastily left the dwelling.

Verity expelled a heavy breath, feeling as if she had just escaped a potential storm. She lie there thinking about the vision that had shown Wrath helping her find her sister and realized that in one of her previous visions Hemera had already been found. Wrath had stood close while she and Hemera hugged tightly. Had Wrath helped her or had he found them after Verity had found Hemera on her own?

Deciphering some of her visions proved challenging while others were so potent in their image that when they proved true, Verity felt as if she was reliving the incident. That particular one was proving to be more challenging. Did she stay and leave along with Wrath? Or did she go off on her own and meet up with Wrath later? Either way Wrath would find them.

So far, she had had no visions of what became of her and her sister beyond that image. She sat up, her thoughts too busy to rest.

Hemera could be lying in the cold snow somewhere, perhaps just outside the stronghold's gates. The worrisome thought had her hurrying to her feet.

Stronghold gates were often opened at sunrise and closed just before darkness fell. What if Hemera had made it as close to the Pict stronghold as she had? She could be out there now lying in the snow freezing to death.

She slipped on her cloak and went to the door. She opened it slowly and peered out, relieved to see Wrath had left no guard at the door. She pulled her hood up and stepped out of the dwelling.

Snow was falling but not heavily and with a determined step she made her way through the village.

Chapter Five

Wrath sat at the long narrow table in the Council Chambers, the High Counsel meeting almost at an end. The last matter to be discussed was who would fill the seat on the High Council of Warrior Commander. Tarn had once held it, but had proven to be no friend to the King, as did Bodu who had held the seat of Master Builder. Both men had proven enemies of the King and had met a fitting fate.

The King had appointed Paine, his executioner, though no longer, Master Builder. He had often helped the King construct small versions of dwellings he wished to build before the actual construction was approved. No one on the council had objected to Paine's appointment, but then the King had the final decision as always.

Wrath thought someone would have been chosen while he was gone, but he had returned to find the seat had remained empty.

"We must fill the position of Warrior Commander," Gelhard said. "The warriors grow restless without someone to command them."

Wrath shook his head as soon as the words left the man's mouth and from the way Midrent, the Tariff Collector's brow went up and the way Ebit's, the Crop Master, eyes turned wide, they were thinking the same as Wrath. He looked to the King and waited.

King Talon glared at Gelhard. "Are you saying that my warriors believe I cannot lead them?"

Wrath placed his hand over his mouth to hide the smile that surfaced when he watched Gelhard turn as white as the falling snow.

"No. No, my King. I meant no such thing," Gelhard said, trying to right his foolish wrong.

"Then what did you mean?" King Talon demanded his voice so strong that it seemed to echo off the walls.

Gelhard stammered, though nothing coherent came out of his mouth.

Normally Wrath would enjoy watching the little man squirm, since he could be annoying at times, but the meeting had gone on long enough and there were still things that needed to be discussed between him and the King.

"I have someone to propose for the position," Wrath said and he never saw Gelhard look so relieved.

"Who is that?" King Talon asked and turned to Gelhard. "Do not think we are done."

Gelhard wisely gave the King a respectful nod and remained silent.

"One of your personal guard, Broc. He is not only a fine warrior, but he has proven to have excellent leadership skills. I believe he would do well as Warrior Commander."

All seemed to agree and King Talon said he would think on it. He dismissed all but Gelhard and Wrath.

Gelhard went to speak and the King stopped him. "Not a word, Gelhard, until I am ready to speak with you. And if you continue to speak foolishly and continue to fail in finding me a wife, your seat on the High Council will be in jeopardy."

Again Gelhard wisely held his tongue.

"What of this woman?" King Talon demanded of Wrath. "Has she brought a plague among us?"

"Verity brings no sickness to us. She has had attacks like the one she suffered today for some time. They cause no harm to others."

"That is good to hear. Have you learned anything else about her?"

"She fears the Northmen may come for her and her sister."

"The Northmen would not dare do something so foolish," Gelhard said with a dismissive wave of his hand.

"Unless there is more to this woman's story than she tells us—in which case—we need to be prepared," the King said.

Wrath saw how Gelhard turned his full attention on the King, prepared to attend to whatever was necessary. The man could annoy, but there was no denying that he was an excellent High Counselor to the King.

"Bring Broc to me, Gelhard. I will appoint him temporarily to the position of Warrior Commander and if he does well, he will be made a permanent member of the High Council."

"As you say, my King," Gelhard said with a quick bow of his head and hastily left the room.

"What do you think this woman keeps from us?" the King asked, stretching himself out of his chair.

It was easy to see why Talon was King. He was not only brave and wise beyond reason. There was a strong, fluidness to his movements that set him apart from others and commanded attention and respect. And the slight lift of his chin gave the appearance of superiority, leaving no doubt he was a man to be obeyed.

Wrath went to stand, for no one sat when the King stood.

"Sit, Wrath, it is only you and me."

Wrath favored when they talked as friends. He remained as he was and watched Talon pace as he always did when his thoughts turned busy. After a few moments, he said, "To stir the ire of the Northmen enough to come after her, I would think it would be something dire."

King Talon stopped pacing. "What if she is not a Pict? What if she is a woman of the Northmen Tribe who grew tired of her husband?"

Wrath had never given such an idea thought and it annoyed him to think it now, though why he did not know. Verity was no different from other women he had protected when necessary, except he had never found the others as appealing as he did Verity.

"Or what if she took something of importance from the Northmen?" the King said, voicing his thoughts aloud.

"Then it was lost to the raging sea, since I stripped her bare and found nothing." That was not quite true. He had found pale, unmarred beauty that surprisingly had aroused him and damn if the memory did not stir him now.

"You need to find her sister and see what you learn from her."

"Verity says that her sister lives mostly in her thoughts and is slow to respond."

"A slow-minded one. No wonder Verity is protective of her and if the Northmen treated her sister badly, it would be a good reason for her to take her elsewhere. If they are Pict, they will have a home here, if not?" The King shrugged, then shook his head. "There is something we fail to see, something this woman does not want us to see. The question is why?" He glared at Wrath. "I will not be left vulnerable in the face of the

Northmen or find myself at war with them for no good reason. Find out the truth."

"I will see to it, Talon."

King Talon walked over to Wrath and sat on the bench beside him. "I can trust you to be honest with me and tell what is being said about me outside these walls."

Wrath expected the question and never had he spoken falsely to his friend. "There is talk that you are not potent enough to be King and it is encouraged by your enemies. Two wives that produced no bairns and now one carrying her new husband's child, leaves doubt to your ability to produce sons that can carry on Pict rule. Many believe you a powerful warrior and can win endless battles, but they are beginning to doubt that you can make sure that Pict blood will run in those who forever claim this land."

King Talon brought his fist down on the table, his deep blue eyes wild with anger. "I will have sons, many sons, and they will spread across this land and leave not only their mark upon it but their blood will run through it as well. Pict blood will always run in those who rule this land."

Another reason that Talon was King was that he spoke with such intense power that you believed every word he said. There was no reason to doubt him, his words made it so.

"Has Gelhard found you a suitable wife yet?"

"There is a woman he believes would make a good queen. He is seeing to the arrangement."

"Her mother has bred many sons?" Wrath asked.

"From what I am told six."

"That is impressive. I am sure all will go well." Wrath hoped it would. Talon had fought hard for his people and sacrificed even more. He was a powerful ruler and most never got to see what a truly good and honest man he was.

Gelhard tried to hurry around Broc as the large warrior rushed into the room before him. "You will wait until you are—"

"Forgive me, my King, I mean no disrespect, but there is a matter that requires Wrath's immediate attention."

"You may speak," the King said.

Broc turned to Wrath. "The woman has left your dwelling and made her way through the village to the gate. She has just left the stronghold."

Wrath was glad the King sprang to his feet, allowing him to do the same.

"Who follows her?" Wrath demanded.

"I did until Gelhard told me the King had summoned me. After that, I had Tarnis follow her."

"Both of you go," the King ordered. "Broc, you will see me when this is settled."

Wrath and Broc sent respectful nods to the King before hurrying out of the High Council Chambers.

Wrath was glad he had ordered Broc to watch his dwelling. He had not wanted to take a chance that worry for her sister would have Verity slipping off to search for her. And his concern had proven valid.

"It was not long after you left that she did," Broc explained. "With the stronghold unfamiliar to her and not calling attention to herself by asking someone the way to the gate, she took a few wrong turns. She was at the gate when Gelhard approached me."

"How did Gelhard respond to you telling him you would not go with him until he brought Tarnis to you?" Wrath knew his men well. Broc would never have left his post without someone to replace him even if summoned by the King.

"He did not have much choice, since I hurried through the gate after the woman."

"You left a trail for Tarnis."

"As he will do for us," Broc said as they stepped outside the gate and saw a deep, long rut in the snow.

~~~

Verity stopped and looked around the snow-covered woods and shivered. She wished it was planting time and the sun was bright and the breeze cool. Their escape would have been far less treacherous, but she and Hemera had had no choice. Her present efforts to find Hemera had proven useless and after searching for what seemed like forever and the sky growing grayer, she knew she should return to the stronghold, but she was not ready to do that yet.

In her worry for Hemera, she had made a foolish decision. She should have trusted her vision. It had been clear enough. She and Hemera had been safe with Wrath. She had had no vision of finding Hemera on her own, so why had she taken such a foolish chance?

The Northmen.

The vision of the Northmen coming for them had frightened her. Had she feared them arriving at the stronghold before she and Wrath could search for Hemera? Had she feared the possibility of the King surrendering her to the Northmen?

She rubbed her head. It ached with far too many troublesome thoughts. From her visions, she had thought she could trust Wrath, but was she deciphering her visions wrong? She wished she never had visions.

"Are you finally finished going around in circles?"

Verity sighed before raising her head. She had hoped to return before Wrath found her gone. "Is that what I have been doing?"

She saw that Wrath was not alone. Two good-sized warriors stood to either side of him. He spoke to each of them, though she could not hear what he said, and they left. He approached Verity and she fought the tickle of apprehension that ran through her as he drew closer. His powerful form and dark garments and hair made him appear more potent against the stark white snow.

"Do you need reminding that I am no fool?" he asked, stopping close in front of her. "I watched how you purposely went round and round, covering every inch of the same ground and snowdrifts. You thought your sister may have met the same fate as you and worried she was out here freezing to death."

He was more observant than she thought. She would have to be careful. "I could not help but see for myself."

"If you had come to me you would have saved yourself worry. I had already sent men out to cover the surrounding area in hopes that your sister would be found nearby."

She sighed with relief, though she would have preferred to smile since his actions had confirmed what her visions had shown her. He would help and protect her and Hemera. "I thought you would think me foolish?"

"Why would I think you foolish? I understand that you worry for your sister's safety and your thought was a wise one."

"Truly?"

"I never speak falsely."

His strong tone alone spoke the truth of his words and she felt guilt nudge her in the side. She should speak

55

as honestly with him as he did with her. But she feared what it might bring.

He took sudden hold of her chin. "You were to rest. You will not disregard my word. You will not leave the stronghold without my permission. You will do as I say."

It was easy for her to say, "As you wish." She had said it often enough through the years, until the words meant nothing to her. They were said to appease those in authority and she would continue to say them until she finally got what she had wished for all these years...her complete freedom.

Chapter Six

"Get up!"

Verity bolted up, her eyes going wide, all sleep gone as she stared at Wrath, anger filling his dark eyes. It had been two days since her arrival here, the snow having prevented them from starting their search for Hemera and though she continued to remain at Wrath's dwelling, they no longer shared his sleeping pallet. She assumed he had found a more welcoming pallet to share.

"Word has come that a Northmen's ship has reached our shore and its leader has requested to meet with King Talon."

Verity found herself unable to respond. She feared this would happen. Her vision had warned her of it, but she had not expected it so soon. She startled when Wrath was suddenly in front of her and she eased back away from him. It did little good. He leaned in closer until she found herself with her back pressed against the wall.

She struggled for words and as she did, she saw that there was not only anger in his dark eyes but concern. It also gathered in the deep wrinkles of his brow, the fine lines that fanned out at the corner of his eyes, and the grimace set at his mouth. Was his deep concern meant for her?

"What is it you fear telling me?"

Fear. He was right about that. She feared him—anyone—learning the truth. She had no words for him, so she kept her lips closed tight.

"How do I protect you, if I do not know what it is I protect you from?" He moved away from her, turning his back on her.

Verity spoke softly, saying what came to her. "I am unimportant."

Wrath turned abruptly. "The Northmen think otherwise." He motioned her off the pallet with a quick snap of his hand. "Come, the King commands your presence."

"I can tell him no more than what I have told you," she said, her insides roiling with the thought of facing the mighty Pict King.

"We will see," Wrath said and motioned again for her to hurry.

"The snow has stopped," Verity said when they left the dwelling. "We can leave and begin the search for Hemera."

"That was the plan until news came of the Northmen." He did not like that he heard concern in his voice, but the news had brought much worry. The Northmen would not come to retrieve slaves they had taken from this land. They would come to claim what was rightfully theirs and that had Wrath concerned and angry. If Verity would just be honest with him, he could help her. Or was that why she was not being honest with him? Did she believe he could not help her?

"We cannot delay our search any longer. We must leave today," Verity insisted.

"We will not be leaving until this matter with the Northmen is settled to the King's liking."

Verity stopped abruptly. "Are you telling me that we must wait until the King meets with the Northmen before we take our leave?"

"If the King so commands it. Now hurry, the King is not a patient man."

She resumed her steps. She had come to understand that few men were patient, most cared little for anything beyond themselves, some were dangerous and were to be avoided and a very small handful respected and cherished women. She believed the King was the dangerous kind that should be avoided. She had yet to decide which best suited Wrath.

The closer they got to the feasting house, the more her insides twisted into knot after knot after knot. It was not only speaking with the King that caused such alarm, it was worry that she would be forced to stay here until the Northmen's arrival. That was not possible. She would have to take her leave on her own if necessary.

They entered the feasting house and Verity saw that the King was speaking with some of his warriors. She caught a word or two and realized final plans were being discussed for Atas' departure today. She was relieved to know Atas was being sent away rather than lose her head.

Verity watched King Talon with apprehension. He frightened her, though it was more his endless power that frightened her. One command and he could end a person's life or make him suffer unbelievable pain. She had seen such power before and the greed that went along with it.

The warriors turned and left after a respectful nod to their King. It was her turn to face the King and she worried her legs were too weak to take another step. She felt Wrath's hand low at her back, urging her to step forward, and she did, though without his subtle urging, she would have remained rooted to where she had stood.

She stopped abruptly a distance away from King Talon, her feet refusing to take her any closer and no amount of urging from Wrath would change that.

"Come closer," the King ordered annoyed.

Wrath waited for her to obey the King and when she did not move and did not respond to his gentle nudges, he took her arm and forced her forward.

"Why do you fear me? And I will have no lies from your tongue," King Talon warned when Wrath brought her to a stop in front of him.

Verity knew well enough to answer the King without hesitation. "I have seen men of your worth do horrible things to people."

"I only do horrible things to people if they deserve it. Do you deserve it?"

The strength in his voice alone had her leaning back and she almost sighed aloud when her back met Wrath's chest. "I do not believe so."

"Then you have nothing to fear. Now tell me why the Northmen wish to meet with me."

A chill lingered in the room, though the large fire pit burned brightly and yet the King wore a sleeveless garment, long that it was and slit from throat to ankles and cinched at the waist with a belt. His arms were not thick with fat, but lean and hard and his fingers long. He could easily snap a man's neck.

She shook her head, realizing she was taking too long to answer. "I do not know." She hoped her lie could not be seen on her face. Sometimes she was good at hiding the truth and her feelings. Other times she failed completely as she had with Wrath. She hoped she would not fail with the King.

"That does not seem likely," the King said, crossing his arms over his chest. "Perhaps you should think on your answer."

"My sister and I were slaves to Haggard, Chieftain of the Southern Region. He does not like losing what belongs to him." It was a partial truth and she hoped it showed.

"You are Pict."

Verity understood the King wanted her to confirm it, and she nodded. "Aye, my King, I was born a Pict."

"I do not take lies lightly. If I find out you lied to me, you will suffer for it."

She had suffered so much already what difference would more suffering make? "I speak the truth." And she did, just not all of it.

"It will take time for the Northmen to arrive here. Until they do, you will remain here. I will send a troop of warriors to search for your sister. You will..."

His words drifted away as she felt darkness begin to take hold of her. Not now. Not in front of the King again. But nothing would stop the vision once it took hold and she had no choice but to surrender to it.

The King stepped forward just as Wrath caught Verity in his arms. He had felt her body wilt beside him and was relieved he had been there to catch her. He lifted her in his arms. Her face was pale, her eyes closed, and her body so limp one would think that death had claimed her. The thought twisted his insides.

"Put her on the table while we talk," the King said.

Wrath was reluctant to let her go, but he had little choice. He did as the King ordered and gently placed her on a table and remained by it, worried she would wake frightened as she had done before when an attack struck her.

"For the Northmen to have arrived on our shores so soon after Verity, I would say that they left not long after her and her sister. And if they gave chase that soon after, when the sea is most dangerous, I suspect that the two women harbor something valuable. I cannot see the Northmen coming after two slaves who have returned to their homeland unless they have done something so grievous that honor bounds the Northmen to seek immediate revenge." The King looked at Verity, appearing as though she lay in dead repose. "That does not seem possible, since she is such a weak woman."

Wrath spoke up. "I believe Verity stronger than most women or she would not have been able to handle this infliction that has been forced upon her."

Verity drifted out of the darkness at the sound of Wrath's voice, his words surprising her, though she did not move. She laid there and listened, letting the two men think she had yet to awake.

"You sound as though you care for her," the King said, "yet I heard that you have spent the last two nights with Simca. Do you turn to her to ease the ache you have for Verity?"

"I do not ache for Verity," Wrath snarled.

"Then why does your temper spark at the mention of it?"

"Need I remind you that you told me she is my responsibility and what I thought a simple problem, which could have been seen to quickly and easily, has now turned into something beyond what I ever thought possible?"

"You can lead the group that will go in search for her sister. I will have someone else see to Verity."

"No, Verity stays with me," Wrath said, trying not to let his anger show. He would not trust Verity's safety to anyone.

"Are you sure of that, my friend?" the King questioned. "The Northmen could not keep hold of her even when they tethered her, which means she may turn out to be far more than you can handle."

Wrath laughed. "There is not a woman alive that I cannot handle and I can assure you there will be no reason to tether Verity as Paine had to do with Anin."

"But would you tether her if necessary?"

"I would do whatever was necessary to keep Pictland safe, my friend...my King."

King Talon's hand came down on Wrath's shoulder and gave it a strong squeeze. "Of that I have no doubt, my friend. Now take Verity to your dwelling, leave her to rest, and return here with Broc so that we can begin making plans for the Northmen's arrival."

Verity moaned softly to make Wrath think she was just coming to. She let her eyes flutter, but did not open them and she whispered his name, "Wrath."

"I am here, Verity. You are safe." He slipped his arms beneath her, lifting her to rest against his chest and cradled her firmly in his arms.

She kept her eyes closed as he walked through the village, afraid if she opened them the tears that were building would spill forth. Hearing Wrath tell King Talon that he would do whatever was necessary to keep Pictland safe, even tether her as the Northmen had done, made her realize that she was not safe here. The Northmen would come and if necessary she would be returned to them. She could not chance that and her vision had warned her of it.

Verity opened her eyes slowly when Wrath placed her on the sleeping pallet.

He looked down at her. "You will rest and worry not. All will be well."

She nodded and pretended to yawn, then turned on her side to hide the tear that had fallen from the corner of her eye onto her cheek. She heard the door close and waited, fighting back the tears that wanted desperately to burst free.

She refused to let them fall. She had no time for tears. She thought on her vision, knowing it would give her strength. She had heard Hemera calling out to her to hurry and she had been shown a path to take and just as she reached for the back of Hemera's hood, a thick mist had begun to swirl around her and she woke up.

With a rough swipe of her hand across her cheek, she rid herself of the single tear that had escaped. She sat up and hurried off the sleeping pallet. She fashioned one of the blankets to wear as a shawl beneath her cloak. She had had little to protect her against the relentless cold the last time. She would not let that happen again. Finding food had been another problem and she had yet to eat today, but she could not linger. She had to leave while it was light and get as far away from the stronghold before they found her gone.

The one thought that worried her was that Wrath may be having her watched. If so, she would have to rid herself of the warrior. She made her way through the village, stopping now and again, pretending to look at something that caught her eye. After the third stop, she knew she was being followed. She made her way to the healer's dwelling, wondering how she would be able to lose the shadow that trailed her.

Bethia smiled, delighted to see her and Verity was grateful when she offered her food and drink. She accepted, not knowing when next she would eat.

A young lad burst into the dwelling and interrupted their chatter, letting Bethia know that his mum had said to come quick that the bairn was on the way.

"Stay and finish your brew," Bethia said, gathering what she needed. After slipping on her cloak, she walked over to Verity and laid a hand on her shoulder. "You should go rest. You look tired. Leave your worries to Wrath. He will see to them."

And he would see to her if it meant placing Pictland in danger and she could not blame him. It was his home. She wished she had a home she could feel so strongly about.

Verity tore a piece from the bread on the table and stuffed it in the folds of the blanket beneath her cloak. She did not like taking what was not hers, especially from someone who had been so kind to her, and she certainly would not take all of it. That would not be right. She would make the piece she took last for as long as she could.

It was not long before she realized it would be impossible to rid herself of the warrior that followed her and she was annoyed her departure would be delayed. She made her way back to Wrath's dwelling. As she reached the door, raised voices were heard and she turned to see that Atas had broken free from the warriors who were to escort her on her journey and was running wildly through the village. She passed nearby Verity and a warrior screamed to the warrior who had been following her to get the woman.

Instinct had the warrior giving Verity a quick look, and seeing her at the open door to the dwelling, he ran after Atas.

Verity blessed the spirits watching over her for this chance. With everyone's attention on Atas, Verity was ignored as she hurried to the stronghold gate and slipped out without a problem. She worried that the snow-covered ground would make it easy for them to track her and she almost smiled when snow began to fall once again. Enough snow to cover her tracks would be perfect, though a raging snowstorm was another matter.

She knew where to go. She had seen the path in her vision. It would take her to Hemera. Then this nightmare would be done...she hoped.

~~~

The sky had darkened and snow was falling once again. It would delay the troop that was to leave earlier and begin their search for Verity's sister. Atas' antics had also caused her departure to be delayed. It would also delay the King's response to the Northmen, which worked to the King's advantage.

All of that had been discussed at the meeting with King Talon. A message would go out to the Northmen when the snow calmed, granting permission for them to travel to Pictland and meet with the King. Messages would also be sent to various tribes to alert them to the Northmen's presence on Pict soil and for other tribes to prepare for a show of strength. The King intended to let the Northmen know the might of the Picts.

Wrath nodded to the warrior guarding his dwelling as he approached. Though slim and shorter than many of the other warriors, Tilden had proven stronger than most, taking down men twice his size. His strength was one of the reasons he had appointed Tilden to guard Verity.

"Go. You are done here," Wrath ordered, thinking Tilden might make a good replacement for Broc as one of the King's personal guard.

Tilden nodded and turned and walked away as Wrath shook the snow from his cloak and opened the door. He was eager to see how Verity was feeling. He stilled, taking in the room in one hasty glance to find Verity was nowhere to be seen. He turned and roared out Tilden's name.

The roar rippled through the village and some people hurried in their dwellings, knowing that the mighty Wrath's temper had been unleashed.

Tilden approached Wrath with caution.

"Where is Verity?"

Tilden appeared confused. "She is not inside?"

"No! She is not."

The strength of Wrath's angry voice forced Tilden to take a step back.

Wrath felt his fury ready to erupt and he fought to control it. "When was the last time you saw her?"

"Standing at your door as Atas ran wildly by us and..." Tilden shook his head. "She was about to enter the dwelling, and someone shouted at me to grab Atas."

"You left your post unsecure?" Wrath asked accusingly.

Tilden raised his chin. "I did. I failed in my duty to watch over her."

"Come with me," Wrath ordered sharply.

Moments later they stood before the King, Broc present as well, having been given the temporary post of Master Commander over the Pict warriors.

Wrath respected Tilden for admitting his failure, though it did not calm his temper.

After listening to Tilden explain to the King what had happened, the King turned to Broc. "You are Master Commander, this is for you to handle. What will you do?"

Broc did not hesitate. "I will have a troop ready to leave shortly to go find Verity and as for Tilden. He will spend three days in a prison chamber and then have two days of double duty. If he cannot survive it, he will no longer be one of the King's elite warriors."

"I will survive it and prove I am not as foolish as I appear," Tilden said.

The King nodded approvingly. "See to it, though wait on readying a troop."

Wrath spoke as soon as he and the King were alone. "I will see to finding Verity."

"I thought as much since this is your failure as well."

Wrath's eyes glowed with anger and his jaw tightened. He fisted his hands so tightly that you could hear the crack of bones. He never failed the King and that the King should accuse him of such, fired his fury.

"Verity ran for a reason and if I was to guess at that reason, I would say she did not want to face the Northmen when they arrived here." The King took a sharp step toward Wrath and while it would intimidate most men, it had no effect on Wrath. "Find her and the truth. I will not be made to look a fool in front of the Northmen."

"You have my word, my King. I will find her and get the truth from her no matter what it takes."

The King dismissed him with a firm nod.

Wrath rushed off, gathered what he needed and was out the stronghold gates as the snow began to fall more heavily. It would not take long to find Verity. She was on foot and he rode a horse. He would find her and when he did...she would regret the day she ever set eyes on him.

Chapter Seven

"Two days," Wrath snarled to himself. Two days and he still had not found Verity. He had been lucky to pick up her tracks shortly after he had left the stronghold, so at least he had some idea of what direction she was headed. The snow had slowed during the night and had stopped completely by first light. That had slowed him down considerably since he had to hunt to uncover any tracks she had left. Still, he thought he would have found her by now. Two days from the stronghold was a good bit of expanse for her to travel.

The longer it took to find her, the more annoyed he had grown at himself. He had thought Verity a helpless woman, treated poorly by those who had taken her captive. Now, however, he wondered over her story that she was a slave and was she truly a Pict? Had everything she had told him been a lie? And if so, what had caused the mark around her neck? And the most disturbing question of all...what did the Northmen want with her?

Wrath pushed the persistent questions aside. He would get no answers until he found Verity and even then he wondered what it would take to get the truth from her. He had to be careful, very careful, when he found her. King Talon had been right when he had suspected that Wrath cared for Verity. It had disturbed him to realize it himself. He had never worried over a woman like he did Verity. And he had never found himself drawn to a woman like he had been to Verity. It was why he had spent the nights with Simca. He had not trusted himself to sleep beside Verity, since he had found himself growing aroused around her far too often.

He shook his head as though he could shake the disturbing thoughts away. He had to concentrate on tracking her and nothing else. He had allowed her to invade his thoughts far too often since meeting her and in ways he had never expected. He had a mission to accomplish and constant thoughts of Verity would not help him find her, and find her he would.

His horse stopped and gave a snort and he cursed himself for having been so deep in thought that he had not paid heed to his surroundings and may have missed something. He thought to backtrack when something ahead caught his eye. It was too far away to be sure of what he was seeing, but it looked like a shelter of sorts. One built hastily of branches and brush.

When he got closer, he dismounted and approached the structure cautiously, not wanting to alert anyone inside to his presence, though the crunch of snow from his heavy footfalls did not allow for that. With no movement from the shelter when he was finally upon it, he knew it must be empty.

As soon as he pulled back a large branch, he saw that he was right. No one was there, but someone had been. He bent down and looked over the pine branches. The branches and pines themselves were not flattened, meaning a heavy person had not occupied this space and there was still some warmth to it.

Wrath was quick to stand and cast a glance around. It had to be Verity who was here and she left recently, which meant she was not far off and there had to be tracks he could easily follow.

He grinned. After stepping outside and searching around the dwelling, he came upon her footfalls. He would find her soon and finally get the truth from her.

~~~

With clear skies and snow no longer falling, Verity worried that her tracks would eventually be discovered. She only hoped she would reach Hemera before then. She had had another vision last night. It was why she had slept much longer than she had planned. It had robbed her of what little strength she had left after plodding through the snow all day.

The vision had pleased her and left her with some hope. Wherever Hemera was, she was safe and appeared content. While Verity hoped to reach Hemera and find safety with her, she was relieved to know that Hemera would be safe no matter what happened to her.

She trudged through the snow, her legs burning from fighting the deep drifts, but she was determined to keep going.

Verity turned her glance up at the clear sky, her brow scrunching. She thought she had heard distant thunder, but there was not a cloud to be seen. Her insides suddenly tightened and she turned and gasped.

There in the distance headed her way rapidly was Wrath and though a good length separated them, she could see his anger in the intent way he rode his horse and, for a moment, Verity thought she saw his eyes glow red with fury.

Instinct to survive took hold and Verity turned and ran, trying to avoid the deepest snow. Her chest pounded wildly, her legs screamed with pain, but she kept going and did not dare look back.

She turned deeper into the woods, hoping the dense forest would slow him down and dared to take a quick glance back. He followed her, a bit slower, but he followed her. She turned and continued running, hoping that somehow she would escape him.

"Stop, Verity!"

She cringed as his strong voice echoed through the forest, wrapping around her as though catching her in his grasp.

"Stop!"

Verity ran faster, the snow not as deep in the dense part of the woods when suddenly up ahead she saw a drop off. She quickly slowed her pace and looked to see that the ledge ran as far as she could see to either side of her. There was no place for her to go. She could run off in a different direction into the woods, but he would easily follow her and wait until she grew too tired to run anymore. She was trapped...unless.

She peered over the edge. It was more a slope than a steep drop and a stream ran along the bottom. He would not be able to follow her with his horse and she could find a place to climb back up further away from him.

"Do not even think about it," Wrath warned.

Verity turned with a startled jump, hearing him so close. His eyes did not glare red, but they sparked with such anger that any moment she expected them to flame with fire.

"I cannot go back with you."

"Because of the Northmen?" he snapped.

"Because of many things. Please let me go—"

"I cannot do that," he said, not allowing her to continue. "You will return with me and you will tell me the truth."

"I am truly sorry, Wrath, but I can do neither."

He never heard his name spoken with such tenderness or heard such a heartfelt apology. She actually sounded as though she regretted her choice. Or

72

was it a choice? She was doing what she must just as he was doing what had to be done. For a moment, he wished it did not have to be that way, but no matter what, he had to return her to the stronghold. The King commanded it and he would not fail his King.

Wrath's insides tightened when he watched Verity take a step back. Even if he dismounted quickly, he was still at a distance where he would not be able to stop her from going over the edge.

His voice rolled with anger as he ordered, "Do not dare step off that edge, woman."

"The choice is not mine."

Wrath dropped off his horse, but too late. He watched Verity disappear over the edge. He hurried to look and was relieved it sloped more than dropped, though the slope was steep enough and would not allow Verity to remain on her feet for long. And she did not. He watched as her stumble turned into a tumble.

He growled beneath his breath and went over the edge after her. Wrath was steady and quick on his feet going down, having traversed slopes like this one before, but not quick enough to catch Verity. She was rolling down so rapidly that he feared she would hurt herself when she hit the bottom. Not to mention the numerous jabs her body had to be taking on the way down. He followed after her as fast as he possibly could, trying to reach the bottom before she did and prevent her from landing in the cold stream.

A thin stapling caught her at the waist and stopped her roll, when she was nearly to the bottom, though only for a moment. It was enough for Wrath to get around her and scoop her up before she could roll any further. He was ready to lash out at her when he saw that her eyes were closed and he felt a sticky wetness at the back of her head.

He carried her the short distance to the bottom and sat, resting her in his lap. He slipped his hand out from behind her head and saw that it was covered with blood. She felt lifeless against him and he grew angry that she had taken such a dangerous risk to get away from him.

She was a stubborn one, but so was he. He would let nothing happen to her. He had told her he would keep her safe and he would keep his word. That was his only thought, not the King and his dictate or the arrival of the Northmen. The only thing that mattered at this moment was seeing to her care. He needed to get her head wound cleaned to see the extent of her injury and provide shelter and warmth for her.

He carried her to the edge of the stream and with handfuls of water he cleansed the back of her head. He turned her in his arms so that he could see her wound. Blood had soaked her gold hair, turning it a fiery red and he feared the worst. After separating the strands of wet hair, he was finally able to see the abrasion. He was relieved to see that the cut was not as bad as he expected, though there was some swelling.

He rinsed what blood he could from her hair, squeezed the water from it and pulled up her hood to help protect the wound. He stood once more with Verity in his arms, holding her close and glanced around. Parts of the glen were heavy with snow while snow barely touched other sections. He spotted an area where rock formation created an overhang and provided a modicum of shelter. He could add to it with branches and brush to help keep out the cold.

He laid Verity on the ground and got busy, starting a fire first to get her warm. He was no soon as done, the flames burning strong, then Verity opened her eyes and winced.

"You have a good bump to your head from your foolish fall," he scolded and realized how relieved he was that she had finally woken.

"You followed me?" She winced again when she slipped her hand in the hood of her cloak and touched the lump at the back of her head.

"You doubted I would?"

"I did not think you would be as foolish as me."

"You make me foolish," he argued, the thought disturbing him.

Verity tried to sit up.

Wrath crouched down beside her, his hand pressing gently yet firmly to her chest to prevent her from moving. "Stay as you are until you feel your strength return."

She had the urge to grab his hand and keep hold of it. She was irrational to think that way, to want to latch onto him and not let go. He was the first man who had ever told her that he would keep her safe and the first man she had ever felt safe with. But he had not come after her to protect her or help her. He was here to return her to the stronghold, to do what was best for Pictland. He would hand her over to the Northmen if necessary and she had to remember that, yet her visions had never shown her that he would do such a thing, unless she had misinterpreted them.

She turned her face away from him, not knowing what to believe anymore.

It irritated Wrath that she looked away from him. "What secret was so important that you lied about everything to me?"

"I am tired," she said.

He leaned down over her, his face close to hers. "You will tell me everything before we reach the stronghold."

75

Her response came from instinct after many years of forced obedience and was meant to appease. "As you wish."

Wrath stepped out of the shelter annoyed, feeling as though he had been going in circles since meeting her. How often had he told her he would get the truth from her and failed to do so? What made him think he could get her to tell him now?

He walked away irritated and searched for a slim branch and once he found the size he wanted, he grabbed his knife, tucked in the strap of his fur leg wrapping, and went to work on carving one end into a sharp point. When he finished, he went to the stream, ready and eager to spear some fish, hoping it would help appease his mounting anger.

The smell of fish cooking woke Verity and this time she sat up with little effort, the sleep having helped restore some of her strength. Her insides grumbled at the delicious scent.

"Hungry?" Wrath laughed, having heard her noisy insides.

She nodded and grimaced as she did, a sharp pain striking at the back of her head.

"You took quite a tumbled and where did it get you?" he asked, handing her a piece of fish.

She took it and ate instead of answering him.

Wrath ate as well and waited until they were near finished to ask some questions. "How many from your tribe were taken captive along with you and your sister? Perhaps the King can negotiate their return."

He had caught her unaware, her eyes widening, but no answer sprang to her lips. She was thinking, but why? It was a horrible memory that one would find impossible to forget. So why was it taking her so long to answer?

"I do not know," she finally said. "Hemera and I were taken away before I could see what happened to the others."

"Surely, you would have sailed with them on the same vessel." Wrath waited for her to respond and when she remained silent, he said, "You are lying to me about your capture. What else do you lie to me about?"

"Please let me go. Trust me. It will be better for everyone if you do."

"Trust you?" He smiled, though it quickly turned to a scowl. "I did once, no more. And now you intrigue me with a pitiful threat. Why would it be better for everyone if I let you go? Trust *me*, I will find out and you may not like the consequences."

No more was said and a while later when Verity stood to go see to her needs, Wrath was right by her side.

"You will not leave my side. You will stay with me, until I say otherwise" he ordered.

"I need a moment alone."

"Only a moment."

He walked a short distance with her and turned his back to her, reminding her once again that he would give her little time. She hurried to pay heed to his warning and get done quickly. She barely finished when he turned around to face her. She went to the stream and rinsed her hands in the cold water, shivering as she did.

Wrath did the same and once he was done, his hand clamped down on her arm, letting her know they were done.

Verity lay unable to sleep. It was not the pain from her head wound that kept her awake, the dull ache having long dissipated. It was Wrath. She wished she could be truthful with him, wished things were different, wished she was free to...she dared not think of it. She had long ago accepted that she would never find *tuahna*,

77

Donna Fletcher

a word used sparingly among the Picts. It was a deep abiding caring that you felt for your mate, one that endured always, but found by few.

She had never thought it possible that she would be blessed to find it and she was foolish to even think it might be possible with a warrior like Wrath. He cared for her now out of necessity and because of his King's dictates. She did not matter to him and he should not matter to her. Then why did it seem like he did?

The pain in her head had been easier to bear than the pain that struck her heart. She was foolish and she had to stop it. She would never have a man care so deeply for her, especially Wrath. She had more important things to see to.

Verity lay there waiting until she hoped Wrath was deep in sleep and would not hear her stir. She sat up slowly and as quietly as she could and looked over at him. He lay with his back to the fire, not moving.

Foolish, Verity, that is what you are, she thought. *Get on with it.*

Her own scolding got her moving and ever so quietly she got to her feet.

"Do not dare think it," Wrath ordered sharply and turned, glaring up at her.

Verity did not bother to lie. She tried to be as honest as possible. "I had a dream about Hemera and I believe she is not far from here. Please, help me find her. Please."

"Lie down!" he ordered curtly as he stood.

She did as told, but then what other choice did she have? She lay on her side, facing the fire, not looking up at Wrath.

Wrath walked around to her and dropped down beside her.

78

Verity jumped slightly when his arm slipped over her waist and he yanked her hard against him.

"Now you will stay put," he said his warm breath tickling at her ear and sending a gentle shiver through her.

Feeling her slight shiver, he shared his fur-lined cloak with her, pulling her closer against him as he tucked the cloak around them. He draped one leg over her two and nestled his face near the back of her neck. A mistake since her pale, smooth skin tempted. He shut his eyes, but the image would not fade and neither would the temptation.

Verity could not deny how natural it felt to have him wrapped around her. It was as though he belonged there and always had. It was a strange and yet comforting feeling. She gave no thought to resting her hand on his arm. It seemed to belong there as well. They seemed to belong together.

She closed her eyes annoyed at her fanciful thoughts about the mighty Wrath. He may not have placed a rope around her neck, but he tethered her all the same with his strong arms, and she would be wise to remember that.

Chapter Eight

"It is not that far, Wrath, please." Verity found herself pleading with him when they woke. "If she is nowhere to be found there, then I will return with you without protest. Please, give me this one chance to find Hemera and know she is safe."

Wrath had given it thought when he woke before first light and found Verity snuggled tightly against him and his arms around her, keeping her close, keeping her from escaping or so he told himself. He had not wanted to admit that he enjoyed the feel of her in his arms. He still did not want to admit it. And he did not want to admit that he was considering her plea.

"The King would be pleased if we returned with Hemera."

"Your head? How does it feel?" he asked.

Verity's hand went to her head and she winced when she touched the area. "It hurts when touched, but otherwise there is no pain."

He considered her words, wondering how truthful she was being with him, since she was desperate to find her sister.

"It is not far," she pleaded again,

"We would reach this place on the morrow?" Wrath asked, trying to convince himself that it was because of the King and not her heartfelt pleas that he was considering it.

"I believe so."

He shook his head. "You believe so? You do not know?" He shook his head again while dousing the dying fire with snow.

"The dream was strong and clear and so far I have had no trouble following the path I saw."

Verity quickly lowered her head as Wrath approached her rapidly. Her breath caught slightly when he stopped so close that their bodies almost touched.

"Look at me," he snapped and her head shot up. "Do not lower your head when I approach you or in my presence."

"I am accustomed to obedience."

"Accustomed to obedience?" Wrath laughed. "If that was so, we would not be standing here now a distance from the stronghold. I do not believe you were ever as obedient as you believe. Or perhaps you are obedient when it is prudent to be so."

"I learned what it took to survive."

Wrath took hold of her chin. "That means you learned how to lie. What lies do you tell me, Verity?" He did not expect silence from her. If anything, he expected more lies, hoped for them, since eventually her lies would reveal the truth. He released her chin and walked away, calling out, "We go find your sister."

Verity followed quickly behind him, keeping her silence since there was little she could say. The truth would eventually reveal itself and Wrath would not be happy with it.

~~~

"My horse waits for us at the top of this rise," Wrath said, staring up at a climb that would not be easy. "At least the snow has stopped and the skies show no signs of more snow, for now." He turned to Verity. "You

81

will follow behind me, step where I step, take hold of what I take hold, and you will tell me if you grow too tired to keep climbing."

Verity nodded and followed behind Wrath as he took the first step. It was slow going, Wrath digging in with each step to make certain she got a firm foothold. He stopped and turned several times to ask if she was tired or if her head hurt and she realized that his intentions were that she get a moment's rest. She also realized that he would have been up this rise with little effort, if it was not for her.

They were near to the top when she felt the familiar darkness begin to close in around her. She hurried and called out, "Wrath!"

Wrath stopped and whipped around, hearing the fear in her voice. His one arm swung out and grabbed her around the waist, while his other hand snagged a thick branch to keep them from falling. He saw her soft blue eyes turn dark before they closed and she went completely limp in his arm. He did not hesitate. With one strong lift, he threw her over his shoulder and continued to climb.

Once he reached the top, he summoned his horse with whistle as he took Verity in his arms and sat on the snow-covered ground. She still had not revived and the longer she lingered in the attack, the more he worried.

He patted her cheek. "Enough now, wake up." When he got no response he ordered firmly, "Wake up right now!" Again she did not stir. Annoyance coupled with worry had him commanding, "Come back to me right now, Verity!" She moved, slightly. Had she heard him? "Come back to me, Verity. Come back to me now!"

Relief gripped his chest when he watched her eyes flutter open for only a moment. They were still a dark blue and he was beginning to realize that her eyes deepening in color was a way of letting him know if the attack still had hold of her. Until her eyes were as they always were—soft blue—she had yet to fully recover.

Wrath heard a snort and looked up to see his horse approach and stop not far from him. He praised the animal for doing as he had taught him, to wait where he had left him unless called, and as he did, he felt strength return to Verity's limbs.

Her eyes opened again and this time they were their usual—soft blue. He ran a gentle finger along her cheek. "You suffered an attack. Stay as you are and rest."

Verity stared up at him. She wanted to speak, to tell him what she saw, but her voice failed her, though perhaps it was her courage. Nothing had looked familiar in her vision, not the area and not the couple she had seen dead. Was it a warning? Would they come upon this horrific scene? And what had happened to the two? It had appeared to be a vicious attack, but why were they killed? And why had she seen it?

"We will return to the stronghold," Wrath said. Verity tried to sit up, but Wrath held her firm in his arms.

"No, please, I am fine," she pleaded. "The walk in the cold will do me good."

"We will ride."

She looked around, her eyes turning wide as she saw where they were. "You kept me from falling and carried me up the rise?"

"It seems I am forever catching you."

No one had ever been there to catch her. Most wanted nothing to do with her when they saw an attack hit her. Hemera had been there for her if she was present when a vision hit, but that had not been very often. To wake in Wrath's arms and feel safe and cared for was unbelievably wonderful and she would cherish it for as long as it lasted.

"I am most grateful that you do catch me, for you are the only one whoever has," she said softly. "I have dropped to the ground far too often and had been left there to wake alone or to find rotted food had been thrown at me."

Anger surged in him to hear she had been treated so horribly. "Never! Never will you be treated so shamefully again. My arms will always be there to catch you and keep you safe." He did not know why Verity tugged at his insides the way she did, and try as he might to deny it had proven futile thus far. And now knowing more of how she had suffered at the hands of the Northmen made him feel even more protective of her.

She kept her eyes on his dark ones. While others might find anger in them more often than not, she found in them a strange tender anger. It was almost as if one could not survive without the other.

"We leave now," he said and stood with Verity in his arms.

The Northmen were a strong lot, but not one of them could compare to Wrath's strength. He seemed to have the power of two or more men. She could feel it in the ease in which he stood with her in his arms or the deep tracks his footfalls left in the snow or how effortlessly he caught her in his arms.

He lowered her on her feet and she braced herself against him for a moment as she found steady footing. Or was it that she always wanted to be near him?

"Feeling unwell?" he asked, keeping his arm around her.

"A bit unsteady, but it will pass soon enough."

He lifted her in his arms and sat her on the horse then mounted behind her, settling her against him. "Now you can rest while you tell me the path to take."

They returned to where Wrath had come across her and she directed him from there. Verity's head dropped on Wrath's shoulder after traveling only for a short time. It took some effort to lift it, since fatigue seemed to be creeping up on her, but she did not want him to think her too weak to continue. Twice more it fell on his shoulder and twice more she lifted it.

The third time her head hit his shoulder, he ordered, "Leave it there."

Verity had no trouble obeying him, leaving her head to rest comfortably on him.

Wrath preferred silence when he rode through the woods. It allowed him to hear everything that went on around him. Not that he expected to hear anything now when the snow was heavy on the ground and few traveled the land. But he would take no chances. While the Unification of Tribes had united the many tribes and settled the constant warring between them, there were still those opposed to a King, at least the present King. But there had been none as strong or as sharp in mind to reign as King Talon.

Until those who opposed him where stopped, there would never truly be peace among the tribes.

An occasional sound stirred in the silence, though nothing that caused Wrath alarm. There had been no time for food this morning and while he had been trained to go without when necessary, he had Verity to consider. She had been denied food by the Northmen and he would not see that happen here among her own people.

He smiled when she stirred awake, her insides grumbling. He had been right about her hunger, but then he was getting to know her well.

Verity raised her head. "How long have I slept?"

"Long enough for hunger to wake you."

Her insides grumbled again and she rested her hand to her middle. "I cannot deny I am hungry, but you must be as well."

"There is a farm up ahead and the couple will be only too glad to share with us."

"You know them?"

"Kinnel and Shona. They chose to farm land away from the stronghold. They often have a good harvest and pay their fair share to the King."

"Do they not fear living so far from the stronghold?"

"Since the Unification of the Tribes there has been little to worry about, but if trouble threatens King Talon sends warriors to escort the outlying farmers safely to the stronghold where they remain until the matter is settled."

The farm came into view and as they drew closer, the sight that greeted them had Wrath urging his horse forward. He came to an abrupt stop, hurrying off the horse, after ordering Verity not to move.

Verity could not do that. She had to see for herself. She had to know if the man and woman lying on the ground, the snow red with their blood, were the two from her vision. She eased herself off the horse and approached the two bodies. The man laid on his stomach, his hand stretched out to the woman lying on her back, her head turned to him and her hand reaching for his, the tips of their fingers touching.

He had crawled to his wife to be beside her in death and tears filled Verity's eyes. She had seen it all in her vision. She had watched him crawl to his wife and her struggle to stretch her hand out to him before she died.

"Do not move!" Wrath ordered.

Verity could not if she wanted to. Pain and sorrow had robbed her of any movement. Why did she have to see such horror? Why could she not prevent what her visions showed her?

She murmured a silent blessing for the couple and looked away, her tears still falling, out of sorrow and helplessness not only for them but for not having been able to prevent their deaths. She turned away, wiping her tears away and saw Wrath searching the ground. He was looking for tracks, looking to see if he could find anything that would let him know who did this.

Wrath looked to see Verity standing by the two bodies, her eyes wet with tears, and he quickly went to her side. His arm went around her and he guided her away, toward the dwelling. "I must see to them."

"What will you do? The ground is too hard to bury them."

"I will place them inside the small shed behind the house and secure it so that no animals can get to them. Once we return to the stronghold, I will send men to see to them. You must see what food you can find for us, then we will be on our way."

"We return to the stronghold?" Verity asked anxiously, knowing it was the wisest thing to do, but after seeing what happened here she was more concerned for Hemera than ever.

"No. There is a small tribe, the Raban, more farmers than warriors, not far from here. They traded often with Kinnel and Shona. We go there to see what they know and to send one of them to the stronghold to return with a troop of warriors. Now go inside and see what food you can find for us to take." He opened the door and ushered her in, not giving her a chance to protest.

Verity stood, staring at the room. It had been torn apart as if someone had ransacked it and a sudden chill ran through her. Some Northmen were known for such destruction, searching for anything worth something. But there was little of worth here and as she looked around she realized that there was no food, not a morsel, to be found.

The door opened and she jumped.

"Easy, Verity, you have nothing to—" Wrath stared at the room.

"They took all the food," Verity said and turned to him. "I see no weapons either."

"We leave now," he said and took her arm to hurry her out of the dwelling.

"You worry they are near?" she asked since the thought also concerned her.

"They got what they came for. They will not return." He had her out of the dwelling and both of them on the horse quickly.

"What if the food and weapons were not enough?" she asked.

"We need to get to the Raban Tribe."

Verity did not need him to say anymore. He was concerned it was only the two of them and if that was so, it was because Wrath suspected there were more warriors than he could deal with on his own. The Raban Tribe would provide them with shelter and safety until the King could be alerted to what had happened and a troop of warriors sent.

They rode in silence, Wrath vigilant to every sound he heard.

Verity did the same, keeping watch over their surroundings and hoping that the visions she had seen that were yet to come to pass meant they would not meet their deaths this day. She wondered if she could be

88

wrong when she saw the dark smoke rising in the sky in the distance.

Chapter Nine

Verity watched as the billowing smoke grew darker and spread higher in the sky the closer they got and she feared the worst, that the whole tribe had been slaughtered. Screams ripped through the cold air at the same time a lad stumbled from behind some bushes and ran toward them.

Wrath reined the horse to a stop and slipped off, hurrying over to the lad who had fallen to his knees, breathing heavily. "What happened?" Wrath demanded, crouching down beside him.

The lad looked up startled, not having realized Wrath was there. His eyes almost bulged from his head as he looked Wrath up and down. "You are one of the King's personal guards. You are skilled with a weapon. We are no match for the mighty warriors who pillage our village. Please! Please help my tribe."

"How many are there?"

"Five and we are no match for their superior strength and skill. I left as soon as the attack started. It is my duty to go to the stronghold for help and to warn our friends Kinnel and Shona."

"Your friends are dead. You are to go straight to the King's stronghold and tell him what happened here and that Wrath needs a troop of warriors."

The lad stumbled to his feet. "You are the mighty Wrath?"

"I am," Wrath said, "and I will save your tribe and you will take my horse and not stop until you reach the King's stronghold." He went and lifted Verity off the horse and helped the young lad on it. "Do not stop," Wrath ordered once again and the lad nodded. Wrath laid his hand on the horse's rump and commanded, "Home!"

The horse took off and Wrath turned to Verity, grabbing her arm and propelling her into the woods. "You will keep your distance from the village until I come for you."

"What if you do not come for me?"

"That will not happen." He stopped, released her, and rapidly began stripping off his garments until he stood completely naked.

Her mouth dropped open and she stared speechless at him. He was an impressive sight to behold. There was no softness to him, only hard muscle. It was as though he had stripped down until his raw strength and power were completely exposed. And along with it came a rage so pure and tangible that it could be seen in his taut muscles growing ever tighter with his every movement and in his dark eyes that raged with such potent anger that Verity took a step back.

"Stay put!" he warned with an animal-like growl and grabbing his sword and knife off the ground, he took off running.

She stared after him, his every muscle rigid and ready for battle as he ran, letting nothing stand in his way. With ease and skill, he ducked under branches, leapt over rocks, and dodged anything in his path that tried to stop him.

Verity shook away her daze, grabbed his garments, hoisted her garment so she would not trip, and hurried after him. It was nearly impossible to keep up with him, so she followed his tracks. She stopped abruptly when he suddenly let loose a horrifying roar that shook the snow off the nearby trees and she shivered, knowing he must have broken past the edge of the woods and into the village.

She hurried forward and stopped when she spotted the village through the trees and she crept closer, careful not to let herself be seen. She watched, stunned by Wrath's fearless actions as he ran right into the heart of battle, straight for the band of warriors. As soon as she saw the warriors' reaction to Wrath's sudden appearance, she understood why he had stripped naked. They stood staring at him, their mouths agape, their eyes wide just as she was doing now. Their shock of him naked and roaring like a demon ready to devour them froze the warriors long enough for Wrath to kill two so quickly that she had not even known he had caught them with his sword until they fell dead to the ground and blood began to pool around them. The other three suddenly came to their senses, but were no match for Wrath. Never had she seen a warrior wield his weapons with the extraordinary skill and swiftness that Wrath did.

The last warrior to fall stared in shock at the blood running from his chest, one last word spilling from his lips as he fell forward. "*Wrath.*"

The people stood staring in silence, their mouths hanging open at the five slaughtered warriors lying around Wrath.

"Your leader," Wrath ordered curtly.

Once again Verity found herself shaking her head to clear it, finding it difficult to believe what she had just witnessed. The Northmen were skilled swordsmen, but they were nothing compared to Wrath's astonishing ability. She hurried and entered the village, no one giving her a glance. They were too busy watching the mighty Wrath talk with their leader a man who wore his age heavily upon his face. His good arm cradled his injured arm and he spoke with respect and gratitude to Wrath.

Verity eased her way around the villagers to hand Wrath his tunic.

He took it, slipped it on, and continued speaking to the leader. "The injured need tending as does the village and the dead need to be seen to after which we will talk, Harran."

Harran, chieftain of the Raban Tribe, nodded and turned to address his people.

Wrath stepped aside and spoke to Verity as he finished dressing. "Did I not tell you to wait until I came for you?"

"You did, but I could not help but follow to see what you would do and..." She bit at her lip, stopping herself from continuing.

"And?" he asked, draping his cloak over his shoulders.

She had stopped the thought that was about to spill from her lips. It almost had alarmed her, for she did not want to admit to him, or to herself, that when she was with him she felt the need to remain close to him and when she was separated from him she felt a strange ache that was only appeased when she was with him again. It was odd and she did not know how to explain to herself, so how did she explain it to him?

"To see you save the village," she said relieved something had come to mind for her to say.

A slight grin touched the corners of Wrath's mouth and he leaned so close to Verity that she saw the rage in his eyes had turned to hot embers that could easily spark to life if even slightly provoked.

"You lie," he whispered, "and one day I am going to learn all your lies and you know what will happen then?"

93

A chill raced through her as she shook her head, her voice caught somewhere in her throat.

He brought his lips close to hers and whispered softly, "I am going to make you pay for each and every one of them. You would do well to remember that before you tell me another lie."

"Wrath! Wrath! Wrath!"

Verity jumped, startled by Wrath's name shouted repeatedly as the tribe honored him, with cheers of his name, for saving them. He turned to the people and let their shouts continue, though not for long. He raised his hand and silence fell quickly.

"It is the King you should cheer, for I serve him and his people. King Talon will see this made right."

King Talon's name was raised in cheers and Verity warned herself to remember Wrath's words. He served the King and would do whatever the King commanded. He would have no choice.

Wrath silenced the crowd and spoke once again. "Tend your injured, see to your dead, and rebuild what has been destroyed in their honor."

Nods circled the crowd as they began to disperse when a woman called out, "You will not leave us yet?"

All stopped and turned fearful glances on Wrath, frightened of what they would hear.

"I will stay here until King Talon's warriors arrive."

The crowd shouted his name once again before dispersing to see to the difficult tasks ahead.

Wrath turned to Verity and she was quick to say, "I have tended wounds. I can help."

"Do what you can, but stay where I can see you."

Verity nodded and went to do what she could. She kept her head turned away as a few men dragged the bodies of the attackers to the outskirts of the village. Her offer of help was gratefully accepted and she soon found herself tending minor wounds. She shed tears with women who had lost their mates and one woman who had lost her son. She watched as the men cleaned away the carnage, pushing away the blood-soaked snow, gathering weapons to be cleaned, and making preparation to burn the dead, since there were too many to keep until the ground thawed.

Verity rubbed at her lower back, a dull ache having settled there after tending the last of the minor injuries. She was about to sit on one of the benches that had held an endless stream of wounded when a scream ripped through the village. All eyes turned to see a mother trying to calm a small lass as she fought to hold her arm for the healer to prick at with a fine bone needle.

The little lass fought with surprising strength and broke free to run straight to Verity. Her red curls bounced around her head as tears ran a path through the grime on her chubby face. She threw herself at Verity, clinging desperately to her leg with all the strength her little fingers could muster.

"Please! Please, help me. They are hurting me."

The lass's mum approached as did the healer.

"Help us hold her down so we can get this done," the healer ordered Verity.

The little lass looked up at Verity with such fright that it twisted Verity's insides. She looked to the healer and asked, "What is the problem?"

"She has a deep splinter in her arm and it must come out," the woman said.

Verity could see that the healer was tired from tending the many wounded and had no patience for the frightened lass. Her long, dark hair sprinkled with gray had fallen loose from its braid, stray strands hanging limply around her face. Blood marred the front of her garment and dried blood stained her hands and was thick under her nails.

"Why not let me see to it? You have far too many wounded who need you," Verity said.

"That I do," the healer agreed. "But it will not be easy since Neva is a crier. Cries over everything she does. "

"You hurt me," Neva said boldly, peeking out from behind Verity's leg.

"There is much pain in life, child. You need to learn that now and suffer through like everyone does." The healer turned from Neva to nod at Verity. "She will hurt you just as I did and when she cannot remove the splinter, you will come crying back to me just as you went crying to her." The healer shook her head, handed the needle to Neva's mum, and walked away.

Neva's mum was quick to defend the woman. "Cora is a good, kind healer. She is simply burdened by so many wounded."

"It understandable," Verity said. "It has been a difficult day for all." She looked down at the lass. "So, Neva , shall I have a look at your wound?"

Her brown eyes widened. "Will you hurt me?"

"Sometimes pain is necessary."

The little lass paled not at Wrath's strong voice, but at the sight of him stepping around her mother to stand in front of Verity. Neva quickly slipped beneath Verity's cloak.

"Hiding will do you no good," Wrath warned and reached down and lifted her up into his arm. The little lass looked ready to burst into tears. "Do not cry!"

Neva's chin trembled as she fought to keep her tears from falling.

Wrath sat on the bench, placing Neva on his leg. "Now let Verity remove the splinter and be done with it."

Neva looked up at Wrath and nodded while her chin continued to tremble.

Verity sat on a small bench that she placed it in front of Wrath.

"Your arm," Wrath ordered, looking down sternly at the little lass.

Neva held her trembling arm out to Verity.

"Did you get this wound in battle?" Wrath asked.

Neva nodded and flinched when Verity touched near the wound.

"Tell me how you got it."

As young as the little lass was she knew a command when she heard it. Her chin quivered the whole time she spoke. "The bad men struck Mum and she did not get up. I could not find Da..." Her tears started to fall.

Verity took the needle from Neva's mum, dipped it in the bucket of water beside the bench to clean the blood off it so she could see the point more clearly and began to gently prick at the splinter in Neva's arm.

"I looked and looked," Neva said, never taking her eyes off Wrath. "I was frightened my da..." She sniffled.

"You were frightened that the bad men hurt your da as they did your mum."

Neva nodded and sniffled back her tears again.

"How did you get your wound?" Wrath asked again.

"I saw my friend Hyde sitting on the ground crying, his head bleeding. I ran to him and pulled him away from the fighting. My arm hurt after that."

"You are a brave warrior, Neva. I would fight beside you any day," Wrath said.

"I am brave?" Neva asked, her eyes widening again, but not with fear this time, with surprise.

Wrath brushed the wet tears off her full cheeks, taking some of the grime with it. "Brave warriors help those in need. You went for help for your mum. You bravely searched for your da and you helped your friend. You are a true warrior."

Neva tilted her head, staring up at Wrath, and smiled shyly. "You are the best warrior of all."

"And you are the bravest little warrior I know."

Her smile widened and her cheeks spotted red.

Verity listened to their exchange, surprised by how Wrath taught the little lass strength yet showed her such caring. He would make a good da one day and the thought saddened her, for she would not know such joy, and certainly not with him. She turned her attention to the splinter and worked as delicately as possible.

"Got it," Verity said after a moment and held up a fairly long splinter.

Neva stared at it surprised, then broke into a big grin. "It did not hurt."

Wrath gave the little lass a poke in the side. "That is because you are a brave warrior."

Neva giggled.

"Some salve and a bandage and you are all done," Verity said.

When all was finished, Neva gave Wrath a hug, slid off his knee and ran to her mum.

"I am grateful for your kindness and help with my daughter. The Raban Tribe is blessed to have the mighty Wrath and his wife among us."

Verity went to correct her as the woman turned and walked away.

Wrath grabbed her arm. "Let it be. No one needs to know what we are about."

She supposed he was right, but it was also not necessary for the tribe to believe them wed.

Wrath walked off and Verity returned to help where she could. She kept Wrath in her sight as he had said for her to do, though it was more from curiosity than obedience. She caught a glimpse of him speaking with Harran. She wondered what he had to say about the attack. It seemed strange. If peace existed among the tribes, then who had attacked the tribe?

She had taken the opportunity while working with the women to ask several of them if any strangers, particularly a woman, had passed this way recently. Their answers were all the same. No strangers had been in the village until the attack today.

Food was prepared and shared among all.

Verity ate as did Wrath, though they did not eat together. Wrath still spoke with Harran and food was brought to both of them while she ate with the women. She continued to help where she could and when dusk drew near, Neva's mum, Deryn showed her to a dwelling.

It was small with a raised sleeping pallet and a bench. The fire pit was thick with flames that warmed the room nicely. The bedding looked fresh and there was a hint of pine in the air. The dwelling had been made fresh for her and Wrath.

"We are grateful for what your husband has done for us and we wanted you both to have a dwelling of your own while you are here," Deryn said.

"We do not wish to put anyone out of their home."

"It is an empty home," Deryn said sadly.

Verity understood. It had belonged to someone who had lost their life this day.

The door opened and Wrath entered.

Deryn was quick to excuse herself and as she left another woman entered with two buckets filled with snow and a cloth. She placed them on the edge of the fire pit and with a hasty bob of her head hurried out the door.

Wrath began to disrobe for the second time that day.

Verity turned and hung her cloak on a peg, keeping her back to him.

"You have seen me naked before why turn away now?"

He was right. She had seen him naked and not just today. She had seen more than just naked men. Northmen slaves lived in the same quarters as the families they served. She had closed her eyes and wished she could have closed her ears against the sounds of mating. One man told her to watch and learn so she would know how to please a man. She never looked, except for one time when the grunts and groans woke her. She had opened her eyes to see the woman she served on her hands and knees on the sleeping pallet and the man on his knees behind her, his hands firm on her backside as he drove his shaft in and out of her with powerful thrusts. After that night, she always made certain to sleep on her side with her back to the Northman and his wife.

"Come and help clean the blood off me."

She, like Neva, knew a command when she heard it. She turned and walked over to him.

He was sitting on the bench and he held the cloth out to her as she approached. "I will not sleep beside you with the blood of battle on me."

The thoughtful gesture was lost to her since she was more concerned with sharing the narrow sleeping pallet with him. They would need to sleep tightly beside each other. Why did that disturb her? They had done so

100

before. Why should she feel a twinge of worry? Or was it worry that she felt?

She took the cloth and turned to the buckets. The snow had melted and she plunged the cloth into the water and shivered. "It is cold."

"It does not matter. The blood must be washed off."

Verity shivered again when she ran the chilled cloth over his back, though he showed no sign of it disturbing him. She washed his back twice, rinsing the cloth each time. When she finished, she gently ran her hand slowly along his shoulders to make certain his body drawings concealed no spots of blood, and she felt him shiver.

"You are cold," she said. "I will hurry and finish."

Wrath did not trust himself to speak. His shiver had nothing to do with the chill of the cloth. He had suffered through far worse cold than that. It was her tender touch that had sent a shiver through him. It had come upon him so quickly that he could not stop it, as did his arousal. He had learned, watching the foolishness of other men, never to let his need control him. Yet now his need was rebelling and all from a simple touch.

Feeling for how he must be suffering through the cold, Verity hurried to wash his arms, though some blood spots needed a stronger scrubbing than others. Her concern for him grew when he once again shivered after she finished running her hands slowly along his arms.

She rinsed the cloth once more and stepped in front of him to see to his chest. Some spots were difficult to reach since he kept his legs closed. Not thinking, she nudged them apart with her knee and stepped between them. She realized then why his legs had remained closed...his shaft was thick and hard, and ready for mating. She stared, never having seen him this size before and could not help but think of him behind her

101

pounding into her as the Northman had done to his wife, and a strangely pleasant feeling tickled between her legs.

"I will grow harder if you continue to stare and you will find me slipping into you fast enough if that longing in your eyes continues to grow."

She jolted back, stumbling, and his hands shot out and grabbed her arms. "What frightens you that you back away from me? Fear that it would happen or fear it would not?"

"I have no wont to mate with you," she said, yanking to free her arm, but his grip was like a shackle around it—strong and tight.

He grinned and yanked her toward him as he stood. "Another lie, and one that will cost you dearly."

She held her tongue,

"You cannot deny what shows in your eyes or what you feel between your legs."

She gasped, her teeth grabbing too late at her lower lips to stop it.

He laughed softly. "Why do you bother to lie when you cannot hide it?"

She dug her teeth into her lip to stop herself from responding, fearful of what she might say or do.

"Nipping at your lip will not help, though a plumped lip makes for a tastier kiss."

She gasped again and Wrath did not wait, he captured her lips with his, his tongue entering her mouth to take command as he swiftly tucked her one arm behind her back and tugged her hard against him with her own hand. His other hand quickly cupped the back of her head and held it firm so she could not pull away.

Verity was so stunned that she did not know what to do, did not know how to respond. Instinct took hold and while she thought to push him away, futile as it was, something else in her begged her not to. She wanted him to kiss her and she wanted to kiss him in return, and she did.

She enjoyed the feel of his lips on hers, the playful taunts of his tongue, the way he held her tight against him, and the pleasurable stirring that spread inside her. Her free arm went up around his neck as her lips begged for more from him.

Wrath had seen desire flare in her eyes and knew she hungered to be kissed. What he had not expected was how hungry he was to kiss her. It was like a burning inside him that needed feeding, yet the more he kissed her, the hungrier he became.

He could not recall feeling such an overwhelming need for a woman that the thought of not joining with her flared his anger. That his need dominated all else annoyed him, as did the reminder that lies came much too easily to her lips.

He ended the kiss, his hand taking strong hold of her chin. "When you cease your lies, I may consider joining with you." He released her and turned his back on her, reaching for the cloth to clean his legs.

His words stabbed sharply at Verity and hurt more than she cared to admit, and she stepped away from him.

"The night grows late and there is much to do on the morrow. Settle yourself in the sleeping pallet and I will join you shortly."

"I will not sleep with you," she snapped, angry at his hurtful words, angry at herself for returning his kiss, angry that she had kissed him because she had let herself care for him. He had no such feelings for her. She met no more to him than the woman Simca whose sleeping pallet he had shared instead of remaining with her.

He swerved around, that ember she had seen in his eyes had sparked to life. "You think I gave you a choice?"

103

"The choice is mine," she said surprised by the defiance in her voice.

"Get in the sleeping pallet," he ordered, taking a step toward her.

She took a step back. "I thought you a kind man."

"You were mistaken."

"I will not—"

"You will," he finished.

The anger mounting in his dark eyes should have been enough to do as he said as well as her custom to obedience. But something inside her refused to paid heed to his words.

She had almost forgotten the word, not recalling when it last fell from her lips, but this time it spewed out sharply. "No!"

Anger flared in his eyes, then he grinned.

Chapter Ten

Verity was caught up in his arms and was flat on her back on the sleeping pallet with him on top of her before she knew what happened. Her mouth sat agape and her eyes spread wide, simply not knowing what to do or say.

"Close your mouth. I will not kiss you again, at least not yet," Wrath said.

Her chin shot up defiantly. "I do not want you to kiss me."

He grinned again and gave a short laugh. "There you go lying again."

"I am not lying," she said and almost bit her tongue, for she had never lied so much in her life since meeting Wrath, but it was necessary. Or so she told herself.

"Truly?" he asked, his grin having disappeared as if her words had shocked him. He brought his face close to hers. "Should I prove you lie?"

Verity snapped her head to the side.

"Your silence speaks louder than any words could."

She did not know if it was courage or foolishness that grabbed hold of her, or perhaps she had been forced to hold her tongue far too long that now she spoke as she pleased and without thought to consequences. "You are cruel."

He laughed again. "No, cruel would have been me stripping you naked and giving you a taste of the pleasure I can bring you."

"I will not couple with you ever and do not laugh at me again," Verity said with an anger that surprised her.

He grinned this time. "More lies."

"Never, ever would I want to couple with you," she said firmly.

He pushed himself off her to sit back and spread her legs apart so quickly that once again she was at a loss to respond.

He slipped his hand beneath her tunic, running his hand up along the inside of her leg. "So you are not wet and ready for me?"

"Stop!" she shouted.

"That is not an answer," he said as his hand moved further up along her leg, stroking softly, squeezing playfully, and tempting unmercifully.

Verity shut her eyes, enjoying his intimate touch, wishing he was touching her because he wanted to, because he cared for her. But he did not and she could not let him continue.

She whispered her surrender, "Aye, you are right." She kept her eyes closed and waited for his words that were sure to sting her.

His hand stopped moving along her leg and she felt him move over her, and she held her breath. He slipped to her side, turning her on her side to face the wall and fit himself close against her back. He spread a blanket over them before he draped his arm over her waist and tucked her back against him tightly.

They would sleep. They would do no more than sleep and Verity breathed a soft sigh of relief.

"We will couple," he whispered in her ear, "*often*."

It was not that words had failed her that kept her silent. It was that she did not trust herself to speak. She feared the truth might slip out and then what? She would feel foolish that he would know that she had begun to care for him. He would probably laugh at her. She should laugh at herself for having any feelings at all for him. She did not truly know him, though she felt she had come to know him through her visions. He had been there to help her in every vision she had had of him. He was always there to keep her safe and he had said he would keep her safe.

He did not, however, say he cared for her. She forced her eyes closed, trying to force the endless thoughts from her mind. She wished the wound to her head still pained her. At least then it would hold her thoughts as she fought against it. But it hurt her no more, unlike the pain she felt when she thought about Wrath and how he would never care for her.

We will couple...often.

He might think that, but Verity knew better. She would not couple with him and walk away like the other women did. It was not possible and so she would *never* couple with him.

She yawned as sleep drifted over her and she let herself be carried off where no constant thoughts would haunt her.

Wrath knew the moment she fell asleep. Her body grew limp and her breathing turned soft. He, however, would not be so fortunate. He was still trying to comprehend how Verity was making him feel. He never hesitated in coupling with any woman who had been wet and ready for him and yet when Verity admitted as much...he had stopped. She had wanted to couple with him and yet she did not, and he would have her no other way but completely willing.

Cruel.

It actually had stung to hear her say that and that disturbed him. He could be cruel when needed, but he had no wish to be cruel to her. What choice did he have when she lied repeatedly to him? Why the lies? That was what disturbed him the most. He did not think Verity was prone to lying. She was doing so for a reason. And he intended to find out, just as he intended to couple with her, when the time was right.

The problem that kept nagging at him was that once he did mate with her, he did not know if he would ever be able to let her go.

~~~

Verity ate with the women just after dawn. An early start was necessary since there was much yet to be done. Men were already busy repairing some of the dwellings damaged by the fire. Layers of pine branches would serve to cover the holes in the roof until it could be properly mended when it was not so cold.

A hunting party left just after Verity had joined the women to eat. One of their dwellings that stored their food had been damaged along with the contents inside. If more food was not found and prepared, the tribe could go hungry.

Some of the women helped the men make repairs to the weapons while others helped the healer tend the wounded and another group saw to keeping everyone fed. Even the children joined in to cart away debris, though they did more running and laughing, but they're young resilience and joy in the face of such hardship was a healing help to all.

Verity saw that although Wrath was busy speaking with Harran, he made sure to keep her in his sight.

"Your husband cares for you greatly," a woman said and the other women around the outside fire pit nodded in agreement. "He rarely takes his eyes off you."

Because he does not trust me. But then she gave him reason not to trust her and that disturbed her all the more.

108

Verity did her best to smile and nod as if she agreed with them.

"He is a powerful and fearless warrior. You must be proud to call him your husband," another woman said.

"I am very proud to have such a brave man as my mate," she said and would have been if he was her husband. But even if he was not, she did believe him a brave man. She needed one as fearless as Wrath to help find Hemera.

The cold lingered and so did the gray skies, but no snow fell. Verity kept working along with everyone else. It helped keep the cold from settling inside her. All was going well, the village repairs doing nicely and smiles returning to many faces.

The smiles vanished quickly when loud shouts were heard. Men and women rushed to gather weapons, ready to fight, and the children were gathered and made ready to flee to safety. One of the hunters who had left earlier suddenly appeared and spoke with Harran and Wrath.

Harran stepped forward and shouted for all to hear. "There is nothing to fear. Go about your tasks."

Sighs of relief were heard and smiles returned, but caution took hold again when shortly afterwards a man was dragged into the village, his head hanging down and the hood of his cloak draped over it. He was deposited in a small dwelling and Cora, the healer, was summoned.

Verity did not need to hear what others were saying to know what was happening. One of their attackers had gotten away and collapsed in the woods. If he could be saved, there was a chance Wrath could find out who was responsible for the attack and if there were more to come.

Wrath came out of the dwelling not soon after Cora had entered and Verity saw that he was headed straight for her.

"Cora says she can use your help with the wounded captive." He did not wait for Verity to consent. He took her arm and guided her to the dwelling.

The man was too big for the narrow bed. His legs hung off the end and his one arm drooped off the side. His head was turned toward the wall, his hood covering most of his face.

Cora looked to Wrath and Harran. "Leave. I will see this done."

Verity knew Wrath's response before he spoke.

"No! Harran can leave but I stay."

"The man is weak he cannot—"

Wrath turned such a harsh look on Cora that she bowed her head and said, "As you wish."

Harran hesitated to take his leave.

"Go," Wrath urged. "Your tribe needs you."

The room was quiet for a few moments as Cora took a dagger and split the man's bloody tunic open down past the middle of his chest.

Verity cringed. She had seen wounds such as his and none had ever survived them.

Cora looked to Wrath. "He will not survive."

"I only need him to wake for a short while."

"I cannot promise you that."

"Do what you can," Wrath said, his firm tone leaving no room to argue.

Cora turned to Verity. "He has slivers of wood in him from whatever he was hit with. I need you to get them out. You have a steadier hand than I do." She handed Verity a needle.

Verity took it and looked around. "Where is the water to first clean him?"

"A waste of time. Pluck out the wood."

"I must clean him first to see his wound more clearly," Verity said.

"He is going to die. Nothing is going to save him. It makes no difference."

"Verity will clean him," Wrath ordered.

Cora once again looked to Wrath. "Then you have no need of me. She can see to what needs doing. I will send someone with a bucket of snow."

"I can see to this," Verity confirmed.

"Go," Wrath ordered annoyed with the woman for leaving the task to Verity.

Cora scurried past Wrath and out the door as he approached Verity.

He reached out and brushed a stray strand of hair off her face. Strands were forever breaking free from her braid and falling around her face. He recalled the one time he had seen it free of the braid. It was lovely and he would like to see her hair that way again sometime. But now was not that time. Now there were more important matters to see to.

"Are you sure you can do this on your own?"

Something inside her sparked at his simple touch. It seemed so familiar as if he had done it often and without thought, as if he cared for her. Not a thought she needed to be having now.

"I have tended wounds before and I fear Cora is right. He will not survive," she said.

"It is important we learn what we can from him."

"I will do what I can, but I fear it will not be much."

The door opened and a man entered with a bucket of snow and an old scrap of cloth. Wrath took them from him and set the bucket on the edge of the stone fire pit. It was not long before the snow melted and Verity sat on a bench beside the bed and began to clean the man's wound.

"I cannot believe he still lives," she said quietly. She worked as gently as she could on him and she

111

wondered if it mattered since he did not move. It was when she plucked the first piece of wood embedded deeper in his wound that he stirred.

Wrath stepped closer.

Verity saw the man's hand that lay at his side on the sleeping pallet begin to fist and she said softly, "I am trying to help you."

His hand stilled.

Wrath reached down and pushed the man's hood off his face and met blue eyes full of anger. "Who are you and what do you want here?"

The man's eyes drifted shut and Wrath took a step away annoyed that he had not remained alert long enough to answer. He caught the sudden flash of movement out of the corner of his eye and swerved around.

The man was sitting up and had Verity by the throat.

Verity tugged frantically at his hand, but she could not dislodge his firm grip.

"He will come for you and he should cut your eyes from your head," the man said and let out a roar, his fingers closing tighter around her neck.

Wrath swung at the man's arm with his fist with such force that it broke not only the grip he had on Verity but split the bone, the crack loud in the small room. The man let out another roar and with his other hand grabbed for the dagger Cora had left on the bed and swiftly plunged it into his neck before Wrath could stop him.

Wrath snatched Verity off the bench and away from the sleeping pallet, depositing her by the door. "Slow breaths," he said as she fought to breathe. He cast an eye at the man, half of him slumped over the side of the sleeping pallet and blood pouring on the ground from his fresh wound.

The door burst opened and Harran and two other men rushed in the room with their swords drawn.

"He took his life when he woke," Wrath explained.

"He said nothing?" Harran asked.

"Not a word. He is yours to dispose of. I want to get Verity to our dwelling. She has suffered a terrible fright."

"Aye, of course," Harran said, nodding repeatedly.

With a snug arm around her waist, Wrath hurried Verity out of the dwelling and along to theirs. He did not release her after shutting the door. "That man was a Northman?"

Verity nodded, still too shocked to speak and not only from being choked, but by who had choked her.

"You knew him."

She nodded again.

"He was not dressed as a Northman."

She shook her head.

"You will look at the men I killed and tell me if they are Northmen too."

She returned to nodding.

He, however, shook his head. "Word was received through the various tribes that the Northmen had only arrived and they must wait on King Talon's word before riding to Pictland. That would take almost a full moon cycle, so how is it that this Northman is here now?"

Verity finally spoke. "He would have had to have arrived here before me."

Wrath released her, though stepped closer to her. "Who will come for you and why did this Northman believe your eyes should be cut from your head?"

Chapter Eleven

Verity knew she could not keep lying to Wrath, but how much did she tell him? How much did she trust him with the truth? What would he do when he learned of her visions? Would he fear her and protect her no more? She chose her words carefully, her hand going to the mark at her neck as she did. "Ulric, son of Haggard, accused me of stealing one of his weapons and insisted that I had planned to use it to kill him. He had me tethered to a post in the middle of the village until he decided what he would do with me. He would be furious that I escaped his punishment and I have no doubt he would follow after me."

Wrath's eyes narrowed, his jaw tightened and he clenched his one hand in an attempt to contain his anger. He was familiar with what happened to those who were tethered or tied to a post before punishment. It was a way for tribe members to express their disfavor with what the person had done. Rotting food was thrown, many spit on the person, and if tribe members were extremely upset they would throw stones or attempt to yank hair out of the person's head.

The thought that Verity suffered any of that disturbed him beyond reason. But so did the thought that she might be guilty of what she had been accused of and if so, had she intended to use the weapon to kill Ulric?

"Did you steal the weapon?" he asked.

"No," Verity said, shaking her head. "I would have been foolish to do such a thing."

"Then why would Ulric accuse you of it? And why would he want to cut your eyes from your head?"

This was where it became difficult to explain it to him. If she was not careful and satisfy his query, he would only ask more questions.

"I do not understand why he would do either." She did not believe her excuse would suffice, but she feared saying any more than that.

"How odd, that he should accuse you for no reason."

He did not believe her and she could not blame him. It was a pitiful excuse.

"What is even odder is that Ulric should follow after a slave that has returned to her home makes no sense. None of what you tell me makes sense."

"What makes less sense is what Ivan was doing here at all and in unfamiliar garments," Verity said not only curious about it, but hoping it would divert the discussion away from her.

Wrath took hold of her arm again. "You will have a look at the men who attacked the village and tell me if you recognize any of them." Once outside, Wrath said, "Tell me about Ivan."

"He was a fierce warrior, but then all Northmen are. Death means little to the Northmen as long as they die with honor as Ivan did. He and Ulric went on many raids together. Ivan and Ulric also were the ones who were sent to trade with the Drust." Her brow furrowed. "I recall hearing that the Drust were angry at King Talon."

"Do you know why?"

"Many things were said, but the one I heard most often was that the King had not kept his word to the Drust. And they believed that a King who failed to keep his word was not a King to trust."

Wrath was glad the misunderstanding with the Drust had been rectified and they could once again be counted as allies of the King, though not all of them. There were Drust who were not in favor of the King. Could there be more unrest with the Drust than had not been revealed? He would make sure he mentioned the possibility to the King.

"This will not be pleasant for you to look upon," Wrath said as they stepped into the woods.

It was considerate of Wrath to warn her, but unnecessary. She had seen more unpleasant things than she cared to remember.

Wrath stopped not far from the bodies and his hand slipped off her arm to take her hand. "A quick look should do. There is no need to linger."

She nodded, pleased that he thought to hold her hand through it, the gesture a caring one or so she wished to believe.

They approached the bodies and one look had Verity shaking her head.

"None are Northmen."

"You are sure?" Wrath asked.

"I am not familiar with any of these men. They are not from my village."

Wrath's brow narrowed and after a moment he said, "Go wait over by that boulder."

Verity did as he said and watched to see what Wrath would do.

He took his dagger and began shredding the dead men's garments. He stopped now and again to stare at something. Verity realized what he was searching for—body drawings. And he had found some.

Verity was not surprised to see the anger in his eyes as he approached her. That a Northman had joined the

116

Pict to attack a Pict village did not bode well, and she feared what it might mean.

Wrath stopped in front of her. "Did you ever hear talk of the Northmen attacking the Pict?"

"I heard nothing, but Hemera heard and shared some of it with me."

"Tell me."

"Haggard and Ulric argued over Haggard's decision to make peace with the Pict. Ulric believed his father foolish. He felt that the Northmen should attack the northern Pict isles and claim them as their own. He then wanted to move further inland and claim more land for the Northmen. Haggard preferred to move in gradually, encouraging his warriors to join with the Pict women and settling in their tribes until the tribes were more Northmen than Pict."

Anger flared in Wrath. The dead men had body drawings from the Ancrum Tribe, a single band of thorns around the upper part of both arms. Their chieftain, Egot, was a strong supporter of the King. Which begged the question, what were Ancrum warriors doing with a Northman, attacking a Pict Tribe?

The other question that begged an answer was what did Verity have to do with all of this?

Wrath and Verity's talk was interrupted when two men appeared, dragging Ivan's body behind them. They stopped abruptly when they saw Wrath.

One man was quick to say, "Harran ordered his body placed with the others."

Wrath nodded and, taking Verity's hand, walked off with her to leave the men to their task.

"The King needs to be informed about this," Wrath said, after entering their dwelling. "We will return to the stronghold as soon as the King's warriors arrive.

"What of Hemera?"

117

"The search will have to wait. This is more important."

"To you, but Hemera is more important to me," she argued, then asked what she knew would be denied, but she would ask anyway. "Let me go search for her while you see to your duties."

"No, I will not allow it. You will not go off on your own unprotected. Besides, I do not know where you and your sister fit into this whole situation, but I believe you both fit in it somewhere and until you tell me the whole of it or until I find out—you stay with me."

Verity went to argue.

"Do not waste your breath. You stay with me." He tossed his cloak on the sleeping pallet. "What else can you tell me of Ulric?"

Verity hung her cloak on the peg, resigned for the moment that there was nothing she could do about her search for Hemera. She also was beginning to wonder if she and Hemera had been allowed to escape. Ulric had arrived on Pict soil not long after them. Had he planned it that way? Had he let them escape, giving him reason to come here and set into motion what could be the beginning of a war with the Picts? But that would seem unlikely, since he had plans for her, and he would not take a chance of losing her to the sea.

"Verity?"

She turned.

"Ulric. Can you tell me more of Ulric?"

This time the darkness rushed around Verity with such strength and force that she barely had time to stretch her hand out to Wrath before it engulfed her completely.

Wrath rushed forward and captured her in his arms quickly. He laid her on the sleeping pallet, leaving room for him to sit beside her and he held her hand tightly as he spoke to her. "I am here, Verity. I will not leave you."

It was strange to hear Wrath speak to her while wrapped in a vision. Never had she heard anyone's voice outside a vision and hearing him say he was there and would not leave her made her feel less fearful and brought her comfort.

A tall, slim woman approached Verity in an unfamiliar forest. Her long white hair, plaited in a single braid, defined her as an elder, yet her lovely face had few lines and wrinkles that came with living long. She had gentle blue eyes and she wore a long, white tunic that skimmed the top of her bare feet. She spoke softly. "Hemera is well. Do not worry. You will be reunited." The woman and her voice began to fade. "Watch."

"Wake up, Verity. Wake up!"

"Listen. Learn."

"You will wake up, Verity."

Was that fear she heard in Wrath's voice? No, that was not possible. Wrath feared nothing. Her eyes fluttered as she fought to open them.

"Open your eyes, Verity," he urged as she continued to struggle to do so.

This vision was different from the others. She had felt at peace around the woman who had spoken to her and she had not wanted to leave her presence. It was the first time she had wanted to linger in a vision.

She felt a hand tapping her cheek.

"Come on, Verity, open your eyes."

Again she heard a bit of fear mixed with his urging and her eyes finally fluttered open.

Wrath watched as her dark eyes turned a lighter blue. He had never seen anything like it and he could not help but wonder over it.

She rested her hand against his chest. "I am grateful that you stayed with me."

"You are my responsibility. The King commands it."

Her hand fell away and she turned her head, pretending to yawn.

He did not know why he responded as he did. Was he reminding himself that that was all there was between them because he was beginning to care for her? Why else would he grow so upset when she went limp in his arms or when she paled as if death had taken her? Never had he worried about a woman as much as he worried about Verity.

He stood, annoyed at his straying thoughts that should be on the problem at hand and not on a woman. He was the leader of the King's elite warriors and that came before all else. "You should sleep. These attacks make you tired and you need rest."

She did not have to pretend the next yawn; it came on its own.

"I go to speak with Harran, though I will make no mention of Northmen. That is for the King to hear before anyone else is made aware of it. Make sure to hold your tongue on that."

"I will say nothing."

"We will talk more later, after you have rested." He grabbed his cloak off the sleeping pallet and dropped a blanket over Verity, then went to the door. "You will remain here until I return." When she did not answer, he turned and saw that she was already sleeping.

He got a sudden urge to go and slip in beside her and take her in his arms, and he grew angry. This had to stop. Northmen were on Pict soil without permission and a Pict tribe had attacked another Pict tribe along with a

Northman. There were much more important matters for him to see to than to dwell on a woman.

He stepped outside glad for the cold wind that caught him like a slap in the face. More repairs were needed to be made to damaged dwellings and weapons made ready if another attack should happen. It was his responsibility to make sure the tribe stayed safe until the King's warriors arrived.

The Raban Tribe was not a warrior tribe. They wielded weapons when necessary, but they were no match against seasoned warriors. They were more farmers, their growing fields harvesting more food than other tribes.

Harran had told him the warriors had entered the village peacefully at first, requesting food, which Harran gave them. It was not long before the warriors turned on them. Their skill with weapons was remarkable and Harran feared the few warriors would defeat his small tribe, killing everyone.

Harran did not recall seeing the large warrior, who had recently succumbed to his wound, enter the village. But with all the chaos and fear that more warriors would arrive, he could not be certain.

Wrath had assured him that King Talon would see the tribe kept safe, but he saw doubt in the elder's eyes. The war was still fresh in many minds. Much blood had been shed to unify the tribes and make them strong so that foreigners could not lay claim to the land again and that those tribes to the south would keep their distance from the mighty Picts.

Someone was trying to destroy what King Talon had managed to build...a powerful Pict nation.

Harran approached Wrath. "My people grow worried that another attack will come, bringing more warriors, and your help will not be enough. I truly believed that the peace King Talon brought to our land would prevail, but now I wonder if peace is possible." He shook his head. "And while I do not condone gossiping tongues, many fear that if the King does not produce an heir soon that someone will seize the throne from him. Someone that will not be as wise and generous as King Talon, and the Picts will once again war with each other. I fear if that should happen, the Pict people will be lost forever."

"King Talon will see us safe."

"I hope your words ring true. I would like to see the King have strong sons who will see that the Picts go on forever in this land. And that in a faraway day from now, my blood still runs in those that follow me. But enough of that, how does your wife fare?"

"She rests."

"That is good. She is a good and generous woman. My tribe is appreciative of her help. But many wonder if she is as good as she appears since she wears a mark around her neck that they question."

"It is no one's concern. Verity is who she appears to be a good and generous woman." He would explain himself to no one, though he and the King had wondered the same about Verity. Good people were sometimes forced to do bad, sometimes horrible, things out of necessity.

"Let us see to the weapons," Harran said wisely, saying no more about Verity.

~~~

Verity sat up after Wrath left. Usually a vision left her tired, but not this time. This time she did not feel tired at all. She felt refreshed. She wondered if perhaps the woman in her vision was a forest spirit and was protecting Hemera. She wanted to believe that. She wanted to believe all would be well, but she feared otherwise.

She scurried off the sleeping pallet and grabbed her cloak, slipping it over her shoulders and hurried out the door. She craved the cold air and the company of others. She did not want to be alone and ponder her problems. If she kept her hands busy, her mind would be as well, especially since she did not want to think on what Wrath would say to her when he found out she had not done what he had ordered.

She had taken only a few steps out the door when Cora grabbed her arm. "I need help."

Verity went with the healer willingly, though she kept a grip on her arm as if Cora was afraid to let go of her. They entered a dwelling and Verity grimaced at the smell.

"This wound cannot be healed. It will take him soon enough, but his mother has not stopped begging me to help her only child. I have others who will live if I tend to them. Do what you can for him," Cora said, pointing to a young man on a sleeping pallet.

The door opened and a woman entered, her eyes filling with tears when she looked at Cora. "You have come to help him. Bless you."

"Verity here is going to help him," Cora said.

The woman shook her head. "No! No! You are the healer. What good will she do my son?"

"As much good as I would do him, Etta."

Etta's tears fell down her wrinkled cheeks. "He will not die. He cannot die."

Cora shook her head. "He cannot be saved, Etta."

Though Cora spoke bluntly, Verity saw the sorrow in her eyes. It hurt her to tell the woman, but lying would not help the woman face the truth.

"Verity will help," Cora said and hurried out of the dwelling.

Verity took off her cloak and dropped it on the sleeping pallet on the other side of the small room. She looked to the woman as she rolled up the sleeves to her tunic. "Could you bring me a bucket of snow and set it on the edge of the fire pit to melt.

Etta nodded, her aged eyes widening with a spark of hope. "Whatever you need I will fetch for you. Please. Please help my son, Rand."

"I will do what I can. Now hurry with the bucket of snow. His wound needs cleansing if he is to survive." Verity pulled a bench next to the bed and braced herself for the smell when she threw back the blanket covering the young man. She scrunched her nose, not at the smell, for it was not as bad as she expected, it was seeing that the leg and wound had never been cleaned.

Etta returned, struggling with the bucket and Verity hurried to take it from her.

"I need clean cloths and I will need the bucket refreshed often," Verity explained.

"The woman went to a basket with a covering on it and returned to Verity with a clean shirt. "I just finished this for him and I will go fill another bucket with snow and keep refreshing them as often as you need." Etta placed her slim hand on Verity's shoulder. "I am grateful to you."

Verity hoped that death was not ready to claim Rand yet. She got busy washing the wounded leg. Rand was warm to the touch, but not hot. If a fever set in all could be lost. Calling on what she had learned from the Northmen and their women, she took some of the snow before it melted and placed it around his neck, hoping to block any fever.

She had also learned that a wound must be cleaned before wrapped. If there were signs of any rot, it had to be dug away.

Rand cried out when Verity began cleaning the wound.

"I mean you no pain," Verity said gently. "I only wish to help you."

Etta entered then and seeing her son's eyes wide open, she rushed to his side. "A bit of pain and you will be fine, son." She turned pleading eyes on Verity to make it so.

"He may need a stick to bite on. I must dig some of the rot out if he is to survive."

Etta grabbed a thick stick from the basket by the fire pit and ordered her son to bite down on it when necessary. She then took his hand and held it tight. "I am right here with you. You are not alone."

Verity admired the woman's strength and how deeply she cared for her son. She set to work determined to save him.

~~~

"Riders approach!" a young lad called out as he ran into the village.

Everyone reached for a weapon, but stilled their hands when they saw who entered the village first— King Talon.

He rode a magnificent beast of a horse that stamped and pawed the ground as if in anger at being brought to a stop. He dismounted in one swift movement. He wore a fur cloak with a black leather tunic beneath that fell to just above his knees and fur wrappings hugged his lower legs down to the tops of his foot coverings. He strode toward Wrath, everyone moving out of his path, the sight of the King frightening as well as thrilling.

"My King," Harran said with a respectful nod as he stepped forward, "welcome to our humble tribe. I had not expected you to trouble yourself over this."

"I protect my people and those that have done this to you will be punished severely. You have my word on that."

"I am most grateful, my King," Harran said with another nod.

"I will speak to Wrath privately, then I will speak to you."

"As you wish," Harran said and looked to Wrath. "You may use my dwelling since your wife is resting in yours."

King Talon turned to Wrath. "First, let us see how your *wife* fares." He once again looked to Harran. "My warriors will make camp on the outskirts of your village. You have nothing to fear."

After more grateful words from Harran, Wrath and the King walked to Wrath's dwelling.

"So you have a wife," King Talon said with a grin. "Was she difficult to find?"

"She gave quite a chase, but I caught her." Wrath was not about to tell him how Verity purposely dropped off the edge of a slope to get away from him. He would never hear the end of it.

"She finally obeys you?"

Wrath stopped at the door to the dwelling. "She does what I tell her."

"Good, we need no more trouble from her, we have enough already."

Wrath opened the door and stepped aside for the King to enter first. He followed the King in and both men stood looking around the empty room.

126

"What was that you said to me? There is not a woman you cannot handle?" King Talon asked with a look that announced he was none too pleased to find Verity had disappeared once again.

Chapter Twelve

It took some doing, but Verity finally had the wound cleaned thoroughly. All sign of rot was gone and the wound was wrapped with fresh cloth. It had been painful for Rand but he had handled it well, his mum urging him to stay strong and fight. She instructed Etta to put snow at Rand's neck and on his brow throughout the night, letting her know it could help in keeping a fever from settling in.

Etta hugged her. "You have saved him and I am forever grateful."

Verity did not want to take her hope away from her. "His chances look much better. Keep the cloth and his leg clean and see that he eats a little something so that he stays strong. I will take a look at his leg tomorrow." She placed a tender hand on Etta's arm. "You need rest yourself, if you are to care for him."

The door swung open, startling the two women and Verity instinctively stepped protectively in front of Etta. Verity was shocked to see King Talon standing before her.

"My King," Etta said, lowering her head.

Verity saw that the commotion had woken Rand and he struggled to try and get up. She put her hand to his chest. "Stay as you are. You are not well enough to stand." He refused to listen and she placed her other hand to his chest to stop his movements.

"Do as she says!" the King ordered and Rand stilled.

"Wrath, see to your wife, while I speak to this brave young warrior and his mum."

Verity quickly moved aside as the King stepped forward, his overpowering presence filling the room. She was suddenly yanked against her husband and she stilled in his arms when she saw the anger in his eyes and felt it in his tense muscles that seemed to tighten around her.

"Verity saved him, my King," Etta said through tears. "The healer gave up on my son, but not Verity. She worked hard and it is because of her that he will live. Wrath is fortunate to have such a caring wife."

The King looked to Wrath. "Yes, he is very fortunate to have such a *good wife*."

Wrath gave a respectful nod to the King and ushered Verity outside so hastily that she stumbled. His strong grip kept her steady as he hurried her to their dwelling.

Once inside, Wrath stepped away from her, shaking his head. "If you were this much trouble to the Northmen, I am surprised they come after you."

His words hurt, but she refused to show it. "Then let me go and I will be no more trouble to you."

"No!" Wrath shouted. "You stay with me. You were to rest. What were you thinking, taking your leave when I told you to stay here until I returned?"

"That was the problem—I was thinking, and I wanted to stop thinking. Lending a helping hand to others keeps my worried thoughts at bay."

"And you did not think to inform me of this?"

"Truthfully, no."

"Truthfully? Now you are being truthful with me?"

Verity sighed heavily, tired of arguing over her every action. "What do you want of me, Wrath?"

What did he want of her? He wanted to stop worrying about her. He wanted to stop thinking that she would have an attack and he would not be there to catch her and keep her safe. He wanted to stop thinking of how inviting her lips were or how soft her skin was to touch. But he said none of that. "I want you to do what I tell you to do."

"And if I do not want to?" she asked, thinking she would never be free to do as she pleased.

"You do not have a choice. "You will stay with me and do as I say. You are my responsibility."

Stay with him. He seemed to be forever telling her of that. *Responsibility.* Another thing he was forever reminding her about. She wished he wanted her to stay with him by choice and for him to be responsible for her as she would be for him if they cared deeply for each other. *Dreams.* That is what they were, dreams that would never come true.

"As you say, I have no choice."

"You will give me your word that you will do as I say."

"I cannot," she said with a slow shake of her head, "for I do not know what the future holds and what choices I may be forced to make."

Her words gave him thought. What choices would he be forced to make in regards to her? It sparked his ire to think that someone else could decide her fate.

He stepped forward, taking hold of both her arms. "You need to trust me. You need to know that I will keep you safe."

Her visions had shown her that, though they had not shown her how she would feel about this mighty warrior.

He did not like seeing the doubt in her eyes or the way her brow scrunched with uncertainty. He never had trouble getting a woman to trust him, but then he never gave a woman any reason not to. So why was Verity different?

Different.

She was not different. It was how he felt about her that was different, and it clouded his judgment. Yet the thought of stepping away from her, leaving another to deal with her, tore at him until he thought he would roar with fury. She had once told him she was where she belonged—with him. And he was beginning to believe her.

The door opened abruptly, preventing any further discussion.

Wrath stepped to Verity's side, their arms touching.

The King's presence overpowered the small room and Verity instinctively leaned against Wrath.

"You did well with the young warrior, Rand. He tells me he will live to fight again for the Picts."

"With a nervous quiver to her voice, Verity said, "I hope that is true."

"You gave Rand the strength to believe it is true and that makes a difference if he is to survive. On one hand, you have proven to be a considerable problem while on the other hand you have proven yourself helpful. If you had not run off, then the Raban Tribe could have suffered a far worse fate than what they did. So, do I punish you or praise you?"

Wrath eased Verity to stand slightly behind him. "I believe there is a more important matter for us to discuss." Wrath did not wait for the King to respond. "Verity knew one of the men who took part in the attack—he was a Northman."

The King folded his arms across his chest. "Tell me."

Wrath explained everything that he had discovered.

King Talon looked to Verity. "Return to Rand and wait there until Wrath comes for you, and do not dare venture anyplace else."

"What if I am needed elsewhere, my King? Do I refuse to help a warrior in need?"

"You dare to speak so boldly to your King?" he demanded his words so sharp they stung.

What had made her speak so brashly? He was King and he would do as he wished to her, whether she deserved it or not, no matter how she spoke to him. His word was law. There was nothing beyond his word.

Verity bowed her head. "Forgive me, my King. I worry should another warrior need my help."

"Do not leave the village or you will suffer, and most unpleasantly."

She bobbed her head and hurried out the door, wanting to distance herself from the powerful King and the anger she had felt growing in Wrath. He was not pleased with the way she had spoken to the King. It seemed that every time she spoke the truth she got herself in trouble and she was already in enough trouble. She shook her head and walked the winding path to Etta's dwelling only to have Cora stop her again.

"I saw what you did for Rand. There is another warrior I have little hope for, perhaps you can have a look at him and see if anymore can be done."

Verity nodded and followed the healer, relieved she was not going against the King's wishes, though concerned how Wrath would feel about it.

~~~

Wrath's glare remained on the closed door. With the King's order, he realized how he would feel if another had say over Verity, and he did not like it.

"You either trust her or you do not."

Wrath turned to the King. "It is not that simple."

"All things are simple. We make them more difficult than necessary." He gave a dismissive wave. "Enough about this woman, I am concerned with this Northman that fought with the Ancrum warriors."

"Verity called him Ivan."

"Ivan," the King repeated as if surprised, "friend to Ulric, son of Haggard?"

"Verity did make mention of that."

"I have never met Ulric or Ivan, though I heard of both when I met with Haggard to discuss peace between our people. Listening to Haggard, I assumed his son thought differently than him. Haggard made sure to mention what a fierce warrior Ulric was and his friend Ivan as well. He insisted that the two of them alone could lay claim to a village."

"If that were true, how could a few Pict farmers wound a fierce Northman warrior so badly that he crawled away from the battle?"

"No Northman would crawl off wounded. He would rather fight to the very end, then to die without honor. Something goes on here. Tarn had spoken of others, before he died, who wanted to see me dead. I was aware there were some who did not want me to be King, but I thought it only a small portion of men who had been opposed to my decision to unify the tribes under one leader. I wonder if they seek the help of Ulric and his warriors to conquer me."

"His father would never condone such action," Wrath said.

"Perhaps or perhaps Haggard had planned it this way all along, letting me think he wanted peace between us and when the time was right, he would send his son to attack."

"That could be why Ulric is coming after Verity and her sister. They saw something they were not supposed to. Their sudden escape from the Northmen, after all these years, would then make more sense."

"Then why not share all they know with us?" The King shook his head. "None of the puzzle pieces fit. A Northman dies not far from a Pict village that was attacked by another Pict tribe. Two Pict sisters who had been taken by the Northmen when they were very young arrive on our shore. One cannot be found and the other one reaches us but tells us nothing. Ulric, son of Haggard arrives shortly after the sisters and requests to see me. Nothing fits."

"There is a piece missing," Wrath said.

"My thoughts as well, but what is the missing piece?" The King remained silent for a moment, then said, "It will take time for Ulric and his warriors to reach us. We will take that time to discover what we can. You will go to the Ancrum Tribe and see what you can find out and while on your way there, you will search for Verity's sister. We may get clearer answers with the two sisters reunited."

"I will take Verity with me." Wrath had not meant it as an edict, but it sounded like one.

The King turned silent once again and Wrath remained silent as well, not ready to offer an apology since he had no intentions of going anyplace without Verity.

"Go find Verity and bring her here," King Talon ordered and Wrath nodded and left the dwelling.

~~~

Verity looked over the aged warrior who grumbled that he needed no attention, he would be fine. Verity did not agree. The arm wound should have been seared immediately. Now it would need cleaning and searing and his skin was already hot to the touch.

"Let me be. I will be fine. It is nothing more than a scratch."

"Hush, Muir," a woman as round as she was short said. "The mighty warrior's wife knows what she does."

"I need no fussing over me, Alvar," Muir said with a scolding tongue to his wife.

"You may not listen to your wife, Muir, but you will listen to me," Cora warned, "or I will see that you feel more pain than you care to. Now let Verity tend your wound."

Muir grumbled, but did not argue with the healer.

"May I show you what can prove helpful when tending such a wound?" Verity asked of Cora.

Cora nodded and watched her every move, helping when necessary.

The door opened and a cold wind whipped in.

"Shut that door you fool," Cora shouted without looking and continued helping Verity.

When Verity was finally finished, Muir surviving the ordeal better than his wife who had cringed more than her husband, she stretched the ache from her back, turning as she did. She stopped, startled that Wrath stood leaning against the closed door.

"The King commands your presence," he said, "though he would want you to finish tending the injured warrior first."

"I can see to what else needs doing," Cora offered and ushered Verity over to her husband. "Verity has been a great help to me. I am grateful to have learned much from her. She would make a good healer."

"Aye, she would," Alvar agreed, "and grateful I am as well for her patience with my husband."

No one other than Hemera had ever expressed gratitude to her for anything she had done until now in this village. "That is kind of you to say, Cora and Alvar."

"It is the truth." Cora gave a nod. "Now be off if you, you don't want to keep the King waiting."

Once outside, Wrath took her hand, and Verity wondered if it was to make certain she remained by his side or was it a natural gesture when he was with her?

"You will be more careful with your tongue in front of the King," he said.

She had been right, he had been angry with her for speaking as she did. "I meant no disrespect."

"I did not think you did, and I would not see you suffer for misspeaking, even to the King."

He would defend her against the King? The thought startled her and made her realize how correct her visions had been. Wrath would keep her safe no matter what.

"I will do as you say."

Wrath laughed. "I would like to believe that."

His laughter and teasing words brought a smile to her face. "I will do my best."

He stopped abruptly and she felt her insides flutter when his hand reached up to tuck a loose strand of her hair behind her ear. It seemed not only a natural gesture, one he did often, but an intimate one as well.

"I do not know what the King wants with you, but I do know that he has ordered us to continue to search for your sister on our way to the Ancrum Tribe."

Her smile burst wider and she squeezed his hand tight, she was so happy. "I am most grateful." They would find Hemera. She had seen it in her vision. She asked quickly, "The King's warriors travel with us."

"A small troop," Wrath confirmed.

"We will find Hemera."

Verity sounded so confident, as if it was already done, that Wrath believed her. They would find Hemera and he hoped when they did, Verity and her sister would be more forthcoming about their escape.

They continued to the dwelling to find the King sitting on the sleeping pallet, though he stood when they entered. Verity stepped closer to Wrath. Never had she seen a man whose presence consumed a room with such power as the King's did.

King Talon looked to Wrath and though he did not say a word, Wrath spoke as if he answered a question. "I am sorry for the delay, my King. Verity was tending another injured warrior."

"Does he fare well?" the King asked, his head turning toward Verity.

"I have hope for him, my King."

"I will speak with Harran and then speak with the injured, but first—" He waved them forward. Once in front of him, he ordered, "Hold out your joined hands."

Wrath glared at him. "What is this, Talon?"

Verity was shocked that he should refer to the King so disrespectfully. Did he not tell her to watch her tongue? She was even more shocked when the King did not reprimand him.

"It is a decision that will keep all concerned safe, for now," the King said. "Now hold out your hands."

Wrath raised their joined hands, though he did not look happy about it.

The King placed his hand over theirs. "I join you two as one until such a time one may want it undone."

Shock turned Verity speechless.

The King looked to her. "For now, this must be. Once all is settled, you or Wrath can see it undone. But for now, you are husband and wife."

"Wrath, come with me," the King ordered and walked to the door and turned. "Go where you please in the village, Verity, but know you are bound to Wrath as he is to you."

Verity turned to Wrath, still unable to speak.

"We will talk when I return, *wife*."

The two men left Verity staring at the closed door. Wrath had not wanted this joining and she had been given no choice. It was not a true joining and she could not let it become one. She would not mate with him. She would find Hemera, then she would have this joining undone.

Her insides churned at the thought.

Chapter Thirteen

Wrath knew better than to question the King on his decision to join Verity and him. He did, however, intend to question Talon his friend, when time permitted. And now was not the time, since Harran approached them as soon as they had left the dwelling.

Harran offered his dwelling to the King while he was in the village and Wrath was not surprised when he turned him down. He told Harran that he would camp with his warriors. Harran attempted to argue, but the King continued to refuse. Pride and support for their King grew stronger as tongues rapidly spread the word that the King was one of them and would sleep on the cold ground as his warriors did. The Raban Tribe was also pleased that the King took time to visit with the injured and how kind he was when Neva yanked at his cloak and held her arms out to him to pick her up.

When he hoisted her up, she giggled and said, "You reach the heavens." She stretched her small arms up, her tiny hands reaching out. "I can touch them." Then she proceeded to tell him how Verity tended her wound and how Wrath taught her to be brave.

"I like you," Neva said. "You are nice." She laid her head on his shoulder, as if intending to stay there.

Deryn hurried to apologize and take her daughter from the King.

"Stay brave, Neva," the King said as he handed the little lass to her mum and she gave him a big smile.

139

Soon after, the King and Wrath sat at the campsite on a long log that had been provided as a bench in front of a large fire pit.

"On the morrow I will see to settling things here and on the next sunrise, we will both take our leave and you will see to your duties and I will return home. I will leave a sufficient troop here and you will take ten warriors with you. We can talk more on the morrow. You should go to your wife now and talk with her."

"Was it truly necessary to join us?" Wrath asked what he wanted to ask since the moment Talon had joined them. "You gave me no choice."

"And the situation gave me no choice. You pledged your fealty to me when I became King, though it was unnecessary since our friendship was stronger than any pledge you gave. While I may have made you responsible for Verity, joining you both makes you responsible in a different way as it does for her. As news spreads about the mighty Wrath having a wife, there is not a tribe that will offer her shelter if she chose to run off again. There is no place for her to turn, but to you." The King turned a grin on Wrath. "Besides, you made the decision easy."

"How so?"

"You care for her whether you want to admit or not. You protect her from me without realizing it, you are there to catch her when an attack strikes her and she collapses, and there are times you look ready to ravish her. This time, I grant you as husband and wife, will let you see if that caring goes deeper than you know. And do not bother to argue with me over it. You know it is true, so see it done and be grateful for a way out of it, if it should prove differently. I gave Paine and Anin no such choice. They are joined for life."

140

"And they want to be. I never saw two people that fit together more perfectly."

"They are a rare couple. Now go to your wife. We did leave her speechless and I am sure she has many questions for you," —the King's grin widened— "unless, of course, you prefer to give her a good poke."

Wrath stood glaring, and realizing his action and that the King still sat, he went to sit.

"Go, my friend" the King said with a dismissive wave of his hand, "though do be cautious of spilling your seed in her, for I will not release either of you if she carries your bairn."

Wrath walked to the dwelling, his thoughts heavy. A spark of anger had flared in him when he had realized what the King intended. Then surprisingly he had felt a sense of relief. Verity's fate was in his hands now. No one could take that from him, unless—Verity had their joining undone. At the moment, that would not happen. The King would not grant her request until this matter was settled. By then her fate would be hers to decide. Or would it?

He opened the dwelling door and shook his head. It was empty again. This time he understood why. If her thoughts were as heavy as his, she would want to get away from them. That meant she went to find something to keep her busy.

Most everyone was inside their dwellings to escape the cold, evening air. It nipped at the face, though it mattered little to Wrath. He had survived bitter cold and days as well as when the sun seemed as hot as a fire pit.

When he left the King's camp area, the warriors had already built three lean-tos and had three fire pits burning strongly. They too knew how to survive the elements with little suffering. They would stay warm and sleep well tonight, as would he wrapped around

141

Verity. He intended to do only that—sleep—unless, of course, she thought otherwise. If she was inclined to join with him, he would not deny her. He would welcome it. Though, he was reminded of the King's warning not to deposit his seed in her. Theirs was a temporary joining and he would not have her take her leave with his child growing inside her.

He tapped on Etta's door and was not offended when she barely opened it. No one wished to lose the precious heat inside.

Etta smiled upon seeing Wrath. "Bless your wife. She left a while ago after checking on Rand. He does well. She is pleased and I continue to be grateful."

"I am pleased for you. Did Verity say where she was going?"

"No, though I saw her walk toward Muir's dwelling."

Wrath was met with a similar greeting and more praise for his wife. Though, it had been a short time that he had begun to refer to Verity as his wife, it seemed natural, as if he was accustomed to it and even more so now that she actually was his wife.

He spotted her when he turned away from Muir's cottage. She was headed toward him, her head down, her hood covering it, and her arms keeping her cloak wrapped tightly around her. She was cold and it would not take him long to warm her. It was a foolish thought since it aroused him. He pushed it from his mind and took strong steps toward her.

Her head shot up, no doubt hearing his footfalls, and she stopped abruptly.

Wrath did not. He went straight to her and scooped her up in his arms, tucking her close against him to let his warmth settle around her. "You are too thin to brave this cold."

He spoke with concern, so she took no offense to his words. "I have braved worse."

"You are my wife. I will not see you suffer needlessly."

"I am your wife for a short time only," she reminded.

"Until that time, you are my wife and you will do well to remember it."

She kept silent until after they entered the dwelling. "I see no purpose in our union."

"The King does." Wrath slipped off his cloak to hang on the peg and went to the fire pit to stoke the flames and add more wood.

What did she say to that? Once again she was reminded that the King's word was law and she had no choice but to obey.

The flames ate hungrily at the fresh wood and Wrath turned to her. "You do have a choice in this, Verity. The King left it for us to decide. You are not bound to me forever. It can be undone." He walked over to her and raised his hand slowly to run his finger down the side of her face and rest it beneath her chin. "But know this, once we couple and I leave my seed inside you, you are mine forever."

Verity felt her breath catch and words were lost to her. He did not speak of caring for her, it was more a warning. Or was he giving her a choice? But the King had already given her one. So why offer her another that would bind them together forever?

The words rushed from her lips. "I do not want to be bound to you forever." It was not what she meant, but she did not have the courage to tell him that she wanted them bound together because they cared for each other, because their hearts were one, because she wanted to hear him whisper the deepest of affections to her...*tuahna*. It was a word spoken so deep from the heart that few had the courage to speak it, let alone feel it.

He brought his lips slowly to hers and kissed her gently, lingering on them with a tempting tenderness. With a slight brush of his lips over hers, he ended the kiss, leaving her lips aching and her body wanting.

"I am here if you want me. I can settle nicely inside you and satisfy you beyond measure." He smiled. "Only if you want me to, but nothing will stop me from kissing you."

Verity could not step away from him fast enough, afraid he would kiss her again and her resolve would weaken. He refused to let her go, being yanked back into his arms. His lips were on hers before she could protest and by then she did not want to. His kiss took command like the mighty warrior he was, settling for nothing less than victory.

He stirred her senses until her thoughts were so muddled that she could do nothing but fall limp against him and savor the kiss. Never had she felt as if she belonged anywhere, but at this moment she knew she belonged right where she was...in his arms.

She was careful not to surrender to him even though he overpowered her and took charge of her senses until she found herself aching for more. It would be easy to surrender her will completely to him, to join with him as husband and wife would, and to have him spill into her and create a new life. But that was not meant to be.

Her heart ached as she eased away from him, reluctant to end their kiss, reluctant to put distance between them, but knowing it was necessary.

"The choice is yours, Verity," he said, "know, though, you are my wife and I will kiss and touch you as I please." What was he thinking? He did not know or he

144

did not want to admit that something inside him did not want to let her go. He got furious at the thought of them separating. He could not deny that feelings for her had been stirring in him. Talon had seen it. Had others?

Strange as it seemed, he also felt that she already belonged to him and there was no choice in the matter, and yet he wanted it to be her choice to stay.

Verity did not respond. She did not know how to respond and she had Hemera to think about. No other thoughts could take precedence over Hemera until she saw her safe.

Verity said words she did not mean. "There can be nothing between you and me."

Wrath smiled. "You deny what already exists?"

She refused to acknowledge his question, for it would prove him right. She snatched one of the blankets from the sleeping pallet and was about to spread it on the ground near the fire pit when he yanked it out of her hand.

"You are my wife and you will sleep beside me." He threw the blanket on the sleeping pallet. "Disrobe. It is time to sleep. We have a busy day tomorrow preparing for our journey."

Sleep naked beside him? She thought not and went to climb into the sleeping pallet fully clothed, fully aware that arguing with him would get her nowhere.

Wrath grabbed her arm. "Disrobe."

"I will not sleep naked beside you."

"Why? Afraid you will surrender to your desires?"

"I do not desire you," Verity snapped.

"Lair! I can feel how much you want me no matter how much you deny it."

Verity longed to tell him that he was right. She wanted him, though it made no sense. She did not know why she cared so much for him when she knew little of him. That was not true. She had come to know him through her visions. He was no stranger to her.

She pushed her troubling thoughts aside and spoke words that hurt her to say, "I do not want you."

"Lair," he accused again, though softly, and yanked her closer to him and kissed her again, quickly this time. "I will not say it again, disrobe." He turned away from her and began shedding his garments.

She turned away from him as well and she began to shed her garments, knowing if she did not he would see her naked by his own hands and that could prove dangerous. Once done, she hurried beneath the blankets on the sleeping pallet and turned to face the wall.

Wrath joined her, his arm going around her to pull her close against him and settle himself around her. Her skin was soft and warm and there was something about knowing she now truly belonged to him that had his arousal from the kisses turning him hard.

"You hide your desire from me. You hide truths from me. Why do you hide so much from me, Verity? What are you afraid of?" he whispered.

She did hide things from him and when he discovered those truths would he be so eager to join with her? Was that what she feared? What would he think when he learned that her attacks were actually visions? Would he keep his distance from her as others had done? Or fear looking upon her? Or worse would he send her away to live in solitude?

"Sleep, Verity, for we have a journey ahead of us that will reveal much," he whispered in her ear. She did not respond and he had not expected her to.

~~~

Wrath spent much of the next morn with the King and Harran, and Verity spent it with helping Cora. She had enjoyed her time here with the Raban Tribe. It had brought back the few memories she had of her tribe. She had been taken so young that there had not been many memories to recall and after a while many had faded until she could not be certain if they were ever real. The few that had stirred in her made her realize how much she had missed her tribe, her home, and how much she hoped to have one once again.

With so much to be done before they took their leave, Verity saw little of Wrath and though her thoughts and hands were busy, she found herself missing him. It was odd how a part of her felt empty without him around. She wondered over it and began to realize that he had been with her and had been part of her through her visions for more moon cycles than she could recall. In a way, he had settled inside her and had become a permanent part of her without her realizing it. He had even helped her to gain the strength to escape. It was no wonder she could not stop caring for him.

She was pleased when she caught sight of him and his eyes settled on her in what she believed, or wanted to believe, was a warm caress.

"You will be carrying a bairn, if you already are not, with the way he looks at you," Cora said, coming up beside her. "Most men have no sense about them. They look to poke their women and be done with it. Wrath looks to satisfy his woman, which in turn will satisfy him far more than a good poke." Cora laughed when Verity just stared at her. "Wise women talk among themselves and listen. It is how they learn."

Watch. Listen. Learn.

The woman's words in her vision returned to her.

"I need to learn," Verity said.

"We all do, though some more than others. Now come, and lend me a hand before you are gone and I can no longer seek your help and knowledge."

Evening fell quickly and after eating with a few of the women, Verity sought the warmth and solitude of her dwelling. Etta had gifted her with a bone comb for saving her son, who was improving even better than Verity expected. She had not wanted to accept it, but Etta had insisted.

Verity had never owned anything of her own and was only allowed to use a comb when given permission. She was overjoyed having one of her own and she told Etta she would cherish the generous gift forever. Her grateful words had brought tears to the old woman's eyes.

With the dwelling quiet, Verity sat on the bed and began to unbraid her hair, eager to comb it. She ran the comb through her long golden hair repeatedly. It felt so good she did not want to stop and knowing she would be able to comb her hair whenever she chose thrilled her.

The door opened and Wrath stepped in and he stopped unable to stop staring at her. Her hair was loose of its braid and the golden strands fell in waves down over her shoulders to rest at her breasts. An image shot through his head of her leaning over him, her golden mane skimming his naked chest, then moving down to tease and tickle his middle, before moving further down for the silky strands to drift across his—he turned around and left the dwelling.

Verity stared at the closed door.

The door swung open once again and Wrath turned a scowl on her. "Go to sleep. We leave early."

He was out the door once again and Verity went to sleep, not because Wrath had ordered her to do so, but because she was tired. She did not know how long after

148

he returned and crawled in beside her, but she woke to find herself nestled against his naked chest, and she returned to sleep feeling safe in his arms.

She woke to an empty bed and dressed quickly and was about to go find her husband when the door opened and he entered.

"Good, you are ready. Join the women and eat and then we take our leave. The King has already departed."

Verity was glad to hear that. She was not comfortable around his overpowering presence. She followed her husband out the door and enjoyed the last meal with the women she had come to know and think of as friends.

It was not long before they were on their way and as sad as it was to bid farewell, Verity was eager to continue her search for Hemera.

Chapter Fourteen

The sky was overcast and the air crisp and Verity was glad to be on the horse with Wrath and tucked against him. She was warm and comfortable.

"Tell me more about Ulric," Wrath said as he kept an unhurried pace.

Verity was only too glad to keep the discussion about anything but them. "Ulric and his father agree on little. Ulric believes his father is growing too old to lead the Southern Region. While Northmen from other regions continue to raid, Haggard has established trade routes with foreign lands. Ulric does not realize what his father has accomplished for his people. Or how his foolishness could unravel all his father had done."

"Do you believe he would go against his father's command?"

Verity bit at her bottom lip, thinking how she could tell him what she knew without revealing other things to him.

"I will not let Ulric hurt you. You have my word on it."

He thought she feared Ulric, but then she did. "Many believe, and fear, that Ulric will attempt to unseat his father."

"Haggard is too well respected by his own men for them to go against him."

"That would not stop Ulric. He would seek whatever means necessary to see it done."

"How was it that you stood in his way?"

Verity should have known it was not only Ulric that Wrath wanted to know about. And the way his eyes glared at her with determination, she knew he intended to have an answer.

"You say you do not know why he falsely accused you of stealing his sword. But I would venture to guess that it was because you somehow stood in his way. What was it?"

His look grew more forceful and Verity was ever so grateful when one of the warriors approached him with haste, preventing her response.

He spoke quickly, "A troop of warriors from the Kerse Tribe approach and they have a prisoner with them."

Wrath called a halt to his troop, wondering what the Kerse were doing in this area, a distance from their home and with a prisoner.

The troop of ten warriors with a large man in tow, a rope around his neck and his hands tied, approached slowly. Grins soon broke out as they recognized the garments of the King's warriors.

Before a word was said, the prisoner stepped forward, glared at Verity, and spoke in the language of the Picts. "Cut her eyes from her head before she sees your fate and steals it from you?"

All the warriors turned to stare at her, giving the man enough time to grab a dagger off one of the Kerse warriors and jab it into his neck and fall to the ground, blood spraying everywhere.

All eyes watched the man choke on his own blood until no life was left in him.

The leader of the Kerse troop, an older man with hair cropped so short he appeared bald, looked to Wrath. "I am Dag."

"I remember you well," Wrath said. "You and your tribe fought bravely to unite the tribes."

"It was an honor to fight beside the man who would be King," Dag said with a firm nod. "We were bringing this man to the King to see what he would want done with him. He attacked our village along with some Ancrum warriors. He was the only one to live and it was not easy to take him captive. His tongue was foreign to us, though hearing his last words, it seems he speaks our language."

"Leave him with us," Wrath ordered. "I will see that the King is made aware of this."

"We have heard rumblings that there are some displeased with the King and wish to see him dethroned," Dag said. "Are the Ancrum among them?"

"A few disgruntled tribesmen from various tribes stir some trouble. The King is seeing to quelling it," Wrath assured the man.

"The Kerse stand ready to help the King," Dag said proudly. "There is talk that he will wed soon. We hope this is true so that his sons may reign after him and keep peace among the Picts."

"The King is appreciative of your loyalty and will call on you if needed. You have done well," Wrath said. "Plans are being seen to now for the King to wed a fine woman whose mother gave her husband six sons."

Dag grinned and nodded as did his warriors. "That is good to hear. I will spread the word." He gave a quick nod to Verity. "What of this woman? The prisoner spoke as if he knew her and he warned against her."

"Verity is my wife," Wrath said as if that was all that needed saying.

"Bless your joining, Wrath," Dag said. "The fool must have thought to use her to distract us so he could grab a weapon."

"That would seem most likely."

"Do you want us to get rid of the body?" Dag asked.

"No, my men will see to it," Wrath said. "The King will be pleased to know how loyal you are to him. If your tribe has not already received word, you should be aware that a troop of Northmen led by Ulric, son of Haggard, Chieftain of the Southern Region has been granted permission to stand before the King at the stronghold."

"What is it the Northmen want?" Dag asked.

"That is not yet known, but King Talon wants every tribe aware of it."

"We stand ready," Dag said and after a few more words, the Kerse were on their way.

Silence hung heavy in the air after the Kerse were out of sight.

Wrath finally turned to his warriors and ordered two to take the body into the woods and leave it for the animals to feed on. He then signaled for the troop to continue riding.

Verity sat silent, dreading the moment he would ask her about the man. He was a Northman, one of Ulric's men, and she knew she could not continue to keep the truth from him.

Once again she was spared when they rounded a bend and she recognized the area from her vision. "This is the area I saw in my dreams."

"You are sure?" Wrath asked.

"Aye, this is it, up ahead," she said excited that she was so close to Hemera.

They followed a slight curve along the trail and Verity gasped when they came upon a dwelling, rotting with neglect and age.

"It cannot be," Verity said ready to slip off the horse as soon as Wrath brought the animal to a stop.

Wrath tightened his arm around her waist, keeping her on the horse. He summoned two warriors to have a look. "There appears to be no one here. Are you sure this is the spot?"

Verity stared at the crumbling dwelling, a large open gap where the door once stood. Her vision had been clearer than most and had showed her a thriving village on this very spot. How had her vision proved so wrong?

Confused and disappointed, all she could do was shake her head.

"No one here," one of his men called out to him, walking out the door, having entered the dwelling from the other side where there was no longer a wall.

"We continue on," Wrath called out and turned his horse away, the warriors following behind him while one rode ahead.

Verity looked around as they rode off, trying to see if perhaps she had been wrong about this place, but everywhere she looked seemed familiar. With her thoughts heavy on Hemera, it took her a moment to feel how taut Wrath's body had grown against hers and how snug his arm had grown around her waist. He was angry and she knew why, but she had been too excited about the thought of finding Hemera to pay heed to what had happened with the Kerse.

"I will have the truth from you, *wife*," Wrath said his anger palpable. "Do not let another lie cross your lips."

Keeping the truth from him would no longer serve any purpose and it was better he learned the truth from her. "He was a Northman."

154

"I assumed that since he knew you." He glared at her, waiting to hear more.

She lowered her head, his angry scowl difficult to look upon.

He gripped her chin between two fingers and forced it up. "I will see your eyes when you finally speak the truth to me."

Fear had kept Verity from sharing her secret with anyone but Hemera and fear now prickled her skin. She stumbled over words until finally they rushed from her mouth. "I do not have attacks; I have visions of what is to come."

He released her chin, his scowl deepening. "You are a seer? You can look into my eyes and see my fate?"

"No," Verity said, shaking her head. "The visions come upon me without will. I never know when they will strike or what I will see. Some are clear and others leave me wondering. It is how I knew your name before meeting you. You were in several visions I had before meeting you and you always helped me."

"Then why not trust me and tell me the truth when we first met?"

"I did not know what you would do. I am not familiar with how the Picts treat their seers. The Northmen seers are not permitted to live among others. They live in remote areas and are available only to those in power."

"The King does not dictate to seers. They may live as they choose, but then he has found none that have been so accurate that he can rely on them," he said.

"It is not always easy to know what a vision shows you. They are not always clear."

"Like the one you had about finding your sister in this area?"

Verity looked around at the tall trees, the boulders half-covered with snow, and the few snowdrifts that the horses avoided. "This is all familiar to me. I saw it in my vision, but there were people here and a thriving village."

"Are your visions more wrong than right?" he asked and was surprised at her response.

"I wish they were more wrong than right, then perhaps they would fade and leave me be." She rested her hand on his arm that circled her waist. "I would prefer not to see what is shown to me."

His instincts had him tucking her closer against him as though he could keep her safe even from her visions.

"Hemera was the only one who knew and she warned me against letting anyone else find out or else I would be sent away and we did not want to be separated from each other. So when the healer questioned me, I told her nothing of the visions. Everyone believed them attacks and in a way it helped, since most everyone stayed away from me fearing they would be inflicted with the same."

"That was why the men paid you no heed," Wrath said and felt grateful that the visions had in a way protected her. "Did Ulric find out?"

"The healer had been growing suspicious and had finally confided her doubts to him. He made it appear that I stole his sword and intended to kill him. That was when he had me tethered to a post, but only for a few days. He locked me away after that, leaving the rope around my neck to tug at for his amusement. He told me that he knew my attacks were visions and that he knew I saw what he planned to do. He warned me to tell no one of anything or I would die."

"You saw what he planned?"

She shook her head. "He was wrong. I had seen nothing of his plans, though now I wish I had. I thought he intended to kill me, but he told me that I could be of use to him. He intended to keep me as his seer, always locked away, always his prisoner."

"How did you escape?"

"Hemera helped me. She had a boat waiting for us."

Wrath wrinkled his brow. "Had either of you ever sailed a boat?"

Verity shook her head.

"You both were fortunate to have reached shore."

Verity gripped his arm. "Maybe Hemera never made it."

"Your visions tell you differently."

"But I was wrong, thinking I would find her here," she said, hope of ever finding Hemera fading.

"Tell me more about your other visions concerning Hemera."

Verity told him about each one.

"From what you say, it would seem that your sister is safe and that you will find her. I think that is what you should hold on to until more is revealed to you."

Verity was pleased that she no longer saw anger in his eyes or that his body felt taut. She had always feared anyone finding out the truth, mostly because what it might mean for her. She wondered then what it would mean for her with Wrath now knowing the truth.

"The King must be told of this before anyone else learns of it," Wrath said.

It would continue to remain a secret for now and that was fine with Verity. She preferred it that way. She wished the King did not have to know about it, for she worried what he might do.

"You nibble at your lip, what worries you?" Wrath asked, running his finger along the side of her face gently to lift her chin slightly.

"What will the King do when he learns of it?"

"Knowing the King the way I do, he will probably want to see how helpful your ability can be to the Picts on a whole. He wants what is good for the Picts. He wants a powerful Pict nation that will battle and be victorious against foreign invaders. He wants Pict blood to run strong in this land long after we are all gone."

"Then I will serve the King if my visions prove helpful to him?"

"We all serve the King, though you will not be held captive if that is what you think."

At least he had showed no signs of fearing her, but he had also made no mention of her remaining his wife, and she did not wish to ask, not now.

Wrath watched her nibble lightly along her lip again. "Have you told me everything?"

"Everything there is for me to tell," she said too fearful to say more.

"You will share your visions with me from now on...all of them."

She did not know if she was comfortable sharing *all* her visions with him.

"By doing so, perhaps I can help you make sense of them."

He wished to help her. She was surprised and pleased that he would help her. No one but Hemera had ever helped her and her instincts had her giving him a quick kiss before saying, "That is kind of you."

"I am not kind," he said gruffly.

"To me you are," she said softly and laid her head on his shoulder.

158

To his surprise, her tender response aroused him. Or was it holding her close in his arms that was what stirred him? Or was it that he was depriving himself from mating with his wife and his body was protesting? He swore beneath his breath. Never had thoughts of a woman troubled him so much. He had no time for such nonsense. He was commander of the King's personal guard and that came before all else.

Then why was Verity more in his thoughts than the King?

"We will continue to search for Hemera?" she asked.

"She will be found."

The strength of his words renewed her hope.

He asked her more about the Northmen, wanting to know as much as he could since a potential battle was brewing. She told him all she knew.

"I have lived with the Northmen for so long that I fear I lost who I truly am...a Pict."

"Never would that happen. You were born of this land. You are and always will be a Pict. No one can take that from you."

"When I woke that day on the shore cold and trembling, all I could think of was that I was finally home."

"And here, *home*, is where you will stay," he said, hugging her close and thinking it was where she belonged, home in his arms.

~~~

They came upon another aged dwelling, though this one still provided some shelter and Wrath ordered camp to be set for the night.

"The roof may have holes, but it will shelter us well enough," Wrath said to Verity after helping her off the horse. "A fire will soon be started, sit and warm yourself while all is seen to."

Verity was not used to being idle or having others do for her. While Wrath went to see to the warriors, she went to the dwelling. An open door greeted her and she slipped around it to enter the small room. The fire pit was still intact and snow had found its way in through the holes in the roof. Part of a wall had crumbled, but there was enough left of the dwelling to provide good shelter from the cold for the night as would Wrath's arms.

She was growing much too accustomed to being with him, but she had felt that upon first meeting him. But it had not been the first time she had met him. She had first met him in her visions. More and more she was coming to believe that she had begun to care for him before she had met him outside her visions? Her feelings for him had not grown fast upon meeting. They had grown gradually with each vision she had had of him.

That was why now, with her feelings so strong for him, that it pained her to think of ever being separated from him. Her hand went to her chest as a slight gasp escaped at the thought of not being with him.

"Verity!"

She turned to see him drop the broken branches in his arms and hurry to scoop her up.

"A vision?" he asked, holding her tightly.

She shook her head, the concern in his eyes, and the way he attempted to rescue her even from a vision brought a smile to her face and lightened her heart.

"Something startled you?"

She was about to say an animal, not wanting him to know her thought, but could not bring herself to lie to him this time. "You."

His brow narrowed for a moment, then he smiled. "How did I do that?"

"You are forever in my thoughts."

"And what are those thoughts?"

She rested her brow to his. "Thoughts I should not be having."

He brought his mouth to cover hers in a gentle kiss. "I have the same thoughts."

A soft laugh fell from her lips. "You have made that clear."

His smile vanished. "We will mate." His smiled returned as suddenly as it had vanished. "I have seen it in a vision."

She laughed again. "Tell me of this vision."

"With pleasure," he said his smile increasing. "You stood in front of me naked, your body so beautiful I could not resist touching you. And once I felt your soft, smooth skin, I could not keep my hands off you. I cupped your breasts and let them rest in my hand, as my fingers teased your nipples hard. I left your sensitive nipples hungry for more as my hands itched to explore you further, gliding down over the gentle curve of your hips and over your middle." He paused and pressed a kiss high on her cheek, near her ear, then whispered. "My fingers eagerly sought the thatch of golden hair between your legs and searched for that little nub that enjoys being touched and teased and by then you were moaning with desire and begging me to satisfy you." His warm breath tickled her ear. "And I did. First, my fingers brought you pleasure, then my tongue, the delicious taste of you grew me harder as did your loud cries. I made you wait no longer, I scooped you up and laid you on our sleeping pallet, spread your legs and—"

"Stop!" Verity said, pressing her finger to his mouth. His words had been as clear as a vision in her head and she had not only seen but had felt every bit of what he had described to her. And now her body was aching for him.

He moved his lips away from her finger and gently took one in his mouth to suck on until a soft moan escaped her lips. He drew his mouth slowly off her finger, his teeth lightly scraping along and sucking the tip before releasing it. "I cannot wait to take your nipple in my mouth and do the—"

Once again her finger pressed firmly against his lips. "You must stop." She moved her finger away quickly before he could slip it into his mouth again.

"We will mate. Nothing will stop that."

"Not here," she said, shaking her head.

"Your choice. I am yours whenever you want me." He lowered her to her feet and brought her hand up to kiss her palm. "Whenever or wherever you want, wife."

Verity stepped away from him and turned and left the dwelling, afraid she would surrender to him there and then. Once outside, she hurried around the dwelling where no one could see her and took great gulps of air. She scooped up a handful of snow and rubbed it across her heated brow.

She feared she would not have the strength to deny him or herself and she worried that once they mated, she would not want to leave him. She would want to remain his wife.

But would he want the same?

Chapter Fifteen

The sun tried to break through the stubborn clouds the next morn as the small troop continued on their journey. Neither Wrath nor Verity had many words to share after last night.

Sleeping had not come easy for Verity, though she had pretended to be asleep when Wrath had entered the dwelling. She had been grateful for the cold, since they had kept their garments on to sleep. Otherwise, she feared her own actions if they had lain together naked.

He no soon as joined her on the sleeping pallet that had been made from brush and pine branches for them, then he wrapped himself around her, tucking her close against him. If he had known she pretended to sleep, he made no mention of it. He simply kept her tight against him, his arm around her, his leg over her two, and it had not been long before his warmth began to seep into her.

She had wondered if sleep would elude him as it had her, but only moments later, she heard a light snore next to her ear. He had fallen asleep without a problem. Naturally, it gave her pause to think that he was certainly not burdened with thoughts of her. After more thoughts and several yawns warning her that she needed sleep, she realized that there had been nothing to keep him awake. He was certain they would join and would wait for her to realize the same.

Sleep had finally won against her nagging thoughts and she slept until the cold woke her. She had turned to cuddle closer to Wrath.

"Are you warm enough?"

Her musings of the previous night drifted away and she returned to the present moment. "Your arms always keep me warm."

"And they always will."

She wished that was so, and though he did sound as if he decreed it, she had grown aware that it was simply his way of speaking.

"Does any of the land look familiar to you?"

Verity looked around, annoyed that she had been so lost in her thoughts that she had paid no heed to her surroundings, and she should have been more vigil. She was disappointed when she had to admit, "No, I see nothing here from my vision."

"It will not be long before we reach the Ancrum Tribe. We will take a different route on our return home so we may cover a different area."

Verity voiced a sudden thought, she hoped might prove true. "Perhaps Hemera took shelter among the Ancrum."

"She could have taken shelter with any number of tribes along the way. Do you think she would have remained with a tribe or would she more likely have searched for you as desperately as you do for her?"

"Hemera would think on what to do before deciding. She is not one to rush into a decision, so she could very well have remained with a tribe until then."

"Does she share your features and your golden hair?"

"No, we are different. Her hair blazes like the setting sun when heat warms the land and it cannot be tamed or contained in a braid like mine. And she seeks solitude more than she does people."

"Could she survive on her own as you did before I found you?"

"I would not have survived if you had not found me in that snowdrift."

"The snowstorm caught me and my warriors unaware as well."

"That is my greatest fear that the snowstorm swallowed up Hemera."

"Perhaps someone found her, and took her to their tribe, as I did you," Wrath said.

Worry creased Verity's brow. "I can only hope."

Wrath's attention was caught by the return of the warrior who rode ahead, scouting the area. He signaled the troop to stop and waited.

The warrior came to a halt in front of Wrath. "Ancrum warriors approach."

Wrath gave another signal and two warriors rode off to the side, disappearing into the woods. The warrior who brought the news also disappeared into the woods.

He gave Verity a quick glance, then turned his attention to the distance as he spoke. "You will say nothing."

"You will ask about Hemera?"

"When I feel the time is right."

"Something worries you about the Ancrum Tribe?" she asked.

"Until I know for sure that rogue Ancrum warriors were responsible for the attack on the Raban and not the Ancrum themselves, I will remain suspicious."

Two of the King's warriors moved up to take a stance on either side of Wrath and Verity. The remaining five fanned out behind them. That the warriors protected them went without question.

Verity pulled her hood down until it almost covered her eyes and waited in silence.

Ten warriors rode toward them at a brisk pace, but Wrath held his ground. He did not move, nor did a muscle in his body. If the Ancrum intended to intimidate, they had failed with Wrath—not so her, a trickle of fear ran through her. These warriors could somehow be involved with Ulric and that could prove dangerous for her and Hemera. Her worry mounted when the troop finally stopped in front of them.

"Wrath, what brings you to the Ancrum Tribe?" the lead warrior asked.

"I have word for Egot from the King, Vard," Wrath said his eyes steady on the warrior. He was a good size, his middle thick, though not tight, but he had strength. He wore his dark hair cropped short and his face was pleasant enough, though his nose was crooked.

"Egot will be pleased to greet you." Vard smiled. "And who is the woman who rides with you?"

"My wife, not that it is any of your concern."

Vard threw back his head and laughed, the sound echoing through the forest. "The mighty Wrath has wed. She must be a very special woman."

Verity pushed her hood back and broke her silence. "I am special; I am Wrath's woman."

Her words surprised Wrath. She had claimed before all, that she belonged to him. She had also failed to obey him, though he could not fault her words.

"Egot will certainly wish to offer his blessings for a fruitful union and provide food and drink for you as well. Follow us," Vard said.

As they traveled along, Verity noticed that the three warriors who had parted from them had yet to join them. Curious, she whispered, "Where are the others?"

Wrath kept his voice low. "They will remain at a distance. Should something happen they will ride and inform the King."

It did not take long for them to reach the village. It was larger than Verity expected and well-tended. A rather large feasting house sat in the middle and that was where Vard stopped.

Wrath reached up and grabbed Verity by the waist to lift her off the horse after he had dismounted. "You will stay close unless I say otherwise."

She nodded and remained at his side as they followed Vard into the feasting house.

Warmth and a delicious scent greeted them as did a man solid and large in body that Vard had gone and stood next to. His hair had been shorn from his head and was completely covered with drawings that also ran down the sides of his face and his neck. Unlike Vard's and the other warriors, who had only a single band of thorns around their upper arms. He also had good features.

"It is good to see you, old friend," Egot said, his large hand closing completely around the vessel he raised. "I hear blessings are in order for you and your new wife."

"I am grateful for your good wishes, but I have an important matter to discuss with you," Wrath said.

"First food and drink, then we talk," Egot said with a smile and waved them to the long table where he sat. "Your wife can join the women." Egot nodded to a table in the corner.

Verity tugged on Wrath's hand before he could protest, knowing he would. He was not a man to follow dictate lightly or to let her from his side.

Wrath wondered why she bowed her head to him, then he heard her whisper.

"I may learn something from the women."

He almost objected, but stopped himself. She was right. Women talked easily among themselves and most men did not realize they saw much more of what men did not want them to see or believed they saw.

He gave her hand a squeeze before she turned to go
and she smiled softly to let him know she would be fine.
She walked to the table, wondering why the Ancrum
Tribe followed the Northmen's rule that women ate
separately from men. It had not been that way at the
Raban Tribe or at the King's feasting house. She
supposed all Pict tribes followed their own established
traditions.

Wrath was given a seat next to Egot.

"Eat and drink your fill," Egot said, "then tell me
how you found such a beautiful wife."

"I plucked her out of a snowdrift," Wrath said.

Egot's grin disappeared and he asked in a whisper,
"You wed a snow creature?"

"She got caught in a snowstorm on her way to
Pictland. I was fortunate to find her."

"She is a fine looking woman, a bit thin, but fine
looking. Feed her well and she will make a good wife."
He turned toward the women's table. "Ethra, see that
Wrath's wife eats well."

"I know how to treat my guests, husband," she
yelled out. "See that you are no fool in front of yours."

Egot shook his head. "Why I care so much for that
woman I do not know."

Wrath had to smile.

They ate and drank until finally Egot said, "Why
has the King sent you to me?"

There were too many ears to hear to Wrath's liking.
"We need to speak privately."

"Come," Egot said and led Wrath to a table in a
corner embraced by such deep shadows that no one in
the feasting hall could see them. Drink was placed on the
table along with their vessels and the servants were
ordered not to venture close. "Now tell me what has
brought you here."

"The Raban Tribe has been attacked by five Ancrum warriors."

Egot glared at him. "That cannot be. You speak falsely." His nostrils suddenly flared and his eyes narrowed. "You think I would betray King Talon?"

"Five of your warriors did."

He shook his head. "I cannot believe it. My men are faithful to their tribe."

"Not the five I killed. There has been a rogue band of warriors from various tribes gathering together to unseat the King. We have caught and executed some, but not all. Have any of your warriors left your tribe or gone missing?"

"We are a large tribe. I do not know what everyone does at every moment."

"You should, any leader should for their own safety," Wrath said.

"After all the bloody battles we fought, after all the Picts who died, I wanted to believe peace ruled. King Talon promised that."

"King Talon promised that he would do all he could to see that peace existed. You know as well as I do that there were those who opposed Talon taking the throne and still do. There will always be those who believe they can rule better and wiser, and we both know there is not a wiser and braver man than Talon to be King."

"I would argue with you if I did not know Talon well and if I had not seen his wisdom and bravery myself. Or the loyalty he instills in the men who come to know him." He shook his head. "There are always those who crave power at any cost or foreign invaders who think to take our land."

Wrath thought of the Northmen, but said nothing. He would wait and see what he could find out.

"Vard keeps watch over the warriors. He would know if any men have gone missing," Egot offered. "I will speak with him."

"I want to be there when you do," Wrath said, making sure Egot understood it was not a request.

Egot nodded. "Tell me more of the attack."

~~~

Verity liked Ethra. She was honest in her word, smiled often, and was not fearful to speak as she wished to her husband. She was as round and short as her husband was thick and big. Her hair was streaked heavily with gray and her many wrinkles did no harm to her pleasing features.

"You must be mighty special to have joined with Wrath," Ethra said, pushing a full trencher of meat in front of her. "Many believed he would never wed, that he would spend his life serving the King."

"Fate had different plans," Verity said and wondered if it was true or perhaps hoped it was.

"I am glad he has wed. He deserves a good woman." Ethra jabbed Verity in the side with her elbow. "Are you a good woman?"

Verity hesitated. Was she a good woman? She had lied to Wrath, run away from him, and it was because of her the King had joined them.

Ethra laughed and jabbed her in the side again. "Since you have to think about it you are not a good woman and Wrath does not need a good woman. He needs a woman who will keep him thinking, wondering, and challenging him or he would grow tired of her and seek another's sleeping pallet."

Verity thought how Wrath had gone to the woman Simca instead of returning to her and his own sleeping

170

pallet. But they had barely known each other, but what did it matter? Yet it had upset her, proving that she had cared for him before meeting him.

Inwardly, she shook the revelation away and turned her attention to see if these women possibly knew anything about Hemera. "You have a large tribe," she said.

Ethra beamed with pride. "We do and we are generous to those who stop only briefly and continue on their way."

"How gracious of you," Verity said. "You must have had people stopping to seek shelter from the snowstorm. It was a powerful one."

"If we did, they left as soon as the skies had cleared, for I saw no one new," Ethra said and the other women around the table nodded in agreement. "Vard would know more about that, since he is the one who would provide them with shelter or turn them away if he thought it best to do so."

"You are well-protected," Verity praised, and Ethra and the other women beamed with pride. "What of women who find their way here? Does Vard see to them as well?"

Ethra laughed. "No women travel alone, except maybe the Lammok women, since they are fierce warriors themselves."

Verity should have known better than to think Hemera was here. She had seen no such village in her vision and she needed to trust her visions. Or so Hemera had warned her repeatedly. It was difficult, since some of what she saw frightened her. She had to trust that Hemera was safe and that they would be reunited, though that did not mean she would give up searching for her. Not knowing how exactly she would find her meant that she had to keep searching until fate finally intervened.

"Only foolish people travel when the land is at rest and the snow falls," Ethra said. "When the land is ready for planting that is when travelers arrive seeking a night or more of shelter."

Could that be why the Northmen were here? No one would expect them now?

Talk shifted to the King, a slim woman asking, "Has the new, future queen arrived at the stronghold yet?"

"I believe arrangements are being seen to," Verity said.

"I hope this one turns out more fruitful than the other two," another woman said.

"Perhaps it is not the women who are barren," one woman whispered.

Ethra laughed. "One look at the King and that would be hard to believe."

"There is talk that one of his previous wives is now with child," the slim woman said.

"Do not go spreading lies, Wilda," Ethra warned.

"Tell Vard and some of the warriors that, since they were the ones I heard talking about it."

"Vard should know better than to spread lies," Ethra said.

"Unless they are not lies," Wilda said.

"Bah," Ethra said with a dismissive wave of her hand. "King Talon is a potent man and will make many fine bairns." She turned to Verity and grinned. "No doubt you will have a large brood with the likes of your husband."

"He is a mighty fine man," Wilda said, her cheeks spotting red.

"He is a mighty fine *husband*," Verity confirmed and wondered if jealousy had her reminding them that Wrath belonged to her, when that had yet to be decided.

Talk continued to shift and Verity enjoyed speaking and laughing with the women, never having known such satisfying companionship. She had also eaten more than she had in some time.

Ethra gave Verity a nod. "Your husband approaches."

Verity turned and watched as Wrath walked toward her. There was power and sureness in his every step and others saw it as well since their eyes followed him in awe.

Egot's voice boomed across the room just as Wrath stopped in front of Verity, "Ethra, show Wrath's wife to the dwelling that has been prepared for them while he goes to see to his men."

"You could not come tell me that, you must scream it at me, you old fool?" Ethra yelled back as she stood.

"Watch your tongue, woman!" Egot warned.

"Be gone with your useless threats," she called out and sent him a dismissive wave.

Verity saw that everyone ignored the squabbling pair as if they had heard and seen such an exchange so often that it was of little importance to them.

Wrath reached out and took her hand, tugging her to her feet and leaned down to whisper, "It is amazing they have not killed each other by now."

"I have thought about it."

Wrath looked to Ethra surprised that she had heard him.

"But I care too deeply for the old fool and I would miss him terribly. Now go see to your men and I will see that your wife is made ready for you."

Wrath leaned down again to whisper in Verity's ear, though much lower this time, "Make ready for me, wife."

He grinned as he walked away and Verity shivered not only from the tingle that raced through her, but from the passion she had seen ignite in his eyes. And she could not help but wonder what he was planning to do.

Chapter Sixteen

Wrath sat by one of three campfires the King's warriors had made, and spoke with Tilden. After having Verity slip away on his watch and having served and survived his punishment, the young warrior seemed eager to make amends and prove himself trustworthy once again. And the King had seen fit to have him prove it since he had brought him to the Raban Tribe and had ordered him to serve Wrath.

"The camp is secure as are the men who wait in the woods," Tilden said.

"They have seen nothing unusual?"

"Only that the village is not as protected as it should be."

"Egot has gotten lazy with age. There was a time he would have punished his warriors and harshly for not seeing to their duties. Now the only things that seem to interest him are food and drink...and arguing with his wife."

"His disinterest shows. Our men in the woods have not been spotted by the Ancrum warriors. I fear the village could easily be raided and conquered," Tilden said. "How long will we remain here?"

"A sunrise or two, depending on what we find out, "Wrath said, poking at the fire with a long stick, "and make sure the men mingle with the Ancrum to see what they can learn."

Tilden nodded. "Do we return home once we leave here?"

"We will take a different path back to the stronghold and see if we can find Verity's sister along the way." Wrath tossed the stick into the flames and stood. "You have done well, Tilden."

He jumped to his feet. "I have done my duty as a King's warrior, no more or less."

"You do more than your share and I saw how you kept a watchful eye on the King while at the Raban Tribe. You have the makings to become one of the King's personal guard, if you make no more foolish mistakes."

Tilden's eyes turned wide. "I would be honored to serve the King in that capacity. And worry not, I will make no such error again."

"I am glad to know that," Wrath said and walked away eager to join Verity in the dwelling provided for them. Thoughts of her had him envisioning her ready and waiting naked in the sleeping pallet, and his hands could almost feel her soft skin. He quickened his step. He had left the decision to her when they would finally couple, but he could always help her decision along.

He smiled and followed the path Egot had told him would take him to the dwelling. Sound and movement had him slowing his pace as he rounded a slight curve in the path. He came upon Vard draped around a woman who was trying to support him as he stumbled with each step he took. That he was deep into his cups was not hard to see.

"Wrath," he cried out, waving his arm and almost falling backward if it was not for the woman steadying him with a firm hand. "Did you and Egot have a good talk?"

"We did."

"All is well then?"

"We will talk tomorrow," Wrath said and walked past him.

A hand gripped his shoulder, forcing him to stop and Wrath reached up, grabbed, and twisted it in one quick movement.

Vard cried out and grabbed his wrist when Wrath released it.

"Lay a hand on me and suffer for it."

Vard wisely took a step back. "I meant no disrespect."

"Then do not show it." Wrath walked off, his scowl deepening. For a man who needed a woman to keep him on his feet while in a drunken stupor, he had gripped Wrath's shoulder with strength and without stumbling into him. There was more for him to learn about Vard.

The incident had annoyed him, but it had not dampened his desire for his wife and his hurried steps showed just how eager he was to be with her. He hid his disappointment when he opened the door and found her pacing in front of the fire pit. It was quickly replaced with concern when she hurried to him and threw her arms around him, her head going to rest on his chest.

Instinctively his arms closed around her and his anger sparked. He was ready to hunt down the culprit who had caused her such distress. "Who has upset you?"

You. Your absence. How did she voice her thought? How did she let him know that she had come to care for him through her visions? And the worse part was now that she had realized it, she wondered if she could ever walk away from him. What then would happen to Hemera?

Try as she might to trust her visions and know from what she had seen so far that all would turn out well, she could not help but worry.

"Tell me, Verity," Wrath demanded once again, his concern mounting and his arms tightening around her as though his strength could protect her even from her troubling thoughts.

Instead of saying what her heart felt for him, she said, "I cannot help but worry over Hemera."

"No one has seen her?" he asked relieved it was no more than thoughts of her sister that had her upset.

Verity raised her head to look at him. "No strangers have passed this way from what Ethra knows. She did mention that Vard was the one who dealt with any strangers that arrived here."

The more Wrath heard Vard's name, the more curious he became about the warrior. From what he had learned and seen so far, it seemed that Vard was more the leader of the tribe than Egot.

He slipped his hand to rest at her lower back and eased her toward the sleeping pallet. Once she sat, he removed his cloak and tossed it on a bench before sitting beside her.

"Did you learn anything else from the women?" he asked.

"They were curious of the King's future wife and also the gossip they heard about one of his previous wives being with child. The warriors must have brought the news home with them, since the woman who spoke of it told Ethra she had heard it from Vard and his warriors."

Wrath definitely would speak with Vard tomorrow.

"Did you learn anything?" Verity asked.

"Nothing significant."

"How long do we stay here?"

"Not more than two sunrises. The different route we take home will pass through the Faelchu Tribe. I can make certain they have suffered no attacks while we search for Hemera."

Verity stood and went to the fire pit, holding her hands out to warm them. "Once again I am grateful for your generous help."

Wrath stood and approached her slowly. "You are cold. Let me warm you."

Verity moved away from him, following the curve of the fire pit so that it remained between them. "I am fine."

He returned to the sleeping pallet and sat, leaning down to unfasten his leg coverings. "You will be fine once in bed where we can keep each other warm."

"The fire warms me," she said, keeping her eyes on her hands and warning herself not to look at him.

Wrath stood again and pulled off his tunic to stand naked.

Do not look. Do not look. Do not look.

Verity moved so that the fire pit was directly between them, the flames preventing her from seeing all of him.

"You cannot stand there all night. Shed your garments and come here to me."

Foolishly she looked through the flames at him and the words on her lips turned to a slight gasp. She could not take her eyes off him. His potent body glistened from the flickering flames that appeared as if they paid homage to him, and his image reminded her of the powerful gods the Northmen worshiped. Her tingle grew and she knew she was in trouble.

"Shed your garments, Verity, or I will."

He was a man of his word and would do as he said, and once he touched her, she feared she would be lost. She already craved his lips on hers and to have him touch her intimately would be her undoing.

Donna Fletcher

"I am not a patient man."

His sharp tone had her slipping out of her garments, though she took her time folding them. Anything to delay—she was suddenly scooped up in his arms.

"You take far too long to join me."

The words rushed from her mouth. "We cannot join"

"Are you trying to convince me or yourself?" He carried her to the sleeping pallet and rested there beside her once he laid her upon it.

There was barely room to move away from him, but she tried.

His hand went to the curve of her waist, preventing her from going anywhere.

"Do not touch me," she warned.

"I enjoy the feel of you," he said, his hand gently following the slight curve of her hip with a soft caress and doing the same to her middle.

Her hand shot out to grab his when he went to cup her breast. "Do you care for me?"

"If I did not care for you, I would not protect you," he said and broke free of her hand to squeeze her breast before teasing her nipple with his fingers.

She grabbed his hand again, fighting the urge to surrender to his touch. "You protect me, as you would others, out of duty. I want to know if you care for me because your heart tells you to."

He got annoyed and spoke more gruffly than he intended. "What difference does it make?"

Verity eased his hand off her and turned on her side to face him. She caressed his chest with a gentle hand. "It makes a difference to me. When I touch you," —her hand drifted down past his middle— "I do so because," —she slipped down further and took hold of his

180

manhood and stroked him— "I care for you more than I have ever cared for anyone."

He did not think it was possible to feel ready to spill his seed so quickly right there and then in her hand. She ignited an overpowering desire in him that he had never experienced before.

"I do not want to be touched out of convenience of being your wife, out of duty to protect me, out of your need for a woman, any woman." She released him and took hold of his hand to press against her breast. "I want to be touched from the depths of someone's heart or not at all." She moved her hand off his and waited.

He stared at her.

"I will give all of myself to you if you care for me that way, but if you do not, then please do not touch me for you will only break my heart."

He stared at her a moment more, then turned away from her, got out of bed, slipped into his garments, grabbed his cloak from the bench, and left the dwelling.

Verity felt tears gather in her eyes. She forced them away. She had cried far too many tears for far too long. She hurt, but she was also relieved to know that he did not care for her in the way she cared for him. She now could take her leave of him when necessary, though it would pain her terribly to do so. She would rather that pain, then the pain of remaining his wife and knowing that he cared for her out of duty alone.

She slipped off the sleeping pallet and back into her garments and returned to the sleeping pallet. She would not lie there naked, vulnerable to his touch, for now he knew how she felt about him. She did not know if she had been wise in speaking the truth to him, but she had had no other choice. His touch fired a need in her that she would not be able to deny and she would only surrender to it if he surrendered as well.

Closing her eyes, she begged for sleep. She did not want to think or feel. She wanted the blessed escape of sleep.

~~~

Wrath's anger pounded the earth with every step he took. When he reached where his warriors camped, those not sleeping quickly gave him a wide berth. He sat by one of the fire pits, an angry scowl darkening his handsome features.

He sat there staring at the flames that seemed to draw back away from him in fright. He was trying to comprehend what his wife had just done. He had told her the decision was hers when they would join and what had she done? She turned the decision on him with a demand he had never expected.

Touch her, join with her, but only if he cared deeply for her.

He was commander of the King's personal guard. He had no time to give to a woman. He was dedicated to keeping the King safe. It would not be right of him to care deeply for a woman. It was why he had kept the company of women who felt the same as he did.

He could not fault her for being honest with him. She was letting him know what she expected from him and if he could not fulfill that expectation, then she asked that he leave her be so that she may find it with someone else.

The thought that another man would touch her sent a wave of fury washing over him and his one hand pushed so hard against the fist he had made that his knuckles popped, sending the sound echoing through the camp. He would kill anyone who touched her.

He shook his head. Verity was looking for something he could never give a woman. She was looking for *tuahna*, a caring so deep that it bound a couple forever. Some believed that when it was found that the two hearts became one and one could not live without the other. It was a rare find and not found or seen often. Paine and Anin had found it and it suited them. It was as if fate had fashioned them just for each other.

Fate had fashioned him a fierce warrior. He would fight to protect the King, to protect Picts, and the land that belonged to them, and one day he would die in battle with pride. It had never been difficult for him to enter battle. If death thought to claim him, then so be it. As long as he fought a good fight, then death could have him. Having a woman he cared for would change that. He would fight not only for the King, but to return home to the woman who had his heart.

He found himself feeling empty when Verity was not with him. Like now, sitting alone in front of the fire when he preferred to be wrapped around her in their sleeping pallet. He looked forward each night to sleeping with her, feeling her warm body coiled around him.

It was where she belonged.

He shook his head again. Was he trying to ignore the truth or was he afraid of it? He gave a harsh laugh, causing the men to glance his way and seeing the scowl still heavy on his face, they turned away.

Fear avoided him. He refused to let it reside anywhere near him and he expected the same of the warriors that protected the King. They had to be fearless, for they had to give their lives for the King if necessary just as he would.

Verity had to understand his position. He cared enough for her that they could do well together. He could give her no more.

He stood and left the camp to the relief of the warriors. He returned to their dwelling, feeling the matter settled. He shut the door and, seeing her huddled beneath the blanket, he added more wood to the fire pit and slipped out of his garments.

He pulled the blanket back to join her and saw that she wore her garments. She made it clear that he was not welcome to touch her unless her demand was met. His anger flared and he had all he could do to stop himself from ripping her garments off her.

He climbed in beside her and she turned to cuddle against him as soon as his body brushed hers. She snuggled her head against his chest and settled there with a soft sigh.

His arms went around her as they always did when they slept together. He was annoyed, though his body showed no signs of it, wrapped comfortably around her. He was where he wanted to be whether he wanted to admit it or not.

He would talk with her on the morn and see this settled—his way.

Chapter Seventeen

Verity sat listening to the women talk, her thoughts more on her husband than what the women were chatting about. He had been gone when she woke along with the sun that surprisingly had risen and shined for a while before clouds settled in once again. She knew he had returned and slept beside her, his scent fresh on her and on the sleeping pallet. She had thought she would find him in the feasting hall, but he was not there and neither was Egot.

"Is it true, Verity?" Wilda asked.

Verity turned to the woman. "Is what true?"

"She pays no mind to gossip as should you," Ethra scolded.

"We should know who our King will wed," Wilda argued.

"I know nothing of the woman who is to be Queen," Verity admitted and nor did she care. Her heart went out to the woman. It would not be easy for any woman to be wed to King Talon.

"If he does not get this one with child, there is a chance he will be King no more."

"Hush your foolish mouth, Wilda" Ethra warned. "We are loyal to the King."

Wilda threw her shoulders back and her chin went up. "I only say what others have said."

"What others?" Verity asked, knowing Wrath would be interested in finding out who spoke unfavorably of the King.

Wilda's eyes turned wide and she looked from Verity to Ethra back to Verity.

Verity caught the slight shake of Ethra's head, a clear warning for Wilda to remember who she spoke to—wife to Wrath, the commander of the King's personal guard—and to mark her words well.

Wilda rubbed her arms as if a sudden chill had settled over her and she avoided looking directly at Verity. "I do not remember. Maybe it was someone passing through our land."

"That is odd. Ethra told me that no travelers have stopped here recently," Verity said, casting a smile at Ethra.

"I heard it a while ago," Wilda was quick to say and jumped up off the bench. "I have chores to see to."

The other women quickly joined her, leaving Verity alone with Ethra.

"Should King Talon be concerned with the loyalty of the Ancrum Tribe?" Verity asked, thinking Wrath would have asked the same himself.

"It goes without question that the Ancrum Tribe is loyal to King Talon and always will be. Before Talon became King, my husband fought in endless battles alongside him and shed much of his own blood for him. My husband will forever be loyal to King Talon and will forever fight beside him to make certain he keeps the throne."

"You think King Talon will lose the throne?"

"We are Pict and proud of it and we want to make certain that descendants of our King always rule this land."

"Surely if the King does not father a child, another Pict King of King Talon's choosing can be appointed."

Ethra shook her head. "Not a King with the noble bloodline of King Talon. His lineage goes back to the

186

first Pict who watched over these lands. His ancestors'
blood runs pure and deep in these hills, lochs,
mountains, and rivers. He is more Pict than any of us
who walk this land."

"How do you know this?"

Ethra smiled. "King Talon's mother was Egot's
sister."

~~~

Wrath stood with Vard in the woods, bow and
arrows ready to catch an animal foolish enough to make
an appearance in the stark white snow. Egot had
suggested a hunt for the three of them, insisting it would
be good for Wrath to become better acquainted with
Vard. Wrath had been in full agreement.

"Look at him," Vard said with a nod to Egot. "His
enthusiasm for the hunt has deserted him and so has his
hunger for battle. He prefers to eat, drink, and argue with
his wife. He is not the strong warrior he once was."

Wrath saw that Egot's once broad shoulders were
now slumped and where he once stood proud and tall,
his stance now was tired as though he had difficulty
supporting his own bulky body. He was surprised, since
Egot had once had such strong stamina that he had put
the young warriors to shame.

"He has grown lazy," Wrath said.

"We all have without battles to fight. Battles keep a
man strong."

"It takes more strength and courage to keep peace
than to battle," Wrath said and seeing that Vard looked
as though he intended to argue, Wrath continued, "but if
it is a battle you look for, then tell me why Ancrum
warriors attacked the Raban Tribe?"

Vard glared at him. "You speak falsely. No Ancrum warriors would attack the Raban Tribe. They are our friends. We trade with them often. They are fine farmers and fair people. The Ancrum would never harm them. Besides, it is forbidden for Pict Tribes to attack one another. Any disputes between tribes are settled by King Talon."

"I speak the truth," Wrath said as if he dared the man to say he spoke falsely again. "I was there and joined in the fight. I killed the Ancrum who dared to break the rules the King has made clear and set forth. No Pict tribe will raise their hands against another Pict tribe to do them harm."

"That is not possible," Vard said, shaking his head. "Ancrum warriors would not go against the King. We are a loyal tribe."

"There are some Ancrum warriors who do not agree with you. Are any of your warriors missing? And I warn you, I will hear only the truth spill from your lips, for I will make certain to confirm, with others, what you tell me."

Vard did not hesitate. "A hunting party goes out every few days. One party is out now. There is no telling when they will return. It could be two sunrises or several, depending on how successful the hunt."

"How many went?"

"Six."

"You told me you sent five," Egot said, joining them.

Vard's brow narrowed, then widened. "That is right. One of the warriors who was to go on the hunt took ill the night before and could not go. Five went on the hunting party."

"You will go to the Raban Tribe to see if the warriors Wrath killed are from our tribe," Egot ordered.

188

"If they are, you will offer my apologies and explain that I did not sanction the attack and that we will send men to help them repair any damage done."

Vard nodded and went to speak and Egot raised his hand, silencing him.

"First, though, you will answer any questions that Wrath has for you, and then you will take your leave and see to this matter without delay."

Vard gave another nod. "I will take a small troop of warriors with me."

"You will go alone," Egot ordered. "I will not see a battle mistakenly started because the Raban think that I have sent more warriors to attack them. You will be humble, helpful, and respectful to the Raban people."

Wrath kept silent about the King's warriors being with the Raban. It was obvious Vard was not pleased with Egot's leadership. He could very well ignore Egot's orders and take a troop with him that could do just as Egot said...mistakenly ignite a battle. Or could that be what someone in the Ancrum Tribe wanted?

Egot turned to Wrath. "When you are done, join me in the feasting house. There are things for us to discuss." He walked off, his gait slow and his shoulders slumped a bit more than before.

Wrath looked to Vard. "I will not keep you long from your task. The sooner you see it done, the better. Tell me, have any strangers passed this way recently? Egot told me you see to those who seek brief shelter here."

"The cold and snow claims the sleeping land, who would be so foolish to travel now?"

"Those who have no choice."

"Who would that be?" Vard asked. "The Picts are settled in their tribes. They war no more with one another and trade is seen to through the King. It is the

Tribal Gathering that brings out travelers and that is not until the land is ready for planting."

"Then it has been quiet here."

"Except for the women's gossiping tongues," Vard said. "They talk endlessly about the King and who is to be Queen and if she will bear the King a child. Has a decision been made on who is to be Queen?"

"That is Gelhard's domain and he has everything in hand," Wrath said.

"That is good since there has been talk that some are not pleased that after having two wives the King has yet to produce an heir to the throne."

"Who dares to say this?" Wrath demanded, anger sparking in his voice.

Vard quickly defended himself. "I heard the women talking. They talk endlessly about the King."

"Spreading lies you mean," Wrath snapped.

"They repeat what they hear."

Wrath took a quick step toward him and Vard jumped back. "Then who did they hear say it?"

"I do not know. Their tongues are always clucking when around one another."

"I will see that it stops," Wrath said, leaving no doubt he would do just that.

~~~

Verity walked with Ethra through the village. She had been disappointed when Ethra would say no more about Egot being brother to the King's mother. She would have liked to have learned more, but Ethra had said that it was not for her to say. It was her husband's story to tell. She simply wanted Verity to know why Egot would always be faithful to the King...they were family.

190

Verity had learned that being family did not always assure faithfulness, but she kept silent.

Ethra stopped now and again to introduce her to some of the women and they would all chat for a while before walking on. Verity took great pleasure in what was common place for the women. She had toiled for others most of her life and had little chance to talk freely with women as these women did.

Verity talked, smiled, and laughed with several women and held a crying bairn for a mum while she saw to another bairn. The little lass had quieted in Verity's arms and the mum encouraged her to keep the bairn contented.

She had tended bairns for the Northmen women and cared for each one of them and they for her. She had never thought she would have bairns of her own, but then she had never thought she would return home and be free.

She and Ethra moved on, having left the little bairn sleeping. After a few more stops where Verity was only too pleased to be greeted and accepted as an equal with the women, Ethra suggested they return to the feasting house for a hot brew. Verity agreed, the cold having started to seep into her.

Verity was about to glance up at the heavy cloud covering that had suddenly darkened an already heavily gray sky when she realized too late that it was not the heavens that darkened. It was a vision that was quickly swallowing her whole and there was little time for Verity to do anything but turn to Ethra before collapsing to the snow-covered ground.

Ethra reached out, but Verity dropped so suddenly that she had no time to prevent her fall. She did not, however, hesitate to scream out, "Someone fetch Wrath!"

~~~

Wrath had caught sight of Verity walking through the village with Ethra as he and Egot had approached the feasting house. She had slept through the knock on the door this morn when a message came for him that Egot wished to see him. He had hoped to speak with her about last night when she woke, but it had not turned out as he had planned. Later he would make sure they talked and he would make sure Verity saw things his way...the way it had to be.

"Have you told me everything?" Egot asked when they settled at the table.

Egot may have gotten lazy when it came to battle, but his senses had remained sharp.

"Or has Talon a secret he wishes to keep?" Egot asked.

"Northmen have landed on our shores and have requested to speak with the King," Wrath said. "The King is spreading word about it now, so tribes can prepare in case it is necessary."

Egot shook his head. "That makes no sense. Why would they sail here now when the sea is not friendly?"

"A question the King has asked himself," Wrath said. He would make no mention of Verity's plight. That was not for Egot to know.

"Talon knows my warriors stand ready for him."

"What of you, Egot?"

"I grow old and slow," Egot said with a brief laugh, "though I will fight to the death for the King with whatever strength I have left in me. I hope it does not come to that. I enjoy this peace that Talon has bestowed on us. I have had enough of battle and bloodshed."

192

"It is a shame others do not agree with you."

"I do not like to think that any of my warriors did as you said, but I have felt the unrest growing among some Picts. And I think they use any excuse to hurt King Talon's favor with the people. That is why so much is being made of Talon having failed to sire an heir with his last two wives."

"Gelhard believes he has found a suitable woman to be Queen."

Egot shook his head. "What Talon needs is what Paine and you have found—*tuahna*." He gave a hardy laugh when Wrath's eyes rounded. "Do not tell me that you do not realize you have lost your heart to your wife and that she has lost her heart to you?" When Wrath continued to stare at him, Egot slapped him on the back and laughed again. "This is one battle you should be glad to have lost. There is nothing like losing your heart to someone special. I do not know what I would do without my Ethra."

Here was something Wrath could respond to. "You two argue all the time."

Egot grinned. "Aye, we do, and glad I am for it. She stirs my blood and keeps me feeling alive with every biting word. And when we are alone," —his grin grew— "her passion fires my heart and my," —he laughed— "I cannot get enough of her."

The way Egot's face lighted with such joy made Wrath realize that Egot was not as slow and old as he claimed to be, though he might have been wrong about his senses with Egot thinking he and Verity has lost their hearts to each other. Or was it something Wrath stubbornly refused to give thought to?

Egot cupped his vessel and his head drooped. "I want that for Talon. I want him to lose his heart to a woman. Then fate will see that he sires an heir worthy of the throne."

Wrath turned his head suddenly, thinking he heard his name being called.

"Is that someone shouting for you?" Egot asked.

They both heard it again, clearly this time.

"Wrath! Wrath! Wrath!"

He leapt to his feet as the door burst open. A young woman, with barely a breath left in her, rushed in screaming out to him.

"Hurry! You must hurry. Your wife has collapsed."

Chapter Eighteen

Wrath vaulted over the table and grabbed the woman's arm. "Take me to her." Wrath kept the woman's steps steady as he held firm to her arm to make certain she did not collapse before they reached Verity. He propelled her through the village, people staring and some following after them.

He stopped abruptly when he saw his wife on the ground, her body lifeless. He released the woman and rushed to Verity. When those standing near caught sight of him approaching, they scurried out of his way, fearful he would trample them, his steps so forceful and determined.

Wrath dropped down beside his wife's prone body.

"Is she with child?" Ethra asked, as if that would explain what had happened.

It would be easier and safer for Verity if Ethra and others thought that and so he said, "Yes." He slipped his arms beneath his wife, taking her gently in his arms to hold her close against him as he got to his feet.

Ethra got to her feet as well. "I will fetch the healer."

"There is nothing she can do. Our healer advised rest when it happened." Wrath turned, wanting to get Verity away from curious eyes and see that she was safe.

"I will fetch other women and we will see to her," Ethra said.

"Mind your own duties, wife, and stay where you are," Egot ordered as he approached. "Wrath will see to his own."

"And what do you know of such things you old fool," Ethra admonished.

Wrath hastened his pace, leaving the two to argue. He would see to Verity, no one else.

"You are safe, wife. You are with me," he whispered near her ear as he approached the dwelling.

Once inside, he laid her on the sleeping pallet and placed his hand against her cheek. It was cold and she looked much too pale to him. She did not make the slightest movement and if he had come upon her without any knowledge of her visions, he would have thought her dead.

Anger surged up in him at the thought and he leaned down and whispered in her ear. "I will have it no other way, wife. Return to me now!" When she did not stir, he raised his voice. "Come back to me! Open your eyes!" Again she did not stir. "You will not leave me. I forbid it!"

He grew more anxious when again she did not respond. He took her hands in his and began to rub warmth into them. "You have been gone long enough. Open your eyes." His insides clenched and he felt something he had never felt before...helplessness.

He was a warrior accustomed to fighting foe, but this was something he could not fight. This was something he had no control over, and realizing that angered him even more.

He lowered his brow to hers and whispered, "You belong to me, Verity." He hesitated a moment. "And I belong to you."

He felt her stir against him and waited for her to open her eyes. When she did not, he coaxed her again with words that surprised him. "You have my heart, though I do not know when I gave it to you or perhaps you stole it when I first laid eyes on you." He could not believe his own words. They sounded foolish to him and yet he spoke the truth. He had lost his heart to her, when and where it did not truly matter. That had seemed amazing in itself, though more so that he would even dare admit it. What he could admit without doubt was that Verity belonged to him now and he would never let her go.

"Open your eyes," he ordered worried he would lose her when he had just found her.

Verity's eyes shot open wide and she sat up abruptly.

Wrath saw the terror in her eyes and his arms went around her as her arms flew around him and held on tight.

"You are safe," he assured her, holding her with a grip that no one could break, but then she clung to him just as tightly. He wanted to know what had caused such fright in her, but at the moment the only thing he felt the need to do was keep her safe in his arms.

She mumbled something in his ear again and again until finally he understood what she was saying and fear hit him like an arrow to his chest.

"He took me from you. He took me from you. He took me from you."

"Who took you?" he demanded ready to kill whoever dared lay a hand on her.

"Ulric. He took me from you." Her body went limp against his as if it was too much of a burden to bear.

"No one will ever take you from me. You have my word on that." Verity eased away from him, though he would not let her out of his arms and when he saw her unshed tears ready to fall, he silently swore to make Ulric pay for the pain he had caused her. "Tell me of your vision." He wanted to be prepared to stop it from happening.

"Ulric was dragging me away, and I was screaming out to you." She shuddered, recalling the scene.

"Where was I?"

"I did not see you. I called out to you, but I never saw you."

"That does not mean I was not there and I will never let anyone take you from me."

"My visions—"

He pressed his finger to her lips. "This one was meant to warn."

She shook her head. "My visions reveal what will be."

"Even if Ulric somehow managed to take you, I would come for you. Never, ever, worry that I would not come after you. You belong to me and I will never let you go."

Verity stared at him, wanting to say many things but finding no words. Or was she afraid of what his response would be? Did he intend to keep her as his wife? If so why? Did he care for her?

You have my heart.

Had she heard him say that or had she simply imagined it?

"You should rest," he said.

She shook her head. "I am not tired." And she did not want to sleep and dream. Sometimes her dreams could be as frightening as her visions and she wished she suffered from neither.

Wrath's hand went to her face, his finger going to the corner of her one eye and catching a tear that had been lingering there. Then he leaned forward and kissed her lips gently.

"You are a brave woman, wife," he whispered and kissed her again.

She got lost in his gentle kiss. His lips did not demand or expect. He kissed her with a caring that squeezed at her heart and sent flutters through her middle.

"I will not listen to your nonsense. The lass needs a woman to look after her, not a man who has no thought to what he is doing."

Wrath's lips fell away from Verity's at the sound of Ethra's voice outside the door, and she smiled when she heard him mutter several blasphemies. It seemed he was as disappointed as she was over their kiss being interrupted.

"I will send her away," he said more to himself than Verity. He stood as Ethra shouted out to him from the other side of the door.

"Wrath, I have come to tend your wife. She needs a woman's care since she is with child."

Verity's head snapped up and she turned wide eyes on her husband.

"No one needs to know about your visions," he said, keeping his voice low so no one heard but the two of them.

That Wrath would let everyone believe that she was with child surprised her, though she did not remark on it. She simply nodded.

Wrath opened the door.

"I tried to stop her," Egot said from behind his wife, "but when the fool woman gets something in her head there is no stopping her."

Ethra turned and jabbed her husband in the chest. "A man is a useless creature when a woman is with child."

Wrath had had enough. "You call me a useless creature?"

Ethra jumped back at the force of his words, bumping into her husband.

"I tend my wife, no other, now be gone or you will know why I am called Wrath!"

Egot took hold of his wife's arm. "Ethra will disturb you no more."

Verity had come up behind her husband and stepped around him to smile at Ethra. "I am grateful for your concern, but Wrath tends me well. I will talk with you later. I am going to rest now."

"I am pleased and relieved to know that," Ethra said, returning Verity's smile. "If there is anything you need, please let me know. I look forward to seeing you after you have rested."

"Now see what you have done, woman," Egot said, hurrying his wife alongside him.

"I have done what I came to do. That was to make sure that Verity was well."

"And insult her husband, commander of the King's personal guard."

"At this moment he is no more than a husband—"

"Who cares deeply for his wife," Egot said. "Did you not see the worry in his eyes as he held her limp body in his arms?"

Wrath shut the door on the squabbling couple, not wanting to hear anymore. Or was it that he did not want Verity to hear?

"You will rest," he ordered as Verity turned to face him. He slipped her cloak off and scooped her up in his arms when she went to speak. "I will hear no excuses."

A soft smile surfaced when he placed her on the sleeping pallet. That others saw worry in his eyes for her made her wonder if he did truly care for her and simply did not want to admit it. Or perhaps he had yet to recognize it himself.

She raised her hand to rest at his cheek. "I do not mean to be a burden on you."

He took her hand, no longer cold, and held it in his. "You are no burden and I will not hear that from you again. We will remain here an extra sunrise to make certain you are well-rested before we begin our journey home."

Verity squeezed his hand. "No, please, I do not want to delay searching for Hemera. And I need no rest. I only told Ethra that so she would leave without worry. And I am sure the King is anxious to hear what we have learned while here."

Wrath worried when her eyes suddenly turned wide. "What is wrong?"

"I was surprised to learn that Egot is brother to King Talon's mother and that the King's blood runs so deep in this land. No wonder so many wish for him to have a son."

"Many believe his descendants were born with this land, his roots far deeper here than anyone else who sees himself fit to be King."

"Have you discovered if there is any here who oppose the King?" Verity asked his long lean fingers slipping over her hand, wrapping around it, and gripping it as if he had no intentions of ever letting her go. And it brought her comfort.

"I am not sure what goes on here, but something does. A hunting party of five warriors, though it was meant to be six, has yet to return, though Vard assures me that no one here would ever be disloyal to the King. It seems questionable that five Ancrum warriors left here and five Ancrum warriors attacked the Raban Tribe, yet were not connected. Then there is Egot. He has changed considerably since last I saw him. He once knew his tribe well, not so much now. It seems Vard leads the tribe more than he does, and I would never have thought that Egot would grow lazy."

"Perhaps he simply grows old," Verity suggested.

"Pict warriors never grow old. They fight until their dying day. Those were Egot's words to me years ago." Wrath grew silent a moment, then shook his head as if clearing it. "Are you sure you feel up to traveling?"

She nodded, hoping he would relent and they would leave on the morrow.

"We leave early on the morrow. I want to stop at the Imray Tribe and see how things are there and if a lone woman has passed their way. I also want to know if they have had any trouble with the Ancrum. If all goes well, we should be home in three or four sunrises."

"What if we do not find Hemera?"

"The search will not stop, though," —he raised his hand to stop her from speaking— "you will not go on every search conducted." Verity tried to sit up, but Wrath pressed a firm hand to her chest. "That is the way it will be."

"How will the warriors know her?"

"You will detail her features and give them a message that Hemera would know could only come from you."

A yawn escaped her mouth before any words could.

"No more talk. You will rest," he ordered and reluctantly released her hand as he stood.

Verity thought to argue with him, but stopped. She had wanted to continue to talk with him, but something told her to wait, and so she did.

Wrath took the blanket bunched at the bottom of the sleeping pallet and spread it over her. "Rest for as long as you need. I will see you later." He leaned down and kissed her brow, not trusting himself to settle his lips on hers since one taste of her would want him seeking more.

Verity was relieved when the door closed behind him, but she was also disappointed. Nothing was going as planned. If she did not find Hemera, the King's warriors might, and then there was Ulric here on Pict soil. And of course there were her feelings for Wrath, which had changed everything.

The more thought she gave, the more she realized that she did not want to leave Wrath. She had found something with him that she did not believe she would ever find with anyone else. And after years of not being able to do as she pleased, she wanted that choice now. She wanted Wrath.

She wondered what Hemera would do if she knew all that had taken place since their arrival here. She did know Hemera would tell her to do as she wanted, but then what of Hemera?

Hemera was never one to act quickly or rush to respond. Verity smiled, thinking how she would not be surprised if that was what Hemera was doing now, not rushing, but taking her time in deciding her next step. She would not worry over Verity as much as Verity worried over her. She would expect Verity to survive as best she could until they were reunited. And she would be right. There was nothing that could be decided upon until they were together again.

Things had changed and she and Hemera would need to decide what was best for them to do from this point on. Her only thought should be of finding Hemera.

Another yawn let her know that her vision had left her tired, whether she thought so or not. She would rest, gather her strength, and do all she could to see Hemera was found and kept safe. Fate would deal with her and Wrath, as it had since she first saw Wrath in a vision.

~~~

Wrath talked with Tilden, letting him know they would take their leave at sunrise and the route they would take. Tilden got busy informing the men and seeing that all was made ready for departure.

Wrath sat by the fire heavy in thought. There was much to report to Talon, though he wondered if he would just confirm what Talon already knew. Talon was a wise King and kept watch over his people. He was aware of what went on throughout the land even if he did not seem like he did. Talon had close friends and allies, no one was aware of, that kept him advised on all that went on throughout Pictland and beyond.

It was one of the reasons he had granted Paine and Anin permission to visit with her family. Paine would form allies with the Wyse Tribe for him and learn of any unrest in the surrounding area.

What news would he bring to Talon? Five Ancrum warriors had turned against the King? Or had someone within the Ancrum Tribe caused unrest? Much would depend on what else he uncovered. He had seen that one of his warriors followed Vard to the Raban Tribe. The warrior would report his findings to Wrath.

Talon would not be happy learning that two Northmen had been found on Pict soil. He wanted no war with them and Haggard wanted no war with the Picts. Or had that been a ruse?

Wrath snapped the slim stick in his hand in two and tossed the pieces into the flames. Anger simmered inside him at the thought that Ulric would attempt to take Verity away from him. She belonged to him now and he intended to make that clear to Ulric when he saw him. And if Ulric disagreed, Wrath would beat him senseless and enjoy doing it for all the suffering he had caused Verity.

Tilden interrupted Wrath's musings along with another warrior.

"John has learned something you should hear," Tilden said.

Wrath nodded for the warrior to speak.

"An Ancrum woman took a fancy to me and we have been talking. She told me that she had seen Vard speaking with a stranger not too long ago. He was a large man with light-colored hair. She came upon them in the woods, though she was not close enough for her to hear what they were saying. And she was too fearful of making herself known, since she felt the meeting was a private one. She never saw the man again after that."

"You did well, John," Wrath said, "though make no mention of it to anyone. It is only for the King to know."

"As you say," John said with a nod.

After the two men walked away, Wrath stood and was eager to return to the stronghold and let King Talon know that Egot's right-hand man could very well be conspiring with the Northmen.

Chapter Nineteen

The sun rose briefly over the land the next morn, enough to begin melting the snow and lessening the burden on the tree branches, before gray clouds blotted it out not long after departure. Verity rode with Wrath pleased they were once again on their way and searching for Hemera. She looked over the land, watching to see if anything looked familiar from her visions or for any signs Hemera may have left for her to find. This time she would be vigilant and not miss a thing.

Wrath watched how intently Verity gazed over the land and how, when something caught her attention, it would bring a smile to her lovely face. He noticed that there was now a slight fullness to her face since he had found her. She had been eating well and he was glad for that. He also noticed how her hand remained resting on his arm and that her body lay against his with ease. It had not taken her long to grow comfortable with him. It was as if she had already been familiar with him before meeting him. It also had not taken him long to become familiar with her and feel at ease with her as well.

It was the feeling that he did not want to be parted from her that was unfamiliar to him. He had never felt that way about any woman he had ever joined with, and he had yet to join with Verity. What then would it be like? Would he feel even stronger about being separated from her? Or would it satisfy him enough to let her go?

"We will mate." He wanted Verity to know that. Or was it he who needed to know?

Her head turned with a snap to look at him. "So you have said and left the choice of when to me, and I have made it clear to you when that will be."

He lowered his face closer to hers. "Laying rules down, wife?"

Verity smiled softly and spoke just as softly. "I am following yours, husband. You gave me a choice and I made it."

Husband.

Never did he think he would be called that by any woman and yet it sounded good to his ears and that annoyed him.

"So you will not join with me unless I care for you from the depths of my heart?" he asked.

"Aye, that is what I said," Verity confirmed.

He lowered his face closer to hers and whispered, "I have no heart." His lips were so close to hers that it felt like he brushed a faint kiss across them and her body shivered against his, arousing him much too fast.

"I do not believe that."

Her faint murmur tickled his lips and with his arousal growing, he could not help but challenge her. "Then join with me and find out."

"And what if you discover you have a heart?"

He threw back his head and laughed. "That will not happen."

"If it did?" she dared.

"I will spill my seed into you and keep you forever." His response was unexpected to his own ears. He cared for Verity; he could not deny that. She tugged at something unfamiliar inside him, but it was not his heart. He had guarded that well. He was tasked with an important role...to protect the King and nothing came before that.

He felt the need to warn her, protect her, or was it himself he was attempting to protect? "I care for you, but you will not now or ever have what I do not have to give...a heart. Know that now before we join."

Did he challenge her? Was he looking to prove he had no heart or to find that he did have one? She did not know, but she would like to find out. She smiled as she asked, "The choice is still mine of when and where?"

"Aye, but that does not mean I will not touch you."

"Or I you?"

Wrath grinned. "You can touch me as much as you want."

"And still not join with you?"

He laughed again. "You can try."

A shout from one of the warriors had both their heads snapping around. Tilden rode forward past them and stopped to speak with the warrior who held something in his hand. Tilden appeared to stare at it as the warrior spoke to him and pointed behind him. After a moment, they both rode toward Wrath.

"What is it?" Wrath asked when the two men brought their horses to a halt in front of him.

The warrior held out a piece of cloth.

Upon seeing it, Verity quickly leaned forward to grab it, almost falling off Wrath's horse as she did, if he had not grabbed her around the waist and yanked her back.

"That is a piece of Hemera's cloak," Verity said, stretching her arm out, attempting to reach for it only to be stopped by his arm that felt like an iron band around her waist.

Tilden took the cloth from the warrior and handed it to Verity.

Verity smiled once it was in her hand. It was not a large piece, only a small square and dark so it could be spotted easily against the snow.

"You are sure it is from Hemera's cloak?" Wrath asked.

She nodded. "I am sure. It is two cloaks in one to keep her extra warm. Hemera stitched it herself, her stitches are not like others. They are small and tight and keep the garment held firmly together."

"Then perhaps she found her way to the Imray Tribe. The path that takes us there appears to have been traveled by not one but many. She could have joined a group along the way," Tilden said.

"But the trail stops suddenly, as if whoever traveled it vanished instantly," the other warrior was quick to add.

Tilden shot him a warning look.

"What do you mean?" Verity asked.

The warrior looked from Tilden to Wrath and waited.

Verity looked at Wrath. "Please, let him have his say. I want to know."

Wrath did not like hearing the distress in her voice and there was no reason she should not know what the warrior thought.

The warrior hurried to speak after Wrath nodded permission. "The tracks I followed brought me to that piece of cloth. I found it in a large arched hole in the middle of a tree that you could walk clear through to the other side. The tracks stopped at the hole in the tree and there were no signs that anyone turned around and went the other way. And the ground on the other side had not been trampled upon. It can mean only one thing." The warrior turned silent as if he did not want to say anymore or feared saying more.

"How far is it?" Wrath asked.

"It is a ways ahead and around the bend, then a bit of a distance off the path and into the woods."

"Take us there," Wrath ordered and the warrior nodded. He looked to Tilden. "Let the others know what might await us."

"What might await us?" Verity asked as Wrath followed the warrior.

"A Wyse Tribe settlement."

Verity shivered. "I only know of the Wyse through the Northmen and they fear the Wyse. I heard them tell tales of seeing one of their own disappear right before their eyes. And all the Northmen did was step through a door of a dwelling that had only partial walls and no roof. He was never seen again. Never will a Northmen step through any type of door on Pict soil that has no wall behind it."

"The Wyse protect this land and always will. They are good people," Wrath said.

"How can that be if they keep people from leaving once they enter a Wyse settlement?"

"No one knows that for sure." He thought about Anin, her mother having been from the Wyse Tribe. He wished he had had the time before he had left on his mission to have talked with her about the Wyse. There would be time when Anin returned to Pictland for him and Verity to learn more about the tribe that seemed more mythical than real.

A fearful thought had Verity digging her fingers into his arm. "Hemera could have stumbled into a Wyse settlement and be stuck there."

Wrath's insides twisted at the thought that Verity would rush through the arched hole in the tree never to be seen again, or until Anin could help free her, if that was possible. "You will not go through that hole in the tree," he ordered sharply.

"But what if Hemera went through it and is now with the Wyse? I must free her. I cannot leave her there."

"And what if she is not with them? One of your visions showed that you reunited with your sister. There is no reason for you to take such a chance."

"This could be how we reunite."

"I forbid you to take the chance," Wrath ordered, an image of her rushing through the hole in the tree to find her sister and disappearing, sparking his anger. "I mean it, Verity. You will take no such chance."

Verity turned silent.

Wrath took hold of her chin, forcing her to look up at him. "Your silence speaks louder than your words. I will have warriors guard you while I see to this." He pressed his finger to her lips when she went to speak. "I will hear no more about it."

Verity knew it was useless to continue protesting, especially when part of her agreed with him. What would she do if she entered a Wyse settlement and did not find Hemera there? Would she be able to leave or would she be stuck there? The thought of not seeing Wrath again upset her and without realizing it, she pressed herself more tightly against him.

"I will not lose you," he said, keeping a strong arm around her. "You will do as I say. I will have it no other way."

It was a command, though a comforting one and one she thought would be wise for her to obey.

It took longer than Verity thought to reach the tree, or perhaps it seemed that way since she was eager to see if anything more could be learned of Hemera. She found herself speechless when they stopped not far from the tree. Even if she had not known that it was a possible entrance to a Wyse settlement, she would have never gone through the arched hole in the middle of the wide trunk.

The sight of it gave her the shivers. The old oak, its age apparent by how high it reached into the sky sat majestically in the middle of a small clearing. Its branches spread so wide at the bottom that it gave the appearance of a roof over the arched hole that looked more like a doorway...but to where?

Wrath got off the horse and helped Verity down. He did not have to tell her to stay close or place a guard around her, since she clung tightly to his arm.

The other warriors dismounted and spread out to either side of Wrath and her, all staring at the arched hole in the tree. No one took a step toward it. They stood where they were and continued to stare.

"I found the piece of cloth inside the hole caught on a sliver of wood," the warrior said to Wrath, breaking the silence.

"You did not go through to the other side?' Wrath asked.

The warrior shook his head and slowly took a step back as if he feared Wrath would command him to do so.

Verity kept her focus on the tree. She had no desire to pass through the hole, though it seemed an easy step to take to the other side, but would it take you there? Or would you vanish?

Wrath stepped forward and she had no choice but to follow unless she let go of him and that she did not intend to do. He glanced at the ground and Verity's eyes followed his and she was startled by the many footprints in the snow that suddenly stopped at the entrance to the hole. How could that be?

She raised her head, shaking it, not believing what she saw and her eyes rounded wide when she caught a flash of something on the other side of the tree. But it could not be. She had to be imagining it? Or was she? Was that Hemera's cloak she saw flying by and had Hemera been in it?

"Did you see that?" Verity asked, letting go of Wrath's arm.

"Did I see what?" he asked, looking where her eyes searched, through the hole.

"A flash of cloth." Verity took a step forward.

Wrath's strong fingers closed tightly around her arm. "I do not see anything and you will not go anywhere."

Verity did as he said, though kept her eye on the hole in the tree.

Wrath turned to talk with Tilden who had stepped up beside him and also the warrior who continued to keep a cautious distance from the tree.

Verity remained staring through the hole and just when she thought there was nothing to see, she caught a flash of cloth again and a sound of familiar laughter...Hemera's laughter. She did not hesitate. She yanked her arm free of Wrath's and rushed through the arched hole. When she got to the other side, she spotted Hemera's cloak lying on the snow-covered ground. She hurried to it, snatched it up, and called out, "Hemera!"

Her voice echoed through the trees and she turned full circle, searching all around her for any sight of Hemera. All she saw were trees being swallowed by a slow approaching mist and that was when she realized that these woods were not the woods she had seen when on the other side of the tree. She stared at the old oak standing majestically, its trunk solid, the hole she had come through was gone.

~~~

Wrath stood frozen as Verity disappeared through the hole and vanished before his eyes. She was there one moment and the next she was no more. He turned to Tilden. "If I do not return shortly, hurry to the stronghold and tell the King what has happened."

He did not wait for an answer, he ran through the hole after Verity.

In all the battles he had fought, he had never known the relief he felt now seeing Verity standing there, turning slowly in a circle, looking lost. When she spotted him, fear suddenly left her wide eyes and a large smile spread across her face and he hurried to her, his arms reaching out for her.

Verity cried out to him, "Wrath!" Her heart beat rapidly against her chest as she ran into his outstretched arms as fast as she could and when they closed around her, hugging her tight, she hugged him just as tight. "You came for me."

"Always."

Guilt washed over Verity and she held up the cloak flattened between their bodies. "Hemera's cloak. I thought I saw her and heard her laughter."

"I saw nothing, but the cloak is proof that you did, though I do not approve of you rushing off away from me."

Verity shook her head. "I thought only of Hemera. She looked around. Now we are stuck, though I see no settlement only a creeping mist."

"Our tracks," Wrath said, pointing to the ground only to see the spots where their feet had tread being swallowed by the invading mist. "Hurry," he urged, taking her arm and rushing her forward as they attempted to keep ahead of the mist.

When the mist swallowed the last of their tracks and began to creep up their legs, Wrath grabbed her around the waist and propelled them both forward with such force that they tumbled to the ground.

Chapter Twenty

Wrath kept his arms locked around Verity, his hand pressed to the back of her head, her face buried against his chest, and his body shielding hers. He released his hold on her only when he heard the familiar shouts of his men.

He was on his feet, taking Verity with him as Tilden approached. He rested her body against his, her legs too weak for her to stand on her own. He signaled to Tilden to bring his horse and when he did, he had the warrior lift Verity up to him after he mounted.

"We leave here," he announced to his men, every one of them all too eager to obey.

Verity shook the confusion from her head and looked up from where she lay cradled in his arms. "Hemera is with the Wyse." She hugged Hemera's cloak to her. "She left this for me to let me know where she was."

"Did she or did she leave it to let you know she was safe?" He watched her brow wrinkle in thought. "We did not escape the Wyse, they chased us away."

"You believe she is safe with the Wyse?"

"Paine had shared what little he knew of the Wyse and of his time with them. If your sister is with them, then she is there by choice and her cloak is proof of it."

Verity turned away, looking out over the land, though too lost in her thoughts to see. What could she do when her sister was with a mythical tribe?

"We will reach the Imray on the morrow," Wrath said and wished he could ease the hurt he saw in her lovely eyes that held far too much sorrow. "If there are no signs of Hemera having been there, then it would add to what we already believe, that she is with the Wyse. All we can do is wait for her to return of her own accord."

Verity remained silent, having no response. She thought back to her and her sister's time at sea when the waters had turned choppy and the heavens had darkened. Hemera had told her then that if fate saw fit to separate them that they would both do what was necessary to survive and find their way back to each other. And that above all else, Verity was to trust her visions, for they would help lead the way.

Thinking on that, Verity wondered if Hemera had discovered that Ulric was here and realized it would be best if she was not around when he presented himself to King Talon. Or would she? She had never been one to back down to Ulric. Why then would she choose to remain with the Wyse?

"Your thoughts are too heavy. Let them be for now." Wrath did not order her to do so, though his voice rang with strength.

"It is easy to say, but far more difficult to do." She looked away from him.

"Your visions show you what will be?"

Her head snapped around. "That would mean I reunite with my sister only to have Ulric take me away?"

He gave her waist a reassuring squeeze. "I told you I will not let that happen."

Fear suddenly gripped her. Why had the thought only struck her now? It had been the way Wrath had not hesitated to follow after her through the open door and into the unknown to rescue her from her own foolish action that had the thought spring into her head. It showed her that he would do whatever was necessary to keep her safe and that thought instilled a fear in her that she had not felt since she had been taken from her home by the Northmen. What if she had screamed out for Wrath in her vision as Ulric dragged her away and Wrath had not come for her because he was unable to follow after her? What if Ulric or his men had badly wounded Wrath? Or worse what if she had been screaming his name because she had witnessed his death?

"I see doubt in your eyes. You do not think I will save you."

She pressed a gentle hand to his cheek and voiced her fear. "You must not place your life in danger to save me."

He kissed her palm and smiled. "I place my life in danger every day for the King. It is nothing more than a chore to me."

Her hand fell away from his face and surprisingly anger sparked inside her. "At least I am an easier chore for you than you are for me."

Wrath found himself startled by her words. "I am a chore to you?"

"A burdensome one."

His anger sparked as well. "Not for long. You can be rid of me as soon as this situation with your sister and the Northmen are settled. Simply say the word and you will be my wife no more." As soon as Wrath said those words he wished he could take them back and that annoyed him even more. What was it about this woman that made him act or speak without thought or reason?

"I will see it done as soon as possible," Verity said and turned away from him to once again focus on the land and once again not see it. He did not care for her. She was his chore and someone to dally with until everything was settled. She was a fool for thinking the mighty warrior Wrath would ever care for her. She willed her tears not to fall, refusing to let him see that he had hurt her.

Wrath was furious and he was not sure why. Or he did not want to admit that the thought of Verity ending their marriage, of never seeing her again or worse, her in the arms of another man had him ready to roar out his anger. It was near impossible to contain his anger when it reached a certain point and he was reaching that point fast.

He had to do something or it would burst lose and she would be renouncing their marriage here and now. That thought only fueled his fury.

"Look at me, wife," he ordered.

Verity turned her head, not because of his abrupt order, but because of the fierceness that rumbled in his voice.

He lowered his face closer to hers. "I forbid you to renounce our marriage."

A warning signaled in her not to argue, but she paid it no heed. "You cannot—"

"I can and I did."

"I will speak—"

"Of it no more," he finished.

But she was not finished. All the years she had not been able to speak up for herself had her fighting back. "I will do—"

"What I command."

"No!" she cried out, not giving him anymore words to steal from her, but having her say.

He glared at her.

"I will not stay where I am not wanted."

"I want you."

The heated intensity of his short response sent tingles rushing over her flesh and raising bumps along it while sending endless flutters to her insides.

"I can see the aching want in your eyes for me and feel the shiver of desire in your body. Until we settle this unrelenting need between us, you will stay my wife."

Verity chose not to respond, it would do no good. There was only one way to make him understand how she felt and that was to couple with him.

~~~

Whispers circled the camp that night, Verity catching a word here or there. By the time she pieced them together, she realized the men were in awe of Wrath and how he had fearlessly followed after her and returned from a place few if any ever did. To them there was no doubt as to why Wrath was the leader of the King's personal guard. They would repeat the tale often to anyone who would listen and Wrath would one day find himself a legend.

How was it that she found herself caring for such a man? She looked over to where he stood talking with Tilden. There was no denying he was a powerful warrior, his strength showing in his every movement. And he not only served the King faithfully, but he was also a friend to Talon long before he took the throne.

She turned her eyes away when Wrath approached her in slow strides. She kept her attention on the campfire that roared in front of her and the bread she nibbled on, not feeling at all hungry, but knowing it was wise to feed her body when possible.

She did not look at Wrath when he sat beside her, though her body enjoyed his warmth when he leaned against her.

"You are angry with me," he said.

"I am displeased," she admitted.

"The truth is not meant to hurt, though it often does hurt to hear."

She turned to look at him. "The truth also hurts when one must admit it."

"I will not argue with you," Wrath said sharply.

"There is no point; the truth will make itself known no matter what either one of us want."

Why that should disturb him, he did not know and he refused to respond to it. He wanted nothing more than to wrap himself around his wife and sleep. He almost laughed at his own lies. He wanted to wrap himself around his wife, but he did not want to sleep. But here and now was not the time and place for them to join.

"What are the Imray like?" Verity asked.

Wrath was glad to speak of something else and settled comfortably next to her as he answered, "The Imray Tribe was formed after the battles to unify the tribes. The tribe is composed of people whose tribes no longer existed after the battles finally ended. Having survived the hardships and losses of the war and with no tribe to return home to, King Talon brought all those people together. They became one tribe and to show their unity, they wear an intricate body drawing down their right arms. It signifies their loyalty to one another while their other body drawings tell of their original origin so their tribes will never be forgotten. They have always been loyal to the King since he saw those punished who decimated their tribes."

"The King has truly united the people of this land," Verity said.

"It was the only way to defeat foreign invaders. If Talon had not stepped forward and convinced the tribes to fight together, this land would no longer be ours. We would live under foreign rule and eventually our people would be no more."

"So you worry for the Imray with what has recently gone on?"

Wrath smiled. "I worry more for the people who would foolishly attack them. Having lost their tribes, they are extremely protective of what they have built together. Anyone who would dare attack them would find out too late that it had been an unwise decision. They also keep close watch on all that goes on around them, never again wanting to be vulnerable to an enemy."

"So they may tell you something you do not know and they would know if Hemera passed their way."

Wrath nodded. "They are a watchful people who can tell us much."

Verity yawned and as if it was the most natural thing for her to do, she laid her head on Wrath's shoulder. He in turn slipped his arm around her, but then it had been the way of things between them of late.

They retired soon after with little more said between them. Verity did not object when Wrath wrapped himself around her, she was glad for it. He not only kept her warm, but she felt safe in his arms. She had not felt safe since the Northmen had taken her and Hemera from their home.

Sleep claimed her quickly and dawn came just as quickly, and they were soon on their way again. It was a dismal day, gray clouds continuing to hover overhead and it remained cold, though not as cold as it had been, allowing for some of the snow to melt.

Imray warriors greeted them along the trail, pleased to see it was Wrath.

"It is good to see you again, Alard," Wrath said, "I hope all is well with you and your people."

"All is good, Wrath," the young warrior, short and burly with a thatch of red hair, said and nodded at Verity. "Someone you found along the way."

"My wife, Verity," Wrath said with such strength that it was almost as if he decreed it an edict, never allowing it to be changed.

Alard smiled, shaking his head. "Minn is not going to like that."

"It is done and cannot be undone," Wrath said.

Verity was surprised to hear him say that since it was not the truth.

"Minn is going to like that even less." Alard laughed. "I will ride ahead and see that things are made ready for your arrival." He laughed again. "And keep Minn calm."

When he rode away, Verity asked, "Who is Minn?"

"A friend of Alard's."

Verity tugged at Wrath's chin to force him to look at her and she ignored the flare of annoyance in his eyes when they met hers. She intended on getting an answer. "And?"

"Minn does not matter."

"Then why not answer me?"

He gave a quick turn of his head, her fingers falling off his chin.

If he thought his silence would discourage her from saying anymore, he was wrong. "If you refuse to discuss it, I will ask Minn."

That had his head turning quickly her way. "Minn has a temper and can be territorial."

"I appreciate the warning, though what reason could she have for turning her temper on me?" Verity asked, smiling.

"Minn and I have much in common and that brought us together on several occasions."

223

"You mated," Verity clarified and wondered why it should annoy her.

"I have mated with many women."

That annoyed her even more. "And I am sure you pleased each and every one of them so much they would be only too glad to mate with you again or as with Minn be territorial and lay claim to you."

"That bothers you," he said with a slight smile.

"Mate with whoever you like, it matters not to me," she said annoyed that she had allowed her feelings to show.

He grabbed her chin, lifting it to plant a strong kiss on her lips. "We are wed and I will not disrespect that and couple with another woman. You and I will mate." He kissed her again. "Be careful around Minn. She is a formidable woman and a fierce warrior."

A fierce warrior.

Verity had no chance against a fierce warrior. She had no fighting or weapon skills. She had not been allowed to defend herself. The Northmen would have beaten her if she raised a hand against them. She should know; she had tried. She had learned what she could from watching others, but she had wished she could have learned more.

The village came into view and it was larger than she had thought. There were many dwellings and a large feasting hall. It appeared as if the whole village had come out to greet the King's warriors and from the way the warriors were bear-hugged and slapped on the back, it was obvious they all knew one another.

Verity smiled at the joyous scene, standing beside Wrath as his horse was led away by a young lad.

"You finally stopped coddling our King and have come to visit," a deep voice shouted out.

Verity stumbled as she hurried to step away from the large hulk of a man barreling down on Wrath. His long, dark hair was braided in thick braids at the sides of his head and he had fine features even though he bore some scars on his face. He was not as tall as Wrath but he was much wider than him. She thought for sure he would plow Wrath to the ground, rushing at him with such fierceness.

She smiled, relieved, when Wrath did not budge as he locked with the large man nor did he flinch when pounded on the back.

"Dalmeny," Wrath said, taking a step back. "It is good to see you, my friend."

"It has been too long," Dalmeny said. "There is much we have to catch up on and I want to hear how the King fares."

Wrath heard what Dalmeny did not say but implied. *I have things to tell you, later in private.* He let it be, though was eager to hear what news the man had.

Dalmeny glanced past Wrath to Verity. "Is this your wife that Alard is telling everyone about?"

Wrath held his hand out to Verity and she took it, stepping forward to stand beside him.

"A strong wind would blow her away and her hair blinds the eyes," screeched a woman.

Verity turned to see a tall woman, thick, though solid and shapely in body with a sword hanging at her side. Her long dark hair was braided on one side of her head and her one arm that was left exposed was covered with an intricate drawing from shoulder to wrist. She had sharp features that caught the eye as did her powerful strides that brought her to Verity and Wrath.

Wrath stepped partially in front of his wife.

"This weak woman will never serve the mighty Wrath well."

225

Verity watched her stop in front of Wrath. She was nearly as tall as Wrath and her muscles as plentiful and defined as his. Wrath had been right. Minn was a formidable woman and no match for Verity.

What Minn did next stunned and angered Verity. She kissed Wrath.

Chapter Twenty-one

Wrath did not stop Minn from kissing him, but he did not return her kiss and when she finished she stepped away from him, scowling. He leaned toward her and her scowl quickly turned to a smile since it appeared as if Wrath intended to kiss her. But he stopped a distance from her lips and spoke in a tone that allowed only those close to them to hear.

"Speak ill against my wife again and I will see you suffer for it. Verity is a good wife. I could ask for none better. She pleases me more than any woman I have known and I will not see her disrespected."

Minn glared at him and kept firm rein on her anger as she said, "Forgive me, I meant no ill will toward your *wife*."

"That is good to hear, Minn, for it would please me if you would befriend her."

Minn's glare deepened. "As you wish, Wrath."

Dalmeny stepped forward. "Come and let us celebrate your visit with food and drink."

Wrath turned and held his hand out to Verity and she took it, sliming, and walked alongside her husband to the feasting hall. She heard Minn follow behind them, her footfalls heavy along with her anger.

Food and drink were plentiful as was talk and laughter, though Verity felt no part of it. These were people who knew one another well. They had fought beside one another in battle and they would again if necessary. And though she was a Pict like them, she had been gone too long from her homeland to join in the fellowship they shared. She sometimes wondered if she would ever feel at home here again.

She looked to Wrath laughing along with Dalmeny. They shared tale after tale as did the others at the surrounding tables. They all were more than friends. They were family. They were one—they were Picts.

"What markings do you wear?" Minn asked as she slipped onto the bench beside Verity.

"I have earned none yet," Verity said and wondered if she ever would.

"Why have you yet to earn them?"

Verity could not help but admire Minn and she could see why the woman would make Wrath a good wife. Beautiful. Strong. A fearless warrior. Familiar with Wrath in ways she had yet to be. She was all that Verity was not.

"You are of age where you should have many," Minn continued before Verity could answer, her smile much too smug.

"Her markings will be my choice."

Verity turned to her husband, surprised and annoyed at his response. She thought him too busy with his own conversation to pay heed to hers. As for her markings? She had had enough of decisions being made for her. What markings she got would be of her own choosing.

Minn persisted. "What of her tribe? Do her people not want her to carry their drawings proudly."

"Enough, Minn!" Dalmeny ordered sharply. "Wrath owes you no explanations."

"Maybe," Minn said with a shrug, "but what about her tribe—"

Dalmeny brought his meaty fist down on the table. "Enough, I said!"

The room turned silent and Minn stood abruptly and sent the leader a harsh look that Verity thought would surely sting the man before she marched out of the feasting hall.

"She is one of my best warriors and most vexing one," he said to Wrath. "I had hoped you would wed her and relieve me of the burden."

Verity knew his words were not meant for her ears, but she heard them anyway, and she listened for Wrath's response.

"Minn was aware I never planned to wed, but Verity changed all that."

If only that was true, but she had not changed it. The king had decreed it and Verity felt the weight of his lie.

"A woman stole you away, stole your heart, and had you doing something you swore you never would...wed. I would say that gives Minn plenty to be angry about." He gave a hardy chuckle. "I would be careful if I were you."

"She can direct her anger at me all she wants, but I will not tolerate her doing anything to my wife," Wrath warned.

Dalmeny ceased his chuckle. "I will speak to her again."

"More firmly this time," Wrath ordered.

Dalmeny nodded. "I will see to it, and now we should talk. A dwelling has been provided for you. I can have one of the women take Verity there."

"One of my warriors will go with them," Wrath said.

Dalmeny summoned one of the women, sitting at a nearby table and when he slipped his arm around her wide hips and smiled up at her, Wrath knew it was the woman he was presently mating with. He had yet to commit to one woman, much like Wrath had, and Wrath wondered if he ever would.

With a flick of his hand, Wrath summoned Tilden, then turned to his wife as the warrior approached the table. "You will go to the dwelling and wait there for me to join you."

Verity was only too glad to comply. She had had enough of the celebration that had turned out to be anything but one. She nodded and went to stand, but Wrath gripped her arm, forcing her to remain seated. He leaned in close and she thought he meant to whisper to her. Instead, he kissed her lips lightly.

"Are you all right?" he asked for her ears alone.

His concerned and comforting kiss softened her annoyance. "I am fine."

Wrath kept his voice low. "I want you more than fine."

Verity was not sure how to interpret that, but her body seemed to and a slight blush turned her cheeks pink.

He kissed her again and whispered, "Later," before turning to Tilden and ordering him to see Verity safely to their dwelling.

Verity went with Tilden, looking back at her husband as they neared the door and seeing that he and Dalmeny were moving to a more secluded spot in the feasting hall. A catch to her insides had her hand rushing to press against her middle. For some reason, parting from him disturbed her and as if he felt her unease he turned and looked at her, sending her a nod that she was certain was meant to reassure her.

She bundled her cloak around her against the cold, not sure if it had turned colder or if her shiver had come from something else.

"Warmth and blankets await you at the dwelling that has been prepared," the woman who walked beside her said. "I can also bring a hot brew for you, if you would like."

Verity had not realized the woman was there, she had been so absorbed in how she was feeling. "I am grateful for your generosity. The food and drink have been so plentiful I have need of no more."

The woman smiled. "I am pleased to hear that. I am Amada. If there is anything you should need, please let me know."

Amada and Tilden left her on her own after Tilden looked inside and around the outside of the dwelling and Amada stoked the fire and spread one of the two blankets over the raised sleeping pallet.

The dwelling was similar to all the other ones she had been in, a sleeping pallet, a small table and two benches, and a fire pit in the middle of the room. She sat on the bed, thoughts of Hemera coming to her. She had heard Wrath ask Dalmeny if a young woman had passed through the village. She had been disappointed to hear him say that if a woman had entered their village, he would not have allowed her to continue on her own with snow so fresh and abundant on the ground.

Upon hearing that, it seemed to add to the belief that Hemera had found her way into a Wyse village. Verity still was not sure if she should be relieved or worried about that. Wrath kept telling her to trust her visions, for they showed Hemera and her together again.

A knock sounded at the door and Verity went and opened it, thinking that perhaps Amada had brought the hot brew anyway. She was surprised to see Minn standing there. The top of the door opening reached only to her brow, forcing her to bend her head if she wished to enter. Verity was grateful that she remained where she

231

was and annoyed with herself for being intimidated by the woman.

"I heard Wrath ask Dalmeny if a woman had passed through the village. No woman has been seen here, but there is someone who may be able to help you. He has recently traveled a distance and may have seen who you are looking for. If you come with me, you can speak with him."

Wrath would not be pleased if she went with Minn and she did not want to go with Minn. She simply did not trust the woman. "You should take this news to Wrath and let him speak with the man."

Minn smiled and snorted. "I knew you feared me."

Verity returned her smile. "You are right. I do fear you and I do not trust you, therefore, I will not go anywhere with you."

Minn grumbled before spitting out, "I am trying to help."

"Are you or are you setting a trap for me?"

"That would be foolish of me, since I have seen Wrath make those suffer who do not heed his warnings."

Still Verity hesitated, not sure of the woman.

"I will go get the warrior who brought you here and he can come with us," Minn said, throwing her arms up before she stomped off.

Verity stepped outside and watched Minn head toward the feasting hall, wondering if she would return or it had been nothing more than a ruse. She turned to go back inside to wait and see for herself, when a hand suddenly covered her mouth, stopping her from calling out and an arm snagged her around the waist, and dragged her away, off behind the dwelling.

"What are you doing here?" the gruff voice demanded.

She was stunned to recognize the voice and realize that it was Lars, another one of Ulric's warriors here in Pictland. She struggled against him and he tightened his grip on her, slamming her back against him.

He pressed his cheek hard against hers. "Keep still or Ulric will find you with broken bones when I drop you at his feet."

Verity winced not only from his arm that was squeezing her middle much too tightly, but from his foul breathe that stung her nose.

"I cannot believe you escaped Ulric. No one escapes him."

Verity dug her heels deep in the snow to leave a trail for Wrath to follow. She suddenly recalled her vision of Ulric dragging her away as she called out to Wrath. But Lars and Ulric were like brothers, did it matter which one she saw in the visions? And Wrath was not harmed or dead. Had she been too far from the village for him to hear her? Was that why he had not come for her? Had he been right? Had her vision been trying to protect her? She had to scream out. She had to alert someone so Wrath would know of her plight.

~~~

"Northmen have been spotted in these parts. The Kerse captured one and plan to take him to the King," Dalmeny said. "Does the King know anything of this?

"No more, the Northman is dead. We met the Kerse on the way here and the Northman chose death over capture. Where else have they been spotted?" Wrath asked, wondering how long these rogue Northmen have been here.

"Not far from the Ancrum Tribe. Egot does not protect his land and tribe as he once did. He leaves it much too vulnerable. Though, I have wondered if someone in his tribe may be plotting with the Northmen. You have not answered me. Does the King know of this? Is that why you are here?"

With the Northmen having been spotted, news would spread. Dalmeny needed to know all of what had happened. Wrath started with the attack on the couple who had been slaughtered and the attack on the Raban Tribe and the Northmen who had joined with the Ancrum warriors. He also told him what all tribes were being told that Ulric and some of his warriors had arrived on their shores and had requested and been granted a meeting with King Talon.

"Ulric chose now to come here when the land is coated with snow and the seas are ready to devour? Something is not right," Dalmeny said, shaking his head. "Ulric made no mention of why they are here?"

Wrath decided to tell him about Verity without letting him know who he actually was speaking about. "No, though we have wondered if it has anything to do with two Pict sisters who had been taken from their home here when they were young and who recently escaped and returned here. One made it to the stronghold and the other we still search for."

Dalmeny shook his head again. "That makes even less sense. Ulric cannot be that foolish to think the King would return two Picts to him. Besides, it would seem the Northmen that have been spotted have been here for a while, so they would have nothing to do with the two sisters."

"King Talon left warriors with the Raban Tribe and the warriors are scouting the land to see what they can find."

"With the Northmen here and those plotting to take the throne from the King, and having no heir to succeed him, it does not bode well for King Talon."

"Have you ever known the King to leave himself vulnerable?" Wrath asked.

"I cannot say I have, but of late, things do not look good for him. With the Northmen on our shores without permission and some already roaming the land, the tribes will begin to doubt that King Talon is capable of protecting them and take matters into their own hands."

"That would be foolish of them," Wrath warned. "The King is a wise man and will see this settled in favor of the Picts."

"I trust you, Wrath, though I will do whatever is necessary to protect my tribe."

"And so will the King, though it will be all the people he protects."

Minn rushed into the fasting hall, yelling out for Wrath, and when she spotted him she rushed to a stop in front of him. "Someone has taken Verity."

Chapter Twenty-two

Verity let her body go limp, making it difficult for Lars to drag her and keep a good pace.

"You will not play games with me," he warned and dropped his hand off her mouth to grab her and throw her over his shoulder.

Before he could, she let out such a loud scream that it reverberated through the woods. She knew the consequences she would suffer, and they came hard and fast. His open hand hit her face with such strength that it sent her crashing to the ground. She had no time to recover from it, since he grabbed her long braid and started pulling her along the ground. Any moment she expected her braid to be torn from her head, the pain so bad it nearly blinded her.

His mistake had been that he thought he had taught her a lesson and she would keep silent. This time she screamed out Wrath's name over and over and over until he turned his hand on her again. Only this time, she was prepared. As he dropped down to deliver another stinging blow to her face, she came up with her head right beneath his chin and sent him tumbling back to land on his backside. It gave her a chance to run and she did, grabbing her braid and keeping hold of it against her chest so that he could not grab it when he followed after her. And he would follow. Northmen never gave up.

She waited to hear footfalls behind her and hoped to see Wrath running toward her. The footfalls came behind her, but not Wrath, and she feared she would be captured once again. It was not long before she was sure she smelled Lar's rancid breath behind her and no matter how hard she tried to put a good distance between them, he gained on her. Any moment she expected to feel his hand on her as he yanked her back and sent her tumbling to the ground, letting loose his anger on her again.

He struck with such suddenness that it stole her breath as she was yanked back and flung to the ground. She scrambled to her feet, knowing he would pummel her if she did not get out of his reach. He got her arm before she could get away from him and as he swung her around, his hand aimed for her face, she brought her other hand up. He grabbed it, releasing her other arm and twisted it hard behind her back, forcing a scream from her. His free hand caught at her neck, squeezing, and turning her scream into a croak.

He shoved her arm up higher behind her back. "Ulric will not mind a broken bone or two."

A terrifying roar suddenly ripped through the forest, sending birds scattering out of the trees and frightening animals out of their shelters. And it sent the Northmen trembling so badly that his hand fell away from her neck.

She remembered that roar and when she caught her breath, she said, "That is my husband, the mighty Wrath, and he is coming for me—and you." He gave her arm another hard yank and she cried out in pain, then screamed, "Wrath!"

Lars released her as he backhanded her across the face and as she fell to the ground, she saw Wrath running straight for her, his dark eyes ablaze with fury, his warriors following behind him and other warriors behind them.

Wrath let out another chilling roar, seeing Verity fall and knowing he would not get to her before she hit the ground. He signaled his men to go after the man he had watched twist his wife's arm up behind her back and his hand strike her face. He would make him suffer endlessly before killing him for daring to lay a hand on her.

His men ran ahead as did Minn and Dalmeny and his warriors while Wrath dropped down beside Verity. He eased his arm under her, and she winced.

"Give me a moment," she pleaded.

Wrath stared down at her, her eyes shut tight, and knew she was battling the pain screaming in her shoulder. He had suffered such an injury and had made sure the man responsible was never able to use his arm again. He would do much more to the man who did this to her.

His anger mounted when he saw bruises forming on each cheek and another forming on her chin. He could not wait. He needed her in his arms. She would be safe there. He gently slipped his arm beneath her, avoiding her injured shoulder and eased her into his arms.

"Tell me what happened." He did not mean it to sound as a demand, but it did.

Verity knew Wrath by now. When he demanded of her, it was more out of concern and that was what she heard—concern. "It was another one of Ulric's warriors. He was surprised to see that I escaped."

"That would mean he had to be here long before you landed on Pict shores."

Voices growing closer had them both turning silent and with a gentle lift, Wrath stood with her snug in his arms.

Dalmeny approached with one of his warriors. "Your warriors and mine are tracking him. My tribe is already prepared to fight if necessary. We need to talk. Our healer can see to your wife while we do."

"I will see to my wife, then we will talk," Wrath commanded and walked away.

"You are needed elsewhere," Verity said as soon as he placed her on the sleeping pallet in their dwelling. "I can tend my own wounds. I have done so for as long as I recall."

He placed a gentle hand beneath her chin. "You have a husband now and I will see to your wounds." He was quick to silence her when she went to speak. "Not another word."

She held her tongue, seeing the anger in his dark eyes mounting as his glance skimmed over her face. She could only imagine how she looked to him and when his hand drifted down to her neck to tenderly stroke it, she wondered if Lars had left a mark there as well.

"Did he do anything else besides strike you?" Wrath asked, his glance lingering at her throat.

She shook her head.

His eyes went to hers. "I will have the truth, Verity."

"Lars would not touch me that way. He would be too fearful. He believes I can see all and know all about him, even his death by simply looking at him. He dragged me by my hair and left some marks on me, but otherwise I am unharmed."

"He dragged you by your hair?"

"I drove my head under his chin and managed to escape him, but not for long. He grabbed my braid and dragged me, but it was enough time for me to scream out to you again. I knew you would come for me."

Wrath sat down beside her and ran his hand gently over her bruised cheek. "I did not get to you soon enough."

"You came just in time. Lars intended to break some of my bones." She realized too late that she should

239

have kept that to herself. Her husband looked ready to roar with rage.

Wrath contained his anger, letting it build to unleash upon the Northman. "He is the one who will find his bones broken."

She tried to soothe his potent anger. "It does not matter any longer. All that matters is that you saved me from worse harm."

"It does matter. He should have never gotten hold of you in the first place."

She rested her hand on his arm and moved the discussion away from her. "We should be more concerned that another Northman has been found here. Also, have you not noticed that the ones we have seen so far can blend easily with the Picts. They do not have hair or beards the color of the sun like many Northmen. They are also trusted friends of Ulric, especially Lars. They are as close as brothers. They have all fought by his side. They are all loyal to him. Why would they be here?"

Wrath took hold of her hand and hers quickly closed tightly around his. "That is a question that has troubled me as well. They have blended much too easily, speaking our language as if born to it."

"The Northmen have traded long enough with the Picts to speak it as well as their own."

"There is much to be considered, much for the King to know. But tell me," he said, "how did this Lars get hold of you?"

"Minn came to tell me that she heard we were searching for a young woman traveling alone and she told me there was someone here who might have seen her in his travels, but that he would not be here for long. I did not trust Minn and would not go with her, so she went to get Tilden to accompany us. Before I could step back inside the dwelling, Lars grabbed me and dragged me away."

He would definitely have a word with Minn. "He had to have been here in the village when we arrived and spotted you."

"That is what I do not understand about the Northmen we have come across. What are they doing here? What are they doing mixing with your tribes? It makes no sense. They always travel together." She was surprised about what she said next. "I wish I had a vision that could explain this."

Wrath recalled her vision of being captured and screaming out to him, he should have paid more heed to it. He should have realized that if she had not seen him in the vision, then she had been taken without him knowing it. "You will stay in my sight at all times."

"Who would have thought that a Northman lurked among the Imray? And is it not better we found out?"

"At too high of a cost," he said and slipped his free hand around the back of her neck as he drew his face close to hers. "I will not see you suffer again." He brushed his lips lightly over hers. "I promise."

A knock sounded at the door.

"Who goes there?" Wrath called out.

"Tilden."

Wrath hurried to open the door. "Tell me that you captured him?"

Tilden shook his head. "We lost him and could not find his tracks."

Anger had Wrath shouting, "You gave up!"

"He would go where you least expect him to," Verity said, stepping from behind Wrath and she was not surprised to see Tilden wince when he looked upon her.

Wrath was quick to order, "Search the outskirts of the village." He turned to Verity and took her hand.

241

"You come with me." She gasped when he tugged her arm to follow him out the door. He cursed when he heard her and came to an abrupt stop, annoyed that he had forgotten how badly her arm had been twisted. He would have rather left her to rest, but he could not bring himself to leave her alone or have someone else watch over her.

"I did not mean to hurt you," he said, releasing her hand and slipping it around her other hand.

"I never thought you did and the pain will fade soon enough."

But not the memory, he thought and could not wait to make the Northman suffer far more than his wife had. He slowed his pace and kept a watchful eye on her as they made their way to the feasting hall.

Minn was whispering something to Dalmeny when they entered and Wrath could tell by the narrowing of his eyes that he did not like what he was hearing.

Wrath looked directly at Minn when he came to a stop in front of them. "Why are you not helping my warriors when it is your fault this has happened?"

Dalmeny looked to Minn. "Why does he accuse you?"

"It was not my fault. Besides, how was it that she was known to this man?"

"Not your fault?" Wrath argued. "You go to my wife rather than me after learning we were searching for a young woman and offer to take her to a stranger to speak with him? Why? What made you think the stranger would know anything? And who else knew of this stranger's presence in the village besides you?"

"Why was I not informed of a stranger entering the village?" Dalmeny demanded.

"He arrived late last night and asked for shelter for a day or two. He was hunched over, his hands gnarled from age—"

"You saw what he wanted you to see—a helpless old man who posed no threat," Wrath accused.

Minn turned an accusing tongue on him. "What would he want with her? What have you not told us about her?"

Before he could answer a warrior rushed into the feasting hall and shouted, "He has been caught."

They all hurried out of the feasting hall to see Wrath's warriors dragging the bloody and bruised captive through the village. His hands were tied and a rope was looped around his neck, not tight enough to choke the breath from him, but tight enough to be uncomfortable.

They deposited him at Wrath's feet and as soon as they did, he staggered to stand.

"I will speak to King Talon and no one else," he said and spit blood from his bleeding mouth, causing Minn and Dalmeny to jump back.

Not Wrath. He stayed as he was, the spit barely missing him, and glared at the Northman called Lars. He would make certain this Northman did not take his life like the other one. He would have that privilege, after he made him suffer endlessly.

"I will speak to the King and only the King," Lars said again, as if he had not been heard the first time.

Wrath took a step toward the man and everyone startled when he delivered such a vicious blow to the Northman's jaw that it knocked him off his feet. He leaned down over him and grabbed the rope around his neck, tightening it. "I will see that you speak with the King, but it is a few days to the stronghold and the

243

snow-covered ground is not easy to travel. I worry that you may suffer *several* broken bones before we arrive."

He released the rope with a jerk, Lars' head bouncing off the ground. He looked to Tilden. "Tie him tightly to a stake until we are ready to leave."

Dalmeny spoke up as Wrath's men pulled the Northman to his feet. "Who are you and why are you here?"

The captured Northman looked to Dalmeny. "That is for the King alone to know, but I will warn you. You have a demon among you. If you have looked upon her, she will possess you as she has possessed Wrath and—"

Wrath delivered another blow to his jaw that sent him to the ground, his body lying lifeless, and he was quickly dragged away with orders to gag him when they tied him to the stake.

"Does he speak of your wife?" Dalmeny demanded of Wrath.

"I warned you there was something strange about her," Minn said. "She has no markings and if she has not earned them yet, then why? Did her tribe cast her out?"

"Enough!" Wrath shouted. "The captured man is a Northman."

"Another one," Dalmeny said, shaking his head. "This does not bode well, Wrath, and what would a Northman want with your wife?"

Verity's past could not be kept secret for long and the Kerse were probably already spreading the news of the Northman they had come across. "Verity was captured by the Northmen when she was young and has served as a slave to them until recently when she and her sister escaped. I would think that he saw her, and he feared that she would recognize him and ruin whatever plans he had for your tribe."

"He called her a demon," Minn reminded.

"To distract you from the truth," Wrath said, "and ignite your fears."

Minn laid her hand on the hilt of her sword. "I fear no demon."

"Then there is nothing for you to worry about either way."

"The King should be warned of his words," Minn said.

Wrath turned an angry scowl on her. "Do you suggest I will not tell the King all that went on here?"

Minn went to step forward, an equally angry glare on her face, but Dalmeny gripped her arm stopping her.

"Minn thinks of the well-being of her tribe and I agree with her. She will accompany you back to the stronghold and hear what you say to the King for herself and learn more of what is going on. If you refuse to let her travel with you, she will make the journey alone."

"Minn is more than welcome to join us," Wrath said, though his annoyed tone spoke differently.

Verity was not happy that Minn would be joining them. Minn did not like her and Verity did not trust Minn. Or was it because Minn cared for Wrath that Verity did not trust her? She was not sure, but she planned on keeping her distance from the woman.

"We will take our leave tomorrow at first light," Wrath said.

"We will talk when we sup," Dalmeny said and turned and walked away.

Minn glared at Verity, as if warning her to beware.

Verity did the only thing she could think of...she smiled.

It annoyed Minn all the more and she turned and followed after Dalmeny.

Verity had no choice but to stay by Wrath's side. He would not let go of her hand. It did not take her long to realize that she had suffered more at Lars' hands than she had first thought. She hurt and the pain was spreading. As her husband finished talking with Tilden, she tugged on his arm. She intended to let him know that she needed to return to the dwelling and rest, especially with them leaving tomorrow. She would need her strength for their return journey home.

Wrath turned to his wife, the bruises on her face had darkened and fatigue showed in her slumped shoulders and the tight lines around her mouth let him know how much she was fighting against the pain. Before she could utter a word to him, he scooped her up in his arms and walked away.

Chapter Twenty-three

Wrath laid his wife gently on the sleeping pallet, wrapping her cloak snugly around her and covering her with a blanket. He went and stoked the fire that had dwindled and left the dwelling chilled. The flames caught fast to the wood he added to it.

He returned to Verity, sitting at her side and once again tucked the blanket around her. "I am a warrior. I have been one since I could first hold a weapon in my hand. My father taught me that strength was the mightiest weapon of all, though the most difficult to learn. Strength demanded more than most people could give. It was one reason I became good friends with Talon and Paine, for both had mastered the power of strength."

Verity felt a tug to her heart that Wrath was sharing something so private with her and she was eager to hear all he had to say.

"I place strength before everything else. Strength made sense to me while little else did. Strength made me the mighty warrior I am today. Strength helped me win many battles. Strength made me the commander of the King's personal guard. To care for someone so deeply that I would give a woman my heart, can rob a man of his strength." He ran a gentle finger over her lips. "I can care for you only so much." He stood. "I will send someone to tend you."

Verity called out to him when he reached the door and he turned. "It takes more strength to care deeply enough to give your heart than it does to go into battle, and the victory is far greater."

Wrath stared at her a moment, then walked out, shutting the door behind him.

Verity smiled. Wrath might not understand why he chose now to tell her that, but she did. This incident had made him realize that he cared for her more than he wanted to admit and her smile grew as she thought about it.

~~~

Wrath walked to the feasting house so deep in thought, he had not noticed that dusk kissed the land. He did not know what made him say to Verity what he did. It had not been a thought when he carried her to the dwelling. His only thought had been to see that she rested and healed from her ordeal.

He shook his head. He was not being truthful with himself. His heart had pounded in his chest when he had seen how tired she was and that once again her pain had been his fault. He could not stand seeing her in pain. He could not stand seeing what Lars had done to her. And he could not understand why his first thought had been to drop down beside Verity and see to her care rather than go after Lars. The warrior in him would have done that. Instead, his only thought had been to see to Verity, take her in his arms and keep her there.

He shook his head again. He cared for Verity, he would not, could not deny that, but care deeply, give her his heart? It would rob his strength. He would not be half the warrior he was. And how she could even suggest that victory of the heart could be far greater than a victorious battle was foolish.

Wrath entered the feasting house with a scowl on his face, his powerful strides sending several people scurrying out of his path. When he reached the table where Dalmeny sat with his arm around his woman, his scowl deepened. He was once like Dalmeny, having a woman that pleased him without thought of the heart, just a poke when needed.

"I need your healer to look after Verity," he demanded.

The woman beside him rose. "I will see to her and also bring her some food."

"Amada is your healer?" Wrath asked.

"And a good one," Dalmeny said, swatting Amada's backside as she walked away. "Sit, drink, and we will talk."

Wrath sat beside him on the bench, taking the vessel, a servant had filled, in his hand. "There is nothing left to discuss."

"Or that you do not wish to discuss? The tribes need to know everything if we are to protect ourselves."

"Did you know everything about every battle we fought to unify the tribes?" Wrath asked, after taking a generous swallow of the potent brew.

"That was different. We were at war," Dalmeny argued.

"War or not, Talon knew what he was doing. He positioned each tribe without the other knowing to march as one against our enemies. Though he may not tell his people everything, he leads them wisely. We trusted him once and he did as he promised, he stopped bloodshed among the tribes, drove foreigners off our land, and unified the Picts. He will not let the Northmen take from us what we have sacrificed to build...a Pict nation."

Dalmeny stared at the half-filled vessel in his hand. "All you say is true, but tell me, Wrath, how do you know Verity is who she says she is? What if she is not a Pict? What if she runs from the Northmen for something other than she tells you?"

"Minn must have filled your head with nonsense."

"She has filled it with questions you should be asking yourself. How do you know who you wed?"

"I know I have wed a good, kind woman, for I have seen her kindness to others. I have seen how worried she is about finding her sister and seeing her kept safe and finally seeing that both of them are home and able to live free. This is not about my wife. It is about Ulric and we should not let anything distract us from that fact."

"Tell me why you wed her and perhaps it will settle this for me," Dalmeny said.

Wrath spoke the truth. "The King ordered it."

Dalmeny threw back his head and laughed. "Now I know all is well and that Wrath is as mighty and fearless as he has always been."

They talked, ate, and drank more and when Amada returned and slipped between the two of them to rest comfortably against Dalmeny, Wrath was quick to ask, "My wife?"

"She rests comfortably. I bathed her sore shoulder with a brew of comfrey leaves and her bruises as well. Her shoulder will have pain for a while, but the bruises on her face will not take long to heal. I cannot say the same for the one just above her waist. It is dark and will take time to fade. She must have fought for breath with how tight he squeezed her."

Wrath downed what was left in his vessel and stood. "I will take my leave since we depart at first light. And I will make sure to let King Talon know how generous and helpful you were to us."

250

"And that we stand ready to fight beside him when needed," Dalmeny added.

Wrath gave a nod and left the feasting house, his strides quickening as soon as he was out the door. His anger grew once again, learning that there was more to his wife's injures than he had thought. He wanted to go where Lars was tied to a stake and begin breaking his bones, starting with his arm. But that would wait, Verity came first.

He stopped abruptly. How many times now had he put Verity before anyone or anything else? How many times had he felt his insides twist with fear when he had thought something had happened to her? How many times had he found himself feeling out of sorts when separated from her? Did he care more for her than he wanted to admit? Could he have lost his heart to her without realizing it? He snorted he was so angry. He was a warrior, a mighty one at that. He had no time for thinking such nonsense.

He continued walking and when he reached the dwelling, he swung the door open. He was shocked to find her standing there naked by the fire, her head shooting up from where she had been glancing down at her side. And that was when he saw the dark bruise. He shut the door, dropped his cloak to the floor, and walked over to her, pushing her hand aside gently. He ran his fingers over the dark spot, that spread nearly from just above her waist to under her breast, ever so faintly, fearful of causing her pain.

Verity stilled, closing her eyes as his fingers explored the bruise with tenderness. She had felt a chill when he had opened the door and the cold air rushed in, but his touch was growing her warm. She wished he would explore more than only her wound. Though her body ached from her ordeal, it ached more for his touch.

251

It had startled her at first, but finally came as no surprise that she cared deeply for her husband. She had come to know and care for him long before she had met him. And it was time for him to see how much they cared for each other.

She reached out and took his hand and slowly moved it to rest over her breast and gave his hand a gentle squeeze while a slight moan spilled unexpectedly from her lips.

"You have—"

"Waited too long," she said and squeezed his hand again.

"I care—"

"Enough," she said and moved his hand to her other breast, a soft moan once again escaping her lips.

"I will not stop once I—"

"Promise?"

"Promise," he whispered before capturing her lips in a hungry kiss as his hand squeezed her breast and his fingers teased her nipple hard.

She gasped, upset when his lips suddenly left hers, but sighed with pleasure when his mouth settled over her nipple and took hold of it to suckle. Her moan grew louder and once again she gasped when his mouth left hers. She was ready to protest until she saw him hastily shed his garments and she saw how thick and hard he had grown. She hurried to press herself against him, wanting to feel his warmth, his hardness, and to have his arms close around her, and they did.

Wrath was so hard and ready for her that he feared he would not last long once inside her. His ache for her was like no other. Never had he felt as he did at this moment. It was not just an overwhelming need to slip inside her and satisfy his ache, it was a need to give all he could to her, share all he could with her, feel all they could—together as one.

He ran his hands down along her backside to squeeze her soft bottom and ease her closer so that his manhood could rub against the enticing thatch of blonde hair between her legs. He had been right when he had told her they would mate often, since he already knew one time with her would never be enough.

He lifted her into his arms and laid her on the sleeping pallet, climbing in beside her. He did not cover them, he wanted to look upon her body. Though the bruising disturbed him, her body was lovely, the sight of her nakedness alone arousing him even more. She was not as thin as when he had first found her. She had plumped up some, not a lot, but enough to notice and his hand reached out to explore every part of her.

"Your beauty steals my breath," he whispered as his fingers roamed over her with a faint caressing touch. "You are so soft, so touchable. I do not think I will ever stop touching you."

"I do not want you to. Your touch pleases me as do your kisses."

He smiled as he brought his mouth to hers and whispered before kissing her, "Then I will kiss you often." His hand continued to explore her body while his kiss sent tiny tremors through her. He stopped suddenly and glared at her. "You will tell me if you feel any pain."

"I will tell you," she said and pressed her hand to his chest, letting it glide across his hard muscles and the swirls and curves of his body drawings, savoring the feel of him. She did not stop there, she let her hand drift down, growing familiar with every curve and muscle and when her fingers swept through the thatch of hair surrounding his manhood, his hand shot out, stopping her from going any further.

"No, I want to be inside you," he said.

She slipped out of his arms and sat up.

He took gentle hold of her arm, stopping her. "What are you doing?"

"I am getting on my hands and knees for you to enter me from behind."

"It is your face I will see when I slip inside you." He eased her down on the blanket, climbed over her and placed her legs over his shoulders as he knelt between them. His hands grabbed hold of her backside and he lifted it just enough so that he could slip his manhood slowly and easily inside her. She was wet and snug and his need so great that he finally could not wait any longer. He pushed into her and she cried out and locked her legs around him as if she intended never to let him go.

He grabbed her backside, squeezing it lightly and began slowly to move in and out of her, but that did not last long. Her own need had her bucking hard against him, and he soon matched her eager rhythm.

Wrath dropped his head back and a growl rumbled deep and low in his chest as he felt himself drawing closer and closer to the edge of releasing inside her.

"Wrath," Verity moaned as her hands gripped the blanket beneath her and she tossed her head from side to side.

His name, a plea on her lips, had him nearly exploding and when she cried out his name again and again, he drove into her harder and harder until she screamed it out as she burst with pleasure, and still he did not stop. His thrusts were strong and quick until finally he came so hard that he exploded in a blinding light, shiver after shiver running through him, sparking every part of him to life with the most intense pleasure he had ever felt.

Still caught in the explosiveness of her climax, she could not believe the sensations that continued running through her. She kept a tight grip on the blanket as she felt the potent ripples wash over her, again and again down to her very core until it faded into tingling shivers, one after the other. Finally, the last of them drifted away, leaving her feeling more satisfied than she thought was possible.

It was when he dropped down on her with a shudder that she realized he was still snug inside her. She smiled and wrapped her arms around him, realizing he had spilled his seed in her. She could not be happier and the thought had her feeling guilty that she could be so happy when she had yet to find Hemera.

Darkness began to creep around her. "No! No!" she cried out. *Not now, please do not let a vision rob me of this precious moment.*

Wrath pushed up on his arms, alarmed at her frantic cries, worried that he had somehow hurt her. Her hands suddenly grabbed at his arms and when he saw her soft blue eyes turn dark, his insides twisted.

Not now, he thought. *Not now.*

"Verity!" he cried out, but it was too late. Her hands fell off him and her eyes fluttered closed.

She was already in the throes of another vision.

Chapter Twenty-four

"Verity!" he cried out again and hurried off her to hastily gather her in his arms and sit on the sleeping pallet with her cradled against him. He worried when the heat from his body did not stop her body from chilling. He reached out for the crumpled blanket and draped it over her, tucking it around her.

He hated when a vision took hold of her. She turned so pale and her body was so limp that she felt lifeless. And he felt helpless. He commanded warriors, fought endless battles, faced death numerous times, and yet sitting here, holding his wife like this, unable to help her in anyway was the most terrifying thing he had ever had to face.

"Hurry and be done, Verity," he ordered. "I am not a patient man. Return to me now." He did not know if she heard him or if his words helped her in any way, but he refused to sit there and do nothing.

His worry grew when he felt her body suddenly chill more than it already had and he slipped his hand beneath the blanket to rub warmth back into her. He ran his hand up and down her arm and along her back. And when his fingers brushed her backside and he felt how cold it was, he not only gave her soft bottom a good rub, but squeezed it several times until it finally warmed.

He spit out several oaths in anger. Her vision had robbed her of the special joining they had shared. The memory would always be tainted with the vision, not of the moment they had finally come together as one.

One.

He had never thought of becoming one with a woman when he had coupled. It was for the sheer pleasure of it. They would enjoy each other and part as he had done many times with Minn. Not so with Verity, he did not want to part from her, just the thought of them separating angered him. She belonged with him and no one could say differently.

"Verity, return to me now," he ordered. She was there with him yet she was not there with him and he would have none of it. He wanted her back this very moment. He continued calling her name, demanding she return to him. And when she did not respond, his worry grew his anger.

~~~

Verity heard voices. They were in the distance and she was fearful of proceeding any further. Besides she was cold even with her cloak on and she stood in an unfamiliar forest. Where was she? Who did the voices belong to? She wanted this vision done. She wanted to return to Wrath.

Sudden warmth shot through her and she was grateful for it as it gave her the courage to move closer to the voices. A few steps took her closer and she peered past a tree to see four men sitting around a campfire. She almost gasped when she saw that the two Northmen who had died was sitting with Lars and Ulric.

"It will not be long before I revenge your deaths,"
Ulric said. "This land will be drenched with the blood of the Picts. I will leave not one standing."

Verity turned away, pressing her back against the tree trunk. Ulric planned to war with the Picts. She had to return to Wrath. She had to tell him. She thought for a moment she heard him call out to her. If that was him, it

257

would mean the vision was fading, she should be waking soon, though not soon enough for her.

She waited, hoping to hear Wrath's voice again only this time stronger. It would mean she would wake soon. When she heard him again, his voice was still faint. Her vision was not done. What was keeping her here? What more was there for her to see?

~~~

Wrath wanted to shake her out of her vision, but he knew it would do no good and he worried it might cause her harm. The only thing left to him was to talk to her, let her know he was there waiting for her, and he would not leave her.

"Though you try my patience, I will not leave you," he said. "You are my wife—" He stopped abruptly about to say she was his responsibility. The thought made him realize she meant more to him. Or had mating with her made him realize that he felt more for her? Somehow, someway she had stolen his heart. He brought his lips to her ear and whispered strongly. "You have my heart, come back to me."

~~~

Verity never felt so present in a vision before. A vision usually came and faded fairly quickly. Lately the visions had lingered a bit longer and she had even talked with some of the people in the vision. The thought gave her pause. Was she to speak to someone in this vision? Surely, she was not here to speak with Ulric.

Realizing the voices had gone silent, she peered around the tree to see that the four men had vanished. She was alone. Or was she? She dared not shut her eyes

258

as she turned slowly and came face-to-face with Ulric. His hand quickly caught at her throat and he smashed her back against the tree. She struggled in vain to pull his hand off her, but she was no match for his superior strength.

~~~

Fury raged in Wrath when his wife suddenly began grasping for air and her hands shot up to grab at her neck as if she was trying to pull hands off her. He was helpless to do anything, though it did not stop him from trying. He placed his hand on hers, adding his strength to hers and helped her yank at the hands he could not see, though when he found out who they belonged to, he would choke the life out of him.

He brought his lips to her ear once again and whispered, "You have my strength—fight."

~~~

Verity knew Ulric and his ways well. She had watched along with others as Ulric choked a person to the brink of death only to release him and begin again. It was a slow torture, the person not knowing if the next time would be his last. And Ulric got such joy from it, as he did now, smiling as he squeezed the breath from her little by little.

"I am not finished with you," Ulric said.

Suddenly, she felt as if a strong hand rested on hers, sharing its strength with her, and she thought she heard her husband whisper in her ear, "Fight." She gladly obeyed and smiled when she saw the startled look on Ulric's face as she pushed his hand off her neck. He began to fade then and she pushed at his hand harder and harder until...

Verity's eyes shot open and she gasped as breath began to return to her.

"Slowly, slowly," Wrath urged, his insides twisting as he watched her struggle to breathe. He rubbed her back gently and kept a hand at her waist and his eyes on every breath she took until she dropped her brow to rest on his chest, her breathing beginning to slow.

Wrath was impatient to know what happened in her vision, but it was more important to feel her resting in his arms and to have her breathing more natural. So he said nothing. He let her be, for now, and kept his hands on her as if he could prevent a vision from taking her away from him once again.

She dropped her head on his shoulder and rested her hand to his chest against the single swirl marking in the middle. The thump, thump, thump of his heart in his chest soothed her, though it was more rapid than usual. It made her recall something from her vision. She had thought she heard him say, *you have my heart*. Had he said it or was that what she wished to hear?

The blanket came around her shoulder along with his arm and he pressed her closer against him. It was good to feel the strength of his strong arms wrap around her and while there were many things she wanted to tell him, there was one more important than all the others.

She looked up at him. "Mating with you was more pleasurable than I ever imagined."

He could not keep a smile from his lips. With all she had been through that was her first thought to say to him? It stirred his heart and aroused him to know that mating with him was foremost on her mind.

He brought his lips to hers and she shivered against him when he faintly brushed his lips over hers. "I feel the same and I intend to mate with you as often as possible."

"I would not mind that," she said softly.

He brushed his lips across hers and whispered, "You are mine now. Nothing will separate us."

Did he mean what she thought he did? Was he telling her they would remain wed? He had released inside her, truly uniting them. But had he meant to? She would learn in time.

She captured his lips in a kiss before his mouth moved away from hers. She groaned softly with pleasure when he responded, taking command and chasing the recent memories of her vision away with his forceful kiss. It was as if with that single kiss he claimed her. She belonged to him and he would never let her go, and knowing that left her feeling freer than she had ever felt. Her worry drained away and her body went completely limp in his arms.

Wrath tensed and pulled his lips away from hers. Verity!"

She was not sure if she jumped and her eyes turned wide because he had abruptly ended a kiss that had spurred that strange little ache between her legs to spread or because he had shouted her name so sharply that she thought she had done something wrong.

"I forbid you to slip into another vision," he ordered, his features turning stern.

"No vision has command of me now—only you." She took his face in her hands and brought his mouth to hers, but before she kissed him, she whispered, "I want you inside me."

Her words hardened Wrath's manhood and he lifted her off his lap to lay her on the sleeping pallet, coming down beside her. That was when he noticed the blood on his manhood and he stilled. "Did I hurt you when I entered you for the first time?"

"A slight pain, nothing more."

"You are sure?"

She smiled. "I am sure." Her arms went out to him. "Now do not keep your wife waiting or she will be most displeased."

"Displeased is something you will never be with me," he said and as he lowered himself down beside her, he was pleased to know that he had taken her maidenhead. He had been her first and no other but him would ever touch her.

His hand whispered across her breast, the palm skimming her nipple and turning it hard with one faint touch. His hand continued to skim over her flesh, touching so lightly it felt like a feather being brushed over her and she shivered when she felt his fingers brush between her legs.

Her hips rose up when his hand disappeared between her legs and his fingers slipped into her.

"You are ready for me," he said and as she opened her mouth to respond, he settled his lips over hers and plunged his tongue into her mouth at the same moment his fingers plunged into her again.

She gasped and soon found her tongue in a frenzy dance with his and it was not long before she felt herself ready to climax and she pushed at his chest, wanting to let him know so that he could slip inside her, but he paid her no heed. She pushed again, feeling herself getting ever closer and closer and his only response was to brush his thumb over the nub buried in the triangle of her sun-colored hair. Her passion almost exploded and if he touched her again like that she would.

He did and she groaned against his mouth as she exploded in a blinding release.

His mouth was off her in an instant and he slipped over and into her in one easy motion. He drove into her as her tingles were rushing through her and when she thought they would fade they came to life again and she found herself near the edge once more.

"This time you come with me," Wrath ordered as he dropped down over her, his hands braced on each side of her head as he slammed against her in a steady and rapid motion. She screamed out so loud that she feared the whole village would hear her, but he dropped his mouth on hers, capturing most of it. And his groan joined hers as he joined with her in a climax so powerful it left them both breathless.

Wrath reluctantly slipped off her, knowing his limp body made it even harder for her to breathe and he lay next to her, his hand reaching out to take hold of hers.

She closed her hand around his as tight as she could, but she was so spent, she barely had any strength left in her. When she was finally able to calm her breathing she said, "I like losing my breath that way much better than in my vision."

Wrath waited until he heard her breathing calm completely, then he turned on his side to face her and drew the blanket up over them to their waists. "Tell me what happened."

His voice held a demand, but it also held concern and, besides, Verity was pleased he wanted to know, wanted her to share it with him. It made her feel not so alone.

She explained it all to him, from waking in an unfamiliar forest, to coming face-to-face with Ulric and what he had said to her. "I felt a powerful hand cover mine and I thought I heard you whisper, "Fight.""

"I did whisper it to you and I placed my hand over yours where you were gripping your neck. It was the only way I could think of to help you."

Her eyes widened. "You broke through my vision and helped me." Tears gathered in her eyes. "I was not alone. For the first time ever, I was not alone in my vision." She threw her arms around him and pressed her face to his chest as she hugged him tight.

Wrath's arms circled her and he thought his heart would break as she wept against him, her tears falling on his chest. He had never given thought to how she must have felt when caught in a vision, alone and isolated with no one to help her. And to hide her visions all those years for fear of being discovered, he did not know where she had found the courage.

He eased her gently away from him and onto her back. "Listen well to me, wife," —he wiped away her tears with his thumb as he loomed over her— "you are no longer alone. You have me. You belong to me. You will never be alone again and you will never be alone in your visions again. I will be there with you—always."

Verity burst into tears again.

Wrath slipped his arms beneath her and pulled her close. How this woman had worked her way into his heart he would never know, but she had and surprisingly he was glad she had. He did not want to think of a day where he would never see her lovely smile. He did not want to think of a day without her by his side. He did not want to think of his sleeping pallet without her in it.

He eased her away from him again and once again wiped away her tears. "I do not know how I have come to care so deeply for you, but I have." He shook his head. "It makes no sense."

Verity pressed her hand to his cheek. "It made no sense to me that I should care so strongly for a man I only met until I realized I knew you long before we met."

His brow narrowed in question. "How can that be?"

"I met you in my visions. You frightened me at first, but I came to see that you would help me and that you were kinder than I first thought. You always protected me in the visions I have had of you and since we met you have not failed to do so, not even in my vision."

"I failed to protect you from Lars and you have the wounds to prove it." He winced. "I should have been gentler with you. I gave no thought to them when we coupled."

"You saved me from a far worse fate with Lars and I felt no pain when we coupled, only pleasure." She could not stop the yawn that rushed out of her.

Wrath took hold of her hand and kissed her palm. "Another thing I failed to realize, how tired visions make you, besides coupling twice and suffering a beating." He winced again, thinking of all she had been through. "You will sleep. We must leave at first light and we will take the direct path to the stronghold. King Talon must be told, without delay, of what you have seen. And Lars will be made to reveal the truth."

Verity yawned again, tiredness creeping up on her, as she said, "He would die before betraying Ulric."

"He wishes to speak to the King. He must have something to tell him," Wrath said, pulling the blanket over them before tucking Verity in the crook of his arm to keep her snug against him.

"I do not understand why Lars said that. He would never reveal anything to the King."

Wrath sprung up out of bed, cursing and reached for his garments. "He has no intentions of speaking to the King. His intention was to survive until he could be rescued." He grabbed his cloak and turned to his wife. "Your vision showed Lars sitting next to Ulric. It foretold of his escape. I will see that a warrior stands guard at this door. Do not open it for anyone but me."

As soon as the door closed, Verity scrambled off the sleeping pallet and winced against the pain in her shoulder as she rushed into her garments, wanting to be prepared for whatever may happen. And part of her worried that Lars would attempt to abduct her once again.

Moments later, the door flew open and Wrath entered with a rush of cold air. "Good, you are clothed."

He reached out to her and she took hold of his hand. He hurried her against him and the anger that glared in his dark eyes confirmed what she feared before her husband spoke.

"Lars has escaped.

Chapter Twenty-five

No sun rose with the dawn just bleak sky and with the escaped Northman still at large, it was a solemn troop that left the Imray Tribe. Dalmeny suggested that a troop of his warriors accompany Wrath for added protection. Wrath refused the offer. It was bad enough Lars had managed to escape his men, but for him to return to the stronghold with support from another tribe would be an insult to the King's warriors. An insult the King would not take lightly.

"Lars and those who helped free him will not attack us," Verity said, after watching how her husband kept intense focus on their surroundings since leaving the Imray village some time ago. "Ulric sent them here on a mission and that is what they will see done."

"Then why try to abduct you?" Wrath asked, keeping a firm arm around his wife's waist. She had barely slept last night with all that had gone on and he was hoping she would sleep in his arms as they traveled. She needed the rest to recover from her vision and from the beating she had taken from Lars. His anger flared and grew every time he looked upon her bruised face and he thought about how Lars had gotten away before he could take his revenge.

"Fear of my visions helping you rather than Ulric would be my guess, though whatever the reason it would seem their mission was more important or else Lars would have attempted to abduct me again."

"Their mission is in jeopardy now that we know they are here among us. And it will be difficult for Ulric to explain why Northmen are here on Pict soil without permission of the King."

"Ulric is no fool. I have seen him explain away things that other men are punished for and often severely."

"His father is an important chieftain and Ulric his only son. He will protect him at all costs," Wrath said.

"Even if he starts a war with the Picts?" Verity asked.

They both turned quiet as Minn approached on her horse.

Minn ignored Verity, keeping her eyes on Wrath. "I remember you telling me that you would never wed, a wife being too much of a distraction to your duties. It seemed your concern was proven accurate last night. The Wrath I knew would have guarded the prisoner himself to make certain he did not escape. And the Wrath I knew would have easily dispensed of the men who helped the Northman escape." Her eyes fired with anger. "I never expected the mighty Wrath to turn weak over a woman."

"And I never expected the courageous Minn to show jealousy." Wrath raised his hand as she went to argue. "Hold your tongue, Minn, I am not finished. It was the Imray warriors who allowed the enemy to slip past them and—"

"And your two warriors who failed—"

"To realize the Imray were not capable of defending their home against a Northman *my* warriors captured." Again he held his hand up to silence a simmering Minn, her neck and cheeks glowing bright red. "And was it not you who failed to notify your chieftain that a stranger, an old man you believed presented no problem, had entered the village? Was that not a duty of yours? The King will want to know all that took place and I will not fail to tell him *everything*. And as for my wife being a distraction—I was wrong. A good wife does not distract. She makes her husband stronger than ever. You should find a good husband, Minn, and let him do for you what Verity has done for me."

"She made you a fool," Minn snarled.

"Jealousy does not suit you, Minn."

Her chin shot up. "I am not jealous. I see the truth while you do not." She turned her horse away and rode off before Wrath could respond.

Verity turned soft, questioning eyes on him. "Do I distract you?"

"All the time." He laughed and she playfully punched him in the chest.

"You distract me," she said, the hand that had punched him now pressed gently against his chest. "My thoughts linger far too often on you and not on concern for Hemera."

"Trust me. Hemera is safe with the Wyse. She is better off being with them than wandering this land alone in search of you. You will be reunited. You saw it yourself."

They both were distracted by Tilden riding toward them.

He reined in his horse beside Wrath. "No signs that anyone is following us have been found in any direction."

"Keep the men alert," Wrath ordered. "I will not have us caught unaware again."

Verity found her eyes closing as her husband and Tilden continued talking. After her head bobbed once, she rested it on Wrath's shoulder and it was not long after that she fell asleep.

Wrath was glad his wife finally stopped fighting her fatigue and slept. She needed rest, having gotten barely any last night, and hopefully it would be a good rest and not a brief one.

He continued speaking with Tilden, making certain all was being seen to as it should be and that they remained alert to any possible problems. Once that was done, Tilden took off to see to his duties.

Minn approached him again and he was quick to say, "I will not listen to you disparage me or my wife again. So unless you have something useful to say to me, be gone."

She did not leave. "I was thinking of the escaped Northman. How is it he speaks our language so well that he sounds born to it?"

"The Northmen have been trading with the Picts for a long time. They have come to know our language as many of the Picts in the north have come to know theirs."

"That would explain it, but what of his arrival before you and Verity? Do not tell me that you have not wondered what reason he had for stopping at my village. I do not believe it was simply to seek shelter," she said troubled by her thought.

"I have thought the same and some of the possibilities disturb me."

Minn nodded. "They disturb me as well. Word spreads about those who feel King Talon is not fit to rule. I fear the Northmen may be searching for the discontent among us."

"Or there is someone who has invited the Northmen here to help him seize power from the King."

"I do not want to believe a Pict would betray his people, but I have seen how greed and power can entice. It is why I pledged my fealty to King Talon. He fought hard to unite the Picts under one rule and chase foreigners from our shores. He is an honest man and sees that the people are provided for and are well-protected."

"Does everyone in your tribe feel that way?" Wrath asked.

"It is not easy to take various tribes and bring them together as one. There are those who miss their tribes and their ways, but do their best to adapt. Others adapted easily, understanding there was nothing for them to return to, and others cling so tightly to the past, I wonder if they will ever let go. Dalmeny does not have it easy being chieftain of a mixed tribe."

"You have not answered me," Wrath said.

With an annoyed shake of her head, she said, "There are some who speak out against the King. Some try to blame him for the loss of their tribe, but all know that is not true. If anything, King Talon saved the tribes from complete extinction and he set a rule down when the Imray Tribe was born. He ordered that the history of the various tribes that became the Imray be told again and again so that they are never forgotten. I never grow tired of hearing them, for the ceremony ends with the telling of how the Imray was born."

"Then there are none you feel would betray the King?"

"I cannot say for sure, for I have seen wise people do the most foolish things," Minn said, grinning at him.

"You are right, for I have seen the same," Wrath said, turning a smile on her as well.

Minn nodded at Verity. "I still think she is too weak for one as strong as you."

"If you give Verity a chance, you will find she is more courageous than the two of us."

Minn snorted as she laughed. "I doubt that."

"Your loss," Wrath said with a shrug.

"Dalmeny will be extra vigilant since the incident with the Northman. He will trust few and watch all and send word to me if he thinks it necessary."

Their talk soon turned to memories they had shared and Wrath was glad that they could talk as good friends once again.

Minn left his side to speak with some of the other warriors she was familiar with and Wrath was content to be left with his sleeping wife. He gazed down on her lovely face for a moment. It surprised him how deeply he actually cared for her. He had been so busy fighting battles and protecting the King that he had had no time for much of anything else. That had changed when Verity entered his life and surprisingly he favored the change. There was a comfort with her that he had not known with other women. And mating with her had brought him more pleasure than he had thought possible.

Verity had not only stolen his heart, but his good sense as well. He had to smile at the thought, though also be careful of it. He was leader of the King's personal guard and that came before everything else. Would she understand that and was it fair of him to expect her to?

Fair or not, she belonged to him now and he had no intentions of letting her go, another surprise to him, but one he had no difficulty accepting.

He shook himself out of his reverie, having lingered too long in his thoughts. He needed to remain focused on his surroundings. He was not of the same opinion as Verity when it came to the Northmen not attacking them. They were a vicious group that could not be trusted. Besides, it continued to worry him that he did not know how many Northmen were here on Pict soil.

Wrath altered the path they took home, avoiding any tribes, knowing if they stopped it would delay their journey home. He did, however, intend to send a warrior to each tribe to inform nearby tribes that Northmen had been discovered in the area, and they should remain vigilant and take extra precautions.

The sky grew darker with clouds and by the time they stopped for the evening a light snow was falling. Fires were started and a small lean-to was erected for Verity and Wrath.

When she objected, telling Wrath she needed no special treatment, he made it clear that he thought otherwise.

"You are still healing from all you have suffered." His hand went to her neck to gently touch along the area where a rope had left its mark. It was healing nicely, though Wrath was concerned it might not completely fade and she would be left with a reminder of her time spent with the Northmen. His hand moved to her cheeks where the bruises were still fresh upon her and it made him wonder how the wound at her side faired. "I will not see you suffer more."

Verity could see that he was still upset that he had not gotten to her fast enough and nothing she said would change that, so she let it be. And later, she was grateful for the lean-to, since the snow continued to fall, though not on her and Wrath.

They woke to gray skies that continued to follow them home as well as a flourish of flurries now and again, almost as if the sky could not make up its mind whether it should snow or not.

Wrath had them push through to the stronghold on the last part of their journey, having them arrive home well after it had grown dark. No one complained, since all were eager to reach home.

He was not surprised to see Broc waiting just inside the gates. He surmised the King would want to speak with him upon his arrival. He would want Wrath to report on his journey and there was much to tell him and much to explain to him about Verity and her visions.

Tilden stepped forward, without being ordered, to escort Verity to their dwelling.

Wrath slipped his arm around her and brushed a kiss across her brow. "Go rest. The journey has been a long one."

While Wrath would have liked his wife to be awake and waiting for him when he joined her, from the slump of her shoulders and her large yawn as she walked away, he did not think that would be likely.

Wrath entered the feasting hall to find it empty except for King Talon. He sat at a table close to the fire pit. He looked deep in thought, staring into the vessel clutched in his hands. He spoke to him as a friend, not a King when he said, "What troubles you, Talon?"

The King kept his eyes on the vessel in his hands as he said, "I will hear all about your journey."

"Aye, my King," Wrath said, hearing the command of his King, not the voice of his friend. "First, let me tell you about Verity."

The King listened as Wrath told him about Verity's visions, detailing some of them, and how they had warned about things that were yet to be. He went on to explain how Ulric accused her of trying to kill him so that he could have her imprisoned and make use of her skills, hence the red mark around her neck from the rope he kept on her.

"Ulric wastes his time if he thinks that I would turn over one of my own people to him, especially a seer. She could be helpful to us in many ways. Does anyone else know of her skills?"

"No. I thought you should know before anyone else."

"Others will find out soon enough, especially with her visions coming on her without notice," the King said. "I will speak with her after she is well rested."

"There is more you need to know," Wrath said and went on to tell him about the two Northmen they had come across. He did not like having to tell the King how the Northman Lars had not only beaten Verity before he could reach her, but that he also had escaped him. "I saw to my wife before the prisoner," he admitted.

"Pict warriors were there as well, they should have made sure the prisoner remained secured as well as Dalmeny's warriors. There is no excuse for this to have happened," King Talon said annoyed, "though I will hold you responsible for it."

"And rightly so," Wrath said. "There is more."

"Good or bad?" King Talon demanded, "since bad is the only news I am receiving of late."

Wrath did not confirm either, he continued speaking, "Verity made me aware that the Northmen warriors who had been found here resembled more Pict than Northmen and they spoke our language as if born to it."

"They blend with our tribes," the King was quick to say. "Ulric plots something."

"That is my thought as well," Wrath said, watching the King as he turned silent, lost in his thoughts. Talon already had surmised something about the situation. Wrath had never met anyone whose mind was as quick as Talon's. He could pull various pieces together and make sense of them long before they fit properly.

"Either the Northmen heard of the unrest among some of the Picts and approached them and offered their help in removing me from the throne or the person who leads those against me approached the Northmen for help." The King shook his head. "A foolish choice since

I believe it is Ulric who is involved with this and that he wishes to show his people that he is stronger and more fearless than his father. Ulric would never let the fool Pict take the throne. He would claim the Pict land for the Northmen and unseat his father. The attacks that have taken place so far, especially the one on the Raban Tribe were to make me look weak to the people."

"Then their attempt failed," Wrath said. "The Raban thought even more highly of you, their King, when you arrived with your warriors and saw to helping them and leaving the warriors to protect them."

"For now, but more attacks will follow. There is no telling how many Northmen are already here, especially if they hide within some of our own tribes. How does Egot do? Has he kept watch on who has entered his tribe?"

"Egot has grown lazy in leading his tribe. It appears that Vard shows more leadership than Egot does. Dalmeny has even complained that Egot has gotten lazy in keeping his tribe protected, which leaves his tribe vulnerable, since the Imray Tribe borders the Ancrum Tribe. The Kerse warriors are also concerned and looking for answers when we met them while on their way to deliver a Northman to you and also to speak with you. One thing I do know for sure is that trouble stirs in that region as does worry and it is not far from the stronghold."

"Do you have any thoughts on who might be the one who leads this revolt against me?"

"Vard comes to mind, since I believe he is keeping things from Egot, who does not see what goes on in his own tribe. He is too busy fighting with his wife, Ethra. Vard also had been seen speaking with a tall stranger in the woods. Egot sent him to the Raban Tribe to offer them help."

"Vard is not a leader, he follows. It is someone much stronger, someone with a thirst for power or perhaps revenge. I must think on this."

Wrath reached out to grab the large vessel when the King went to take it and pour himself more wine.

"Leave it, Wrath, we sit here as friends now not King and servant," Talon said and poured himself wine. "Have you discovered where Verity's sister might be?"

"I believe so," Wrath said and explained what had happened when he followed Verity through the door.

"Anin would know if Verity's sister is with the Wyse. As soon as she and Paine return, we can find out for certain."

"I have no doubt she is. Her sister left her cloak as a sign so that Verity would know she was safe and she was not to worry, though she will continue to worry until she and her sister are reunited."

"Tell me how it goes with your wife." Talon smiled when after a few moments Wrath had not responded. "She has left you speechless?"

"She has done more than that," Wrath said and refilled his vessel.

"You finally realized you care for her?" King Talon asked. "I was wondering how long it would take you to surrender."

"I did not surrender," Wrath said and downed a good portion of wine.

King Talon laughed. "Wait until Paine learns of your capitulation."

Wrath cringed. "Wait until you lose your heart." He shook his head angry with himself for not thinking before he spoke and for his words wiping the laugh from Talon's face. "I am sorry, Talon. You deserve better than to be stuck with a woman whose chief task is to bear you an heir."

277

"It does not matter, my friend. There is no woman who can match my unquenchable thirst for mating or could tolerate my temper. It is better I marry out of duty than to condemn a woman to such a harsh union."

"When will the future queen arrive?" Wrath asked.

"Not soon enough," Talon said as he stared down at the wine in his vessel. "I received troubling news earlier that no doubt will have spread through the village by the morrow and will soon spread across the land. My second wife, who I arranged a good marriage for when ours ended, is now with child."

Wrath did not know what to say, though he thought what most everyone else would think upon hearing it, that the King was incapable of fathering a bairn. How then could Pict rule survive? This was not good for the King and would only serve to help his enemies.

"Go and be with your wife. We will talk again on the morrow."

Wrath did as his King ordered, for it was no longer his friend speaking to him.

Wrath took quick steps to his dwelling, entering quietly in case she was asleep and was disappointed to find she was. He would not wake her, though his need for her had grown with each step he had taken. She was tired and there were her bruises to consider. He slipped out of his garments and when he went to slip in beside her, he realized she was not asleep.

She was in the throes of another vision.

Chapter Twenty-six

Verity stood frozen from where she watched in the woods, unable to move. Her legs felt like they were encased in a block of ice rather than the minor snowdrift she stood in. She struggled to free herself and the more she struggled with no success, the more her worry grew. She heard shouts and the thunder of horses' hooves as they pounded the ground.

"Find them!"

Verity felt an icy shiver run through her. She recognized the voice. It was Ulric. Was he after her and Hemera? But where was Hemera? She turned her head, searching the woods around her, hoping to spot her sister. She did not see her and her worry soared as she struggled again to break free.

Ulric was getting closer, his shouts growing louder. She had to get away, she had to.

Wrath had no choice but to throw his leg over her two to keep them from thrashing wildly about. Her actions alarmed him. She had always lain still, not moving, looking almost as if death had claimed her when in a vision. It had been a cause of much worry for him, but now with the way she was thrashing about, he feared she was fighting someone. He had helped her before in one of her visions, but he was not sure how he could help her now.

Verity heard rustling behind her. Was someone approaching? She swung her body around as far as possible, trying to see and almost fell over. Her fear grew. Was it an animal scurrying about or one of Ulric's warriors? Or was it Ulric himself? She had to break free. She had to get away from whoever was behind her.

Wrath spoke to her as he did when other visions had struck her. "I am here, Verity. I am with you. You are not alone." She suddenly stilled and he kept talking to her, reassuring her that he would stay with her. "I will stay with you. I will let nothing harm you."

Verity stopped her struggling when a whisper tickled at her ear. "You are not alone." It was Wrath; he was with her. But how did she get back to him? How did she break free of this vision? She recalled what Wrath had once said to her. "The visions warn." What was she being warned of in this vision?

The crunch of snow grew louder behind her. Someone was getting closer, much closer. She shivered when she felt a brush of someone's warm breath upon her neck. Her eyes widened like full moons and she gasped when a hand reached around in front her. Before it could grab hold of her, she shoved with all her might against the snow that encased her feet.

Wrath was about to clamp down on her legs as she tried to break free once more, when the thought hit him that instead of helping her, he was hampering her by keeping her legs locked still. He threw his leg off her and set her legs free.

*Verity broke out of the snow and ran, fingers brushing her shoulder as the hand tried to grab her. She took only a few steps...*when her eyes fly open and she let out a loud gasp.

Wrath wanted to grab her and hug her close and calm her fears, but with her gasping for air, he let her be.

It was not long before she rolled on her side and into his arms, pressing herself as close as she possibly could against him. She wanted nothing more than to lay there in the protection of his powerful arms. She would have to tell him about the vision, since she believed she understood what it was trying to tell her, but for now she wanted only the shelter of his arms.

Wrath did not care if these visions warned of things to come. He would prefer she not have them. He continued to hold her and continued to remain silent while her breathing eased and her body lost its tautness.

It was a while before Wrath felt her at ease enough to speak with her. "You must be exhausted with this vision following so closely on the last one. Has this happened often to you?"

That he asked about her before inquiring about the vision touched her heart. Her lips brushed his naked chest as she turned her head up to look at him. "My visions increased with time, more so in the last twelve moon cycles and even more so since arriving here. I wish I had more warning before they struck, but the darkness descends and consumes me so quickly that I collapse where I stand." She smiled. "At least this time I was on the sleeping pallet, waiting impatiently for you."

"Were you now?" he asked with a smile of his own. "Waiting impatiently for me?"

She nodded. "I have gotten far too accustomed to sleeping in your arms to find any comfort in an empty sleeping pallet." She turned her head as a yawn rose unexpectedly.

Her words enticed as did her naked body so snug against him that her nipples, hard from brushing against him, poked teasingly at his chest. But her yawn and her body wilting against his had him thinking she needed to rest more than she needed to mate.

"You will sleep well in my arms tonight between the laborious journey and the intense vision. Tell me about it. I am curious, since you are usually so still when in your visions and yet you thrashed about in this one."

281

She should be pleased that he was thoughtful and would have her rest instead of couple. He could be like one of the Northmen she had served. He would force his wife almost every night and complain afterwards that she had not pleased him and force himself on her again later. She had been glad her time with the family had been brief.

"Verity!" he barked and she jumped. "You did not answer me. I thought you were slipping into another vision."

"I was thinking how thoughtful you are."

He barked at her once again. "It is a mistake for you to think that of me."

"Why?"

"I am a warrior and I do what must be done even when it seems unkind. When you see that, and you will see it more often than you will like, you will think differently of me. So it is better if you do not think of me as thoughtful. Now enough talk of something I am not. Tell me of your vision."

Verity did not agree with him, but she did not argue with him. She turned to lie on her back and his arm, around her waist, went with her as she did. She lay quiet a moment before she spoke. "I know what this vision warns of."

Wrath remained silent, waiting for her to continue, though he gave her waist a slight squeeze to remind her that he was there and would not let go of her.

"I was in the woods, I do not know where, and my feet were stuck in a snowdrift. I should have easily been able to get out of it, but it was as though my feet were frozen solid in the snow. I heard horses and voices shouting and I recognized Ulric's voice. He shouted for his men to '*find them.*' I knew he meant Hemera and me. I looked around for Hemera but did not see her. The

282

horses and voices got closer and closer and then I heard a noise behind me. Someone was approaching me, but I could not turn and see who it was. I struggled to break free from the snow, but it was useless. I could feel the breath on my neck of the person behind me. I believe it was Ulric. I fought with all my strength and just as his arm came around in front of me to grab hold, I broke loose." She shivered. "His fingers brushed my shoulder as I got away and was finally released from the vision."

It was not lost to Wrath that he had kept her legs restrained and could have well been the cause of her not being able to move. He said nothing to her, but he would be more vigilant of how he handled her visions from now on.

"What is the warning?" he asked, though he had his own thought on it.

Verity rested her hand on his arm. "That Ulric is unaware that I am at the stronghold and separated from Hemera since he still searches for the both of us as though we were together." She gave his arm a slight squeeze. "It also warns that he is closer to the stronghold than we know since he was about to reach out and touch me."

Wrath thought the same himself. "I must alert the King."

She nodded. "I will wait for you to return."

"I do not know how long I will be. You will sleep and I will hear no arguments about it." He gave her a quick kiss and hurried off the sleeping pallet, though tucked the blanket around her after he did. Then he hastily slipped his garments on and with another warning for her to sleep, he left the dwelling.

Wrath was surprised to find the King still sitting where he had left him. He had thought he would have disturbed him while he was with a woman, since there was not a night he did not have a woman share his sleeping pallet, though they seldom remained the whole night.

"Something is wrong?" King Talon asked when he saw Wrath approach.

"I entered my dwelling to find my wife in the throes of a vision. It seems that Ulric and his men are closer than we thought." Once again he took a seat opposite the King.

"Your wife's vision is accurate. Ulric and his warriors are about four sunrises from here."

"So the Northmen were on Pict soil longer than they let us believe. It is good you sent warriors to track the Northmen as we discussed before I left." His voice turned stern. "Tell me you alerted your personal guard as soon as you found out how close the Northmen were."

"You need to ask when you know I am adamant about rules that I have established being obeyed, especially the ones I set for myself. And that means making certain that my personal guard is kept abreast of any possible danger that may threaten my safety."

"When did you plan on making me aware of this turn of events?"

"I am telling you now," the King said curtly. "More will be discussed when the council meets on the morrow. I continue to wonder if anyone else who has a seat on it intends to betray me as Tarn and Bodu did." The King shook his head. "This cannot go on or the people will lose trust in me and that is what my enemies want, for then they can sway the people to their side. Whoever leads them is no fool and keeps himself well hidden, though I would not be surprised if he was right in the open, declaring his allegiance to me while his minions work in the shadows for him." He shook his head again. "Why are you here when you should be with your wife, mating? The Picts will need more warriors to keep hold of our land and foreigners off our shores. You will have sons as strong as you and perhaps daughters with your wife's skill, both will help secure the Pict nation."

"Only if Verity and I choose to remain wed."

"You have lost your heart to her and you have spilled your seed in her. I knew you would as soon as I advised you against it. Now you are bound to each other, unless... I can undo it if you wish."

"No," Wrath insisted, "and nor will you undo it for Verity if she should ask."

"Why would she ask when she obviously cares deeply for you?"

"She has yet to see the true me."

"I think she has seen more of the true you than you have. Now go to her. The Northmen will not be knocking on our door just yet."

Wrath stood and went to leave, then stopped. "War with the Northmen may be inevitable."

"Not, if I can help it."

The King's words gave Wrath hope, for he knew he would do everything in his power to prevent war with the mighty Northmen.

Wrath purposely kept his steps slow as he made his way back to the dwelling. He wanted to make certain that Verity was asleep before he returned, so he would not be tempted to mate with her. On the morn would be time enough, though his stiff manhood told him otherwise. He might have to see to it himself if he was to get any sleep tonight.

"Your steps are slow for a man who now has a wife to warm his sleeping pallet. Are you not eager to poke her?"

Wrath stopped and turned to see Simca, the woman who had pleasured him many a night. Theirs had always been a mutual joining with no thought of it being anything more. She was far different in appearance than Verity. Her features were sharper, her hair dark, her body full and shapely. He had enjoyed his time with her and he did not think that she would be upset that he took a wife since he had not been the only warrior Simca had coupled with. Yet he had detected an abruptness, bordering anger, in her voice and that he would not tolerate.

"Is that sharpness in your tone for me or because you could not find a warrior to give you a good poke tonight?" he asked his tongue just as biting.

She stepped closer to him. "You gave me the best poke out of them all."

Wrath grabbed her hand as it reached out to slip past his cloak. "You will find another to please you."

"Not one of your skill."

She went to press against him and Wrath pushed her away as he released his hold on her. "My skill pleases only my wife now."

Simca ran her tongue over her lips slowly and drifted closer to him once again. "Does she enjoy the taste of you as much as I do?"

Wrath cursed when he felt himself grow harder, no doubt what Simca intended. Though, the image that her words evoked was not of her. It was of his wife's mouth that pleasured him.

"Enough, Simca," Wrath ordered. "It is my wife I have a need for, not you."

Simca shrugged. "I will be here when you grow tired of her. Or if you miss the taste of my mouth on you." She grinned, turned, and walked away.

This time, he cursed her. She knew all too well what she was doing, then he cursed himself again for not being able to control his body's response. Something he

286

had easily been able to do before meeting Verity. He shook his head and continued walking. He stopped at the door to his dwelling, let out a deep breath, and entered.

Chapter Twenty-seven

Wrath walked over to the sleeping pallet and saw that his wife was sleeping. She was turned on her side facing him and looked so peaceful he almost did not want to climb in beside her and disturb her. He also worried that once he took her in his arm, he would not be able to stop touching her, her lovely body far too tempting.

He disrobed, his eyes remaining on her as he did. The blanket had slipped down, revealing one breast, the nipple so soft that his tongue ached to take hold of it and turn it hard.

With a shake of his head, Wrath sat on the edge of the sleeping pallet. If he joined her now, hard as he was, he would not be able to keep his hands off her. He had only one choice, if he was to leave her alone to get the rest she needed, and that was to pleasure himself. He had not done that of late, since he had always managed to find a willing woman.

Now he simply wanted his wife.

He released another deep breath as he moved his hand to stroke himself. He would hurry and be done with it and join his wife and not bother her with his need. He shut his eyes and the image of her naked, her legs spread wide, ready for him, excited him all the more and he grabbed firm hold of himself.

He was so lost in pleasure that he did not hear Verity stir behind him and sit up, then get up on her knees to peer over his shoulder.

Verity stared for a moment, blinking her eyes to clear the sleep from them. When she saw what her husband was doing, she gently trailed her hand down his arm.

Wrath stilled, feeling his wife's hand slowly move along his arm as she came around from behind him to sit at his side. She gently eased his hand off himself and replaced it with her own, giving his manhood a tender squeeze, then began to stroke him. He shut his eyes for a moment, enjoying her light, teasing touch. It was when she took a stronger hold of him that he knew he could not let it go on for long. And he didn't.

He grabbed her around the waist and hoisted her over his lap, her legs going around him and the muscles in his arms straining as he hovered her over his manhood.

"Slip me inside you."

Verity was only too pleased to reach between her legs, grab hold of his stiff manhood and give it a couple of tugs before rubbing it against her.

"Verity, so help me," he warned with a growl.

She smiled and eased the tip of him inside her.

Once she did that, Wrath yanked her down on his lap, the full length of him disappearing inside her.

She dropped her head back with a gasp, only to raise it and look at him wide-eyed when his hands took firm hold of her bottom, squeezing her cheeks as he brought her up and down on him with a force that had her crying out, not in pain, but with pure pleasure.

She placed her hands on his shoulders holding tight as he continued to bounce her up and down on him, forcing moans and groans of sheer delight from her. She tightened her grip on him as her pleasure grew and she gasped loudly when he suddenly yanked her off him, tossed her back on the sleeping pallet, grabbed her bottom and pulled her to the edge to take hold of her legs and spread them apart, and plunge into her.

She cried out and continued to do so as he slammed into her over and over and over until she screamed out his name as she burst so hard she did not think she would stop coming.

And she didn't. She had no chance to since Wrath continued to plunge into her and as he groaned louder and louder, getting closer and closer to coming, he sparked her passion to life once again and she followed him into another blinding burst of pleasure.

Verity wrapped her arms around his neck as he bent over and slipped his arms around her waist and pulled her up against him, his manhood still snug inside her, then slipped his hands to grip her bottom and holding her firm, he turned and sat on the edge of the sleeping pallet.

She kissed him lightly on the lips. "You please me, husband."

"Not half as much as you do me, wife." Wrath kissed her, though not lightly.

Verity was overcome with happiness and it showed with the smile that sprang to life on her face after the kiss ended, but it was quickly stolen by a large yawn.

"I should not have disturbed your sleep," he said, running a finger gently across her lips, "but I am not sorry you did." A frown suddenly marred his handsome features. "It pains me to say I was wrong, since I am never wrong."

"Wrong about what?" she asked curiously.

"About us mating often." He kissed her lips lightly. "Often is not nearly enough."

She smiled about to agree with him when another yawn stole her words away from her.

"Enough talk, we will sleep now," he ordered abruptly, concerned that he had robbed her of much needed sleep."

Verity was quick to shake her head. "I will not be able to sleep comfortably until you tell me what the King said about my vision."

Wrath would have preferred the news about Ulric to wait, but since she asked, he would not keep it from her. "He was impressed that you saw what he already knew. Ulric and his men are only a few sunrises from the stronghold."

Verity's face paled and she shuddered, and Wrath cursed himself for not waiting until morn to tell her. He stood and hurried her down on the sleeping pallet and joined her, slipping the blanket over them before taking her in his arms.

"You have nothing to fear," Wrath assured her. "You are my wife and I will keep you safe. You are also a Pict. The King will not allow you to be taken from our land."

"Ulric is a cruel man and will stop at nothing to get what he wants."

"It has been a tiring journey, fraught with difficulties. The morrow is time enough to think on all this," Wrath said. "It is time for sleep."

Verity did not argue, she snuggled against her husband, pleased she was safe in his arms. He was right. The morrow was soon enough to think on Ulric. Though, a question followed her into sleep...why was Ulric truly here on Pict soil?

~~~

Wrath walked to the feasting hall under gray skies while an icy chill not only stung his cheeks but

291

threatened more snow. He smiled. More snow meant more time spent in his dwelling with his wife. He had woken early, donned his garments, and was about to leave when she woke.

"Kiss before you go," she had said.

His smile broke into a soft laugh. It had turned into much more. He hurried his steps, eager to eat before the High Council convened.

Wrath entered to see Simca talking with Broc, her hand going from patting his shoulder to caressing his cheek. She had wasted no time in finding another warrior to pleasure her.

"When do I get to speak with the King?"

Wrath turned to Minn standing behind him.

"Forget I was here?"

Wrath grinned. "You are definitely not a woman a man forgets."

Minn smiled. "That tongue of yours pleases in more ways than one."

"Let me introduce you to Broc," Wrath said with a nod toward the warrior.

"Who is the woman who cannot keep her hands off him?"

"That's Simca. She sees to the food preparation."

"It looks like she is about to feast on Broc."

Wrath laughed.

Simca turned a scowl on Wrath as he and Minn approached the table.

A smile quickly replaced her scowl when she turned to Broc. "I will see you later."

Broc did not respond to Simca as she walked away, he looked to Wrath.

Once seated, Wrath said, "This is Minn. She is from the Imray Tribe. She is a skilled warrior and a good friend."

"I am honored to meet you, Minn."

"Watch out for that woman," Minn said with a nod in the direction where Simca had gone. "She cares only for herself."

Broc laughed. "That suits me fine."

Wrath and Minn laughed along with him. The three were soon lost in talk and laughter and enjoyed the hardy fare set out on the table before them. They all stood when King Talon entered the feasting hall from the High Council Chambers, Gelhard at his side.

The King did not look pleased.

"Minn," King Talon said, acknowledging her with a nod, "it is good to see you again."

Minn bobbed her head. "As it is to see you, my King."

"Come, we will talk now. Wrath and Broc will join us," the King commanded and the three followed the King to the High Council Chambers.

Verity entered the feasting hall just as the door to the High Council Chambers closed. Not seeing her husband or anyone else, she assumed the council meeting had started. Wrath had told her, though it was more an order, to linger and not rush to the feasting hall when he left her feeling quite satiated earlier. She did as he had said, at least for a while, stretching sore limbs and enjoying the memories of mating with her husband. Then her insides had begun to grumble, reminding her that it had been some time since she had eaten.

She smiled at the change, not in the feasting hall for it had remained the same as the last time she had been here. It was she who had changed and she was pleased she had. She was not as fearful as she was before, but then the unknown had loomed large in front of her. And she had feared people learning about her visions. Now Wrath knew and she was alone with that burden no

293

more. And best of all, she was wife to the mighty Wrath, a brave warrior she had met in her visions and had lost her heart to.

Her stomach grumbled again and she hurried to a table where bread, quail eggs, and a crock of gruel sat. She stared at the food for a moment, thinking how it was not that long ago when she had been imprisoned by Ulric and given little food to eat or how she had almost starved after arriving on Pict shores and searching for Hemera. Now she had food aplenty, but she still had not been reunited with her sister. She missed Hemera, but she had missed her sister while living with the Northmen as well. They had been kept separate, Hemera having been placed in the chieftain's dwelling and she with a family who worked her day and night. She saw little of Hemera, but once she was moved to another family to serve, closer to the chieftain's dwelling, she got to see her often and it made each day a bit more bearable.

Tears welled in her eyes and she dropped the piece of bread in her hand, her hunger having faded.

"What is wrong?"

Verity jumped at her husband's abrupt tone. She looked to see him hurrying her way and her heart swelled at the sight of him. His handsome face was twisted in anger, which she now understood was actually concern...concern for her. And seeing his powerful strides, the formidable muscles in his chest and arms that strained at the black wool garment he wore, gave her a sense of security. He would keep her safe and he would do the same for Hemera when Verity was finally reunited with her.

Wrath dropped down on the bench beside Verity, his arm circling her waist. "Has someone upset you? Did someone speak ill of you? Do you not feel well? Tell me so I can squeeze the life out of the fool for bringing tears to your eyes."

Verity laid her head on his shoulder, not wanting him to see her tears.

Wrath laid a gentle hand beneath her chin and lifted it, forcing her to meet his eyes. He muttered several oaths while wiping at her tears with his thumb. He kept hold of his anger, saving it to unleash on whoever caused her this suffering.

He kissed her gently. "Tell me, wife."

Verity sniffled back her tears. "I miss my sister. She defended me without hesitation as you do, though she suffered for it."

"I care for your sister already and I will see her kept safe. That I promise you." He wiped the last of her tears away. "Eat and know all will be well."

Voices caught both their attention. The council members entered, talking while making their way to the Council Chamber for the meeting.

Wrath gave a squeeze to her waist and a quick kiss. "Do not wander off. There is an icy chill that stings the flesh. Stay where it is warm and—"

"Go," she said when she felt him hesitate to leave her. "I will see you when you finish."

"Eat," he ordered with a smile as he stood.

"As you wish, husband."

"An obedient wife, how wonderful, now if only I could find one?" He laughed as he hurried away.

Verity found that her appetite had returned and she ate. When she finished, she thought to wait for her husband, but she did not know how long he would be and she did not want to continue to sit and do nothing. She decided a walk through the village would suit her.

She wandered through the village amazed at her freedom to do so. There would be daily chores she would soon have to see to, but they would be done not for someone else, but for her and her husband and eventually their bairns. The thought brought a smile to her face.

Her walk turned even more enjoyable when a couple of women stopped to talk with her. She was being accepted not only as Wrath's wife but into the tribe itself.

She was so pleased to finally be home, finally have a home, finally be a Pict once more.

Bethia approached and Verity stopped to talk with the woman.

Bethia glanced with a frown at her face. "You took a beating. It would seem a few days ago from how the bruises have faded some. Are the ones I see the only ones you have suffered?"

"There is one at my side," Verity said and placed her hand where it was. "But it is fading quickly and causing me no discomfort."

"I can only imagine what Wrath did to the person who dared to raise a hand to his wife."

"He did not get the chance," Verity said, not knowing how much the King would want others to know about the Northman.

"Otherwise all goes well with you and Wrath?"

"All goes quite well," Verity smiled and leaned closer to whisper, "as do my visions."

Bethia smiled as well. "That is good to hear. Secrets are too much of a burden to keep."

They talked a bit more, then Bethia leaned closer and whispered. "Do you know a woman follows you? She does not look familiar."

Verity was glad Bethia confirmed what she suspected. At first she thought it was her own worries that had her thinking someone trailed her, until she spotted the familiar face more than once. "I thought so, though I could not be sure until now."

"Shall I make Wrath aware of it?"

Verity laughed lightly. "He is probably the one who forced the task upon her."

They were about to part when Bethia asked, "Tongues wag about the King's second wife. Is it true?"

Verity found herself shaking her head, wondering what Bethia meant. "I have heard nothing about his second wife."

"There is talk that she, now too, is with child just like his first wife."

"I had not heard that," Verity said.

Bethia said what Verity thought and no doubt what most were thinking. "This does not bode well for the King. I must be off. I have two women who recently gave birth who I must look in on." She smiled and reached out and patted Verity's middle. "Soon you will be growing large with a bairn, having such a potent husband like Wrath."

Verity pressed her hand to her middle and thought how much she wished that was so. She had never thought it would be possible, but now...

She smiled as she walked, enjoying the crisp air that turned her cheeks rosy and made her bruises appear less prominent. She hastened her steps a bit, tucking her cloak closer around her and suddenly ducked around the side of a dwelling. She waited a moment, then popped back around, startling Minn who nearly bumped into her.

"It is your husband's doing," Minn said before Verity could berate her. "He told me I owed him, since it was my fault that idiot abducted you."

"I believe I am safe here in the King's stronghold," Verity assured her.

"I believed I was safe once, then I learned there is truly no place that is safe."

"What happened?' Verity asked as she continued walking, an invitation for Minn to follow, and she did.

"It was when Talon fought to unify the tribes, to bring them together instead of destroying one another and leaving ourselves vulnerable to foreigners. Fighting among the tribes had slowed and Talon was having some success in keeping the tribes from fighting and slaughtering one another. Unfortunately, the Drust was bitterly against the tribes uniting and they went on a rampage, attacking tribes that were in agreement with the unification. My tribe was one of the tribes they slaughtered until not a person was left."

"How horrible for you," Verity said, tears stinging her eyes at her terrible loss.

"Talon went after them, killing those who took part in the attack and destroying much of their village. It is why he supplies them with necessities now, since nothing was left. I know Talon warned that we all had to forgive the blood spilled between us if we, as a people, were to survive, but it is difficult for me to do, so I keep my distance from the Drust and have little to do with them as much as possible."

"Are you the only one left of your tribe?"

"Yes." Minn said and tossed her cloak back over her left shoulder and pushed her sleeve up, holding her left arm out for Verity to see an intricate weave of never-ending, interlocking circles that ran around her wrist.

Verity stared at it, for some reason it looked familiar to her, but she made no mention of it. "Something to pass on to your bairns one day," she said.

"It is a solid, powerful tribe I want my bairns to know, so I will do all I can to make the Imray Tribe a strong one. I also want a King who can keep us from slaughtering one another and foreigners from invading our land, which is why I pledged my fealty to King Talon and will fight beside him whenever necessary."

Shouts caught both their attention and Verity could not help but shiver when I young lad ran past them, shouting, "The executioner has returned!"

Chapter Twenty-eight

Verity and Minn hurried along to the feasting house.

"I am eager to meet Paine's wife," —Minn laughed— "knowing Paine, I wonder who would marry him."

They both stepped back startled by the large man who rushed past them and into the feasting house. Verity barely got a look at him, he flew by her so fast. Though from the angry scowl that marred his fine features and the double-sided battle axe he gripped in his hand made it appear that he was ready to execute someone.

Minn grabbed her arm. "Come on, something is wrong."

Verity hurried alongside her, fighting to keep pace with her strong strides.

They entered just as Paine knocked two of the King's personal guards to the floor, threw open the closed door and entered the High Chamber Council. Minn let go of Verity's arm to hurry to the open door to hear what was going on.

"I need warriors," Paine demanded. "My wife and the woman, Hemera, we brought with us, have vanished in the woods."

Upon hearing her sister's name, Verity pushed her way past Minn and into the High Council Chamber to grab Paine's arm. "Hemera was with you."

Paine glared down at the woman, then looked to her hand that was squeezing his arm tight, as if warning her to release him.

Verity paid him no heed. "Is she well? Where did you find her? How could you lose her? Why did you not take better care of her and your wife?" She realized that she had erred when she finally got a close look at him. His cloak was thrown back and she could see the body markings on his neck that disappeared down beneath his tunic. His hair was cropped short around the sides and back of his head and what was left atop was no more than a thatch of dark hair. His bold green eyes glared with such intensity that she almost took a step back away from him, but her worry for her sister held her firm. Wrath suddenly appeared by her side, easing her hand off Paine and gently pushing her to stand to his side and slightly behind him.

"*My wife*, Verity and Hemera's sister, means no disrespect. She is upset that she has been unable to find Hemera."

"If I was not so upset over my own wife missing, I would find it humorous that you had a wife or perhaps more fitting that you actually found someone who would wed you."

Wrath took a step forward. "I was wed like you and Anin, by decree of the King and given no chance to object."

His words cut Verity like the sharp blade of a knife.

"Not that I object. Verity stole my heart and I care much too deeply for her to ever let her go."

Verity felt her heart swell with joy. That he should announce how he felt about her before so many people, solidified what he had claimed. He would never let her go, and she would never let him go.

"Enough!" King Talon shouted, his fist crashing down on the table. "Tell me what happened, Paine."

Paine walked to stand in front of the King. "Hemera wandered into the Wyse settlement and Anin's grandmother, Esplin, advised her to remain there until it was time for her to leave. The other morn Esplin announced that that time had come and that I should escort Hemera

to the stronghold." He shook his head. "Once we were close I made sure to follow the path where the stronghold sentinels would see us. Esplin warned me that our return journey would not be easy and that I should trust my instincts. When I came upon the first sentinel who guarded the far outskirts of the stronghold and found him dead, I knew our journey home would be fraught with difficulty."

King Talon held up his hand, silencing Paine and turned to Broc. "When did the sentinels in that area change posts?"

"No more than a sunrise ago," Broc said.

King Talon turned once again to Paine and nodded for him to continue.

"The second attack came before we reached the second sentinel, but by then I had sent Anin and Hemera to hide—"

"Hide? Off on their own with no one to help them?" Verity called out as if he had done the most grievous thing.

Paine turned and glared at her once again, though it was a much more annoyed glare. "Bog is with them." He turned to continue speaking with the King.

Verity went to speak again, wondering if this warrior Bog was strong enough to keep two women safe, but Wrath yanked her against him and warned her to remain silent with a strong look and a shake of his head. She wisely held her tongue.

"I assume you dispensed of the troop of warriors since there was no worry for your wife and Hemera?" the King asked.

302

"It did not take me long to see them finished, though it was long enough for Anin, Hemera, and Bog to vanish without a trace." Paine's face tightened in anger. "I told Anin to remain close but out of sight. I searched, but to no avail. I could not find them."

"How are we to find them, if Paine cannot?" Gelhard asked, stepping forward. "And how is it that this troop came upon our sentinel? They hide themselves well enough."

"Not from those they know. Do I assume correctly, Paine, that the troop that attacked you was composed of warriors from various Pict tribes?" the King asked.

Paine nodded. "It is difficult to distinguish your enemy when most are Pict."

"A large troop should be sent immediately to search for the women and for any other culprits who wait out there to do the stronghold harm," Gelhard said.

King Talon's fist came down again on the table only harder this time. "Do you think I cannot keep the stronghold safe, Gelhard?"

Gelhard shook his head. "No, my King, I but advise you."

"Your advice is wrong in this situation. You think with anger, not wisdom. The stronghold is secure, but it will not be if we send a large troop of warriors out in search of two women."

"I do not need a large troop, Wrath will do," Paine said.

Wrath stepped forward to show his eagerness to help Paine, and Verity went with him.

"She will not come with us," Paine said with a nod to Verity as if he knew her thought.

"I will join you in the search," Minn said, walking over to stand near Paine.

"It is good to see you, Minn, and I welcome your help," Paine said.

"I will go too," Verity said, refusing to be left out of the search for her sister.

"No!" Wrath and Paine cried out in unison, and Minn smiled.

"Verity will go with you," the King ordered, and Verity smiled.

"She will be in our way and slow us down," Paine protested.

Wrath agreed with Paine. "Verity is not needed on this mission."

Minn chimed in, "They are right. Verity is not needed and would only be a hindrance rather than help."

"It is done. I will hear no more. Verity goes with you." King Talon ordered. He looked around the room at all there. "Go and see to your tasks and continue preparation for the Northmen's arrival, and, Broc, a word before you go. And the lot of you will stay," he said to the four in front of him as he walked past them.

Paine kept his voice low as he turned to Wrath. "You have your wife beside you. I want mine beside me."

"I will see that we both return to the stronghold with our wives by our sides," Wrath assured him.

"Is she a good wife?" Paine asked with a nod at Verity.

"Since I know the both of you well, I take pity on the two women for being stuck with such poor excuses for husbands," Minn said.

Verity listened to what some would think was an insulting exchange of words between the three, but Verity heard differently. The three were friends who had been through troubling times together and had become stronger friends along the way. She envied them their friendship. And though her husband had said nothing to her about going with them, she could tell by the pinch of his brow that he was not pleased about it.

"We can waste no more time. We must leave now," Paine said as the King approached and Broc left the room.

"Paine, you said that most of the warriors that attacked you were Picts," the King said as he stopped in front of him. "Does that mean some appeared foreign to you?"

Paine nodded. "Two had no body drawings. I looked to see but there were none. The others were from various tribes."

"If there is time, Verity will see if she recognizes them as Northmen." King Talon turned to Wrath. "And perhaps she will be able to tell us something else while on the search."

That the King alluded to Verity's visions annoyed Wrath. Searching for Hemera and Anin was no time for Verity to have a vision. He would have to make certain she remained close by. There was something else disturbing Wrath, but he needed Minn and Verity gone to speak his mind.

Paine seemed to be of the same thought. "We have no more time to waste. "Minn, go and have the horses made ready." He looked to Wrath.

Wrath was about to tell Verity to make herself ready to leave when a sharp rap sounded at the door.

Annoyed at being disturbed, the King called out sharply, "Who disturbs my meeting?"

One of the guards outside the door responded, telling the King that one of their warriors had arrived with important news.

The King bid him to enter.

When Wrath saw that it was Corbin, the warrior he had sent to follow Vard, he was eager to hear what news he brought. And he saw that Verity was as well, her eyes brightening.

The warrior bobbed his head after stopping in front of the King. "I followed Vard as Wrath bid me to do and he never went to the Raban Tribe, he went to join a small group of Picts camped in the woods. He remained there until a Drust warrior arrived and they all took their leave together. I followed for another day and they appeared to be headed north."

"Go feast and drink, Corbin. You have done well," the King said.

Wrath spoke after the warrior was gone. "Someone is amassing troops for an uprising."

Minn shook her head. "I would have never suspected Vard to be part of such a traitorous plan."

Verity addressed Paine. "Please tell me that this Bog who is with my sister and your wife can keep them safe."

"Bog is a wolf and he has saved me more than once from predators."

Verity stared at him, not knowing what to say. "How could a lone wolf protect two women?"

"Bog has been protective of your sister since meeting her. He will keep her safe as well as Anin," Paine assured her, then looked to the King. "We waste time."

"More than you know," King Talon said. "Ulric and some of his Northmen will arrive here in a few sunrises."

"We leave now," Paine ordered just as another hard rap sounded at the door.

Before a response could be given, Gelhard rushed in and looked to Paine. "Your wolf has been heard."

306

While all rushed out of the High Chambers, the King silently gestured for Gelhard to remain behind.

Bog's lone wail sent shivers through everyone more than the bite of the frosty air, and Paine felt it more than anyone. The wolf was beckoning him, letting him know he was nearby and as soon as he left the stronghold, Paine followed the continuous wail through the woods.

Minn was surprised that Verity kept pace with them, but then she herself would have run until there was no breath left in her if she could reunite with family.

Verity ignored the ache in her legs and the pain that stung at her side as she hurried alongside her husband. He turned his head her way several times, though said nothing. He was keeping watch over her, knowing how important it was for her to finally get to her sister and see that she was safe.

Tuahna. That was what she felt for him deep in her heart. It gripped tight and would not let go and she did not want it to. They were one and always would be. All she needed now was to be reunited with her sister and all would be well.

She kept glancing about, searching, hoping she would see her sister. When two figures came into view a distance ahead, she almost stumbled, but Wrath's hand shot out, grabbing hold of her arm and steadying her. It appeared as if one was trying to support the weight of the other as they stumbled along.

When the hood fell off the one woman, Verity almost shouted out with joy. No hood could ever contain her sister's red, wild curls that sprung out from around her head and fell well past her shoulders and down her back.

"Anin!" Paine shouted and ran straight for the woman Hemera was supporting.

307

Donna Fletcher

Verity was so overjoyed to see her sister that it propelled her past Minn and Paine before her husband could stop her, but she was brought to an abrupt halt just before she reached Hemera by a large, black wolf who jumped in front of her snarling, warning her away.

"Call Bog off, Paine," Wrath shouted, familiar with Bog's protective nature for those he deemed part of his pack.

It was Hemera who the growling wolf responded to. "It is all right, Bog. Verity is good. She will keep us safe."

The wolf moved aside just as Paine hurried past them both to scoop his wife up in his arms.

Verity paid them no heed. She hurried to Hemera and they flung their arms around each other, hugging tight, and letting happy tears fall. Talk would be saved for later when they were alone. At the moment, they wanted only to hold on to each other and not let go.

Paine ignored the sisters' reunion and looked at his wife, then at her slightly rounded stomach, then back at her. "The wee bairn?"

"Is well," she said with a soft smile. "It is my leg. I gave it a twist when walking, but thankfully Hemera was quick and prevented my fall and has been helping me ever since."

Wrath and Minn approached, turning their back to the couples as they kept a watchful eye all around them.

"What happened? What kept Bog from responding to my summons?" Paine asked, pressing his wife close to him, needing to feel her warmth and smell deeply of the rich scent of pine in her hair that she had got last night from the sleeping pallet he had made out of pine branches for them.

Anin kept her voice low. "We spotted two men and Hemera recognized them as Northmen. We hid, not

308

knowing if there was more lurking about, possibly setting a trap, so we purposely kept our distance from you. I was relieved when you summoned Bog and I knew all was well. We took hasty steps to get to the stronghold and alert the King, thinking we would find you along the way. That is when I twisted my leg and Hemera was burdened with my weight."

"You are no burden and Hemera is a fit woman, though I owe her much for helping you."

"We should go," Paine and Hemera said in unison.

"Danger lurks about," Hemera said with a shiver and took hold of Verity's hand and gave it a squeeze.

Wrath was pleased to see Tilden arrive, leading a troop of warriors. He made the decision not to take the chance and have his wife look at the dead Northmen. Instead, he saw them all escorted back to the stronghold, the warriors having circled them at Tilden's command to keep them protected. The young warrior would make a fine addition to the King's personal guard.

Once past the stronghold gates, Paine took Anin to their dwelling to tend her leg, though Bethia was sure to arrive once she heard what happened.

Wrath knew Verity would want time with her sister, but he also knew the King would not permit it until he spoke with both of them first. So he was surprised when Tilden told him that King Talon would speak with them later.

He escorted his wife and her sister to their dwelling, their clasped hands remaining tight as if they feared they would lose each other if they let go. A pang of jealousy struck him. While he was pleased his wife was happy, he also realized that he would no longer have Verity to himself. He would have to share her with Hemera. And where would she stay? There was no room in his dwelling.

309

Without letting go of her sister's hand, Verity stretched her other hand out to him and he took it, locking his hand around hers tightly.

"Could you give us some time to talk?" she asked, remnants of her tears still shining in her eyes.

He hesitated, annoyed that she had not introduced him as her husband, but held his tongue and gave a sharp nod. "I will return later."

"Promise?" she whispered softly.

Her whisper drifted around him like a longing only he could satisfy and chased away his annoyance. "Promise," he murmured and kissed her hand. He looked past her to Hemera, and it struck him how different her features were from her sister's. "Welcome home, Hemera."

She stared at him a moment before responding with only a nod.

Wrath left them alone and walked toward the feasting house. He was relieved the hunt for Hemera had finally come to an end. It freed him to think on other things like questions some of the King's remarks had stirred in him.

Something was brewing and Wrath intended to find out what it was.

He entered the feasting hall. It was empty and there was not one of the King's personal guards in sight. Had the King left the feasting hall? He went to the High Council Chambers and found that empty as well.

It was odd that the King would not be here. He should be waiting to hear from him and Paine and to speak with Hemera before anyone else did. Why was he not here?

Wrath was about to leave when he heard a noise on the second floor. He did not hesitate, he hurried up the stairs and heard hushed voices coming from the small room a short distance from the King's sleeping chambers. Worried the King might be in danger, he threw open the door.

Chapter Twenty-nine

Wrath stared at Vard standing not far from the King. Instinct would have had him jumping in front of the King to protect him, but something warned him against it.

"You enter my private chambers without making yourself known?" the King demanded, a glint of anger flaring in his eyes.

Wrath retaliated with a spark of anger of his own. "You leave me no choice when I find not one of your personal guards lurking about yet hear voices coming from your private chambers. You made me responsible for your safety and I will do whatever is necessary to do my duty, especially when you do something foolish like dismissing your personal guard."

Vard stepped back away from the pair as the King took a hasty step toward Wrath.

"You are fortunate I call you friend," the King said, stepping so close to Wrath that their bodies almost touched.

Wrath planted his face near on top of the King's. "You are fortunate to have me as a friend and one who speaks so honestly to you. Now I will take my leave and post two of your personal guard outside the door. And I warn you...do not dismiss them again. They have been trained to see only what you wish them to see." He turned and went to the door.

"Wrath!"

His sharp command had Wrath turning around.

"Stay. It is time for you to hear the truth," the King ordered.

~~~

A rap at the door sounded just as the sisters were about to sit on the sleeping pallet to talk.

"Make yourself known," Verity said as she went to the door.

"It is Minn."

Verity hesitated for a moment, recalling what happened the last time she had opened the door for the woman.

"I have brought a hot brew," Minn said as if she instinctively knew what Verity was thinking.

Verity opened the door.

Minn handed her a flagon, a cloth wrapped around it and two vessels. "To warm up your sister."

Verity got the sense that it was more a peace offering than it was for her sister and she appreciated Minn's effort in offering it. "I am grateful, Minn."

Minn nodded and walked off, Verity watching her go. Her heart went out to the woman. She had come close to never seeing her sister again and the possibility had filled her with dread. Minn lived with the pain of losing not only one member of her family, but her whole tribe every day and there was nothing that would change that.

Verity shut the door and returned to her sister, filling the two tankards with an inviting scented brew.

Hemera reached out eagerly for the tankard her sister handed her, wrapping her hands around it and sipping at the steamy brew.

"Are you hungry?" Verity asked, silently admonishing herself for not thinking of asking sooner.

Hemera shook her head, her flaming red curls bouncing as she did. Her eyes, bright green from her tears, searched the room with curiosity.

Verity waited, not bothered by her sister's silence. Hemera did not speak without thinking on her words first and rarely did she respond quickly to anyone. Some believed her slow, but Verity believed her sister wiser than most.

"Is this your home now?" Hemera asked, turning to Verity.

Verity nodded. "The King wed me to Wrath, though he left it to the both of us if we wished to commit or end the union once we found you and all was settled." Hemera did not respond and feeling a sudden guilt stab at her, she said, "We can be safe here, have a home here, be free here. Wrath is a good man and the people generous." She lowered her voice. "The King frightens me. His power overwhelms, but he will see us kept safe."

Hemera looked around again, saying as she did, "It is a fine home." She turned to look directly at her sister. "There are Northmen here. "I saw them. They have come for us."

Verity shivered, Hemera's words sounding as though she declared it so and nothing could change it.

Hemera shook her head as if questioning her own words. "But how do Northmen walk on Pict soil without being discovered?"

~~~

King Talon half sat on the edge of the narrow table in his private chambers, his arms folded across his chest, and looked to Wrath. "I knew there would be those who would continue to oppose the Unification of the Tribes even after it was settled. After Tarn and Bodu's betrayal, I realized that opposition to the unification went much deeper than I had anticipated and I looked to those I had planted in various tribes to alert me to any suspicious behavior. Egot never grew lazy in ruling the Ancrum Tribe. When he discovered some of his tribe were speaking ill of their King, he went to Vard, the warrior I had planted there, and they formed a plan to discover who was behind it." The King nodded to Vard to speak.

"I knew nothing about the attack on the Raban Tribe until you told me nor did Egot. We would have stopped it, if we knew. I made it known I was not pleased with Egot and his leadership. It was Menton, the warrior who had claimed he was too ill to join the hunting party who had begun to speak with me, extending his disappointment in Egot to the King as well. It was why I was so shocked when you told me of the attack. Not one of those warriors mentioned anything about disliking the King. These traitors hide themselves well, leaving only one exposed and it is his chore to search for others to join them.

"Menton approached me and asked if I would be interested in speaking to others who not only felt as I did, but were willing to do something about it. I agreed and told Egot of it, keeping him apprised of what I learned in case something happened to me. Egot, in turn, informed the King. Egot purposely sent me to the Raban Tribe to apologize to see what Menton would do when he learned of it. Menton did not waste any time in telling me to go and speak with someone of importance. I was shocked to find it was a Northmen."

~~~

Verity would have preferred to speak to Hemera about anything but the Northmen. She was anxious to know what had happened to her after the storm had claimed their boat and deposited them on land. And she was curious about her time with the Wyse, but that was all insignificant to the Northmen being on Pict soil.

Verity told her what she had been dreading to tell her. "Ulric and some of his warriors are here and have asked permission to speak with the King. It was granted and they will arrive here sooner than expected. But there is nothing for us to fear. We are Pict and Ulric has no rule over us here."

Hemera looked away and brought the vessel to her lips to sip at the brew once again.

Verity rested her hand on her sister's arm. "We are safe here."

Hemera shook her head as she turned to her sister. "No one is safe from Ulric."

~~~

"The Northmen are working with whoever it is who is attempting to overthrow the King," Vard said.

"You have no idea who it is?" Wrath asked

"It is a well-guarded secret. I wonder if the Northmen even know who they deal with," Vard said.

"Now you understand why I dismissed my guards," the King said. "From what Vard says, it will be difficult to trust anyone among us. That does not count you and Paine. I trust both of you with my life, but it was best I kept this to myself until I had more proof of my suspicions. And I also wanted to know if Verity or Hemera could have been planted here by Ulric. I do not believe they have been, but to make certain, I intend to

316

have Anin use her talents to tell me something about them."

"Anin will confirm what a good and trustworthy woman my wife is," Wrath said.

"It is good you do not object," the King said.

"Would it matter if I did?" Wrath asked.

"No," the King said, "Vard must leave here without being seen so that he may resume his mission."

"I assume since you got him in here without anyone seeing him, you will see to his departure as well," Wrath said.

"It is not for you to concern yourself with. Now go tell Paine that just before dusk I will see him and Anin in the High Council Chambers and you, Verity, and Hemera as well."

Wrath nodded and turned to Vard. "You have my respect for taking on such a difficult task and I wish you well. I also commend you for keeping silent to me when I all but accused you of not being loyal to the King."

Vard smiled. "It actually helped my mission. Tongues wagged about it and it helped Menton to trust me even more."

"Good luck, my friend," Wrath said and after clasping arms with Vard he left.

He went directly to Paine's dwelling that sat a distance from the others. Paine and Anin soon would move to the Master Builder's home, a larger dwelling than most and Paine would continue his duties as executioner until someone was found to take his place—a nearly impossible task.

The news was received as Wrath expected—with anger.

"Anin has suffered an injury and she needs rest," Paine argued.

"I would feel the same if it was Verity, but the King commands it," Wrath said and looked to Anin. She sat up on the sleeping pallet, her injured leg covered with a cloth that had probably been soaked with a special brew to help the pain and any swelling. "You and the bairn are well otherwise?"

"I feel quite well and I do not mind being of service to the King. He has been good to me and to Paine." She reached her hand out to her husband and Paine took it and sat beside her on the pallet. "It will be a good excuse to be carried in your arms, a place I most often want to be."

Wrath watched how Anin's words and her gentle smile melted Paine's anger. He had thought Paine foolish for allowing Anin, then the future Queen, to affect him so, but now having lost his heart to Verity, he understood.

There was no controlling the heart once another touched it. Anin had touched Paine's heart and Verity had touched his. He wished Talon could know the same, but that would never be.

"I am so pleased you have found a good wife, Wrath," Anin said her smile wide. "I look forward to meeting and getting to know her. I am sure we will be good friends."

"I am sure you will find her a kindred spirit and I will say no more, since the King wants to hear from you about Verity. I will take my leave now so that you may rest. I will see you at the High Council Chamber just before dusk," Wrath said, reminding them as he headed out the door.

Wrath went to his dwelling, wanting to let his wife know about the King's summons. He found her and her sister where he had left them, sitting on the sleeping pallet talking.

"I do not wish to interrupt your time together, but you should know that the King has summoned you both, and Anin and Paine as well, to the High Council Chambers just before dusk," he said, hoping his wife would be less concerned knowing Paine and Anin would also be there.

Verity felt her insides tighten. "What does he want?"

Hemera answered more quickly than Verity had ever known her to answer. "He intends to have Anin touch us and see what she can tell him."

Verity stared at her sister, then looked to Wrath, then turned to her sister once again. "Whatever do you mean?"

"Anin has a gift, born of her mother's tribe, the Wyse. When she touches people she feels what they feel and she also sees things about them. Her grandmother, Esplin was teaching her how better to control it. I spoke to Esplin about you and she told me that you can be taught to control your visions as well. She would be only too pleased to teach you." She turned to Wrath. "It pleases me to know that you care deeply for my sister, visions and all."

Verity did not hear them, all had gone silent around her, though no darkness chased after her. It was her own worries that had her drifting off. Her visions often disturbed her, seeing things about other people when she had no right to. She did not like the idea that Anin would touch her and know about her.

"I am curious as to what happened to you after the storm struck at sea," Wrath asked, leaning against the door with his arms crossed to listen.

His words pulled Verity out of her musings, for she too was curious to know what had happened to her sister. She cast an eye at her husband and a yearning settled over her. He had removed his cloak and his muscles grew taut as he crossed his arms against his chest and she could not help but strip him naked in her mind. A foolish thing for her to do since she grew aroused at the image she was now unable to get out of her head. If they were alone, she would have shed her garments and gone to him and he would have lifted her and—she shook her head. When she looked at her husband again, he was wearing that smile that tempted and teased and all but shouted *I know you want me, why deny yourself?*

Later, wife, he mouthed as Hemera filled her vessel with more brew before she spoke.

"There is not much to tell. I woke to find myself alone on the shore. I was soaked through and had to get warm and soon after I found myself with the Wyse Tribe."

Sounding as if she had not given much thought to search for her sister, he asked, "Were you not worried about Verity?"

"Why should I have been? I knew she would come across the warrior she had seen numerous times in her vision and that he would help her. She talked about you, when able, often enough. You never failed her in her visions, so I trusted you would not fail her when you met. Now that I have satisfied your curiosity, satisfy my concern. Why are there bruises on my sister's face?"

Verity had forgotten all about the bruises. Why had Hemera waited until now to mention them? Did she believe Wrath had raised his hand to her?

"It was Lars," Verity said quickly and went on to explain what had happened.

Hemera remained quiet after Verity finished until she finally asked, "What will the King do about this?"

"Protect his people," Wrath said.

"The Northmen are a vicious lot, though not very wise," Hemera said, looking at no one in particular, appearing as if she spoke more to herself.

Wrath was going to answer when he caught his wife shaking her head.

Verity stood and took the vessel from Hemera and as she did Hemera moved back on the pallet to rest her back against the wall and pull her knees up to her chest. And there she sat, staring.

Verity went to Wrath, his arm shooting out to snag her around her waist when she got close and ease her up against him.

"I have missed you, wife," he whispered near her ear before nibbling on it.

It tickled in more ways than one and she found herself aching to be alone with him, but right at the moment she had Hemera to think about.

Wrath did not expect the worry he saw in her eyes and he whispered, "What troubles you?"

Verity looked over at her sister, her head tilted to the side as she remained lost in her own world.

Wrath released her and grabbed their cloaks, draping hers over her shoulders before throwing his around his shoulders. He opened the door and with a hand to the small of her back, eased her out of the dwelling. Once he closed the door behind him, he took her hand and began to walk. "Now tell me what troubles you."

"I think only of myself."

"What nonsense do you speak?" he scolded gently.

"I am overjoyed that Hemera is finally here and safe, but she will have to share our dwelling and—"

"No, Hemera will not be sharing our dwelling. I will speak with Gelhard and see what dwelling is

321

available. And we will see her comfortably settled there—this evening."

"It would be cruel to leave her alone after just being reunited."

Wrath tried to stop the words from coming out of his mouth but they slipped out anyway. "If you do not want your sister spending this evening only, I can find a sleeping pallet elsewhere for this eve and this eve alone only."

Anger sparked in Verity. "And whose pallet would that be?"

Wrath grinned. "With that murderous look in your eyes, I would say sharing a pallet with the animals might be the safest place for me."

Verity stopped walking and wrapped her arms around her husband's middle and laid her head on his chest. "I do not want to be parted. I want you next to me in our sleeping pallet each and every evening of our lives." She sighed. "I am a terrible sister."

"We can settle this easily. We will sleep together and we will fix a sleeping pallet on the floor for your sister."

Verity raised her head to look at him. "But then we cannot—"

He pressed his finger to her lips. "Do not remind me. We do this for your sister. As you said it is not right to leave her on her own when she has just returned to you." Wrath cast a glance to the sky. "Dusk will settle soon. We need to get to the High Council Chambers."

They returned to the dwelling to find Hemera running her fingers through her red curls, trying to tame them some.

"We must go," Verity said.

Hemera picked up her cloak off the sleeping pallet to drop over her shoulders. Before she joined them at the door, she stopped and stared for a moment.

"Is something wrong, Hemera?" Wrath asked.

"I am most grateful that I now have a home here, but," —she hesitated— "forgive me but I cannot abide sleeping with other people in a room. A small place, enough for a sleeping pallet would be fine. I hope my request has not offended you."

Verity wondered what remnant was left of her sister's time with the Northmen that had caused her to make such a request. Her heart went out to her and she hoped there would come a time Hemera would speak with her about it.

"That will not be a problem, Hemera. I will see to it for you," Wrath said.

Wrath could not keep a smile from his face and, with much guilt, neither could Verity as they followed Hemera out the door.

Chapter Thirty

Paine and Anin were already in the High Council Chamber when Wrath arrived with Verity and Hemera. The King had yet to arrive, but then Wrath knew that before entering since two of the King's personal guards were not outside the chamber door.

Verity hesitated to approach Paine, not Hemera.

"Where is Bog?" she asked Paine.

"He is outside, keeping himself busy while he waits for us."

Hemera nodded and after asking Anin how her leg was, wandered around the room.

Wrath nudged his wife over to the couple, whispering, "Paine looks fiercer than he is."

Verity did not believe him. He looked like a frighteningly fierce warrior to her. He was as thick with muscles as he was covered in body drawings from what she could see peeking out from the sleeves of his tunic and the ones that ran up his neck. And he was the executioner, meaning he had taken many lives with that double-sided battle axe he had been carrying when she had first seen him.

"Paine, Anin, my wife Verity," Wrath said as he seated her across from them at the table, then sat beside her.

"I am so pleased to meet you," Anin said. "Hemera spoke so often about you that I feel as if I know you. I am sure we will be good friends."

Her gentle voice soothed and her lovely features captivated, but still Verity did not feel at ease, knowing

324

that when she rested her hand on her, she would know more than Verity wanted her to.

"I am pleased to meet you and I am forever grateful that you welcomed my sister into your tribe and kept her safe."

"Hemera is a wonderful woman. My grandmother adores her."

"So does Bog," Paine said with a slight scowl.

"Jealous that Bog likes Hemera better than you?" Wrath asked with a laugh.

Paine never got to respond, the King entered the room and before they could hurry to their feet, the King ordered, "Stay." And he took a seat at the head of the table.

Verity moved closer to Wrath and his arm rested at her hip and his hand on her leg, and she was grateful for his comforting touch. She did not know why the King frightened her so much, though whenever she saw him, she could not help but think him a cold and uncaring man. He did have fine features, almost too fine. It was as if he had been created by the gods the Northmen worshiped. Even the strange drawing that ran down the one side of his face did not distract from his exceptional features, though it did send a chill through her.

She watched as his eyes went around the room and she felt her stomach roil when she realized...

"Verity, where is your sister?"

"Hemera was here a moment ago," Wrath said, his head turning to search the room.

Paine agreed, having a look as well.

"She is not here now," the King said annoyed. "Find her!"

Before Wrath and Paine could get to their feet, Hemera entered the room with Bog.

"Bog remains outside," the King ordered.

Hemera stared at him as if she did not understand him, then said, "It is cold out."

"He is a wolf," the King said.

"It is cold out," Hemera repeated.

"He is a wolf," King Talon repeated.

"You need reminding of that since you have repeated it twice?" There was no ridicule or malice in her tone. It was as if she simply asked out of curiosity.

Verity went to rush off the bench to her sister and offer an apology to the King.

King Talon stilled her with one word. "Sit!"

Wrath looked to the King and spoke low. "Do you recall our discussion about Hemera?"

King Talon thought a moment and remembered she was slow-minded. He nodded, then spoke with a commanding tone, but not sharpness. "Bog is only allowed in here on special occasions."

Hemera smiled. "Wonderful! It is a special occasion that Verity and I have been reunited, so Bog is allowed to stay." She walked to the table, Bog remaining by her side and when she sat, the wolf sat beside her, leaning his body against her leg.

There was complete silence in the room and Verity noticed how Anin's hand went to rest on her husband's arm as if attempting to calm him. She wished she could go and sit beside Hemera and help her watch her words.

"Let us be done with this," the King said and everyone nodded except Anin.

The King looked to Hemera and Verity rested her hand over her husband's, squeezing it.

"Hemera, what can you tell me of the Northmen?"

She thought a moment before answering, "Some have evil hearts and some are good men."

The King waited for her to say more and when she did not he asked, "Why would they follow you and Verity here?"

"I have been wondering about that."

Again the King waited for her to say more and when she did not he asked, "And what do you think?"

"I have not had enough time to think on it."

The King was growing impatient and it showed with the spark of annoyance that lit in his eyes and the sharpness that returned to his tongue. "So you can tell me nothing?"

"I have made you angry."

Verity spoke up, too worried for her sister to remain quiet. "Hemera and I have talked about the Northmen and we do not know why they are here."

"He did not ask me why the Northmen were here. He asked me why they would follow us here," Hemera said.

"Why do you think the Northmen are here, Hemera?" King Talon demanded.

"Why are you angry?"

"Answer me," he demanded again.

Hemera sighed. "The Northmen are here to find a way to conquer you and take your lands. The Northmen go nowhere without thought of conquering. Now will you stop being angry?"

King Talon was about to snap at her and caught himself. "Aye, Hemera, I will stop being angry." She smiled at him and he realized what a beautiful woman she was, but though she was a woman, she spoke more like a child and he had to remember that.

Hemera suddenly stood. "You need no more from me. Bog and I will take our leave now."

"I am not finished," the King said once again fighting to keep hold on his annoyance.

"Then continue," she said and turned to go, Bog following close beside her.

"Hemera!" King Talon called out.

She turned. "I forgot. You wanted Anin to touch me so that she may tell you about me and what she sees." She waved her hand at Anin and smiled. "She can tell you everything, since she touched me when I arrived at the Wyse Tribe to see if she could help me find my sister." With that Hemera was out the door before anyone could stop her.

Verity quickly offered her apology. "I am so sorry, my King, Hemera means no disrespect and—"

The King raised his hand silencing her. "I understand why you were so anxious to find her. She will be safe here."

"You have my everlasting gratitude, my King," she said with such relief that she sagged back against her husband.

The King turned to Anin. "Is there anything you think I should know about Hemera?"

"Hemera is kinder than most I have met and she has a," —she hesitated a moment— "unique mind. She will bring you no harm, only," —again she hesitated— "wonder."

"That she will," the King said with a shake of his head and turned again to Verity. "Give Anin your arm."

Verity wanted nothing more than to take her leave as Hemera did, but the King would see Hemera protected and for that she would let anything be known about her. She stretched her arm out to Anin.

Her touch was soft and the gentle look in her eyes never wavered.

As soon as Anin's hand slipped off Verity, the King ordered, "Tell me."

"Verity is kind and trustworthy like Hemera. Her heart belongs to Wrath and always will. It did shortly after she had met him in her visions. She has great power that she has yet to harness and will be of much help to you, but...the Northmen want her badly."

"Why?" the King asked.

"They believe her skill can help them conquer you and they fear if she remains with you, she will help you conquer them."

The King nodded. "I wish to speak to your husbands alone. Wait for them in the feasting hall."

Paine stood and went to lift his wife.

"I can walk. I may limp a bit, but I can walk," Anin insisted and Paine scowled.

Verity hurried around the table, after giving Wrath's hand a squeeze. "I will help her."

The first wince had Paine ready to scoop Anin up, but the look she shot him warned him not to dare touch her.

"Wince again, wife, and I will carry you whether you like it or not," Paine said.

Verity slipped her shoulder under Anin's arm as she helped her take the next step and Paine scowled when his wife sent him a smile.

One of the two guards at the door, closed it behind them and when Verity spotted Minn sitting at a table in the feasting hall alone, she headed toward her.

Minn hurried off the bench and went to help Verity with Anin.

Once Anin was seated comfortably, Verity said, "I will go see if Hemera is hungry." She hurried outside. Darkness had fallen and she was glad for the torches high atop the wooden poles that lit the area. She looked about, and not seeing her sister, grew concerned. She reminded herself that the stronghold gates had been closed and that the wolf was probably still with Hemera. When her sister was hungry, she would join them.

She returned inside to the two women and was soon smiling and laughing with them. Experiences were shared and tales told, food eaten, and drinks enjoyed. Though, she did not know the two women well, she was glad she was getting to know them and looked forward to calling them friends.

"I am starving."

Verity turned with a smile upon hearing her sister. "Come join us. There is plenty."

Hemera hurried around the table and sat beside Minn, across from her sister and Anin, and reached for a quail egg and a piece of bread. "I came across a dwelling that would do well for me. It sits removed from other dwellings and would give me the quiet I prefer."

Anin smiled at her. "The executioner's dwelling."

Hemera nodded. "I recalled you telling me how you and Paine would be living there no more and how pleased you were that the Master Builder's dwelling was closer to other dwellings."

"That dwelling is for the executioner," Verity said, thinking it was not a good place for her sister to live.

"I have thought on this," Hemera said. "It would only be until another executioner is chosen and in the meantime I am sure something else can be found for me. For now, however, it would do."

"It would be the King's decision," Anin said. "I think it would be wise to wait until the morrow to approach the King about this. I will speak to Paine and have him speak to the King on your behalf. But you are welcome to stay at the Master Builder's dwelling tonight, if you would like."

Hemera's face brightened. "Aye, I would very much like that."

Verity was glad that at least tonight's sleeping arrangements had been made and she need not worry about her. The dwelling was not that far from Wrath's place, so Hemera would be close by.

They chatted more, though Hemera mostly listened. And she was the only one who noticed that Tilden hurried into the hall and after speaking with the guards at the door to the High Council Chambers was allowed to enter. It was not long after that he emerged only to rush out of the hall.

After Minn yawned several times, she said, "Time to take my leave and get some sleep." She stood and turned, the hem of her sleeve snagging on the hilt of her sword. She pulled it off and shoved her sleeve up to keep it from snagging again as she reached for her cloak on the bench.

A hand suddenly coiled tight around her wrist.

"You better have a good reason for grabbing me like that," Minn warned as she turned her head to look at Hemera.

Hemera released her and pointed to the drawing that circled Minn's wrist. It was a circle within a continuous circle, connecting to another continuous circle that wrapped completely around her wrist. "Forever connected—the Alpin Tribe."

"Aye, Alpin Tribe is my original tribe that was decimated during the battles to unify the tribes. I am the last Alpin."

Hemera smiled and shook her head. "No, you are not. Verity and I are from the Alpin Tribe."

Minn felt her legs give way and she dropped down on the bench.

Verity stared at her sister. "You remember that? I barely remember anything of our tribe, though Minn's marking did look familiar."

"Mum had the exact drawing on her wrist. She would tell me of the Alpin and what a proud and brave tribe they were."

Minn looked to Hemera and Verity. "I have family again."

Verity was surprised to see tears form in Minn's eyes. She did not think Minn ever cried and it touched her heart. She reached her hand out across the table and Minn grabbed hold of it.

Hemera laid her hand on top of theirs. "Mum would be happy to know that we have truly returned home to our tribe."

"We are forever connected as the drawing shows. I will protect you with my life," Minn pledged as if sealing a pact.

Verity and Hemera repeated the same and a tear fell from Minn's one eye.

"You must have your wrists marked so all will see that the Alpin Tribe survives," Minn said.

Verity nodded along with her sister. She was shocked and thrilled to discover not only her past but to find someone that was still connected with it. She had to ask, "Do you recall the Northmen attack on the Alpin Tribe?"

Minn shook her head. "The Northmen never attacked the Alpin Tribe."

Chapter Thirty-one

Verity had no time to question Minn. A summons came for her to join the meeting with the King. Verity and Anin were instructed to go to their dwellings that their husbands would be longer than expected.

As Verity and Hemera helped Anin to her feet, Broc and Gelhard entered the feasting hall and the doors to the High Council Chambers were immediately opened for them. Two more men hurried into the hall, along with Tilden, and were also let into the room.

"The King has convened a High Council meeting. Something is amiss," Anin said.

It was a slow trek to Anin's dwelling, Bog joining them along the way and keeping close to Anin. Hemera saw to settling her on her sleeping pallet and Verity tended the fire pit. After making sure all was good with her, the sisters took their leave.

Verity took Hemera's arm and they walked in silence at first.

"It is good to be together again," Verity said, hugging her sister's arm. "I have missed you so much."

"You should not have worried so much. Your visions showed we would get the help we needed," Hemera said, leaning her head to rest briefly against her sister's. "I am glad Wrath is the good man you saw him to be. Perhaps now you will trust your visions."

"I am learning to."

"I am truly happy for you," Hemera said, her wide smile proving it so.

"One day you will find someone to care for you and be as happy as I am."

"I am happy now, for being free of the Northmen brings me more joy than any man could."

"Aye, I feel the same joy at finally being free," Verity agreed. "It was odd that Minn should say that the Northmen never attacked our tribe."

"We are here," Hemera announced, stopping and paying no heed to her sister's remark.

Verity looked to see that they were standing in front of a dwelling that was impressive in size. Though, she had passed it often enough she had paid little attention to it. Seeing it now, she thought it a good dwelling for Paine and Anin, especially with his recent status of being made Master Builder.

"I will stay here until Paine and Anin move and then I shall reside in their old dwelling," Hemera said as if it was the most joyous news.

Verity did not like that Hemera planned to live in the executioner's dwelling, and she hoped to speak with Wrath and find her another place before that happened.

They entered and Verity was surprised that there were two rooms. One held a table and two benches that could easily seat four people and a narrow sleeping pallet that barely looked big enough for one. The other room held a sleeping pallet large enough for more than two people.

Verity was glad that Hemera wanted her to stay and talk. Sometimes her sister preferred being alone than to being with others, but it had been too long since they had been apart and there was much for them to discuss. They talked and talked and talked, thinking of nothing but this time together and the future. They let their time with the Northmen remain in the past. When they both yawned at the same time, they laughed and decided it was time to sleep.

After giving her sister a tight hug, Verity took her leave and was glad when she finally disrobed and crawled into her own sleeping pallet. As much as she would have liked to wait for her husband to return, she could not keep her eyes open and she fell asleep shortly after pulling the blanket over her.

Repeated shouts woke Verity and she shook the sleep off her and hurried into her garments. Her husband's scent was not on her. He had not returned to their dwelling last night and she feared what might have kept him. Once outside, she did not have to ask what was amiss.

"The Northmen approach! The Northmen approach!"

Verity quickly went in search of Hemera, but she was not where Verity had left her last night. She was about to search for her when she heard her husband shout her name. She turned and he held his arms out to her and hurried toward him.

"There is nothing to fear," he said as he caught her in a solid embrace. "Ulric approaches with a small troop and we are well prepared for him. The King will receive him and two of his warriors. Once it is done, Ulric will be escorted to our northern shore and sent on his way."

It seemed simple enough, but knowing Ulric she did not think it would be as simple as Wrath made it seem.

"Hemera is not where I left her," she said.

"She is safe in the stronghold. The gates have not opened yet. She is probably with Bog somewhere. A good thing since he will keep her well protected." Wrath kept his arm around her as he turned her to walk alongside him. "We go fetch your cloak before we go to the feasting hall and wait for Ulric's arrival."

Verity had been so concerned with getting to Hemera that she had not realized she had forgotten her cloak.

Once inside their dwelling, Wrath grabbed her cloak from the peg and draped it around her shoulders, pulling her closer to him to kiss her lips gently. "There is something I have been meaning to say to you, and I do not want to wait any longer to say it." His voice dropped to a whisper as he brought his lips close to hers. "*Tuahna, wife, tuahna*. Never have I felt for anyone as deeply as I feel for you. You are part of me and I am part of you. Nothing and no one can ever change that. We are bound together forever and I will have it no other way. *Tuahna*," he whispered again and kissed her, not gently this time.

His kiss stole her breath and his words her heart, and when it ended, she labored to say, "*Tuahna, husband, tuahna*."

He rested his brow to hers. "I will let no one harm you. *No one*."

Verity cupped his face in her hands. "I am most grateful to have found you."

His smile teased. "How grateful?"

Her smile matched his. "I will show you later."

"I will make sure to dispatch Ulric with haste."

A rap sounded at the door before it flew open.

Paine stood there, Anin beside him and Bog beside her. "The gate opens."

Wrath took his wife's hand and they followed alongside Paine after he scooped his wife up in his arms.

"I can walk," Anin said.

"You are safer in my arms," Paine said, "and that is the end of it."

Anin did not argue.

336

"Have you seen Hemera?" Verity asked more concerned now, since seeing Bog with them.

"No," Anin and Paine said together.

"I cannot find her." Verity eyes darted wildly around her, hoping to spot her sister.

Wrath snapped his hand and Tilden was suddenly walking beside them. "Tell the men to watch for Hemera and when you see her bring her to me."

Tilden nodded and hurried off.

Verity thanked her husband with a generous smile and stepped closer to him when they entered the feasting hall, never having seen it so crowded. Warriors stood shoulder to shoulder along the walls of the hall and the High Council stood off to the sides of the King who stood directly in front of the long table at the far end of the room.

It was easy to see why he was King. His stance was regal, his chin tilted up just enough to demonstrate his authority. He wore a near ankle-length tunic of fine cloth, the color of the rich dark earth and it was belted at the waist. His long dark hair was pulled back and tied tight with a strip of leather. It made the markings on the side of his face more prominent and the King appear more imposing than he already was, if that was possible.

The King summoned them with his hand, directing Paine to seat Anin, then stand to his one side. Wrath and Verity were instructed to stand to his other side. And there they stood, waiting.

Verity kept waiting for the door to open and Hemera to be escorted in by one of the King's warriors, but it was not Hemera who entered when the door opened...it was Ulric.

She could not help but shiver as his mighty steps brought him closer and closer.

He was not as tall as Wrath, though he did not lack height and though slim, he was strong. She had seen him squeeze the life out of a man with no more than his hand. His long hair was similar to hers in color and his beard a slightly darker color with small braids running through it. His eyes were deep blue and while his features were not as fine as Wrath's there was something about them that drew one's attention and held it.

"King Talon," Ulric addressed the King when he stopped in front of him.

The King's acknowledgement was curt. "Ulric."

"I have—"

"Why do Northmen walk Pict land without permission?" the King demanded.

"I requested—"

"I will tolerate no lies," the King ordered, anger sparking his tone. "Northmen, other than the warriors with you, have been spotted on Pict soil."

"I do not—"

"The Northmen intruders have been killed." The King took a quick step forward. "Do you still wish to lie to me?"

Ulric glared at King Talon, his eyes narrowing in anger. "A band of rogue warriors who believe this land belong to the Northmen. Much like the rogue warriors who fight to dethrone you, a King—they feel—unworthy to rule."

"Lars feels you so unworthy, he turns against you?"

Ulric clenched his one hand at his side. "Lars will suffer far worse than the others if I find this is so."

"For once you speak the truth. When Lars is found, I will turn him over to the executioner."

"I will search the land, find him, and see him punished," Ulric ordered as if he was King.

"You will leave Pict soil, under escort, and not set foot here again. Your warriors will be found and executed, punishment befitting traitors."

Anger was creeping up Ulric's neck, scorching it red and spreading to his cheeks.

"And if you think to battle me over this, know that Girthrig and Lammok warriors surround your men outside and the Drust surround your camp not far from their shores. They have since the day you landed."

Verity did not show her surprise at the King's remark, though it had surprised her. It meant that the King had to have planned this as soon as he had received word of the Northmen's arrival on Pict soil.

"I have no wont to battle you. I will collect what I came for—what is mine—and take my leave," Ulric said.

"Your rogue warriors will be dealt with and harshly. There is nothing for you to collect."

"You have something else that belongs to me."

"What is it that you believe I have that belongs to you?" the King demanded.

"My wife."

Chapter Thirty-two

Ulric pointed to Verity. "She is my wife. I will take her and be on my way." He stepped to the side of the King to approach Verity.

Wrath stepped forward as he pushed Verity behind him, shielding her and as he did he heard her whisper, "He lies."

"Take another step toward *my wife* and I will kill you." Not for a moment did Wrath believe Ulric, and while Verity need not have confirmed it, it pleased him that she did.

Ulric turned angry eyes on Wrath, then looked to King Talon. "Verity cannot be his wife. She is wed to me and I will have her returned to me. She fills your head with lies. No doubt she has claimed she is Pict." He pointed at her. "She is no more Pict than I am. Do you see any markings on her?"

"I see a mark left from a rope being kept around her neck like a slave," King Talon responded sharply.

Ulric's retort was just as sharp. "A fitting punishment for a wife who disobeys her husband."

"If she is such a troublesome wife, why do you wish her returned to you?" King Talon demanded.

"Like you, I keep what is mine and Verity is mine." He turned a grin on Wrath. "Besides she pleases me in many different ways."

Wrath wanted to pound Ulric until there was nothing left of him, and it took all his strength to stop himself from doing so. Instead, he leaned close to the King and whispered in his ear, "I took her maidenhead."

How to prove it, he did not know, but at least the King would know for sure that Ulric spoke falsely.

"It would not be wise to keep a man's wife from him," Ulric warned.

"Do you threaten me?" King Talon demanded.

"Do you deny me my wife?" Ulric challenged.

Verity felt a chill race through her. Would Ulric go to war over her? No, she would only be the excuse he needed to go to war with the Pict. What of the King? Would he go to war to save one lone Pict?

"Prove to me Verity is your wife," the King said.

Ulric grinned as if he already tasted victory. "My men were there at the ceremony that united us."

King Talon shook his head. "Your men would lie for you. That proves nothing. Tell me something about Verity that only a husband would know."

Ulric stared at him speechless.

"Does she snore when she sleeps?" King Talon asked.

"She breathes softly, but does not snore," Wrath answered and Ulric looked from one man to other with contempt.

King Talon continued questioning. "Does she welcome you to her sleeping pallet?"

"Most eagerly," Wrath said quicker to respond than Ulric.

"This proves nothing," Ulric shouted. "She is my wife—"

"Prove it," the King demanded once again.

"My word is not good enough?" Ulric challenged once again.

"There is a simple way to learn if he speaks the truth."

All eyes turned to see Hemera standing on the top step of the second floor. All eyes widened along with curiosity. What had she been doing in the King's private chambers?

"The dim-witted one," Ulric said with a laugh. "Pay her no mind since she makes little sense when she speaks."

"If I make no sense, what difference would it make if I spoke?" she asked, walking down a few steps.

Ulric laughed again and the two men with him laughed as well. "See, she does not even understand that her words would be wasted."

Hemera stared at Ulric a moment.

"And it takes her time to understand most words and respond. Is. That. Not. Right, Hemera?" Ulric asked, speaking to her as if she could barely understand him.

"Is it not the King's decision to hear me or not?"

"Enough!" the King ordered with a shout. "Come down, here, Hemera, and have your say and be quick about it."

Verity wondered what her sister would say since there were times Hemera did not make sense. She only hoped this was not one of those times.

Hemera walked down the steps and Paine stepped aside so she could stand next to the King.

"Have your say," King Talon ordered once more.

Hemera smiled at Ulric. "Verity has a mark since birth in a place only a husband would see. Let Ulric describe it."

"How do you know of this mark?" Ulric challenged.

"We are sisters and bathed in the stream when the sun was hot," Hemera said and turned to Verity and they shared a smile.

"Do as Hemera says and describe the mark and tell me where it is on Verity," the King demanded.

Ulric's lower lip began to twitch and once again his neck began to flame red as words seemed to fail him.

The King waited a few moments before saying, "Obviously Verity is not your wife. I would ask why you have lied to me, but I would get only more lies from you. Your father and I have forged an agreement so that our tribes may live in peace and trade may flourish between us. I will not jeopardize that over the foolish actions of his son." Ulric went to speak and the King shouted, "Silence! I will hear no more of your lies. You will be escorted by Pict warriors all the way to your ship where you will take immediate leave. Your *rogue* warriors, if that is what they truly are, will be hunted, found, and executed. And when next I meet with your father, I will discuss this incident with him, for I do not trust you to tell him the truth."

"You have not heard the last of this," Ulric threatened.

"You had better hope I have," the King warned. "Now be gone. You are not welcome here."

Ulric turned and left with his two men, all the Pict warriors filing out behind them.

"They will not be left alone until your warriors watch the Northmen's ship disappear in the distance," Broc assured the King and with a nod, he followed the last of the Pict warriors out of the feasting hall.

The High Council members left as well, except for Paine and Wrath.

Paine hurried over to his wife who was already on her feet and walking over to join the group. He scowled at her and she smiled, resting her hand on his arm for support and he relented, not scooping her up in his arms to carry her, though he did slip his other arm around her waist.

343

"How wise of you, Hemera, to have Ulric describe Verity's mark," Anin said.

"Aye, wiser than you know," Wrath said, "since Verity has no mark."

The three women smiled and laughed, but when they saw the King scowl, their laughter quickly faded.

The King looked at Hemera. "What were you doing up in my private chambers?"

"Exploring," she said innocently.

"Listen well, Hemera," the King said, pointing his finger at her. "I forbid you to go anywhere near my private chambers." He held up his hand when Hemera went to speak. "I forbid it and my word is law." He turned to Verity. "Keep your sister in tow. Now go, I wish to talk with your husbands."

Paine reluctantly turned over his wife's care to the two women, each taking her arm and supporting her as they left the feasting hall.

"Where is your cloak?" Anin asked of Hemera as they stepped outside.

Hemera glanced at each of her shoulders and thought a moment. "I believe I left it on a bench in the feasting hall." She scrunched her brow. "Or maybe I did not put it on when I left my dwelling this morn."

"I will go see if it is at your dwelling," Verity said, "if not I will look in the feasting hall." Not that she wanted to go there and disturb the King, but it was cold and Hemera needed her cloak, the one she had returned to her only recently. "Stay with Anin, she needs your help," she ordered Hemera and hurried off.

Verity was disappointed when she did not find Hemera's cloak in her dwelling. She was even more surprised and upset when she saw Hemera, the hood of her cloak up on her head as she headed for the open gates where a line of warriors, three across, were filing out of the stronghold behind Ulric and his troop.

Verity kept her eyes on her sister and when Hemera slipped through the open gate, Verity's heart slammed in her chest, and she hurried after her. She could not make sense of why Hemera would leave the stronghold or leave Anin, knowing she needed help.

Verity brought herself to an abrupt halt.

Hemera would not do that. That may be Hemera's cloak a distance ahead, but it was not Hemera wearing it. She turned and ran, realizing it was a trap and hoping it was not too late. She had only gone a short distance when two men jumped out from either side of the path at her and when she saw who one of them was, she ran faster.

Chapter Thirty-three

"You have had the Girthrig and Lammok warriors follow the Northmen since landing on our shores, have you not?" Wrath asked the King.

"Did you truly think I would trust the Northmen on our land without watching them? The Northmen are no fools. They did nothing to stir suspicion that they were here for anything other than to speak with me. They contacted none of their fellow warriors who were already here. I believe that group landed far from where Ulric did and with our focus on Ulric, we failed to look elsewhere. I imagine they intended to meet up somewhere along our shores."

"We cannot cover all our shoreline," Paine said.

"No, but I am making certain that word is spread that Northmen are infiltrating some of our tribes and to be alert to unknown travelers."

"Do you think Ulric's father, Haggard, knows what his son has done?" Wrath asked.

"I doubt it. Haggard knows peace will serve both our lands well," the King said.

Minn entered the feasting hall and did not wait for permission to speak. "I think there is a problem. I saw Verity leaving the stronghold and I believe she was following her sister, though when I came here to tell you, I saw Hemera helping Anin inside her dwelling. I think someone wanted Verity to believe she followed her sister."

"Guards!" Wrath shouted and two of the King's personal guards appeared out of the shadows. "Let no one near the King."

"I go with you," the King commanded.

"This could be a trap to get to you," Wrath argued.

"I will not run nor cower from those who are after me."

"We do not know how many are out there."

"One or two perhaps," the King said, "anymore would have been spotted."

"Then I can dispatch them with ease, though I will take Paine and Minn to ease your worry," Wrath said. "But you, my King, will stay here or you will make my task more difficult."

King Talon acquiesced, understanding what Wrath said. He was duty-bound to protect the King at all cost, even if it meant his life. If the King joined him and was put in a position where Wrath would have to choose between saving the King or saving his wife, there would be no choice. Wrath was an honorable warrior and he had pledged to protect the King. Talon would not put his friend in that position.

"Go and bring your wife home," the King ordered and turned to Paine. "I will have guards look after Anin and Hemera."

Paine nodded and hurried off with Wrath and Minn.

~~~

Once again Verity found herself running from Lars and once again he caught her and flung her to the ground.

"We have no time to waste," the other man said, Verity not recognizing him. "We need to be far gone from here before they realize she is missing."

347

His words while frightening were also helpful. She could not let them take her far from the stronghold and with no time to spare, she let loose with a blood-curdling scream that echoed through the woods.

Verity ducked out of the way of Lars' hand as he swung at her, hitting nothing but cold air. She let loose with another scream, knowing she had little time before he either gagged her or knocked her out.

He shoved her hard to the ground, his hand going to the back of her head to keep her face planted in the snow, making it difficult for her to breath.

"We have to go. Someone had to have heard her," the other man urged.

Lars pulled her head back roughly and as he did, he placed a knife to her cheek. "I will cut that pretty face of yours every time you scream."

Verity did not hesitate. She let loose with another scream, which turned into an agonizing cry as she felt the blade slice along her jaw.

"Are you crazy?" the man cried out. "Gag her and be done with it. We need to leave here now unless death is what you want." He handed Lars a small cloth.

Lars swiped it out of his hand, annoyed, and shoved it hard into Verity's mouth, causing her to gag. "Spit it out and I'll cut you again before gagging you again."

Verity left the gag in her mouth, though she struggled against him when he took her arm, forcing her to walk.

"Pick her up," the man ordered and hurried off ahead of Lars, too afraid to linger any longer.

Lars did exactly what Verity wanted him to do. He grabbed her and flung her over his shoulder. She turned her head so that the blood from her wound dripped down, staining the white snow as Lars walked. After seeing that the blood was leaving a good trail, she worked the gag out of her mouth and let it drop to the ground. She made no noise. She waited, confident Wrath would find her and, strange as it was, hoping she would continue bleeding until he did.

Lars suddenly stopped and Verity could feel that he was turning his head as if anxiously looking for something or someone.

"Neddle," Lars called out. "Neddle, where are you?"

Verity listened for a response and none came.

Lars took a couple of steps and called out once again. "Neddle."

Suddenly a horrific roar ripped through the air and Verity was flung off Lars' shoulder and she hit the ground hard. Hands grabbed at her, dragging her away, then yanking her to her feet and rushing her off and when she was finally able to see who had helped her— "Minn."

"You are safe now," Minn assured her.

Verity smiled her thanks and quickly turned her head and saw her husband running straight for Lars. While there had been a rage in Wrath when he had attacked the warriors who had descended on the Raban Tribe, it was nothing compared to what she saw now. It was as if his fierce fury empowered him with unbelievable strength and skill beyond what he already possessed. Lars could barely match Wrath's vicious sword thrusts, since they struck at him so rapidly. Blood began to drip from various places on Lars' body, his arms, his sides, his face.

Verity noticed that Paine had joined her and Minn, and when she saw his battle axe dripping blood, she knew Neddle was dead.

Her eyes returned to her husband and she was not surprised to see Lars drop to his knees, his sword falling on the ground beside his limp arm. Blood was spreading rapidly out from spots on his tunic to cover nearly the entire garment and his fur leg wraps. Wrath had chopped away at him piece by piece.

Wrath stood before him. "I would like to leave you here to bleed slowly so that the animals would smell you and come feast on you while you still lived, but I will not take the chance that you may have friends nearby who would attempt to help you." Wrath dropped his sword, grabbed viciously at the hair atop of Lars' head, pulled the knife from the sheath at Lars' belt, and sliced his throat from ear to ear. He released him with a shove. Lars fell backward on the ground, the white snow staining red with his blood that rapidly began to pool around his head and he choked and spurted as his life drained away.

Wrath did not turn away from Lars until he was sure he was dead, then he looked for his wife and when he saw her, he hurried over to her to take her in his arms, but stopped and took hold of her by her shoulders, his fury that had tempered some rising again when he saw the blood dripping from her wound on to her cloak. He had been too late to protect her, to keep her safe.

Verity knew his thoughts by seeing the hurt and anger in his dark eyes and before she could explain to Wrath, Paine spoke.

"We need to leave now. It is not safe. There were more tracks than those of two men and troops must be sent after them. Much could be learned if only one was captured."

Wrath lifted his wife up into his arms, tucking her close against him and without another word from any of them, they took off.

Once in the stronghold, Paine went to alert the King and Minn went to get the healer and Hemera.

Wrath settled Verity on the sleeping pallet in their dwelling. He discarded her cloak to the ground. He would not see her wear it again, the bloody stains forever a reminder of...

"You did not fail to protect me," Verity said softly.

Wrath remained silent as he lifted her chin to examine her wound. Only a little blood dripped along the slim cut that ran along her jaw on the right side of her face.

"Are you in pain?" he asked abruptly.

"You did not fail to protect me," she repeated.

Gently, he placed his hand beneath the wound as if his touch would take her pain away and heal the injury. "You should have never suffered this."

"I did not have to suffer it. I did so on purpose."

Wrath sat beside her on the sleeping pallet, his brow scrunched and his hand leaving her face to rest on her arm. "What do you mean?"

"Lars told me to stay quiet or he would cut my face. I wanted you to have an easy trail to follow, since I worried that Lars and the other man would split and take separate paths and you would not know which tracks to follow. Blood is easy to follow in the snow."

Wrath shook his head and lowered it slowly to deposit a tender kiss on her lips. "You are a brave woman, Verity."

"No, I am not brave," she said. "I was full of fear."

He raised his head. "And rightfully so, Lars would frighten anyone."

She pressed her hand to his cheek. "It was not him I feared. It was never seeing you again. Never having you hold me again. Never joining with you again. Never—"

His lips silenced her with a soft kiss. "We belong to each other and *never* would I let us be separated. I would find you no matter where you were. You have my heart, wife, I cannot live without you, nor do I want to. You are stuck with me—"

Verity brushed her lips over his and smiled, "Forever."

Wrath returned her smile before he ran his lips over hers as he whispered, "And ever and ever and ever."

Chapter Thirty-four

One moon cycle later

Wrath hurried to his dwelling, the snow that had started falling at dusk, growing heavier. The High Council meeting took longer than usual since the council celebrated the newly appointed member not only of the council, but of the King's personal guard as well. Broc had been made Warrior Commander and Tilden had been appointed to the King's personal guard.

Tilden had trained with the other personal guards for the last moon cycle and had done exceptionally well and the other guards were pleased to have him join them.

After the meeting had finished, Wrath went to see how Hemera was doing at the executioner's dwelling. The move had been made only a few sunsets ago and already his wife was worrying about her sister being too far from her. Anin must have thought the same since Paine had been there when he arrived at the dwelling.

He had to laugh when Paine, with a scowl, had offered Hemera to come sleep at their dwelling in case the snow worsened, which was what Wrath was going to suggest. He had been glad when Paine had asked first. Hemera had refused and hurried the two men home to their wives.

Paine had commented on how strange Hemera could be at times and Wrath had laughed and said, "Unlike you who is not at all strange?"

Paine had punched him in the arm and smiled, something Wrath was glad to see him doing more often, and walked off.

After that Wrath could not get to his dwelling fast enough. He was eager to wrap his naked body around his wife's naked body and...the thought of what they would share grew him hard and he hurried his steps.

He opened the door shocked to see his wife standing on the other side of the fire pit, running a wet cloth down the front of her naked body. Her lovely skin appeared golden through the flame's flickering light.

"Hurry and shut the door, the cold chills me."

Wrath quickly did as she asked, seeing that her nipples had puckered even tighter from the cold than they had been. He dropped his cloak on the bench that sat by the door and hastily shed his garments before going to his wife and taking the cloth from her.

"I need to finish—"

"I will do it for you," he said and placed a light kiss on her lips.

Verity laughed softly. "It is not washing you will do to me with that wicked glint in your eyes."

"I promise I will wash you first."

She rested a tender hand to his cheek. "Since you always keep your promises to me, I will let you wash me." She laughed again. "Though, I think you punish yourself."

"Then take mercy on me, wife." He kissed her palm lightly and she shivered. "And on yourself."

"Be quick," she pleaded.

He was all too willing to comply. He was relieved to see that the rope burn on her neck had faded considerably and would be completely gone eventually. The scar along her jaw had healed better than Bethia had expected, but that was due to Hemera's care. She had made her sister keep a cloth against the wound with some sort of mixture in it. She refreshed the mixture now and then and each time she did the wound looked much better. The scar had now faded to a thin line, the redness gone. All her bruises had healed and her body was fuller now with more tempting curves and plumper breasts.

He had always thought her beautiful, but now... "You are more beautiful than ever, wife."

"And more fortunate than I ever thought I would be, to have such a wonderful, caring, and patient man for a husband."

"Patient?" he asked with a smile that tempted.

"Much too patient," she whispered and kissed him.

Wrath dropped the cloth, scooped her up in his arms, and carried her to the sleeping pallet, the heat of his body chasing the chill from hers. They kissed, they touched, and they joined together as one and whispered the one word to each other that came naturally to their lips before sleep each and every night.

Tuahna.

THE END

King Talon's story, The King & His Queen, coming 2017.

Titles by Donna Fletcher

The Pict King Series
The King's Executioner
The King Warrior
The King and His Queen (2017)

Macinnes Sisters Trilogy
The Highlander's Stolen Heart
Highlander's Rebellious Love
Highlander: The Dark Dragon

Highlander Trilogy
Highlander Unchained
Forbidden Highlander
Highlander's Captive

Warrior King Series
Bound To A Warrior
Loved By A Warrior
A Warrior's Promise
Wed To A Highland Warrior

Sinclare Brothers' Series
Return of the Rogue
Under the Highlander's Spell
The Angel & The Highlander
Highlander's Forbidden Bride

The Irish Devil
Irish Hope

Isle of Lies
Love Me Forever

The King's Warrior

Dark Warrior
Legendary Warrior

The Daring Twin
The Bewitching Twin

Taken By Storm
The Highlander's Bride

About the Author

Donna Fletcher is a USA Today bestselling author of historical and paranormal romances. Her books are sold worldwide. She started her career selling short stories and winning reader contests. She soon expanded her writing to her love of romance novels and sold her first book SAN FRANCISCO SURRENDER the year she became president of New Jersey Romance Writers.

Drop by Donna's website www.donnafletcher.com where you can learn more about her.

Made in the USA
Middletown, DE
24 October 2017